The ORDER of the ROSE

ALYSHA KING

The Order of the Rose

First published 2013
This edition published 2020

ISBN: 978-0-6485003-0-8

Dedicated to my parents for their encouragement,
to my friends for all their inspiration,
and in memory of my grandmother,
Nancy Skilton, for introducing me to the wonderful
world of reading.

A Poem

Friendship is a sunset
That gently envelops the eternal heavens with flaming
clouds and blades of light from pinpricks in the sky.
A gift of beauty measures in awe that is wrapped in
the wings of the nightingale's slumber.

Friendship is a melody,
The softest, sweetest aria, smooth as the snowflake's whisper
in a tune more tender than silk icing sheathing trembling seas.
It is carried on the silver winds, echoing through the
sequined palace walls of our mind's endless gaze.

Friendship is a mountain
That is born with the glowing broth of moonstone's shiny pane,
cooled and hardened for life to make it its home.
The swollen wave stands old and wise, knowing more generations than life itself,
and under its chalky layers of envy is a heart more solid than gold.

Friendship is a stream
That swirls and sparkles, the glitter-eyed ice chasing
its unknown destiny through the soaked sand and rocky nests.
Its mellow tears bringing life like no other and splashing its laughter
on shallow banks that wild glaciers once touched.

Friendship is a rose,
The purest white of a stallion's mane with petals lighter than
tiptoes on a cloudy shore and fragile limbs of forest's grudge.
Its sweet musky scent guarded by the armour of the gardens
loyal shepherds silently sharpening clawless stings.

Yet, friendship is a poem
Of flowers and songs, laughter and jest, beauty and life.
A gathering of timid words in hope of a saviour's voice to
give freedom to the withered soul.

~ Sara Connellan

Prologue

It has been many years since there was peace in the Realms, and many more since white magic reigned. Balance in the universe has been lost; very little good remains while darkness covers all. The struggle of these forces created a war more terrible than any other, and slowly, evil consumed everything. Nothing escaped its clutches. Darkness triumphed and what little hope that remained, died. Peace became a memory. The memory became a dream, and, all too soon, those dreams died also. The People were forced into the Realm of Commoners, the realm where even their white magic was considered evil. Fearfully, they were made to hide their magic, not only from the Commoners but also from the dark forces that still sought them. Their freedom was taken from them. They now have but themselves left, their will to survive...

Those who exist in the Realm of Commoners hide in buried cities, built beneath the earth's surface for safety. Fear keeps them from surfacing, afraid of fear itself. And out of those who surface, few escape the horror that awaits them. These cities were the only way of surviving, but these havens are slowly beginning to disappear...

It began in the Realm of Wizards – the Mystic Realm. Since the beginning, the council had ruled, a circle of the wisest and most powerful sorcerers in the realm. The Centre City became the realm's kingdom, the council its main rule. The sovereignty of Benjamin Merilius had been considered the strongest in a fair age. His council was powerful beyond all, and as one, they governed the Mystic Realm fairly and justly. They made their strength known throughout the two Realms. They warned their enemies of their might. But the council became blinded. Their followers were deceived...

A force stronger than Emperor Merilius and more sinister than the

Darklands had begun to creep over the Centre City. Talk of a powerful adversary spread throughout the lands and anxiety gripped the hearts of the civilians. But despite this, the council remained steady. They ignored the warnings and it was their confidence that led them to their fate...

From the shadows emerged an enemy, a sorceress, the likes of which had never been seen before. She tricked the people of the realm, gave them false hope. She gained their trust and with their help, she overthrew the council. She destroyed the Orb of Power, the energy that till then had kept balance within the Realms. Stability within the Realms shattered and chaos broke out. The sorceress harnessed the position of power and wreaked havoc with the sole intention of allowing evil to gain full supremacy over both worlds. She enslaved the People and destroyed freedom. She created a lurid reality in which the People were forced to work in slavery, forced to live lives of excruciating pain. Her council began their reign, a time which was to become the darkest period in the history of the Realms.

However, there was one person who stood against her. One person formed an alliance against this new council. Lady Fianna Parnell, the youngest of the councillors, fought this new rule. She formed an alliance with those who had escaped slavery. She gained followers who joined her in her mission to destroy what had become a malicious Empire and campaigned to bring freedom to her people. The fight became a war, and it soon was the war to end all. For almost three decades the battle raged on, spilling out into the Realm of Commoners. Catching the eyes of Commoners, the Empire soon had the advantage of witch burnings, ridding many of the alliance through the hatred of the Common realm. It was a dark period for white magic, and this fight was taking its toll on Lady Parnell. Her Order was slowly dwindling. The power of the Empire was growing stronger, and eventually it claimed full rule. It almost destroyed Lady Parnell and her followers. Their fight for freedom was almost lost...

Yet, when all seemed hopeless, there was one last group of warriors. They were the very last of the rebel fighters, and they were the People's last hope...

Chapter One

The Order of the Rose

The morning frost was fresh on the leaves as the sun began to rise over the hidden valley. About a dozen people were creeping silently up the side of the valley, cautious not to disturb the peaceful surroundings. They were unusually dressed, somewhere between a commoner and a Traveller, though the latter was very rarely found without some kind of wagon or transport, and the former was rarely found sneaking about the countryside so early in the morning.

It just so happened that these people were neither. They were magical folk and their reason for being there was something neither a commoner or Traveller would be party to. Suddenly, the foremost member of the group held up a hand, signalling them to halt. Something had called upon the attention of their leader and he looked about, his eyes darting to the line of trees that loomed ahead of them. A strange flicker of light danced at his fingertips, but after a moment he shook his head and extinguished the sparks, motioning for the others to continue.

This group of unusual people were not just any magical folk, and there were indeed many of those to be found. No – these were members of a rebel order, sorcerers and sorceresses that fought ferociously against the Empire, a growing society of dark witches and wizards that was ruled over by a sinister sorceress. The Mystic Realm, a realm beyond this one, was once a world where most respectable wizards, witches and magical creatures had resided before the Empire's initial conquest. It was, however, no more.

These witches and wizards were the final act of a powerful rebel sorceress, Fianna Parnell, who had been the first to stand against the Empire. She had named her Order delicately after her favourite flower, the rose. It contained her own hidden message meant only for her Seekers: they were as roses, seemingly harmless but for their hidden thorns. Each was distinguishable by a single gold triangle that hung around their necks, imprinted with their name. These necklaces were a symbol of hope to those who supported them and a reason to kill for others, but the Seekers would never be rid of them.

The Seekers' prime purpose in recent times was to find the opening to The Mystic Realm but had so far been unsuccessful. The Empire had succeeded in concealing it from the minds of the normal wizards, hiding it from any possible detection. The Seekers had been forced to search for it based only on vague rumours and instinct. The closure of the opening prevented the passage of wizards between the two realms, trapping them in either slavery or confinement. This morning, the Seekers were once again on the hunt for the other realm, believing that they were closer to it now than they had ever been before...

As they continued on up the hill, three young children trailed closely behind them.

"Ji! Kat! Carey! What do you think you are doing?" Jenny Lee whispered harshly.

Jenny and her husband, Robert, were the leaders of this last remaining group of Seekers. They were the most determined to find the sorceress Malevolence, the sorceress at the centre of the Empire. They knew with strong confidence that with her downfall, the terrible arrest on the magical community would end. With so few in the Order active, this had become their sole purpose and aim. If they were to continue fighting, they would have to aim high if they were to aim at all.

Carey gave her a withered look.

"*Mother*, we're tired! I hate these early mornings. Why must *we* go?"

Carey Lee was a short, nine-year-old who had inherited her mother's shoulder-length honey-brown hair, and her father's round face and deep-brown eyes.

"You are a member of this order, are you not?" her mother asked firmly. Carey nodded sullenly. "Yes mother."

Jenny pursed her lips. "Then please at least act like one, Carey. You know what we are trying to accomplish."

Carey scowled even deeper. She had been a member of the Order since the day she was born, for her parents had been part of it long before her time. It was both privilege and curse and their purpose was never far from her mind.

Her comrades and friends, Ji Binx and Katrina Lawrence had been in the Order just as long as she. Ji's dark brown hair ruffled slightly in the morning breeze as he walked along side her, his pale, blue eyes glinting with excitement. Carey enjoyed being around Ji; his happy-go-lucky attitude brought light to even the darkest of times and he had a knack for witty remarks. His brother, Zacharia, was fourteen-years-old, but when placed side-by-side, he was almost indistinguishable from Ji. They were both quick with their reflexes and their senses were sharp, which to an outside wizard could be very deceiving and dangerous on their part.

Kat was much different to Ji. She tended to be quite dominating and liked things done her way. There were high hopes for her in the Order as her skills with magic were far beyond the expectations for her age. This was owed to an unwavering confidence that had bestowed itself within Kat's being – she believed she could and should do everything. She had caught up with her mother, Jiani, her long black waves of hair shining brightly in the early morning light. Her mother was nodding along, half listening, glancing nervously at the thicket of trees that surrounded them. Jiani preferred the rush of combat to the suspense of the hunt.

Carey, Ji and Kat were the youngest members of the Order but weren't yet skilled enough to take up arms against Imperial wizards and witches. Kat despised not being allowed to blow up everything and anything. Her father was the only one able to stop her from doing so. He was more worried that she'd blow herself up instead, so she had to settle for her speciality – a simple, yet effective stunning hex.

Carey's older twin sisters, Jody and Laurel were nearby and had heard her complaints.

"Stop whining, Carey, none of us need your complaining right now," Jody snapped, staring at her through penetrating blue eyes.

"And if you don't stop wandering we'll be late, and don't blame us if you get caught because you weren't concentrating!" Laurel hissed at her, shaking her head, her brown hair flicking into her eyes.

Carey was just about to ask what exactly they'd be late for but was silenced by a warning look from her mother. Jody and Laurel had become overly bossy and increasingly secretive of late and Carey couldn't help but wonder why.

"Just writing to friends," they would mumble, turning away to talk in whispers.

Carey didn't believe them though. She didn't even know if Jody and Laurel had any friends outside the Order. She knew something was suspicious but every time she interrupted, they'd snap at her to leave.

Carey gazed around at the quiet (and in her opinion, boring) surroundings, wishing she were back at the hidden city, Durn Pien, trying some of Clarett Mihion's muskmelon tarts. These days they hardly stopped, and Carey dreamt of the feasts waiting for them at the next city.

She felt an itch start to tickle her nose and she lifted her hand to her face. Carey tried to stifle the sneeze, but was too late and it expelled itself with quite a force.

"Oh no – a–A–*ACHOOOO!*" Carey spluttered. The sound echoed slightly through the trees and for her disturbance, she received a few disapproving glances.

She sniffed and Carey wiped her face clumsily on her sleeve. Looking up, she spotted a small movement in the bushes ahead. She stopped dead, her heartbeat quickening slightly in her chest. Her Seeker-born instinct stopped her at the slightest hint of unsuspected action, but after a moment's panic, there were no more disturbances within bushes and she let out a slow breath of relief.

"It was nothing... nothing. Don't be silly," she muttered to herself as she livened her pace, catching up to Ji.

The group had begun climbing under the low branches of some willow trees and Carey found herself in a hollow, enclosed by the tree's large roots. Carey shivered; it was very dark within the hollow. The willows cast eerie shadows, the gnarled branches creating patterns that appeared much like watching figures.

Kat's father stopped abruptly up front. There was some sudden rustling up ahead, and he silenced everyone. Stealthily, he went to inspect it. An eerie breeze fluttered through the small clearing and everyone shrank back into the dry cold shadows. They watched as Peter Lawrence crept ahead, hands outstretched and ready. Carey bit her lip; her mouth went dry. Was it the same thing she had seen before, she wondered? She squinted, trying to see what it was. She gasped.

Out of the shadows emerged a large group of dark, hooded figures, and within a blink of an eye, they had surrounded the nine Seekers. Carey's parents took guard. Carey could hear her mother, bellowing curse after curse, a string of spells that she had never before heard her mother use. She wasn't aiming them at the hooded figures though; her curses flew past them. Carey spun around. Who could she possibly be fighting? She tried to see but it was impossible. Then, as quickly as they had started, they stopped, falling to the ground with two dull thuds. Their fall brought Carey crashing back to her senses. She thought of just one thing: escape. Just as her parents had taught her, Carey ducked, trying to weave through a gap in the circle of intruders but was gripped roughly by the hair and flung back towards her group. In unison, the intruders produced a blinding light.

In an instant, invisible bindings pinned the Seekers' arms hard to their sides. Their legs sprung together, and they all fell awkwardly to the ground, one by one, strangled by the magical clasps. Carey screamed as her arms locked tightly to her sides and she collapsed along with her comrades. Panicking, blind with confusion, she struggled, arousing clouds of dust. She kicked out, but a strong force stopped her, gripping her so hard she couldn't move. Carey desisted, but her heart continued to pound painfully against her ribs.

Carey twisted in her bindings and peered into the gloom. Her mother's shouts ceased and there was silence. From within the trees, emerged a tall silhouette of smoke and shadow. Darkness grew and within moments, an eerie darkness had filled the clearing and the temperature had dropped to an icy chill. The figure was shrouded in dark ragged material that covered every inch of its body. The cloak fluttered and flickered as though caught in a slight breeze; the tattered ends were wisps of black smoke that melted into the moist morning air. They moved with a sinister grace, almost gliding and without haste. Where a mouth would have been, the shroud flickered with the breath of the one behind the eerie covering. A cold shiver ran up Carey's spine and she shook uncontrollably. An unsettled flurry rumbled in her stomach.

An abrupt wind blasted through the clearing with a swirl of dead leaves and dust as the ominous figure turned its featureless face towards the Seekers. It was surrounded by energy of hatred and ill-will, an energy so strong that it made Carey's arms prickle and heart stand still.

"Release Jody and Laurel."

The voice was artificial, hollow and sharp. It was a woman's though, quiet as a whisper and rasped like the wind blowing through a dry clearing. The sound intoxicated the air, stung at the Seeker's faces and bit at Carey's heart. It made Carey gag and wretch but the bitter sensation did not leave her.

Two of the hooded Imperials turned to Jody and Laurel and made a downwards slicing action in the air with their hands, releasing the two girls. Dusting themselves off, Jody and Laurel walked calmly over to the tall, shadowed woman and bowed reverently.

"Here they are, your Ladyship - the last active members of the Order of the Rose," they said, indicating them with a small gesture, "as you requested."

There was a short stunned silence in which Carey's stomach dropped; the sensation of plummeting into an endless darkness filled her. She closed her eyes, blinking away a wave of dizziness that was threatening to engulf her.

"Jody? Laurel? What is happening here? What are you doing?" Jenny demanded, staring at them in both anger and bewilderment.

The energy around the shrouded figure changed; Carey felt a wave of sadistic amusement wash over the group. She knew with a sudden realisation who this woman was – it was the sorceress. It was Malevolence, the very person her parents were trying to find. Carey knew very little about her, but what she knew was enough: Malevolence was a force of darkness, corrupt and evil.

Malevolence stood before them and lifted one of her thin, gloved hands, turning the palm towards the Seekers. A strange sensation drifted over Carey and suddenly there was a voice. Carey yelped as her hair prickled, electricity running along the inside of her scalp. Malevolence's voice was inside her head, cold and empty, whispering in harsh tones.

"*Welcome to a new era, Seeker,*" it echoed. Carey whimpered as another shock ran along her hairline. The others were also trembling and twitching in reaction to this horrible sensation, shaking their heads in a bid to rid themselves of the voice reverberating within their skulls.

Malevolence continued to address the group. "*Welcome to the new world, my pathetic adversaries. Once again, it seems to me that you are unaware of the changes which your realms, or should I say my realms are experiencing. You have left me with the satisfaction that I am succeeding in the wake of your ignorance. You have failed for the very last time, although it could be seen that you never were succeeding and were a hopeless case from the very beginning...*"

Carey's eyes began to water with pain as she experienced another shock. She wanted to scream but the sensation was so strong that it was suppressing all other senses. The voice spoke again.

"*As you may see, I have acquired an extraordinary advantage that you failed to realise you possessed. Let me enlighten you all. Jody and Laurel Lee, daughters of your ill-fated leaders, are my faithful devotees, my insiders,*" Malevolence's voice proclaimed with a hint of sadistically-achieved happiness. "*They have been providing me with information for almost six months now about your deplorable Order and its pitiful attempts to overthrow my Empire. My Empire will not be destroyed, I will not see my dynasty destroyed by your almost non-existent group of pestilent rebels. You are a mere nuisance, a pest and I have taken the necessary steps in order to rid myself of your race. Your efforts have done nothing but try my patience, however intelligent and organised you may believe yourself to be. You never saw and never learnt. Your efforts were and still are useless. I have released Laurel and Jody from the abysmal existence in which you had entrapped them. They have finally realised how truly pathetic your campaign has been and have risen above their former selves to achieve something far beyond your own efforts."*

Carey's father looked up incredulously at his two eldest daughters whose faces were lit with wide smiles of victory.

"Laurel… Jody… you betrayed your own family… but… how… why? How could you do this?" he stammered, pale faced.

"Father… We chose this path because Malevolence possesses powers you could never achieve. She gave us something that has enlightened us in regards to your… situation. She has given us power beyond anything you could offer. We have come to realise that you are fighting a losing battle. We *couldn't* have you standing in the way of absolute victory for the Empire, we simply couldn't. We just couldn't have you tarnishing their power," Jody explained slowly, expressionless and emotionless.

Carey looked on, shocked that her sisters, her own two flesh and blood sisters that she had known for a lifetime, had just handed their family over to the Empire. A wave of heated anger rushed over her – she loved her sisters but at this very moment she felt a deep sense of loathing towards them. However, this newly surfaced abhorrence towards her siblings was struggling with a terrible fear, scattering her emotions. Carey began to struggle against her bonds, squirming around on the ground in blind fear, but her restraints held tight. Her fear turned into panic and a great torrent of emotions welled up inside her, working their way up into her throat. Carey gasped as the build up of mixed emotions spilled over and she began to sob in self-pity. Sensing the child's distress, Malevolence glided over to her, her aura prickling with so much hatred and disgust that the hair on the back of Carey's neck tingled. Carey hung her head, shaking uncontrollably from her anger and fear, tears streaming down her face. She saw the sorceress come to a halt in front of her and Carey felt the touch of a thin, gloved hand under her chin. Malevolence lifted Carey's face and Carey recoiled – Malevolence was so close that Carey could hear her ragged breath and feel it against her skin. The tear running down her cheek froze and stung Carey's face.

"Hush child," the voice rang through Carey's head again. *"Your tears fall in vain for they cannot redeem your family's honour, or what little they had!"*

Carey shook her head. "No!" she heard herself cry out.

At once, a sudden wind caught Malevolence's cloaking and she made a sudden swift movement. She struck Carey hard over the head with the back of her hand and Carey fell heavily. She felt her face starting to redden and sting with pain and humiliation. Biting back a sob, she tried to pull herself back up into a sitting position. She was weak and Carey squeezed her eyes shut, trying to separate herself from the chaos that was building up around her. She knew what was happening – they were trapped. They had come to a terrible end which could be the only reason why Carey's usually calm mother suddenly went into furious hysterics.

"Jody – Laurel – make her stop! Look what she is doing! Look what *you* are doing. You are a disgrace... you..." Jenny screamed, shaking violently, her eyes aflame.

Laurel and Jody ignored their mother.

"What is wrong with you?!"

Kat had finally regained herself. Ji had recovered from his state of shock and he had joined her, supporting her with mutinous stares. Carey wanted to cry out to them, to tell them to stop, for even though her two companions were much more courageous than she, Carey felt a deep sense of foreboding that something terrifying was to happen today.

Malevolence's featureless face turned towards the defiant child and Kat flinched. Wisps of black smoke were rising from the thin ragged ends of Malevolence's mantle, accompanied by a horrifying energy that made the Seekers shrink with fear.

A blue flash illuminated Kat's face and a blast of wind struck them. Malevolence appeared as a spectre would, her ominous cloak flaying wildly. There was a moment of confusion and then Carey blinked; Kat was lying unconscious on the ground. A silence fell over the clearing as Malevolence calmed and glided back to the top of the clearing.

"You have all stretched your luck much... too... far. Your diminutive Order has infuriated me for long enough," her voice rasped in barely a whisper. "Fianna Parnell was an idealist who did not know her boundaries. Therefore, I made them for her. I claim power here, and still you think you have a chance. Now, if you make any attempt to redeem yourselves, I will ensure that your children are punished for your actions."

And with that last chilling threat, the last of the Seekers were led away up a slope to the nearby village, where their final fate awaited.

Chapter Two

The Miracle

Carey's head spun as they walked up the hill. Ji had regained his strength, fighting against the grasp of the wizard restraining him. Carey allowed herself to be led along, the pain of her last punishment still fresh in her mind. Her parents were walking in front of her. Carey wanted desperately to run to them, to forget she was a Seeker and to simply be a nine-year-old girl who just wanted her parents' comforting touch, but Carey knew it would be impossible. She would never be let near them as long as they were alive, for Malevolence had neither the heart nor concern for them.

She saw Ji's holder give him a quick clip under the ear to try and silence him, providing Ji with a reason to curse out loud. He stopped struggling however and fell silent in spite of himself. They soon found themselves being directed up the front stairs of a rickety old broken-down two-storey house. It seemed ancient; the windows were boarded up and the shutters hung off their hinges. Every step creaked under their weight and the inch-thick dust and dirt flew up around their ankles.

Kat was still unconscious and was being carried roughly up the stairs. They were forced up another flight of stairs within the dark, inhospitable dwelling that looked as though it hadn't been lived in for a good few years and walked a short way along the landing. They reached a small room and were marched into it. There was no furniture within the four small walls and the lack of windows had turned the air stale and humid. They were bound and left with five of the Imperials to guard them. The door slammed shut and they were plunged into semi-darkness, the only light coming from a low-burning oil lantern hanging by the door. The guards stood their posts, their hoods shadowing their faces. Their presence frightened Carey terribly, so trying not to think about it, she instead decided to observe their new surroundings, taking it all in silently. Looking around, she couldn't think of a worse fix to be in. The invisible bindings were bruising Carey's ribs, and she was finding it increasingly hard to breathe. Carey tried pulling her arms away from her sides, but received another hard slap across the face for her troubles.

"No moving, girl!"

Jenny Lee snapped angrily, drawing the wizard's attention away from Carey. Honouring her mother's actions, she stopped trying to escape. She silenced herself, ignoring the sneers and sadistic grins the guards bore as they watched her. Carey was weary and confused. She had never encountered anything her parents couldn't handle or escape from. This failure came as a shock and she struggled to comprehend the enormity of this situation.

No-one moved or spoke again. Kat continued to lay motionless in the dirt and dust and Carey knew that their parents were all deep in thought.

They must have been in there for about an hour before Malevolence returned to the room, flanked by three of her wizards.

"Bring me Oliver and Meela Binx. I understand you hold some very important information in regards to the Order and its activities," she leered in her harsh whisper. Meela shook her head distraughtly. "No? You should know better than to refuse my biddings." Malevolence extended a slender gloved hand and Zacharia winced. Carey knew what Malevolence was doing – the pain brought on by her invasive mind- technique was unlike anything Carey had ever experienced.

Zacharia's face contorted in anguish as Meela and Oliver were pulled from the floor and pushed towards the door. Meela struggled, pained by Zacharia's suffering. "Stop, stop! I'll go, please! Zacharia!" she screamed, pulling herself towards Zacharia, fighting desperately against the Imperial holding her. Her method achieving the desired outcome, Malevolence lowered her hand and Zacharia slumped sideways, gasping for air. Breathing heavily, Meela Binx was dragged from the room, along with her distraught husband and Malevolence followed, the door snapping shut behind her.

Carey peered over at Zacharia and Ji; Zacharia had recovered but was lying still, muttering something inaudible beneath his breath. Ji was staring at the floor, unable to comfort his brother and stricken with grief. His courage had evaporated with the cries of his desperate mother and he was clearly distressed. Unable to face her companions for the agony it caused her to see them like this, Carey went back to inspecting her dilapidated surroundings. She scrunched her nose up at the sight of the peeling paint flaking from the mouldering walls. Sighting a small crack in the wall, Carey followed the progress of several odd-coloured insects as they emerged from the crevice and made their way to the gap under the door. In addition to the abysmal state of the space, Carey couldn't help but smell the foul stench that was wafting from the grimy floorboards, making her slightly nauseous.

Why had her sisters done this? Why had they left them like this? Carey couldn't believe what was happening. Was there any chance they would escape this? It didn't seem possible and it brought terrifying thoughts to her mind. She had heard the stories of half-crazed wizards that had escaped from the other realm. She could hear the fear in their voices as they spoke of the slave colonies and of the desolate wasteland they had been forced to work in, day after day. There would be no doubt or question that they would all be sent to this hellish world – or worse. Carey began imagining all kinds of terror when she forced herself to stop, feeling the beginnings of a great headache approaching. She groaned audibly and lay down on the disgustingly grubby floor, receiving a disapproving grunt from one of the guards.

It seemed like an age before two of the hooded wizards returned, reluctantly supporting two very weak people; Oliver and Meela were deathly pale. **THUMP!** They were flopped down onto the floor violently.

Zacharia turned his head away from his parents and glanced up at the ceiling. Ji was devastated.

"What happened?" Carey whispered, leaning towards Ji with wide eyes.

There was a long pause. Ji bit his lip but didn't say anything. Zacharia took a deep breath.

"It's... torture," he answered shortly. "They've been tortured."

Carey gasped. "What? Torture? Is that when...?"

Carey didn't have to finish her sentence. She had overheard her parents discussing the horrific interrogation techniques of the Empire. She had heard that word, *torture.*

"I've seen it before..." Zacharia answered. "They go into their minds... make them feel unimaginable pain. Pain breaks down barriers, unlocks secrets within their minds. I met a man once... it was exactly like this. Malevolence needs to know what they know. If she was successful, then she may know now," he said in a very forced voice.

It was upsetting to see Zacharia like this, so different to his usual persona. A depressed air settled over the room like a heavy blanket. Their parents had been silent the whole time and Carey knew they were deep in thought, reflecting on their dire predicament. The guards seemed to take delight in all this though. They sneered at the group with a mounting confidence that made Carey feel ill.

After another hour of gloomy silence, Malevolence appeared at the door again, this time accompanied by Jody and Laurel.

"Bring Peter and Jiani Lawrence," she said brusquely.

Jody and Laurel stalked over to Kat's parents, released them and led them sharply out of the room. With steely expressions, Peter and Jiani disappeared through the door, determination etched on their faces. Malevolence paused for a moment as if surveying the Seekers. Carey felt the room darken for a moment before Malevolence turned and exited the room without a second glance towards her victims.

Kat had begun to stir and she opened her eyes feebly, blinking dazedly up at Carey and Ji. She sat up as best she could, grunting in her effort. A bright purple bruise was forming around one of her eyes, causing one side of her face to swell. Kat squinted around the room, first at her new surroundings, and then at Ji's parents, who were now lying still upon the wooden flooring. Kat stared round-eyed at them, agape. She turned to Ji.

"W-what happened?" she asked faintly. "Oliver and Meela – uh – oh…"

"The Empress… she hurt them, to – to get them to tell her stuff," said Ji, sounding even more pathetic than Zacharia.

Kat was terrified. It looked as though she was trying not to believe what lay before her. She turned her head sideways, searching the room.

"Where's *my* mother and father?" Kat asked, looking from side to side, suddenly panicking. "They're not here. Where are they?"

Carey looked to her parents as if to ask them what to do, but her mother had already taken the initiative. "Kat, dear, please don't be alarmed. You must stay quiet, all right? Your parents are currently downstairs but they will be back soon. Kat? Katrina, are you all right?"

First her face went a deathly shade of white; then she began to shake her head; and then…

"What! What – no… n-no… hey c-can't… Where! WHERE! What is happening to them? I want to know! Where are they?" Kat screamed.

The guards advanced threateningly, but this did not stop Kat's cries of despair. Carey, Ji and Zacharia were petrified, hoping her screams did not carry downstairs.

"Kat – KAT! Stop it Kat, *please*. Screaming will not help them. Please, just calm down."

Carey's mother tried to calm her but Kat was beyond comforting and was now crying noisily, shaking with remorse. The guards that had advanced on her were unsympathetic and one of them reached down and pulled her up by her collar. Despite this, Kat did not stop. One was raising his hand to curse her when a loud bang echoed from somewhere downstairs. They all stopped and listened. Kat was thrown down harshly and the Seekers breathed a sigh of relief. They soon heard footsteps on the landing and the door swung open. Kat's mother and father were pushed into the room. Malevolence entered behind them, bringing an air of sadistic excitement. The atmosphere within the room was electric and the feeling made Carey gag again. Something had heightened Malevolence's emotions and it had a clear effect on the Seekers. Zacharia's face showed murder.

Malevolence turned her featureless face towards them. She towered above the Seekers, her shadowy figure belittling them where they lay. She raised her hand and Carey braced for what was coming.

"Perhaps the finest point in your miserable lives, I must admit," the voice prickled along Carey's scalp painfully. *"I suppose you will never truly realise how important and valuable your information so far has been. Although reluctant to provide it, I have other means of extraction at my disposal. I do hope you will therefore make it easier on yourselves..."*

Carey stared up at her, suddenly terrified. She had realised something that had not yet occurred to her; *her* mother and father were next for...

She felt a lump rising in her throat and a dry sob escaped her mouth before she could stop it. Carey stopped herself before another one could force its way out, but Malevolence had noticed.

"Worried are you?" she added, the feeling intensifying, making Carey wince in pain. *"Perfect. Those who stand in the way of my victory deserve to suffer the consequences of rebellion. Now, only two people remain. Only two people left to be... of service. The leaders of the Order of the Rose – Jenny and Robert... Lee,"* Malevolence's voice hissed, the Empress herself slowly turning towards the only two conscious adults left in the room.

Lost for words, Carey watched as her beloved parents were led away like the others, stone-faced and silent. Malevolence's spectre-like form followed and Carey breathed easier as the nauseating sensation lifted from her body. She could hear Kat breathing shallowly, almost hyperventilating. Ji was quiet, the shock of the events around him obviously taking its toll. They all seemed a little disconnected, hesitant to look at one another. Eventually, Carey's anxiety got the better of her and she fainted...

After a while, Carey didn't know exactly how long; she awoke from her unconsciousness, mainly from the foul smell coming from the floor but also from a crash that had issued from the room below. Furrowing her brow, she listened closely for further movements, pressing her ear hard to the floor. She heard another two thumps. Then, with a burst of colour, the door was flung open, bouncing back hard against the wall. Malevolence stood in the doorway, outlined by the brilliant light. Her shroud was whipping about wildly and Carey felt the sting of Malevolence's emotions that were emanating intensely around the room. Malevolence turned to face the door as Carey's mother and father were dragged in and dropped to the floor next to her. Small, red blotches riddled their pale skin.

"Now I have you here all together, I have something to say," Malevolence rasped eerily, pointing her finger towards the lifeless Seekers.

Their parents blinked and sat up, determined not to give Malevolence the satisfaction of showing any weakness. Malevolence drew herself up to her full height, a terrifying figure, commanding the full attention of the Seekers. The hair on Carey's arms prickled as Malevolence took a rattling breath. She spoke in barely a whisper but her voice echoed with victory.

"Your insignificant and impertinent campaign against me and my empire has endured long enough. It has cost us both valuable members. However, before you now stands the leader of the victorious, declaring you as the defeated. I have, though, no desire whatsoever to destroy you despite the extent to which I loathe you," she rasped steadily and calmly, her voice sounding like nails scratching on cold metal. "I want you all to live with the knowledge that you have lost everything and all you have left is nothing. Your world, your determination, your hopes will be dissolved. I sincerely hope that I never have to deal with your *kind* ever again. Be this your last view of this world, for I intend to never let you cast your eyes upon this land ever again. Your type of freedom does not exist anymore and you will have to realise that very soon."

Malevolence turned from the Seekers and faced her guards. "They have provided me with what I need. I see no need to prolong the inevitable. Also, release their bonds. I see no need for them anymore, considering... Just finish it. I have more important affairs to settle."

Feeling faint, Carey watched as Malevolence swept from the room, her cloak billowing out behind her. *Finish it? What did she mean by 'finish it'?* Carey didn't quite understand. It was a few seconds later though that Carey got her answer. The Imperial wizard walked to the room's centre, released the Seekers reluctantly with a wave of his hand then held out his palm, as if offering something. Everyone looked on reluctantly yet with a small hint of curiosity. A small golden ball about the size of an apple appeared in his hand. It had strange markings on its shining surface, a foreign language Carey did not recognise. The sphere was etched with thin, curling, elegant lines. The wizard tapped it once with a long, slender finger and the ball began to revolve slowly. The wizard then glared at the dishevelled group before placing the golden orb on the floor and turning on his heel. The group gazed curiously at the unusual item with a feeling of foreboding.

"Mother, what is it?" Kat whispered.

"I'm… I'm not sure. One of Malevolence's inventions, I believe. I've never–"

Jiani broke off. Sharp rays of light had split the thin, swirling veins on the globe's surface. The glow illuminated their faces as they sat spellbound by the sight. A surely magical power was keeping them from pulling away. The light flitted over them like sunlight on water as the ball began to spin faster and faster. The outer shell was shifting, breaking into smaller segments. There was a small spark and the ball swelled to twice its original size. The split contours widened; burning rays burst from within, flooding the room with its light. Carey threw a hand up to shield her eyes, as did Kat and Ji next to her. Carey squinted hard in order to watch the revolving orb that had captured the Seekers' attention so effectively. Carey's heart was thumping hard as she watched this terrifying spectacle climax. It was now spinning so fast that it was a stinging blur.

"Kat? Ji?" Carey whimpered, and she pulled herself towards them.

They huddled together, watching in trepidation. The beams of light grew brighter, more startling, reaching to the darkest corners, filling every fissure in the room until the golden ball became almost invisible behind the glowing shafts. Then, as if Carey was seeing it in slow motion, the globe sparked once more, and it splintered into a thousand tiny pieces.

Carey screamed. She saw the pieces fly as the sphere exploded, releasing a dazzling bowl of blistering light. Carey clung to Ji and Kat as the intense white light engulfed the Seekers. It drowned out her mother's cry of surprise with a disorientating silence; it was as if someone had clapped a pair of invisible earmuffs over her ears. A multitude of sensations overwhelmed Carey. Something strange was happening to her skin, something warm and prickly. The white haze that had filled the room suspended Carey, the substance around her supporting her weightlessly as the strange tingly feeling on her skin grew warmer...

Then it was gone, leaving her blinking bemusedly. She rubbed her arms but the feeling was gone. What was that strange sensation? Was it from the light? Looking down past her arms, she saw an unexpected sight. Glancing up, Carey was met by a shocking surprise. She, Kat and Ji were still in the foul, decaying room, but they were the only ones; the room held no-one else. Carey's eyes smarted with tears.

"What was that?" Carey heard Kat say.

"Where is everybody? Why are we still here?" Ji asked, his forehead wrinkling with confusion.

Carey shook her head. "I don't know. That – thing did something," Carey whispered in reply, blinking back a tear. Her parents were gone and she had a terrible feeling that they were no longer in this world but somewhere much more terrifying. But why hadn't Kat, Ji and herself disappeared along with them?

All of a sudden, Kat yelped, causing both Carey and Ji to jump with fright.

"What?!" Carey asked, startled.

Kat was staring at the door. "We... look... Malevolence... we have got to get out of here. We – we can't... what if Malevolence finds out we're still here?" she managed to say in barely a whisper.

"But we'll never escape them!" Ji whispered in despair.

"We can't let them get us Ji!" Kat said shrilly, moving towards the door. "Do you just want to stay here and wait for them to come and get you?"

"I didn't mean–" Ji began to protest but Kat cut him short.

"Then c'mon!"

Carey nodded. If they waited there any longer they'd be in big, big trouble. "All right. I don't see anything. Shhh..."

Quietly, the three of them peered cautiously around the corner. The landing seemed deserted but a shuffle of footsteps alerted them of someone climbing the stairs.

"There's someone coming!" Kat said. "We have to go now! On the count of three. One... two... *three!*"

Carey rushed out onto the landing and they began sprinting down the hall. The wizard's head bobbed into view on the stairs and he shouted in alarm. Adrenalin running through her, Carey thundered towards him. Before he could make a move, the three children ran into him and the four of them went tumbling down the stairs. Carey felt her head hit something sharp as the world turned upside down. Her foot connected with someone as they thudded painfully down the flight of stairs. Coming to an abrupt halt, Carey moaned, grasping her head, but Kat and Ji were already pulling themselves out from under the wizard who had one mighty big bruise on his head. Realising he was out cold, Carey began to untangle herself from him but her foot was trapped beneath the hulking Imperial.

"Kat! Ji! I'm stuck!" she cried out and the two of them raced to pull her free.

They were just about to make for the door when a deafening crash issued from behind them. They spun around and there stood Malevolence in all her fury. She threw her hands over her head.

"Duck!" Ji shouted, and they narrowly missed being hit by a violent curse that crumbled the wall behind them.

Carey did a sort of awkward roll and flung her arms up, covering her head from the falling rubble. The ceiling kept falling and she screamed. Kat was scrambling backwards, trying to flatten herself against the wall; Ji had huddled himself into a ball to protect himself against the debris. Squinting, Carey lifted her head. Through the swirling dust Malevolence appeared, coming to a halt just to Carey's right. Carey rolled over and saw Kat cowering in the Empress' shadow, scrambling at the wall in a frenzied panic. Malevolence began to raise her hand slowly, curling it into a fist. Kat gripped her throat and she began to rise from the rubble. She flailed her arms, spluttering and whining incoherently. Carey bit her lip, watching hopelessly, her mind void of any ideas that could help Kat. She saw Ji move out of the corner of her eye and saw that he held a large chunk of rubble in his hand. Carey moved her hand and she felt a large stone beneath her fingers. Considering it only for a second, Carey picked up the stone and summoning all her strength, threw it at Malevolence just as Ji tossed his. Malevolence sensed this though and she dodged these deftly, the rocks passing through nothing but smoke. *She moves like a phantom* Carey thought, but she didn't have much more time to ponder this, for their strategy had proved successful. Malevolence had lost her grip on Kat and she dropped to the ground, coughing and wheezing. She doubled over, hugging her chest in pain.

"Ji! NOW!" Carey screamed and Ji stumbled forwards.

He grabbed Kat around the middle and began hauling her out the gaping hole in the wall. Malevolence had turned to Carey and Carey stumbled back away from her. There was a rumbling as another large piece of the ceiling collapsed between them. The churning dust and rubble gave Carey the chance to flee. Carey pulled herself up and she ran to catch up with Ji and Kat who were already out the door. There was a crunching behind them and Carey whipped her head around to see two more Imperials come dashing out from the ruins.

Having no idea where they were running to, Carey followed Kat in hope that they could maybe put enough distance between them and the wizards following them. They reached the village outskirts and with feet thudding heavily on the dirt road, they ran past some startled villagers. Reaching a marketplace, Ji, Kat and Carey pushed their way through the busy village street. It was crowded and Carey reached for Ji's hand, desperate not to lose them. They fought their way through stalls and groups of people watching entertainers. Carey could hear the roars of the enraged Imperials and the cries of indignity from the villagers as they were pushed aside. The people around them towered above the three children and Carey gripped Ji's hand even harder.

They were moving through the central pavilion when Carey heard a loud bang. People began to scream and there was panic as the villagers scrambled for safety, jostling the three young Seekers around. In the confusion, Carey's hand slipped and she cried out in dismay as her hand slid from Ji's.

"Ji! Kat!" she hollered as she pressed past terrified villagers but her words were lost in the commotion as a second, louder bang sounded out across the square.

Carey began to panic as she searched the frenzied market for her companions. The screams and shouts of terror filled her ears so much that she could not hear her own voice calling for Kat and Ji. She lost her footing as someone much larger than she was, dashed past her and she fell hard to the ground. She yelped in pain as someone trampled her fingers. Glancing around, there was nothing more than feet and dirt and she screamed one last time. "Kat! Ji!"

Through the turmoil, Carey felt a hand on her back; it gripped her and pulled her roughly to her feet. She spun around only to find to her complete dismay that it was one of the Imperial wizards who had been pursuing them. He grinned with yellow teeth and Carey tried to scream, but it was lost as the chaos around her dissolved and she sunk into darkness…

Chapter Three

The Lost Seeker

C arey woke with a start. Rubbing her head, it took her a few moments to realise it had just been a dream. But it had seemed so real. She looked out the window; the tiny courtyard was cloaked in darkness and the sky was tinged blue. Carey could feel the cold air of dawn through the crack beneath her windowsill. The dream was still vivid in her mind, but it was disjointed and confusing. She had been having this dream for a long time now. Bits and pieces would flash through her mind, making no true sense but they were coming faster now. Was there something behind these strange recurring dreams? Who were these people she dreamt of, night after night? She felt she knew them. The situation though... witches, magic...

"Impossible..."

Carey shook her head dismally and turned her head to watch a bluebird fly over the garden shed below. As she watched, a pang of longing blossomed in her chest. It had been six long years since she arrived at the orphanage, and she longed to be out. She longed for freedom. The orphanage did not favour her; she didn't seem to fit in there. The problem was that she didn't know where she belonged. As strange as it seemed, Carey had no memory of who she was before she was nine-years-old.

Carey had woken up in the Monaghan Hospital with her head wrapped in bandages, an enormous headache, and absolutely no memory at all. "Where am I?" was the first thing she had asked one of the nurses bustling by.

"You're in the Monaghan Hospital, Carey dear."

"What?" Carey asked dumbly, sitting up.

"You're in the Monaghan Hospital–"

"No, not – not that. Who am I? What did you call me?"

"Carey. Your name is Carey, deary," the nurse answered, sweeping over to take her temperature.

"Is it? But… how do you know?" Carey asked anxiously, trying to push the nurse's hand away from her forehead.

"It was on this necklace of yours," she said, giving into Carey's persistence. She held a small, triangular-shaped necklace up for Carey to see. "Do you want me to put this into your little bag here?"

Carey looked curiously at it, having never seen it before in her life.

"Um… what? Er… yes… please… thank you."

Terribly confused, Carey found the presence of two women by her bedside one day even more perplexing. One was dressed in a perfectly starched grey dress and had the foreboding presence of a military officer by the way she held her strong-jawed chin and wide square shoulders. The other was tall and thin but her appearance was quite the opposite. She wore long black clothes; a long flowing skirt, a high-collared long-sleeved blouse and silk gloves. She also wore an odd kind of bonnet with a thin black veil that dangled delicately in front of her face. Carey thought she looked more like a widow in mourning than the Headmistress of Saint Kathleen's Orphanage for Girls. Her name was Ms de Valera and she reminded Carey dreadfully of someone she might have known once before, but Carey's memory was so damaged, that she had little chance of remembering anyone. The other woman was Ms Rorx, the orphanage's overseer.

Carey left the hospital accompanied by Ms Rorx four days later. She was taken to live at the orphanage; Carey had hoped almost desperately that it would be better than the loneliness of the hospital. When she first walked into the orphanage, Carey remembered seeing the other girls in their lessons as she passed the first-floor rooms. She remembered walking into her small, dark and rather pathetic little room at the top of the stairs to the left. It consisted of a very small and very dusty mirror that hung next to the door, a narrow cupboard that stood against the right wall and a low, spongy bed that was situated right under the window that leaked every time it rained. The room had a slightly musty smell about it, but Carey had been glad to have her very own room.

She hid the bag containing the necklace under her mattress as soon as she had arrived. Carey wasn't allowed jewellery in the orphanage and she wanted to keep this to herself. It was the only thing she had from her past and she wanted to study it, find out what the strange symbols on its surface meant. A tiny inscription on the back read *The Order of the Rose*; what *The Order of the Rose* was exactly was a complete mystery, but she kept it to herself. She couldn't risk asking anyone about it. Ms Rorx was merciless in regards to punishment and Carey soon learned that Ms de Valera was a force not to mess with.

Carey's first meeting with the other girls of the orphanage occurred when she went down to breakfast the very next morning. Adrianna Rinaldo, a tall, blonde-haired girl and six other girls around Carey's age stopped her at the bottom of the stairs. Adrianna looked Carey up and down, her lips pursed as though she had just eaten a particularly sour lemon and her eyes narrowed dangerously. The other girls stood there, leering at her with extreme dislike.

"So *you're* Carey," Adrianna said curtly, leaning against the wall. "I'm Adrianna Rinaldo. My parents died in a forest fire when I was six. What happened to *your* parents?"

A horrible sneer spread across her face. The other girls waited eagerly for Carey to answer.

"I – er – I can't remember my parents... I – lost my memory. I don't know," Carey replied nervously.

Adrianna's expression changed instantly from hateful to pure loathing and she flexed her fingers as if resisting the urge to slap her.

"You don't belong here, you know, so don't think you do. You're not an orphan," she spat at Carey, turning on her heel and stalking away, the other girls in tow.

Feeling very perplexed and troubled by what Adrianna had said, Carey crept into the kitchen and ate her somewhat pitiful breakfast of burnt toast and cheese. It had seemed that Carey's hopes of ever having friends had hit rock bottom. She was now completely alone. And now, so many years later, she found herself as alone as she had ever been. None of the younger girls liked the older students (Adrianna made sure of that) and the only person Carey could talk to was Miss Griffith, the cook.

"Carey, m'dear, they're jealous. Jealous because they can remember how their parents died and you can't. Jealous because you don't have that memory to live with and they do and because you were able to forget it all. That is all there is to it."

Carey liked Miss Griffith. Even if she was hopeless at cooking, she was the only person Carey could trust.

The sun had begun to appear over the distant horizon and Carey heaved herself out of bed. Miss Griffith would be up soon to give her the list for the market. She was under orders from Ms Rorx to provide Carey with the lowest of jobs and loathed the task of giving them to her. Carey would sweep, mop, dust and travel to the market every morning before anyone else was awake. They were assigned to her for some unknown reason, but to do them rather than not, was much better than to endure the wrath of the orphanage's overseer. Luckily Ms Rorx was a little less harsh in the absence of the Headmistress. For strange, unknown reasons, the Headmistress would leave for weeks on end and then return in a worse fury than when she left. There were certainly rumours in the orphanage on where and what Ms de Valera got up to on her travels but Carey was less than interested. She didn't care because when Ms de Valera went away, she was relieved of the terrifying feeling that plagued her when the Headmistress was there. She agreed with the other girls when it came to the Headmistress. There was something very mysterious about her for the fact that she rarely made an appearance at the orphanage and that she only ever spoke to the girls when something of grave concern required her attention. There was the fact that Carey felt she knew something more about the Headmistress than the others but it was a mere feeling and she knew how crazy she would sound if she told anyone about this.

There was little to keep Carey from leaving this horrific dwelling but the orphanage was Carey's only 'home', if you could call it that, and if she rebelled, she'd be cast from it with nowhere to go. She'd be an outcast with no money and no status. She would be the lowest form of society. As hard as it was, Carey had to accept this and reminded herself of it every time she had the urge to run away.

Carey pulled her pinafore over her shirt and buttoned it up the back. She was just buckling her shoes when there was a sharp rap on the door. Before she could answer, the door burst open and Miss Griffith entered.

"Morning, Carey. Here is your list for this morning."

"Thanks, Miss Griffith," Carey said, taking the piece of paper in her hand.

"Oh, and I must warn you, Carey. Ms Rorx knows that you talk to the stall keepers and she's not liking it. I would be careful if I were you. I have an inkling that she has told the Headmistress."

Carey paled. "The Headmistress?" The bottom of her stomach churned. "Oh... um ...thanks. I'll be careful."

Carey drew her shawl around her shoulders and placed her school beret on top of her blonde head. Staring into the mirror, she grimaced. "You can do it, Carey. It can't get any worse than this... can it?"

* * *

The markets were always a colourful affair. The stall holders strung up bright banners and festival tents throughout the dismal streets of Monaghan, lighting up even the darkest of its corners. Carey found this early morning event comforting and it uplifted her spirits as she strolled through the tents devoted to brilliantly dyed clothes, scarves, jewellery and home wares. Music echoed down through the masses of people as the Music man played on his vast array of bizarre instruments. This morning he was playing a funny sort of stringed instrument that looked more like a long thin washboard with three strings down its front. He was pulling a bow that was bent like an archer's bow and the strings hooked under those of the long wooden board. The high-pitched notes curled into quick two-step tunes that had many of the townsfolk bobbing along in time with them.

Carey reached the food stalls and consulted the list, looking around for the items as she read each one. She walked over to O'Donnell's Food Emporium and began picking out what she could.

"Good marnin', Carey. What can I do ya for?"

A tall, firmly-set woman with a brightly painted bandana wrapped around her head had appeared from behind a curtain at the back of the stall. Carey gave her a rare smile. "Good morning, Clera. How are you?"

"Good, good. Are you on a day off?"

Carey laughed humourlessly. "I don't get days off. No, I was just getting the daily list of goods for Ms Rorx."

"Again? Doesn't she get anyone else to do it? I've only ever seen *you* get it for her," Clera asked as she rearranged some purple eggplants, the many rings on her fingers glinting in the early sun.

Carey shrugged. "I don't know, Clera. She only picks me because of the Headmistress. She doesn't like me or something. It's like she knows something I don't, you know?" Carey said, picking up a clove of garlic and placing it in her basket. "It's like I'm different to all the other girls and she likes to punish me for it."

Clera nodded in understanding. "Well, whatever it is, Carey, I don't see it. Ya seem perfectly normal to me."

"Thank you, Clera," Carey said, rummaging around in her purse. "Well, here. How much do I owe you?"

"Oh, yer not goin' to stay an' talk for a bit?" Clera said with slight disappointment.

"Not today. Ms Rorx knows I've been stopping to talk and she's furious. I think she's told the Headmistress as well," said Carey. "I'm not so sure I want to endure that kind of abuse again."

Clera nodded again, her brown hair bobbing at her shoulders. "Ay. I remember you telling me of her fury. I won't keep you then. Don't want you gettin' in trouble again. That'll be two pence an' four shillings, thank you," she said, accepting the coins from Carey and waving her off. "An' Carey!"

Carey turned around. "What?"

"If you ever need a job, you know, to get away from that awful place, just come to me an' I'll get you somethin'."

Carey smiled again. "Thanks Clera. I'll think about it. And say hello to your brother Marcus for me!"

Clera laughed. "'E'll like that! Bye!"

Leaving the vegetable stalls in a slightly better mood than she had been in earlier that morning, Carey wandered back to the orphanage, admiring the clothing stalls. The cleverly stitched fabrics and beautifully embroidered tunics fluttered on the racks and hangings, splashing the gloomy grey cobblestones with brilliant contrasts. Carey stopped at one of the silk stalls. She ran her hand over one of the scarves, marvelling at its delicate patterns. Casting about at the tent's other items, she saw hundreds of peculiar contraptions and wares standing upon the many different tables. There were brass pots carved with elegant peacocks, teapots that were covered in silver orchids, an array of tiny handle-less teacups and a large golden flower of which the petals would open, revealing the many spice cups. Carey was looking down at a zebra carved board when she heard a tinkling in front of her. She looked up and a jewellery-clad, frizzled-haired woman, wearing a luminous yellow dress appeared before her. Carey smiled slightly at her; her appearance was most strange.

"Greetings, m'dear. Do you see anything you favour?" the woman asked, flashing an almost toothless grin.

Carey shook her head slightly, then realising how rude she must seem, said, "I was just looking, thank you."

"Are you sure? This particular one came from Ahmedabad, India and is very rare," the woman said, pointing to the golden flower. "Or if you like, a more exotic choice is this teapot, made by a medicine man in the Americas."

Carey shook her head again. "No, no. I was just looking. I'm – oof!"

Carey was suddenly bumped from behind, sending her almost headfirst into the woman's displays. She spun around to see a brightly dressed girl dancing animatedly to some music. A boy was playing music by her on the ground, a coin dish at his crossed feet. Something glittered at his throat, something that looked oddly familiar. The girl flicked her long, dark hair back out of her face, tapping her tambourine in time to the tune issuing from the boy's pan flute. The girl caught Carey's eye and winked. Disgusted, Carey turned back to the woman at the stall; the stall keeper noticed her expression.

"I am guessing – you don't like Travellers?" she asked with the smallest trace of a smile on her face.

Carey considered her carefully. "I don't favour their type. They're… uncivilised."

The woman grinned, flashing her remaining teeth at Carey. "Not all is as it seems, m'dear. Not until you look a little closer."

Carey stared. "What do you mean? They're horrible so what else can they be? Why would anyone disguise themselves as Travellers? Travellers are lower than… than me even."

"And what are you then, hmm?"

"I'm an orphan," Carey said sullenly. "But at least I know things. I don't have to steal and wander the streets to make a living."

The stall keeper nodded slowly then pulled down a light blue scarf from its hangings and handed it to Carey. "Then all I can give you is this."

Carey frowned and looked down at the scarf. "Pardon? All you can… I cannot accept this."

"Take it. It's her favourite colour." The woman looked at her with great excitement.

Carey looked at her, slightly confused. "Whose?"

The woman grinned. "Your mother's of course. I hope you find them. I know you will."

"What? My mother? Is? You must be mistaken. My mother is…"

But the woman had disappeared. Bewildered, Carey turned from the stall, still clutching the scarf. What did she know of her mother? The woman made it sound as if Carey's mother was still alive. But that was impossible. If she was still alive, Carey wouldn't be in an orphanage being treated so badly. No parent would leave their child to such torment...

She looked up at the Travellers – *Not all is as it seems.* What was the woman trying to say? "It's nothing," Carey convinced herself and she stuffed the scarf into her basket.

* * *

Everyone was already eating breakfast by the time Carey arrived back at the orphanage. Voices were floating into the front hall from the kitchen, as was the smell of overcooked tomatoes and sausages. Carey decided to skip breakfast and hurry up to her room, anxious to hide her scarf. If she was found with it... Carey shuddered at the possible consequences. She was just climbing the stairs when a scathing voice caught her from behind.

"Been out begging again, Carey?"

Carey stopped and turned; Adrianna was leaning against one of the bottom railings.

"What do you want?" she asked bluntly.

Adrianna grinned shrewdly. "You're late again. Were you out talking this time or were the pickings slim–"

Adrianna's eyes widened as she spotted the corner of the silk scarf protruding from over the basket's lip. Carey tried to stuff it back under the food but Adrianna was quicker. She bounded up the stairs and snatched it from Carey.

"Oh my God. Where did you get this? This is... oh my gosh... it's silk!" she said, holding it up.

Carey tried to grab it back but Adrianna held it out of her reach. "Adrianna! Give it back, it's mine!"

"Yours? You wouldn't have enough money to buy something like this!" Adrianna said, now running her hands through the smooth fabric. "No one here does."

"It was a–"

"You stole it!" Adrianna screeched ecstatically. "You stole this scarf from one of the stalls!"

Carey could feel the anger rushing to her face. She could see what was running through Adrianna's distorted little mind. If she could make it look like Carey stole the scarf, Carey would almost for certain be thrown out of the orphanage. For Adrianna, it would be a dream come true.

"Adrianna, if you don't give it back, I'll–"

"You'll what? Hit me with your coin dish?" Adrianna laughed derisively. "You are in so much trouble. You're not even supposed to have stuff like this. And to make it worse – you stole it!"

Adrianna ran down the stairs before Carey had time to think and she dashed down the hallway, the scarf in hand. "No!" Carey pleaded, and she started after her. "Adrianna!" But Adrianna wasn't listening. She was running full pelt towards the Headmistress' study. Carey saw the Headmistress' travelling cloak hanging up in the hallway and her heart skipped a beat. She was back. The very thought made Carey run faster and she caught Adrianna just as she reached the door.

"Give it back!" she yelled, latching onto Adrianna's arm.

"Get off me! I'm taking this to Ms Rorx! You are going to be in so much trouble. She'll *have* to tell the Headmistress this time!" Adrianna cried back, trying to pull her arm away from Carey, but Carey wasn't letting go that easily.

The two of them were now wrestling for the scarf, Carey almost on top of Adrianna as they banged against the hallway walls, tumbling backwards. Adrianna seized a handful of Carey's hair and pulled in an effort to get free. Carey screamed with pain, but she did not relent.

"What is going on here?"

Adrianna threw Carey from her back and stumbled back to her feet.

Carey looked up from the floor to see Ms Rorx towering over them. Gulping back a rush of fear, Carey jumped to her feet, dusting herself off quickly.

"I asked you both a question," she said in a dangerous whisper. "What is going on here?"

The other girls were peering out around the kitchen's door. One of them whispered to another and they both stared at Carey, eyes gleaming maliciously. Adrianna burst into an explanation.

"Ms Rorx, I was just going upstairs to get my books, and I found Carey with this–"

She held up the scarf for everyone to see. The girls at the door gasped. Carey clenched her fists in fury. Adrianna continued quickly, not wanting Carey to interrupt. "She stole it from one of the stalls at the market and was just going to go hide it with the rest of her secret stuff."

"What! I did not steal it! A lady at the market gave it to me," Carey said angrily.

Ms Rorx walked slowly over to Carey, towering over her. "She gave it to you... and why would she do such a thing?"

Carey opened her mouth then closed it again. What was she going to say, that she was given it because it was her mother's favourite colour? Carey dropped her gaze. "I don't know. She just... gave it to me."

Ms Rorx paused dangerously. Her nostrils flared. "I see. Adrianna, what is this 'secret stuff' you speak of?" she asked.

Carey glanced up at Adrianna; she grinned malevolently back at her. "Carey has a necklace. It's hidden under her mattress."

Carey stared open-mouthed at Adrianna, feeling as though she had just been slapped hard across her face. How did she know about her necklace? Ms Rorx was silent for a moment and Carey waited for the blow.

"My study. *Now*."

Carey gazed down at the floor and headed for the study, feeling Ms Rorx's gaze upon her back. Carey entered the dark study and sat down heavily on the edge of one of the large wooden chairs that stood in front of the enormous oak table. "We'll see about this," she said and she left them alone as she went to investigate.

Carey continued to stare at Adrianna. Adrianna had just given her most prized secret away. She had destroyed what little hope Carey had left and this burnt Carey deep inside. A deep sense of loathing built up inside her that was unlike anything she had ever felt before. She had never hated someone so much in her life. She wanted to jump up and kick Adrianna in her blonde curly head.

"How did you know about my necklace?" Carey asked through gritted teeth.

Adrianna smiled sickeningly. She was sitting on the edge of her chair, her hands clasped in her lap. "Carey, everyone has their own little cache somewhere. We all have our own secrets. Yours was just easier to find. But really, Carey, under your *mattress*?"

Carey glowered in a disbelieving rage. The *nerve...* "What were you doing in my bedroom in the first place?" she demanded, trying to keep her voice down. She didn't think it entirely wise to start another blazing row right there in Ms Rorx's study, especially with the Headmistress having just returned.

"It's very strange though, isn't it?" Adrianna went on to say, ignoring Carey's question. "Did you steal it too? Oh... wait, you couldn't have. It has your name on it, doesn't it? Very unusual, that is."

"And what about it?" Carey hissed, her fingernails digging into her palms. She could feel the heat rising in her face, her ears burning in ire.

"Well, if you didn't steal it, where did you get it from?" Adrianna asked, raising her eyebrows. Her face was gleaming with spite.

Carey bit her lip to stop from launching herself on Adrianna. "I've had it ever since I got here, so I didn't steal it. And what's it got to do with you anyway? Why do you care?"

Adrianna smiled as if she was teetering on the edge of revealing something big. She was wringing her hands excitedly. "I've had a look at it, your necklace. The markings on it. They're very... strange, aren't they? I've only ever seen writings like that once before."

"And where exactly did you see them then, hmm?" Carey said, though with a little trepidation. What did Adrianna know that she didn't? She was looking annoyingly superior, her head tilted to one side.

"I saw them used by a witch once," Adrianna said shortly but with great triumph.

"A what?" Carey spat. She wasn't sure if she had heard her properly. Was this Adrianna's sad idea of a joke?

"A witch. You know – they dress in black and ride broomsticks. They cast spells on people to make them do whatever they want. They brew potions and use them for their black magic. Witches have even murdered people before, you know–"

"Stop it! Just stop it! What are you saying? I am not a witch!" Carey cried. "How can I be? They're evil. I'm not – I'm not–"

"You're not what?" Adrianna asked sadistically. Her eyes were glinting maniacally.

Carey's stomach dropped like a lead weight. "I am not a witch."

"But how do you know, eh? You don't have any memory of before you came here. You don't know where you got the necklace from. You don't even know your last name. You only know your own name because it's on that necklace. For all we know, you could be," Adrianna said simply but harshly.

Carey didn't say anything. She couldn't. She didn't want to say anything that Adrianna could twist into this ludicrous story of hers. This was sick, disgusting. She wasn't a witch. She wasn't evil. Even so, if Carey really was a witch, she'd have powers, wouldn't she, and Carey knew most definitely that she had no special talents what so ever. She was just a normal, boring person, just like everyone else. Adrianna was surely just being horrible, making up these – these… lies.

Adrianna continued to speak. "Imagine if Ms de Valera heard about this? She hates witches, you know. I heard Ms Rorx say so. She thinks they're the most disgusting things on the face of the earth. Did you ever wonder why she doesn't like you? Think about it. Maybe she knows," Adrianna said cruelly. "You're different to everyone else. You're… odd. It's not like it's hard to see you're not like… normal people. We can all see it. And what if the town found out? What if *people* found out what you are? You know what they used to do to witches?"

"I am not a witch," Carey said quietly. "I am not a witch. This is completely absurd."

"If you say so," Adrianna said with her arms crossed resolutely. "I still think that necklace says it all."

If Ms Rorx had not entered at that very moment, Adrianna might have found a vase cracked over her pretty little head. "Adrianna, you may leave," she said as Carey quickly put the vase by the window back down. "You. Sit," she pointed at Carey, and she sat obediently.

"So, how long were you going to keep this from me? Hmm? You know *perfectly* well that students are not allowed jewellery, perfectly well. I thought you of all people, Carey, would obey the rules of this orphanage, having suffered punishment before. I will have to confiscate this," Ms Rorx said, holding Carey's necklace up. *"And* I will have to inform the Headmistress of this blatant disregard for the rules."

"But it's mine. Why can't I keep it?" Carey said miserably, watching her necklace dangle in the air.

"You see Carey, in orphanages, possessions are dangerous. If one person has something, everyone else will want something too. I just can't have you parading this… necklace," she said as if repulsed by the very sight of it, "around the orphanage. Considering it is real gold."

"So what if it's made of real gold?" Carey asked impudently, not really noticing what she was saying.

"Excuse me?" Ms Rorx asked harshly.

Carey shrunk back. "N-nothing," she stammered, lowering her eyes.

"This necklace is an expensive piece of jewellery. It does not belong in an orphanage," she hissed.

"But – but, it's all I have! If I can't have a memory, why can't I have this?" Carey cried.

"Because your past is not one worth having," a voice bellowed from behind her, filling the whole room with a terrible sound. Carey's ears resonated with Ms de Valera's words like a deafening roar and she spun around. There the Headmistress stood, framed in the doorway, her long black attire fluttering slightly, making her look even more terrifying than usual. An unusual sickness filled Carey and she was suddenly dizzy. Goose bumps rose on her arms as the temperature in the room seemed to drop a few degrees though Carey could never fathom how this always seemed to occur when the Headmistress entered the room. A darkness crept inside Carey and the hairs on the back of her neck stood up.

"Wha – ?" Carey whispered.

There was a silence in which Ms de Valera turned from Carey and glided over to the curtained window to stand next to Ms Rorx. Carey's heart was pumping hard, waiting for an answer, but it seemed that Ms de Valera wasn't going to dignify Carey with a response. She remained with her back to Carey. Ms Rorx stood with her head tilted towards her, as if waiting for something. There was a moment of silence before she looked up at Carey with her steel-coloured eyes.

"As punishment for this," Ms Rorx said, "I will be taking this to the markets tomorrow where it will be sold to one of the merchants–"

"It's mine though…"

"Not anymore it isn't."

"No! It has my name on it! I've never even showed it to anyone else. Give it back!" she screeched, losing herself completely.

Before she knew what she was doing, Carey lunged at Ms Rorx, arms reaching for her necklace, but Ms de Valera knocked her arm quickly out of the way. She pushed Carey back against the window with an alarming amount of strength. Carey clutched the curtains and stared, horrified, up into the faceless terror that was the Headmistress. Ms Rorx stepped up and the Headmistress turned to her, as if to say something. Ms Rorx hesitated for a moment before pulling Carey towards her by the scruff of the neck.

"Now listen here. I am the overseer of this orphanage and you will respect what I say. As extra punishment for this insolence, you will do all of the other girls' chores. *All* of them," she said, savagely.

"But you can't sell my necklace!" Carey cried desperately, tears streaming down her face.

"Go!"

With that, Ms Rorx threw her from the room. Carey stumbled, bleary-eyed into the front common room. She flopped down into a chair and wiped her face clumsily on her sleeve. Her frustration was thudding at her chest. She wanted to scream, the urge was so overwhelming. Carey gripped the arms of the chair so tightly that she thought she might rip holes in them. She stared up at the ceiling, feeling that she couldn't take much more of this abuse, this inexplicable hatred. Everything was against her; it was as if the whole world hated her. All the terrible things from her past in the orphanage came flooding back to her like a torrent of burning waves – the taunting, the unfounded punishments, the loneliness… The pounding frustration was ebbing only to be replaced by a furious determination. Carey grit her teeth, deciding then and there that she would get her necklace back and she would make her escape. She couldn't make herself see reason, she refused to. Carey didn't care. She didn't care that she was an orphan with no future if she escaped. No future was better than remaining in this nightmare. She had made up her mind. It was final.

Carey gazed out of the window and stared moodily into the garden, looking from the tall, green shrubs to the rose bushes. She sat for several moments, her mind racing, trying to devise a plan of escape. Carey was just about to get up from the chair when a movement in one of the bushes caught her eye. She stopped and stared, her eyes on the bush. Again there was movement. Cautiously, she rose from the chair; she tilted her head to one side, trying to get a glimpse of what was stirring within the bushes.

Placing her feet quietly on the floor, she tiptoed over to the window; she pressed her face up against it, trying to get a better look. All of a sudden, out of the bushes came a tall, brown-haired boy about Carey's age – the boy from the markets. He crept across the garden, evidently not trying too hard to keep himself from being seen at all, and knelt beside another shrub. He waved to someone back on the other side of the garden then busied himself with admiring a nearby rose bush. Carey stepped behind the curtains as she caught sight of another person; the dark-haired dancing girl. She ran low across the yard to join her companion, something dangling obviously from her neck. Carey observed them silently as the two intruders discussed something animatedly in the bushes. She was amazed at their daring. Travellers were ill-favoured by most people, including herself, but to come near the orphanage – Ms Rorx would be furious, not to mention Ms de Valera. The two youths seemed not to care whether they got caught or not though. Their faces conveyed neither concern nor worry. Suddenly the boy turned his head and looked directly into Carey's eyes, smiling.

Carey glared at them, her mouth open in disgust. "Urgh," she muttered, yanking the curtains closed.

Thudding footsteps were approaching the study now and Carey sat back down quickly. It was Miss Griffith coming to give her her list of chores. She gave Carey a mop and bucket and rattled off her tasks before leaving without giving Carey a second glance. Looking back at the closed curtains, Carey sighed then dragged the mop and the bucket resolutely after her as she prepared herself for the long day ahead.

Chapter Four

Truth Be Told

C arey finished her last chore around eleven o'clock that evening after almost a full day's work and walked out to the kitchen to put her cloth away. After clipping the hedges, cleaning the bathrooms, sweeping, dusting, removing the spider webs and mopping the floors, she had just enough energy left for what she was about to attempt. Carey had been fine-tuning her escape plan all day, her desire to get out of there as soon as possible fuelled by Adrianna, who kept walking her dirty feet across Carey's clean floors. Every chance she got, Adrianna would sneer 'witch' in her direction until Carey felt she was going to burst with anger. This had been the absolute last straw; Carey was possibly more determined than before to rid herself of this place.

Carey left the dark kitchen and crept on tiptoes down the moonlit hallway. The floorboards creaked only slightly beneath her feet and she tensed every muscle in an effort to soften her steps. The other girls were now fast asleep as was evident from the loud snoring and squeaking of beds as their occupants rolled over in their slumber. Carey stopped just outside Ms Rorx's bedroom, her heart beating so loudly against her chest she thought she might wake her up. She looked around warily for any hint of intrusion; Carey wanted no disruptions from midnight wanderers. She clasped the cold doorknob and turned it slowly, trying hard not to make any noise. After an anxious moment, she had it open just a crack. Carey then slipped silently into the room most of the girls avoided.

Ms Rorx's room was quite large and beautiful compared to her own dingy little room. A magnificent four-poster bed stood against the left wall; dark green velvet curtains hung from each side, save for the one facing Carey. Alongside it was a small, polished wooden bedside table on top of which stood a small blue lamp and several different ornamental boxes. The room looked quite out of place within the orphanage with its rich tapestries hanging from the walls and its beautiful wooden carvings.

Carey could see Ms Rorx's chest rise and fall as she slept soundly beneath her covers. Her thin brown hair was strewn messily across her face and pillow. A long open window faced Carey on the opposite side of the room; its dark green curtains were billowing out from the wind. Moonlight fell across the stained oak floorboards and across the large wooden cupboard that was leaning against the right wall. Carey searched the room, squinting through semi-darkness. She moved a little closer to the bed and as the curtains fluttered up from the window, a strip of moonlight reached the bedside table. A glint of gold caught Carey's eye and she saw it lying there amidst the odd assortment of trinket boxes. Grinning, Carey padded over to the table and snatched up her necklace victoriously. Unfortunately, it caught another, heavier gold chain and before Carey could catch it, it fell loudly to the floor.

An unearthly sound erupted around her. A howling burst forth from the very walls and Carey stumbled. Ms Rorx's eyes snapped open and she sat bolt upright in her bed. Carey stared horrified. She backed away as the orphanage's overseer threw herself out of bed.

"What have you done!" she screamed over the top of the howling but Carey couldn't speak. She couldn't think for the screeching was getting louder. She looked around wildly. It filled her ears with an unmerciful ringing that itched its way into her head. She clapped her hands over her ears and staggered a little, still clutching her necklace. The room began to rattle and the floor began to shake beneath her feet. Carey let out a terrified yelp as the curtains whipped about her. Ms Rorx neither moved nor said anything else; she was waiting. Then Carey saw it; her heart skipped a beat.

From out of the darkness, came a dark, foreboding figure. It emerged from the darkness, like a ghost. The curtains furled around it, the light dancing across the faceless phantom as it moved slowly and purposefully past Ms Rorx and towards Carey. She backed away quickly and came up against the door, which had slammed shut. She fumbled for the doorknob as the noise grew even louder, vibrating inside her head painfully. The figure was the most terrifying thing she had ever seen, shrouded in black and with no face at all. It was almost hypnotic; she could not tear her eyes away because it was familiar; nightmarishly familiar…

Ms Rorx gave a shout that brought Carey crashing back to her senses. Heart pounding, she turned and flung the bedroom door open. The screeching ceased and Carey's head was cleared of the terrible invasion. She made a desperate sprint down the hallway, slip sliding on the freshly mopped floor. As Carey ran towards the front doors, lights flickered on upstairs and she could hear the voices of the other girls. Adrianna was at the top of the stairs and she shouted something that sounded like "malevence!" but Carey kept running. Reaching the front doors, she fumbled with the locks, her hands damp with sweat. She glanced nervously back down the hall and with a final slide of metal, she unlocked the door. Carey heard Ms Rorx's shouts reverberate off the walls of the hall. Adrenalin running high, Carey threw herself out onto the landing. It would have been too dark to see if there had not been a full moon that night. Squinting, she slammed the doors shut, jumped the stairs and ran down the moonlit street as fast as she could, almost tripping in a deep pothole. She heard a bang as the doors of the orphanage bounced open. Ms Rorx was undoubtedly pursuing her. Carey ran faster, her feet pounding painfully on the hard ground as she took herself further from the ghastly scene she had witnessed. She turned a corner and found herself on the highway. It stretched before her like a dark snake into the night, bare and revealing. She had to hide herself. To her right was a small grouping of trees and bushes. Her eyes now adjusting to the dim moonlight, Carey swerved off the side of the road and flung herself behind a large shrub. Carey crouched low, trying to hide as best she could. Her breath was heavy and she clutched her side, a stitch developing painfully beneath her ribs. Straining her ears, the crunch of footsteps on the loose dirt alerted her of someone coming. Sure enough, a few moments later she saw Ms Rorx's bare feet run past. Carey let them disappear into the dark before taking a deep, steadying breath. Her heartbeat was beginning to slow and she leant up against a nearby tree, staring up at the stars with immense relief. She had done it, she had escaped…

It seemed like hours before she heard Ms Rorx return. She then waited a little longer; she had not come this far to get caught. After making sure there was no chance of this happening, Carey climbed out of the shrubbery and began walking. She had achieved her goal, but Carey did not want to simply escape from the orphanage; she wanted to be as far away from Monaghan as possible. She walked for hours along the dusty road beneath the round glowing moon until she was so sleepy and her feet were so sore that she had to stop or risk passing out from exhaustion. Carey found a soft clump of bushes by the highway in which to sleep and carefully concealed herself amongst them. It didn't take long for her to fall asleep. The stars swam before her eyes as she gazed up through the branches and she fell almost instantly into a deep fitful sleep.

* * *

Carey awoke a little before dawn; the frost was still fresh on the ground. She had barely slept, owing to the hard ground and the strange surrounding wilderness. Carey sat up cautiously, rubbing her eyes. She looked around warily and slowly got to her feet. The dirt road stretched before her like a long, brown snake. It looked demanding, the nearest possible respite being a farmhouse several miles away at least. Carey noticed the vast fields of wheat and vegetables that were growing on either side of the road, soft yellows and greens cloaking the countryside. *The orphanage must be miles away by now*, Carey thought as she bent down to pick some wild berries off a bush to eat.

The sun began to warm up as Carey started walking. She was beginning to wonder where she would actually go when three men stepped out from behind a towering oak. They were all rather dirty and their clothes hung off them in tatters. A foul smell met Carey's nose. She lowered her eyes, hoping just to walk on by without any trouble. One of the men walked towards her and stepped in front of Carey, blocking her way.

"Ex-excuse me," Carey stammered, stepping to the left to walk around the man, but he too, stepped to the side and again blocked Carey's way.

"Tom, Michael, 'ow much do you think we'll ge' for this one?" he called over to his friends, who sniggered back, their hungry eyes fixed on her. The one blocking her way turned back to Carey. "Where's your mother and father, li'le girl?" he asked her, leaning forward.

"I'm – I'm not a little girl," Carey said, shaking slightly, "and my mother and father are waiting for me in Dublin."

"Is tha' so?" the man sneered, looking Carey up and down.

Carey's mouth became quickly parched. Her heart quickened. "Yes… that's-that's right… And you better not do anything to me either. My father is a royal guard and he'll catch you, you know. They will put you in the dungeons." She stood up a little straighter, trying to draw up some courage in the face of these men. Carey wasn't about to give up her new-found freedom so easily and she certainly did not want these filthy kidnappers taking it from her.

She looked passed the scruffy layabout and saw the other two progressing towards her. The fellow blocking Carey's way suddenly advanced on her and made a grab for her arm. Carey began to stumble backwards, but before she had moved even one step, a stream of silver hit the man in the middle of his stomach, making him double over in pain. Carey spun around in surprise and saw the Travellers from the garden standing behind her. The girl had her hand outstretched, pointed towards the three men, who were now running as quickly as possible in the opposite direction.

Carey stood stunned, looking at the girl in amazement. A wide smile spread over her defender's face and she walked towards Carey, holding her arms out. She reached Carey and gave her a big hug before retreating and beckoning the boy over. Carey observed them both, not sure of whether to be disgusted or relieved.

"Er… um… who are you?" Carey asked, slightly put off by their behaviour. What was that silver light that had hit that man? Was it some kind of flare?

"Carey," the girl said. "Carey, it's us."

Carey stared at the girl, completely confused. "I'm sorry, I – wait a moment. How do you know my name?"

"That's because… we used to be… Carey, don't you remember?" the girl asked, her smile fading.

Carey shook her head, still staring. The girl looked sideways at the boy who shrugged.

"You have to… I… It's us, Carey, Kat and Ji! Kat Lawrence and Ji Binx! Don't… don't you remember?"

She was starting to look worried. Carey stepped back away from them. She didn't like this. How did these *Travellers* know her name?

"Look, I don't know how you know my name or what you just did, but I'm just going to leave now, all right?"

The boy Ji took a tentative step towards Carey. "Carey," he said calmly. "Carey, it's us. It's…" he stopped then changed his approach. "We're your friends. Please, just listen…"

"Friends? I'm sorry, I really don't remember…" Carey said, continuing to back away.

The boy looked at his companion in desperation. The girl, Kat, whispered something urgently to him.

"Please stop," he urged Carey. "Please. If you don't remember us… then how about your parents? Do you remember anything about them?" he asked.

Carey stopped. "What?" she said, shaking her head. "My mother and father are dead–"

"No, they're not," Kat said.

Carey's heart skipped a beat. "What?"

"They're not dead. They're alive."

Carey took a step forward. "How are they alive? How do you know this?"

"Is there anything you remember, about us I mean?" Ji pressed on, ignoring her questions. "How about Malevolence? Do you remember her?"

"Malevolence? Who's Malevolence–"

"How about the marketplace? That day...?"

Carey just stared at him. His words sparked a faint memory, though it was one of a dream...

"I lost my memory when I was nine-years-old," she said, continuing to stare at Ji, watching his reaction. "I am an orphan and have been ever since I can remember. I can't remember my last name, or anything before that time, let alone my mother or my father or this Malevent or Malevence or... I'm sorry, I don't understand... You say you know who I am and that my parents are alive. I just can't..."

Carey took a deep calming breath, settling the nerves that were jangling inside her chest. "Who are you?"

It took all her willpower to ignore the feeling inside her that told her to run. It was all too strange, disturbingly so. These people said they knew her parents, that they were alive and that they knew who she was. But if that was so, why had it taken them so long to come forward? Why had they left her in that orphanage for so many years? Did they really know who she was? They were Travellers after all. What did Travellers have to do with her?

Ji and Kat talked in low voices for a moment, turning their faces away from Carey.

"Okay," Kat said with a deep breath. "We're going to start right from the beginning. You're a witch, a sorceress, Carey, your mother and your father are sorcerers and your older twin sisters are witches too. Your mother–"

"Hold on a second," Carey said, taken aback. "What did you say?"

"You're – you're a witch," Kat said hesitantly. "You're one of us."

Carey shook her head stubbornly. She said a witch – that couldn't be true because... What Adrianna had said came flooding back to her in a horrid rush. If what this girl said was true, that would make Adrianna right and that would be too much for Carey to bear. She was trying to escape from all that. "No. I am *not* a witch. I am not one of... *you*. Witches are evil and if you think you're going to make me believe..." Carey began backing away from them. She had to keep moving – she was losing time. "I'm leaving."

"Carey wait!" Ji said, walking towards her.

Carey quickened her pace. "Leave me alone!" she cried over her shoulder.

Kat started after her. "But Carey you don't understand–"

"No, *you* don't understand! You don't know me! So just leave – me – be!" Carey yelled, her voice turning shrill.

"But that's the thing, Carey, we do."

Carey stopped and turned. "Is that so? Then please, tell me!"

Kat and Ji were looking at her desperately.

"So? What is it that you know?" Carey snarled.

She stared hard at Kat, willing her to say something, daring her. Carey was ready for a fight.

"You want to know about your family," Kat started. "You want to know where you came from, your past."

Carey laughed airily. "Oh really–"

"But," she cut across Carey's remark, "a part of you doesn't, because what kind of people are they, if they abandoned you to be brought up in such a terrible place? What kind of people are they, to do that to you?"

Carey's heart quickened. "That's not..."

Kat's speech quickened. "Even so, if you're anything like us, your curiosity will never rest until you've found them... until you really know..."

Carey's heart was in her throat now. "Know what?" she asked in barely a whisper.

"Whether the reason you're all alone is because they didn't love you, or because of something much worse, and I *know* you secretly wish it is the latter of the two," Kat said, taking a step towards Carey.

Carey didn't say anything – she *couldn't* say anything. It was all true. Kat had just laid out in front of her everything she dreaded, everything she lay awake thinking about, night after night...

"How do you know this?" she asked. 'How do I know this is not just some trick?"

"Because, Carey, we *are* you. The only difference is that we know that our parents did not abandon us. We've finally found you, after all these years. We're not going to let you disappear again."

"But what you said before, about me being a… being a witch," Carey hesitated.

Ji nodded. "That is true."

Carey frowned. "But it–"

"Look, Carey, we are not what you think. Not all witches are evil, not all of them. We are white wizards. We hate evil, just like you," Ji said patiently.

Carey bit her lip. "How can I trust you? How do I know this is real?"

Ji tugged at a thin strap that was around his neck. A necklace fell from the neck of his shirt. It was the same as Carey's; an engraved golden triangle on the end of a thin, leather strap. He held it out to her.

"This is why. You are part of an Order – an Order that is dedicated to the destruction of evil and Dark magic. You're the heir, Carey. Your grandmother created this Order. Her power was passed on to your mother and father, and now, now that they are no longer able to possess this power, we need you. We are the only ones left of this Order, and we can't do this without you," Ji said passionately, gazing unblinkingly into her eyes.

Carey didn't know what to say. She just stared. Ji's necklace was the same as hers, right down to the markings on the surface. It glinted in the sunlight, willing her to believe. She reached inside her pocket and took out her own necklace and looked down at it, the conflict in her mind subsiding slightly. Could it be true?

There was something he said, however, that niggled at her.

"What happened to my parents?" Carey asked, still clutching her necklace in her hand. "You said they could no longer possess their power or something. They're still alive?"

Kat continued. "There are different worlds Carey. There is our world and this world. Our world, the Mystic Realm, Terra Saga, the world of magic has been overthrown by the Dark magic and is ruled by the most powerful Sorceress of all the ages. All that was once good has been forced from it or enslaved. This world, the world of men, of Commoners, became our only refuge, but the Sorceress wasn't satisfied in having taken one world. She had to destroy all white magic, whether in this realm or the Mystic Realm.

But your grandmother, Lady Fianna Parnell, began the Order–"

"The Order of the Rose," Carey said vaguely, looking down at her own necklace and Kat nodded.

"Yes, the Order of the Rose. She founded this Order in a valiant attempt to rid the Realms of the Empire that had formed and its Dark magic that was cloaking our worlds. But it was failing. It was then that she decided that she would shift her focus to destroying the one that had created this terror – the Sorceress herself, Malevolence."

"Your mother and father were part of a select group," Ji continued for Kat, "that would carry out this mission, but when we were nine-years-old, we were caught, or rather, betrayed. Our families were sent to the Mystic Realm to be enslaved – all but your twin sisters. They were the ones who had betrayed us to the evil Sorceress." Ji's face contorted with hatred, as did Kat's at the mention of Carey's sisters' betrayal. "We were the only ones to escape from the spell that day but only us two got away. We got separated in the marketplace. We tried to find you but you had disappeared. As for your memory, we can only guess that the guards following us did something to you."

Ji paused, giving Carey a moment to process everything he was telling her. "After that, we didn't know where you went. We had thought that Malevolence had got you, because you just... disappeared. But after searching for Malevolence for the past six years, we finally found you, and you just happened to be being held in that orphanage by... well Carey, you were being held there by Malevolence herself."

Carey looked back down at her necklace. Her head was spinning with all this information. She was a witch for one, and one third of what remained of a rebel Order. And oddly enough, everything about this that might have seemed strange made sense. Now she knew why Ms de Valera and the Ms Rorx hated her so much and why she had felt so much like an outcast. But Adrianna had been right. Had she just guessed, or did she really know?

"But why did Ms De Val – I mean... *Malevolence* keep me in the orphanage all this time if she, you know, hated us? That is, 'cause I think... she did hate us, didn't she?"

Kat and Ji started walking and Carey walked along side them, waiting for an answer. Ji nodded. "Oh yes, very much. She hates us with every fibre of her body. Even when we escaped, it was close. She would have rather have killed us all than waste time catching us and sending us away again. She almost did that once already."

Kat was biting her lip pensively. "I believe she was keeping you for a reason. There must have been something between us that saved us from Malevolence's curse that day. There must be some sort of power between us that she doesn't want us to have. Perhaps if she kept you away from us then that power could never be used again, if it is in fact something between us. And if you were unable to remember, then you wouldn't try to look for us, or pose any kind of threat to her."

"*But* it could also be that she was using you to lure us there so she could finally send us all to the other realm in one go – either that or destroy us. We guessed that a possible reason why Malevolence never just sent you to the other realm was because she wanted to catch us all at the one time, rather than one by one," Ji added intelligently.

"Yes, well that too," Kat admitted.

Carey stopped walking, opened her mouth, and then shut it again in thought. She mulled this information over while Kat and Ji looked at her uncertainly, most probably hoping that Carey would believe them. Carey looked back at them. She wasn't sure what to think now. There was a lot to consider, but it did make sense, even if it was completely outlandish. Carey had dreamt of the time when she would find out about her history, when she would discover who she really was. If this was true, if she really was what they said she was, then maybe this was the way to find it. She would finally discover her past. Besides, it's not like she had any real future anyway so what was there to lose?

"So Malevolence has been keeping me in an orphanage for the last six years, to keep me away from you or whatever Ji just said, thinking that we had some inexplicable power… or because she's just too impatient? You're joking, right?"

"Well not quite but…"

Carey shook her head. "I really must be dreaming, because I actually believe you," she said smiling nervously.

Kat laughed, greatly relieved. Ji grinned widely, tucking his necklace back inside his shirt.

"Well, we better make a start for it, shall we? Malevolence will find out sooner or later that we've found you, Carey, so we have to be careful. She has spies everywhere. Plus, when she does find out, there's no telling what she'll do. But don't worry, it's going to be all right. We've lasted this long at least," Kat said reassuringly. "And Carey… it's great to have you back."

It was strange. Carey didn't quite know what to think just yet. Everything was still a blur, slightly surreal. It was like a dream that felt all too real to actually be one. However, she knew one thing for sure – she was all of a sudden extremely happy, which was something she hadn't felt in a very long time.

Chapter Five

Dæmons of this World

Magic proved a lot more difficult than Carey had expected.

"I *am* a witch, aren't I?" Carey asked Kat and Ji miserably, examining her fingers as if to find something there that might explain why she had not been able to produce even the smallest exhibition of magic.

"Of course you are Carey, don't worry," Kat said supportively. "It's been a while since you've done magic remember."

"Well actually, no, but I'll take your word for it," she said, screwing up her nose and concentrating on the small candle Ji had produced for her to light.

"Now just remember, it has to come from right inside," Ji coached. "Concentrate fully on your intention, okay? Imagine the magic flowing from within you and rushing to the tip of your fingers – that's it!"

A rush of red sparks had shot from Carey's fingers and set alight the patch of grass beside the candle, which Kat quickly stamped out. "You did it!"

Carey beamed. Now that was more like it.

"Ok, try again. This time, aim more for the candle," Ji smiled, repositioning the candle in front of Carey.

Carey nodded sarcastically. "Yes yes, if you say so. All right, here goes."

She pointed at the candle and Kat and Ji fell silent. She screwed up her nose in concentration and tried to summon the magic again but it was gone.

"Oh no!" Carey cried and Ji rolled over laughing while Kat made to comfort her once again. "This will get easier, won't it?"

"Of course it will, and stronger. Soon you'll be fighting off Imperials with the best of us," Kat assured her, although the prospect of actually fighting anyone sent a thrill of fear through Carey's body. "Once you master your magic, you will be able to control its strength and purpose. Most Imperials shoot to kill because their magic is laced with dark magic. It is easier to kill if you possess that kind of evil."

"So you've never killed anyone?" Carey asked with wide eyes.

Kat grimaced. "Never intentionally, but accidents happen..." she trailed off and Carey decided not to push her. It was clearly not something she wished to discuss.

"Shall we try again, then?" Ji suggested, shifting the conversation away from Kat.

With the thought of murderous Imperials in mind, Carey nodded determinedly. "Yes, let's."

* * *

Carey worked harder as they moved further away from Monaghan. They travelled the open roads past small thatched villages, vast wheat fields and into deep, menacing valleys before reaching a dark and forbidding forest.

"Do we really have to go in there?" Carey asked fearfully, casting her gaze towards the tops of the towering trees that stood before them.

"Of course. This is perhaps one of the most important parts of our trip," Ji answered, but his eyes were also wondering warily about the darkness.

"In this forest is our parents' oldest friend and confidante, Madame Guise. She is powerful in the art of divination and is helping us find the window into the Mystic Realm. She believes that if Malevolence is destroyed, then the whole of the magical world and the Mystic Realm will be restored, and peace will finally reign again after the many decades of living under the dark rule of the Empire. Lady Fianna also believed this, which lead to the formation of us – the last Seekers," Kat said.

"Oh... so Madame Guise can see the future?"

Kat shook her head. "No, not the future, just what might happen if someone is ready to take the action needed. Fianna took her advice very seriously and so... here we are," she said, arms outstretched.

"Wait," Carey said, mulling this over. "So we're the product of an order formed in the past for the sake of something that might happen in the future – ohhh," Carey felt dizzy. "That's just–"

"All right, Kat. I think that's enough information to mess with Carey's brain for the time being," Ji laughed, clapping a hand on Carey's shoulder. "All this talk about the future is enough to give anyone a headache. I just get a headache thinking about getting up tomorrow rather than what will actually happen!"

Kat didn't share his view so easily or light-heartedly.

"You're not taking this seriously enough, Ji," she said irritably. "Carey needs to know this if she is to truly help us."

"*You're* taking this too seriously, Kat. It's already been a mind-blowing few weeks for Carey. I don't think she needs any–"

"Oh really Ji! We don't have the t–" Kat said sternly before Ji cut across.

"Time? Kat! We've had six years of searching already and suddenly we have no time? Oh come on, really?"

"Well we don't, Ji. She'll know we're here by now! We don't have the upper hand like we did before and you should know that," Kat spat throwing her hands up into the air. "You know what she's like. She can kill you faster than you can think!"

Ji raised an eyebrow. "You don't think I know that? *You don't think I know that?* What in mercy's name – geez! It's just that... well, you know... oh, for Potter's sake, come now Kat! It's just a little forthcoming don't you think?"

Carey bit her lip, unsure of whether to interrupt or not as this was all a little awkward. She was fine with Kat telling her all this but the she also agreed with Ji; it was all so overwhelming. She didn't want to make it look like she was taking sides though; Kat did seem awful angry.

"No, Ji! I won't 'come on'! This is important! This is – oh, I give up. You don't understand! You *never* understand!" Kat said shrilly. "And after all this, I thought you would!"

Kat was fuming. She stormed off into the forest's darkness, yelling back at them, "*Come on!*" before disappearing. Ji frowned.

"Oh I wish she wouldn't do this! Sorry, Carey. It's been difficult, you know, with everything... I just wish she wouldn't do that though! There are Dæmons in there," Ji said, sounding exasperated.

"Well you did kind of – what? What's a Dæmon?" Carey said, slightly alarmed as Ji started towards the forest. "What do you mean?"

"It's a–" Ji began, but was cut off by a high-pitched, blood-curdling scream.

"Kat!" Ji and Carey cried in unison, and they took off at breakneck speed towards the screams coming from deep within the forest.

Carey ran behind Ji, dodging the low branches of the tall oaks and sprinting over the moss-covered logs that lay in her way. She heard a loud deafening shriek echo from within the trees. It sounded terribly like a large animal and its shrieks continued to fill the forest, making Carey's hair stand on end. She tripped over a large protruding root that she didn't see in her rising panic and almost tumbled head over heels. Her heart had begun pounding hard against her ribs. She felt a little hesitant as the creature's howls grew louder and louder.

Carey ran from behind a humungous tree and found herself in a small, round clearing. Lying in the centre of the clearing was Kat; she was bleeding freely from a long deep gash up her right arm and her leg was positioned very awkwardly. The worst, however, was towering high over Katrina, bearing down on her. It was enormous, about ten times the size of any man Carey had ever seen. The beast had the head, chest and front legs of a gigantic burly black wolf. Its long barbed tail was scaly like a snake's and it whipped through the air lethally. A pair of large, black bat's wings, ending with long sharp talons, beat noisily, battering the trunks of the towering trees; leaves fell around Kat in a whirlwind of foliage. Carey stared, transfixed as the monster vanished in a whiff of smoke then reappeared only metres above Kat. Kat flung her arms up above her head to shield herself as the creature swooped down on her; it picked her up like a rag doll and threw her up against a tree.

"Kat!" Carey screeched. She was shaking with horror.

Ji ran towards the creature, his hands outstretched, ready to attack. "Get to Kat and use a shield! I'll try and hold it off!" he yelled at Carey.

Doing as Ji had said, Carey sprinted towards Kat. The animal flew at her and she hurled herself to the ground; she wasn't fast enough though. The wing of the beast hit her, the talon slashing her side as she dived at the ground. Blinded by pain, Carey crawled awkwardly towards Kat who lay unconscious on the ground. She could hear the blasts of Ji defending them, one after the other. The monster was avoiding Ji's curses, disappearing then reappearing again and again until it was merely a haze, reappearing for only a fraction of a second each time. When Carey reached Kat she stopped. She held her hands over Kat and tried to clear her mind. The prickle of magic ran from her fingers but it wasn't strong enough. She was so shaken by fear that it was hard for her to concentrate. A screech sounded close by and Carey heard Ji shout in alarm. She bit her lip and willed the magic to shield Kat from the terror that flew not ten metres above them.

A white wave of silver erupted victoriously from Carey's hands and it spread, covering Kat. It shimmered innocently in the midst of the din. Carey hoped that it would last. She turned now to help Ji but to her immense horror, Ji was laying sprawled on the ground, blood staining the back of his shirt. The beast was flying overhead, bearing down on Carey menacingly, low, growling noises resonating around the clearing. Carey raised her hands to attack but hesitated. A strange sensation was tingling in her skin, a warm prickling. It was slight at first but suddenly grew stronger. It spread all over her body, from her chest to her arms, to her fingers, then all the way to her toes. Carey felt an unfamiliar burst of confidence as she stood there, facing the beast. Her eyes darted across the clearing as it disappeared. She suddenly knew where it was going to appear next...

The thing materialized right above her, flapping its gigantic wings. It was so close that Carey could see the string of saliva dangling precariously from its sharp pointed teeth. As the creature swooped down on her, Carey took hold of her new-found strength, summoned all her magic and forced it upon the animal.

The creature was so close now that it was unable to avoid it. Intense red sparks hit it and for a moment it was suspended in the air before it exploded into a thousand glittering pieces. Carey fell forward onto all fours, gasping for breath as the monster's shimmering remnants fell down around her. The magic that just a moment ago had surged through her body, strengthening her, was gone, leaving her exhausted and weak. The adrenalin was ebbing and with its departure, Carey began to feel the pain in her side. New blood was blossoming all over her pinafore. She ripped a strip of material from her hem and wrapped it tightly around her waist to suppress the bleeding. Carey stood up gingerly and proceeded towards Ji, who was moaning in pain. Doing the same for Ji, Carey helped him stand.

"Don't worry – urgh. Madame Guise's wagon shouldn't be too far. She can help us then."

It took both Ji and Carey's efforts to revive Kat. The ordeal had almost killed her. The gash along her arm had gone so deep that they could see the bone and her leg had suffered a fracture so bad they could see the bone sticking through the skin. It caused her so much pain that she had passed out before she had even hit the tree. They bound her wounds as best they could but all they could hope for was that Madame Guise was not far away...

Kat was very weak and after using every energy reserve they had to revive her, Carey and Ji weren't much better. All three of them leant up against the trunk of an enormous oak and closed their eyes with weariness. After a few minutes' rest, Carey turned to Ji.

"Ji," said Carey wearily. "What was that thing?"

Ji sat up slowly, wincing from the pain. *"That,"* he said, "was a Dæmon... a type of spirit that can have an effect on the real world. We've seen a few, yet, having said that, this one would have to be one of the nastier ones. It's unfortunate that they are not *just* Dæmons."

"What do you mean?"

Ji sighed and closed his eyes. "They are the Empire's... they set them free..."

Chapter Six

Old Friends

After a while, they decided it was no longer safe to stay where they were and made the painful decision to keep moving. With Kat's leg bandaged and bound with a makeshift splint, Carey and Ji helped her to her feet.

"Madame Guise will be able to help us more with this but at least this is better than nothing," Kat said as she tested her leg tentatively. "Ouch. That's nasty."

As they hobbled along the dimly lit forest path, Kat relived the moments before Carey and Ji had come to her aid.

"I wasn't really paying proper attention, which was my fault really. It was stupid – I was being stubborn, but... well, I was walking along the path when I heard it. The flapping of those wings was bearing down on me. It was there before I had even turned around fully. I tried to stop him with a curse but he landed on top of me. His talon ripped through my arm before I could hit him," Kat laughed nervously. "I felt incredibly weak. It was as if something was draining me. My mind went blank."

"The mind-control..." Ji said softly.

Kat nodded. "I should have been ready for it. I knew what it could do. I could only watch as it came at me again. I couldn't even run..."

Kat stopped to take a breath and to rest for a moment.

"What do you mean by mind-control?" Carey asked, waiting for her.

"The Dæmons have the power to drain anything of its magic and make them easy prey just by using their mind," Ji answered for Kat.

"But... *you* were still able to use your powers in its presence though. How did you do that?" Kat said, looking at Carey inquisitively.

Carey frowned, unsure of how to explain what had happened back in the clearing. "I don't know really. When I was face to face with it, something really quite odd happened. This strange... *feeling* spread all over my body and I was given this great surge of energy. It was really quite strange. I know it sounds odd, but I can't really describe it. I was as if I could do anything. I wasn't even panicking," Carey said, wrinkling her nose at how strange her story sounded.

Kat and Ji were looking at her with great interest.

"What?" Carey asked, frowning back at them.

Kat pursed her lips in thought. "I don't know what to say Carey. Some wizards and witches possess within themselves unique powers, something that not all wizards can do. Perhaps this is something like that..."

Kat trailed off in thought and Ji nodded in agreement.

"That could be true... that could be..."

Intrigued by their comments, Carey felt a spark of confidence within her, something that rarely happened. She had always thought that she was a terribly normal and rather boring kind of person but now she felt a little less common and a little more unique.

Carey obviously hadn't spoken for a few moments, having wandered into her own little world because Kat and Ji had started talking about the Dæmon again.

"...what was I talking about... where were we–"

"You and mind-control."

"Ah, right. Well after I collapsed, it simply picked me up with its claws as easily as if I weighed nothing! I heard its shriek – it was so loud... and then it threw me down so hard that it broke my leg. It just snapped... like a twig. Mm," Kat winced and clutched her leg. "I watched it as it came back, as it turned on me again. It threw me up against that tree. I was so afraid it would kill me–"

"Yes, we saw that. It's a wonder that it didn't, Kat," Ji said earnestly and with a noticeable degree of pity.

"Well... now it's over and thanks be that nothing terribly bad happened–"

Carey raised her eyebrows and Kat shrugged. "Well at least we still have all our limbs. All right, come on... Madame Guise will be waiting for us. There may be more of them, and since we can't move faster than a wretched snail, we need to get to her as quickly as possible," said Kat with a tone that clearly said she was not happy with her state of being at the moment.

Carey forced herself to keep moving, helping Kat as she struggled to hobble on her damaged leg. Looking ahead, Carey marvelled at the fact that she was part of something so unbelievable. She wondered at how Kat and Ji could just talk about what had happened as if it were normal. But then again, they were accustomed to all this – it *was* normal.

Carey continued to mull this over in a slightly dazed manner as they carried on, which was quite all right, because at least she wasn't concentrating on the pain in her side.

They continued on, walking quietly through the shadows of the thick trees. The light in the forest was shady and the trees showed little mercy to the scattered flora struggling to capture the sun's rays. They saw very few animals, only insects, including a large quantity of spiders, swarming all over the place, and despite the warm weather, the shadows were cold and bitter.

Carey was just fantasising about a warm blanket and a cup of tea when Ji nudged her and said, "We're here."

They had reached another small clearing where the trees weren't so thick. Carey spotted a wagon on the opposite side. Judging by the grass that was growing high and thick about its wheels and the ivy vines creeping up its sides, the wagon had been there for many years. The polished wood was painted with bright colours; blues, reds, yellows and greens brightened the dull grey of the surrounding woods. The door was emblazoned with a large gold star. Puffs of smoke issued from a thin tin chimney stack and the fire within tinted the red curtains orange, throwing animated shadows of the people within.

Something at the wagon's end caught Carey's eye. A great pure white horse-like creature was grazing in the cool of shadows by the wagon's rear. Carey walked over to gain a closer look – it seemed too large to be a real horse. As she drew closer she realised something very strange about it – it had *wings*. The creature lifted its head and surveyed Carey with a pair of bright blue eyes that seemed vaguely familiar to her. Carey lifted her hand tentatively to the creature – BANG!

The door flew open, making Carey jump: surprised by the sudden noise, the winged horse turned and trotted around to the other side of the wagon.

"Ah! Carey Lee! *Finally!*"

A rather short and equally thin lady had appeared at the door and was looking at Carey with utmost delight. She wore a red and white spotted handkerchief atop her head and a puffy-sleeved, yellow midriff blouse. The skirt she was wearing reached down to her ankles and was composed of odd bits of material sewn together with a very large stitch. Small round earrings hung from her earlobes and her long, blonde hair fell down around her waist in delicate plaits. Her large eyes shone with excitement behind a small pair of square glasses that were set upon a long, thin nose. Carey supposed that this was Madame Guise but was somewhat taken aback. She was much different to what Carey had imagined. Carey had imagined a large plump woman holding a crystal ball, not this small, thin woman that more or less resembled a mouse.

"Yes?" Carey said uncertainly.

"Carey, m'dear! Oh I thought I'd never see you again. You were a most unexpected premonition, most surprising," Madame Guise said, beaming.

"Oh! Er – Carey, this is Madame Guise," Ji said with a start, noticing Carey's confused expression.

"Uh huh," Carey said dazedly then realising how rude she must seem, extended a hand to Madame Guise. "Hello," said Carey, shaking Madame Guise's hand with a smile.

A sharp pain ran up her side. "Ouch!" she whimpered, doubling over.

"Oh, dear me. Are you also hurt? I don't know. I should have seen it really. Master Ji and Miss Katrina have always had the knack for attracting more trouble than they're worth. Come in, come in! I'll fix you up and in the meantime, we need to talk. Oh it's been such a long time... " Madame Guise said, beckoning them inside.

They all sat around a small scrubbed wooden table in the corner and Carey surveyed the inside of the wagon. It certainly was unusual. The interior was twice as big as a normal wagon; the kitchen housed a large, wood-burning stove where a fire was crackling away steadily. A number of dead fouls hung from the roof along with numerous other peculiar plants and pickings. On either side of the wagon were six beds, one on top of the other, set into the walls and lined with intricate carvings.

Madame Guise fussed over them a little, dressing their wounds and applying soothing balms. She fixed Kat's broken leg in an instant then scurried around the kitchen, fixing something that contained a number of herbs and spices.

Carey continued to inspect the wagon. Behind the table was a shelf that held an array of what looked like potions, tarot cards, rune stones and crystal balls. Carey lowered her eyes to a picture mounted on the wall beneath the shelf. It was of a small group of people. Her eyes travelled from each of the eleven people then came to rest on the three young children at the front.

"That's us, isn't it?" Carey asked slowly, intrigued by the sight of this photograph.

Madame Guise placed mugs of a greenish liquid in front of them. "Yes. That is you and the other members of the Order. It was taken in the earlier days of the forming."

"The forming of what?" Carey asked.

"The last hope, my dear. You were the last hope for the rebellion. Here," Madame Guise said, taking the picture down from the wall, "take a closer look."

Carey took the photograph. She knew they were a special group, the last Seekers, but a last hope?

"We were the last hope? The *last?*" she whispered.

Carey observed their small group with a mixture of admiration and pity.

"That's my mother and father on the left there. And there's Kat's," Ji said, pointing to the four people along the back row. "I remember this day. It was hot and I couldn't sit still. My mother was so annoyed…"

Ji's mother and father stood tall amongst the Seekers, smiling proudly alongside their comrades; Kat's mother seemed slightly nervous but her father appeared positively ecstatic. In the front were two older girls, exactly identical in everything including their scowling faces. Carey presumed they were her older twin sisters, Jody and Laurel. A boy of about fourteen years stood at their side wearing a smile that was remarkably similar to Ji's.

"This boy here… is he your brother?" she asked Ji.

He nodded. "That's Zacharia. He was fourteen there," Ji said in a strange voice.

Carey looked back down at Zacharia's frozen portrait. She tried to imagine what it would feel like to lose someone like that, but she couldn't. Carey couldn't possibly imagine without the memory of her family. She had no recollection of such a feeling – it was like searching for a memory that wasn't really there. Beside Zacharia stood the last two adults of the group.

"My mother and father…?"

"They were brave wizards, your parents. They fought many battles and risked everything they had for the freedom of the People. We may never truly appreciate how great they were," Madame Guise said with a small smile.

Carey gazed down at the two people grinning at her from the photograph. Her father's arm was around her mother's shoulders and her mother had her hands placed on Carey's shoulders. Carey ran her hand over the face of the picture, trying desperately to remember them. A tear of desperation began to roll down her cheek.

"Madame Guise. Have you any news on Malevolence yet? Do you have any idea about where she might be?" Kat asked, breaking the silence. With everyone's attention on Madame Guise again, Carey bowed her head to the table and quickly dried her eyes.

"Hmm… Her mind is clouded at times, especially at the moment,"

Madame Guise answered, holding her hand to her brow. "Her thoughts are scattered and divided. It is difficult to decipher them. My greatest fear would be that she has sensed my intrusions and has disbanded her mind's thoughts.

"However," she continued, turning to Kat, "I have seen in part a great island. Now I have no confirmation as to which island it is but I have a suspicion that it may be Aran Island. Spies loyal to the Order contacted me not long ago informing me she had been present in Burtonport and was speaking of some place west of there."

"Did they say what she was doing there in Burtonport?" Kat asked.

Madame Guise shook her head. "Unfortunately they did not. The wizard I am in contact with has been wary about his position. The Empire is beginning to suspect people–"

"Suspect them? Suspect them of what?" Ji enquired.

"Well, you see, the People are becoming restless. The Imperial Court has become suspicious. They are beginning to doubt the loyalty of some Imperials–"

"In other words spies," Kat piped up.

"Yes, spies – spies that have been unable to escape the Empire since the days of the Order. Loyal to us, these spies have been able to tell the People plans and secrets from within the Empire itself. My spy is unfortunately not high enough to know anything of any true importance but never mind – his help is help nonetheless. However, I don't think the spies are the main cause of this unease within the Empire or amongst the People. I feel that there is some other reason behind the disturbances."

"Another reason?" Carey asked, joining in the conversation. "What kind of reason?"

"I am not sure but I sense it is something big. The People have no power in the other realm so they have been reluctant to rebel as the chances of a victory would be slim. But with this… it seems that whatever it is, it has finally stirred them into action. It is a means by which they can fight."

Madame Guise's words rang into silence. Carey didn't really understand what she meant but she could see that it had an impact upon her friends.

They sat, deep in thought, Kat with her brow furrowed and Ji biting the end of his thumb in contemplation. Carey felt a little understudied in the matters of this world to truly know what Madame Guise had meant.

"Could this mean a prophecy of some sort?" Kat suggested finally. "If there was one, promising some release, then perhaps it would be just enough to make them want to fight."

"That's exactly what I thought," Madame Guise said, adjusting her glasses and leaning forward on her chair. "But I cannot find any such prophecy, unless it is so old it was destroyed by the Empire in their purging of the old council. I am searching for anything that might justify the movements of the People but until then, I'm afraid we're all just flying blind."

"If such a prophecy exists though, do you think that perhaps maybe the Empire is aware of it, that perhaps their knowledge is the reason behind their suspicions?" Ji asked, frowning.

"No," Madame Guise said. "No, I don't think so. If they knew, they would be more than suspicious. They would have acted by now and not without force. I will keep searching for it, though. If it is an old prophecy, it may prove difficult to find the keeper, if they are indeed still alive. Malevolence will not act until she knows her suspicions are founded. She is not one to chase after a rumour."

Kat leant back on her chair and Carey blinked. She was finding it difficult to keep up; it was confusing, more so than any other conversation they had had before.

"So this could be a danger to us?" Kat enquired.

"Yes, most definitely. Now here is a map. Use it carefully. Remember, Malevolence has spies and huntsmen everywhere trying to find you. My guess is that Malevolence thinks you are behind the sudden strength of the People and if there is indeed a prophecy, she will attack you in order to get her hands on it. Since the Seekers' disappearance, Malevolence's power and tyranny has every witch and wizard in this world and the other, bound with an incomparable fear. No one is free from the dread she has instilled, even those who claim to have freedom. Therefore, she is not about to let go of that power freely, especially to some rumour. Those of the People that have not been drawn in by her, are in hiding, and those who were not so lucky to escape are enslaved by her in the Mystic Realm. Therefore, you must assume that any witches or wizards you meet on your journey are most likely to be on Malevolence's side. We must keep this idea of a prophecy as speculation though. It may be that her loyalists are looking for something quite different so stay on your guard. Do not let it waver.

"Now," said Madame Guise, taking a deep breath, "you must be starving after travelling all day long, especially with those horrific wounds. And drink – that medicine will help. I'll go and prepare some food."

"No no, let us," Ji said, placing a hand on Madame Guise's arm to stop her from getting up. "We'll do it."

Not long after, numerous plates of food lay upon the table; mountains of vegetables and juicy chicken that Kat and Ji had prepared, with a little magical help, produced wonderful smells, making Carey's mouth water.

"Well, help yourselves," said Ji, grabbing a chicken leg and tearing into it.

Picking up a piece of chicken for herself, Carey turned to Kat as Ji and Madame Guise started talking amongst themselves.

"What did you all mean by prophecy before? I'm not sure I quite understand," she asked.

Swallowing a mouthful of food, Kat answered. "Sorry Carey. I keep forgetting that so much of this is new to you. We believe it might be a prophecy that has the People restless because, until now, there has been very little to give them hope. The Order was officially disbanded when the Empire caught our parents all those years ago. We are considered more of a nuisance than a real threat by Malevolence and I doubt very few people actually know the truth of that day, which is exactly how the Empire would like to keep it. So if there is a prophecy, if something has been Seen, then it would give the People a reason to look for rebellion. A hero is what they need right now, someone they can rally behind. We've seen it happen before. It's a bit of a stretch but the People have no power where they are and it's really the only possibility we can think of."

"How can we know for sure?" Carey asked, intrigued by the idea of some miraculous hero.

Kat shrugged. "We'd have to find someone who had heard it first-hand or even the one who made it. We might get lucky but right now, we just have to go on what we've heard."

After eating their fill and discussing a little more of the possibility of a prophecy, Madame Guise suggested that they turn in for the night.

"You've had an eventful day and have a very long journey ahead of you. You'll need the energy," Madame Guise whispered to them as they climbed into their separate bunks and pulled their patchwork quilts over themselves.

They each murmured their goodnights and although Carey's mind was bursting with thoughts, she found herself drifting immediately off to sleep.

* * *

The sun had barely cracked the horizon when Carey woke the next morning. She lay in her bunk staring up at the bottom of Ji's bed, listening to his breathing in the early morning silence as the remnants of a dream faded before her eyes. From the corner of the wagon came a cough; Carey lifted her head to find Kat sitting quietly, wide awake.

"Kat?"

"Morning," Kat said, sitting forward. "How did you sleep?"

Carey grunted as she rubbed her eyes. "Hmm... not too badly, I suppose. You?"

"I don't sleep much," Kat said, stretching her arms upwards. "I haven't for a while now. It's become more of a habit now than anything. You were dreaming, just now. Nothing too bad, I hope."

Carey sat up in her bed and swung her legs over the side. "Was I talking in my sleep or something?"

"Just a little. You were mumbling and twitching a bit."

Carey closed her eyes and sighed. "It's always the same. The day our parents were taken. My sisters' betrayal, our escape. Always the same."

"Do you ever dream of anything else?" Kat asked, leaning forward.

She shook her head. "I wish I did."

"And I wish I could have a lie-in but that's not going to happen either, is it?" came a croaky voice from above them.

Ji's head poked over the side, squinting through the semi-darkness. "You do realise the time, yes?"

"Sorry Ji," Carey said, rolling out of her bed, but Kat clicked her tongue.

"Stop being such a baby, Ji. It's time to get up anyway."

Ji groaned as he rolled awkwardly down from the top bunk. "One day. One day I'll get to sleep past dawn…"

After a quick breakfast with Madame Guise, the trio gathered their things and made their way out into the clearing which was just starting to gather light from the distant sun.

"Madame Guise, thank you again so much again," Kat said as she slung her satchel over her shoulder. "As usual, you've been very helpful."

"Remember to keep that map safe. Memorise it as soon as you can, then get rid of it," Madame Guise warned.

They each shook Madame Guise's hand in thanks then, just as they turned to leave, Madame Guise called out to Carey.

"Oh! Hold on one moment," Madame Guise cried, suddenly remembering something. "For all the life of me, how could I forget, when after all this time…" she mumbled to herself. "You almost forgot something."

Madame Guise bustled down the wagon stairs, waving for Carey to follow.

"I forgot something?" Carey asked tentatively.

"Yes, yes. Before… well, before that unfortunate day… Where is she? Whenever you don't need her… FIREFLY!" Madame Guise bellowed towards the sky.

Carey stared quizzically up at the trees, wondering what on earth she was looking for when a flash of white sunlight hit her eyes as the canopy was broken. Flying down from the tops of the trees was the dazzling white horse Carey had seen grazing beside the wagon the day before. She watched in wonder as it landed gracefully beside her, folding back its beautiful wings to its body.

"This is Firefly, a gift given to you when you were very young. It was thought that these Pegasus-like creatures were extinct, but your mother

68

and father saved this one from a horrible fate during the Dark War. They are immortal creatures, loyal and good, a faithful friend until the end," said Madame Guise, patting Firefly on the muzzle. Carey stood gaping at the beautiful creature with its white-gold hair and sparkling blue eyes.

"She's mine?" Carey asked, amazed at her good fortune.

"All yours," Madame Guise smiled. "Now you had better move along. Katrina is looking a little impatient."

"Well I do think we should be getting along," Kat said with her hands on her hips.

"Right then! Best of luck, and let no harm befall you on your journeys," Madame Guise said, shooing them along. They looked back and waved as they turned the first corner.

Kat dropped her hand sadly as Madame Guise slipped from view. "I just hope we'll see her again."

Chapter Seven

Destruction and Discovery

They walked in relative silence for a short while, each lost in their own thoughts. Carey was preoccupied with Firefly, taking in every detail of the magnificent creature that walked beside her. Her coat, which had appeared white at first glance, was almost a bright shimmering pearl, the light causing a ripple of shades across her flank. Her mane was like silk to touch and so light that Carey imagined this was what running a hand through a cloud must be like. Her mere presence was much different to that of a normal horse. Firefly exuded intelligence, as if she was aware of the situation. Carey didn't even need to guide her; she matched their pace perfectly.

They walked for some time, Ji whistling an unfamiliar tune softly to himself as Kat glided along the path, her steps barely making a sound. At one point she reached out and punched Ji in the arm in an effort to silence him, but all she got was a loud protest and continued whistling, except a few decibels higher. Carey smiled at Ji's cheek. He seemed terribly apt at diffusing tension which, she guessed, must have become a coping mechanism after so many years.

They came over a rise and Carey looked up to see a most welcome sight. "Look! Kat, Ji, look! Light up ahead!" she said over Ji's tune.

They were approaching the edge of the forest to Carey's great relief and saw before them a small town. Carey smiled at the sight of civilization again but slowed down when she saw the horrors that lay beyond the perfect line of oak trees. Her jaw dropped as she came level with Kat and Ji, who had stopped short, their eyes on the most horrendous sight Carey had ever seen.

"What... but... is... oh my."

Kat, lost for words, looked down at the devastated village that lay before her. Half the town had been destroyed, left in smouldering ruins, while the other half had been pulled apart. It appeared that nothing had been left untouched. Burnt houses rose from their ashes like the tormented skeletons of some immense creature, contents of homes were scattered in the streets and Carey could still hear the screams and cries of people as they wandered through the devastated town. Kat walked over to a house that was still reasonably intact. "Hello? Hello? Anyone in there?" she called, leaning through the doorway.

A scared whimper echoed from within and Ji entered cautiously, Carey and Kat close behind. A middle-aged woman was huddled, cowering and bleeding in a corner of the back room. She was staring at the three of them with large green eyes and her voice quivered in pain as she spoke.

"It's all right. We've come to help," Kat said quietly, moving slowly over towards the woman.

The woman looked at Kat warily through narrowed eyes then closed them as a racking cough took her over.

"They came... in the darkness..." the woman muttered, her breath becoming ragged. "They were searching... searching for them..."

"For who?" Ji demanded softly, kneeling down beside her.

She looked at him for a moment. "They came for them... the Seekers... aargh..." she moaned, curling in pain. "But I thought..."

Kat curled her finger around the leather strap of her necklace and tugged so it fell from within the collar of her shirt. The witch's eyes fell upon the golden triangle. "You...?"

"Yes, they want us. We are those Seekers," Kat said almost bitterly as she looked upon the witch in pity.

"Then this means... aargh... that you are finally together – then?" she asked in painful hope.

Carey nodded as the witch looked up at them with tears in her eyes.

"Oh how w-wonderful! So long, so long have we wait – aargh!"

Her scream cut through Carey like a knife, awakening her from the shock of this situation.

"Can we not do anything for her? Can we not stop her pain–"

"No… no, you can't. The arrow which pierced my flesh is tainted with – with some kind of magic that w-will not let it heal…" the woman muttered through gritted teeth, her hand clutching her side where the arrow must have hit her. "Mmm… I will die soon, I am sure of that…"

Carey knelt down beside her as Ji tried to comfort the woman. "There must be something…" she whispered.

Kat shook her head. "She's right. The creatures who serve Malevolence use weapons that inflict wounds that even a skilled wizard cannot heal. I've seen it before."

"It doesn't seem as bad now though," the woman moaned. "I have – lived to see the return… of our champions. Aargh!"

Carey looked on hopelessly, desperately. The witch gasped for air. "You have returned… and now… you must… fight… like you – fought… before…"

Her last word was born on her last breath and the grey-haired witch slumped side-ways, her face slack.

Carey clapped her hand over her mouth. Ji leant over and closed her eyes. *"Ressing Pias,"* he muttered in a language Carey didn't recognise. Kat sighed and turned away.

"You're – you're not just going to leave her here, are you?" Carey asked, her voice shaking.

"We can't do anymore for her–"

"We're not going to bury her or anything?" Carey cried, shocked that Kat and Ji were just going to walk away.

"Carey, understand this. If we move her, we leave traces of ourselves behind for enemy eyes to find. It is harsh, I know," Kat said, reading the horrified look on Carey's face. "But it's just how it has to be. We can't leave any of ourselves behind to be found."

Carey bit her lip, trying to hold back the sudden wave of emotion that was spilling over her. Kat and Ji had told her stories of the horrors they had faced, the dangers they had escaped, and she had not fully appreciated the gravity of them until this moment. She felt sick, as though she wanted to throw up at the very thought of abandoning that poor woman but the others had already turned to leave. A lump rose in her throat and, before she could stop it, a sob escaped her throat. Kat and Ji turned at the sound.

"How much more is like this?" Carey asked in a small voice. "How many more people will die because…"

Kat's expression softened as Ji walked back over to comfort her. "I'm sorry we can't do anything, but they'll know. They have ways. It's been like this ever since it started. We've been fighting this war for a long time and as long as it continues it will take the lives of those who least deserve it. I'm not saying that it's easy – I want so much to give that woman the final respect she deserves – but we need to be careful with everything we do. It is our people who are dying and we are the last of those who can do anything about it. We are the last of the Seekers and just being that brings hope to them. The mere fact that we are still alive gives them something they have not had for a very long time – a defender. That's why we can't leave any trace of ourselves for Imperials to find. We can't risk being caught."

"It's not always like this, I promise," Ji said, giving Carey's arm a calming squeeze.

His reassurance didn't do much to ease her horror but Kat's speech made sense. With everything they had told her about the Empire, she did not want to be the one to let them down and give them away. With a sigh, she nodded and followed the other two out, taking care not to glance back at the woman in the corner so as not to weaken her resolve. She certainly hoped Ji was right and that it wouldn't always be this terrible.

They picked their way through the remaining rubble until they reached the town's outskirts. The screams and cries continued to emanate around them but they were beginning to subside. Carey stayed a few steps behind, her mind racing with the terror of this day, how it had turned so horrid all of a sudden, when she saw something small move out of the corner of her eye. She whipped her head around but there was nothing but smouldering stone and wood. Carey narrowed her eyes and looked over the ruins, searching for signs of life. She could have sworn she had seen something move amongst the rubble. Then she saw it again; a small form within the piles of stone and wood.

"Kat! Ji! What – ?" Carey started but stopped abruptly. The figure had disappeared again.

Kat and Ji had stopped ahead of her. "What is it?" Ji called out.

"Um…" Carey stammered, searching. "I think… I…"

But the thing had vanished. Carey frowned and shook her head. "Erm… never mind. It's nothing."

She took one last look at the ruined village before hurrying to catch up to Kat and Ji.

"Are you sure you're all right?" Kat asked, raising an eyebrow.

Carey forced a smile. "Sure. Fine."

"Well let's get going then. We have a long way to go."

* * *

They continued on, with nothing but their thoughts and the increasingly dismal weather to keep them company. One particularly dim afternoon, Ji spotted a resting point just as the sun was disappearing – a large and rather old-looking castle set atop a small but steep hill.

"We could stay there," Ji suggested, turning to them.

"We could," answered Kat, considering the castle with squinting eyes.

Carey stared up at the castle, feeling a little apprehensive. Ji took the lead, waving for them to follow him up the slightly sloping path to the castle. Carey left Firefly at the foot of the hill, hiding her with a little magic, and the three of them stumbled up the path. Tripping on hidden roots and rocks all the way, they reached the large stone staircase that led to the door. They came to a halt on the landing in front of two huge double oak doors and gazed up at the castle. It felt a little derelict and there was an eerie air about it; a shiver of goose bumps ran down Carey's spine. Ji stepped forward. "Hello?" he called up at the windows. "Anyone home?"

Carey thought she saw a flutter of movement in one of the top windows just as Ji reached over to open the doors; except, he didn't quite grab the handle. For a moment it seemed as though he had lost his footing, but there was something like fear on his face. His eyes widen with surprise as a small "oh!" escaped his lips. Carey and Kat watched in horror as Ji fell straight through the door.

"JI!" Kat screamed as she tried to catch hold of him but failed.

Carey stood stunned. She stared at the spot where Ji had vanished but there was nothing. He had completely disappeared.

Chapter Eight

Behind a Mask

Carey couldn't breathe; her mind was racing. Kat held her hand up just short of the door and ran it the length of it as if searching for something. Her breathing was ragged and shaking slightly, her complexion pale beneath her dark hair. Then, without warning, she started screaming at the high wooden doors. "JI! JI! Are you there! JI! Answer, PLEASE!" There was nothing but silence.

Then, without warning, a loud, desperate pounding began echoing from within. The two Seekers jumped backwards, startled, but it had stopped, just as suddenly as it had started. Carey and Kat held their breath, waiting. Then came a sound they did not expect. Through the thick wooden doors came the faint sound of laughing.

"Kat? What's happening?" Carey asked, confused, but Kat didn't answer.

She was listening closely to the sounds coming from within, leaning slightly in towards the door. She looked terrified, her eyes darting around. Carey waited anxiously for a few tense moments, and then Ji's voice called out to them.

"Kat! Kat, I'm all right, but you won't believe who's here!"

Then a different voice yelled out to them. "How's my girl?"

"OH! Oh, JEREMY!" Kat screamed in excitement, her face breaking into an ecstatic grin. "Carey, it's Jeremy! Oh my...!"

"Just walk through the door, Kat! It doesn't hurt or anything," the new voice came. "It's just an illusion."

Kat hesitated for a moment, then with a resolute sniff, walked straight through it.

Carey felt a jolt of nerves somewhere in her stomach.

I don't like this, Carey thought to herself, a tingle of goose bumps running down her spine once more. *Something doesn't seem right.* Shaking her head, she took a deep breath.

Carey took a step forwards. It felt like walking into a strong wind. Carey pushed through and stumbled into a brightly lit foyer. A marble staircase stood before her, going upwards and then promptly splitting in two. There were countless doors lining the walls of the hall above, which mirrored the lower level with their red banners and tapestries. Kat and Ji were standing at the foot of the stairs talking to a well-built, red-haired man with very pale skin.

Carey approached them slowly, taking in her surrounds. Her eyes travelled, first to the stone walls with their spider web cracks and crumbling corners, then to the marble floor that seemed as though it hadn't been properly polished for some time, then up to the cobwebbed chandelier that hung high above their heads. As she joined the others, Jeremy looked up at Carey with bright blue eyes and smiled. His smile was so wide that Carey could almost count every one of his straight white teeth.

"I don't believe it. Where did you find her?" he asked.

"In an orphanage outside Monaghan and being kept there by no other than Malevolence. It was a wonder that we found her at all, wasn't it Kat?"

Carey saw something flicker in Jeremy's eyes; she frowned, not really knowing why.

"Jeremy, aren't you going to show us around?" Kat asked happily, linking her arm with his.

"All right, come into the kitchen first and I'll make you a cup of tea. You all look dead on your feet," said Jeremy, leading them through an open door to Carey's left.

The kitchen spread before them, housing a large wood stove, a massive polished wooden table and chairs, and a mass of hanging pots, pans and poultry. As Jeremy went to put the kettle on the stove, Carey lent over the table to speak to Kat and Ji. "So, who's this Jeremy then?" she asked, leaning on her crossed arms while trying to sound casual and unconcerned.

"His name is Jeremy Shultz-"

"Another old friend then?"

"Yes."

"All right then."

"He's a little older than us and has been our friend for a *very* long time. We haven't seen him since you disappeared – since we all disappeared I guess – but we hear from him from time to time," Kat explained. "He's really clever, quite the inventor. The door illusion is obviously one of his. He used to make us laugh when we were younger with jokes and tricks he'd come up with," she laughed, her eyes glistening with memories.

"Hope you're not talking about me now?" Jeremy asked, placing a tray of tea on the table.

"Only the good things," Kat smiled, passing the tea-pot to Ji. "So, what have you been doing? We haven't heard from you in a while."

"Well, I've only been living here for about a year and a half. Mother and father inherited it from someone in the family line. It seemed like a good place for them to settle down, stop travelling. Of course, I wasn't one to stop running around all of a sudden, as you can possibly imagine, but then again, they seemed happy."

"I know what you mean. By the way, where are they?" Kat asked, looking around as if to see Jeremy's parents there somewhere.

The same strange flicker Carey had noticed before echoed in Jeremy's eyes. His face fell. Kat gasped, covering her mouth with her hand. "Jeremy, they're... they're not... dead... are they?" she asked in barely a whisper.

Ji gave a small convulsive twitch that nearly upended his cup.

"It was the Empire. My parents – they knew too much about the Empress and what she was doing. They knew information that could have destroyed the Empire. It happened about... a year ago, or so. I was travelling at the time and didn't know until I returned. I don't know how the Empire knew, but when I found them... they had no chance. I knew it was the Empire almost immediately. They were marked, the goat's head, on the side of their neck."

"Why didn't you tell us this?" Ji asked, alarmed, his face deathly pale.

"Well, I… I guess I didn't want to let the Empire to… to know I could do something about it by… bringing you into it…" replied Jeremy, but Carey found his excuse very unconvincing.

There was a long, awkward silence. Kat cleared her throat.

"I'm so sorry Jeremy. I feel like this is something of our fault–"

"No, Kat, no it's not. Don't ever think it's your fault. It's mine and mine alone. If I had been here… perhaps I could have saved them…" His voice trailed off but Carey couldn't help but notice the lack of conviction in his voice. The sorrow that penetrated his dulcet tones seemed false and insincere but as Carey looked over at Kat and Ji, it seemed that she was the only one that thought this. There were some burning questions she wanted to ask this Jeremy fellow but she just couldn't find the courage in front of Kat and Ji.

"Um… look, I have to go do something. There's a nasty draught up on the third floor that I was in the middle of fixing when you showed up and it needs to get done, now that it's so cold… I shouldn't be too long but if I don't see you before you head to bed, your rooms are up on the balcony to the right."

There was a slight note of urgency in his voice but, just like everything else, Carey seemed to be the only one that noticed. Jeremy waved his hand and the empty cups flew over into a bucket on the bench. He then turned and started walking over to the door.

"I shouldn't be too long. Make yourselves at home," he said.

Carey frowned at him as he left. "I have a funny feeling about this," Carey whispered.

"Funny as in 'ha ha' funny, or strange funny?" Ji asked, looking a little perplexed.

"Strange funny. He seemed so odd, don't you think? I'm going to have a look around."

"Carey, he's our *friend*. What's so strange about him?" Kat asked, shrugging her shoulders.

"I don't know. Just, how he was acting. He didn't seem sincere at all, about anything. Especially about his parents' deaths–"

"What? That's a terrible thing to happen and it would be hard for anyone to talk about something like that. You should know that!" said Kat fiercely, but Carey ignored her and kept going.

"Not only that, but he didn't say *why* they died, only that it was his fault. What could he have possibly done to cause his parents' deaths?"

"Well," said Ji slowly. "Now that you mention it, he did seem a bit anxious."

Kat coughed, exasperated. "What are you thinking? He has helped us so much in the past and this is how you treat him?"

"Yeah, well there is something not quite right here Kat, no matter how much you don't want to believe it." Carey stood up.

Leaving an infuriated Kat behind, Carey walked out into the foyer again. Torches were now lit on either side, casting a mellow light over to the stairs. They flickered eerily, throwing devilish shadows up onto the high stone walls. The sight made Carey's skin crawl. Listening carefully, she heard the faint rumble of voices from somewhere above.

"Who can he be talking to?" Carey whispered to herself, tiptoeing softly up to the left corridor. The doors coming off the balcony were all closed and none of them showed life from inside, but just as Carey made to turn back, a small stream of light caught her eye. A faint glow emanated from *behind* a hanging tapestry. Carey stopped and stared. Cautiously she crept over to the tapestry and slowly lifted up one corner. Behind the tapestry was a dimly lit stairwell that sloped down towards a door at the end. Carey lifted it a little higher watching for any sudden movements within. Looking over her shoulder, she stepped down onto the first step and again heard the voices, but closer this time. Listening intently, Carey flattened herself against the wall, hiding herself in the shadows. Slowly, she edged down the corridor. A sliver of light came from a crack between the wall and the door at the end. Carey leant around it and peered into the mysterious room beyond.

It was a large living room, lit only by the light of an enormous fireplace.

Two long shadows lay across the floor, their owners standing by the open fire. A burst from the fireplace lit up the scene. Carey swallowed a gasp.

"They're here, Your Highness," Jeremy said.

"Perfect. And Carey, is she here?"

"Yes, Your Highness. Is there anything you need?"

"Just keep them here. You have finally proven your worth, Jeremy. I will expect you to follow this through. You must not fail me, not now that we finally have the remaining Seekers."

"Yes, Your Highness. You have nothing to worry about. I will not fail you."

Carey listened with baited breath, her heart pounding painfully in her ears. It was a trap. Kat and Ji had no idea and Malevolence had them exactly where she wanted them. She could feel panic beginning to rise in her throat, the tingle of anxiety rippling across her skull. She turned on her heel and ran light-footed back up the passageway as fast as she could. She flung herself out onto the balcony and sprinted along it desperately. Grabbing onto the banister, she swung herself down the stairs, jumping the last few steps and slipping ungracefully on the polished floors in her haste.

"Kat," she panted, as she burst through the kitchen door. "Ji... Malevolence is here... in a hidden room... Jeremy's helping her... we've got to go..."

Shocked by her initial entrance, it took them a moment that seemed like an age to register what Carey had said.

"What? Carey, where? Are you sure?" Ji asked, standing up.

"Up to the left, behind a tapestry," Carey answered, out of breath.

Ji strode over to the door and disappeared. Kat looked up at her.

"It's not true. Tell me it's not true," she pleaded with Carey. "This is Jeremy, he can't have-"

"It is, Kat, but there's no time to talk about this now," Carey said, pulling her out of her chair impatiently.

They hid out of sight waiting for Ji to return. He came back a few moments later. "Jeremy's coming, he's right behind me."

"What! What do we do?" Carey whispered in terror.

"Just - just try to act normal all right? Quick! Sit back down-"

The door swung open and Jeremy strode through, running his fingers through wet hair. "Ah, nothing like a warm shower, hey?" he asked as he sat down next to Carey. Carey grinned forcibly and Kat said, "Mmm… can't wait for one of those myself."

"So, anyone for more tea?" he asked.

When no one answered Jeremy pressed on. "Why so quiet? You guys couldn't keep quiet a second ago. What's wrong?"

Now quite nervous, Carey glanced at Ji anxiously. "Um, it's – it's nothing. We're just tired, that's all."

There was another awkward silence. Carey saw Kat's eyes flit towards the door. It was only a small movement but it was enough for Jeremy to notice. Carey ducked a split second before Jeremy could grab her, knocking her chair clear across the room. Kat was already at the door with Ji close behind her. Carey found herself furthest from the door and Jeremy had noticed this too. There was fire in his eyes as he charged at her. He dived at her but was knocked sideways by Ji who rammed him from the side. Both of them went head over heels, smashing the stone wall. Jeremy was up before Ji could pin him but Kat did so with a single shot.

"Carey! Go!"

Jeremy was writhing in pain, a web of burning red spreading from where Kat had hit him. Ji freed himself and gave Carey an urgent shove towards the door. She ran from the kitchen and across the foyer, scanning it quickly with her eyes. Kat was already halfway across the floor when it was made apparent that Jeremy was back on his feet. Ji was flung out of the kitchen door, skidding across the marble floor. Carey and Kat stopped to help him when a voice echoed across the room.

Malevolence had emerged from behind the tapestry and was looking down on the Seekers below. For a brief moment, Ji, Kat and Carey stared back before Kat's voice rent the air.

"RUN!"

She dodged in front of the other two and sent a flash of magic flying towards Malevolence. Ji ran to the front doors and tried to jerk them open.

"They're stuck!"

Carey spun around, trying to find another escape route. Kat was struggling to shield herself as Jeremy joined Malevolence in her attack. Ji ran back to join Kat in her battle. Carey spotted a stained glass window to the back of the foyer, beneath the balcony. Without a second thought, Carey ran at Kat and Ji, grabbing them around their waists and pulling them towards the window. A flash of light whisked past Carey's ear, shattering the pane of glass a split second before they went flying through it. There was a moment where they were suspended in air before they hit the ground, rolling down a grass embankment.

Ji whistled hard and Firefly appeared at their side, tossing her head nervously. The three of them leapt onto her back and with a swift nudge, Firefly spread her wings and they lifted from the ground. Carey looked back to see Malevolence emerge from the castle; she raised her hand.

"Watch out!" Carey screamed.

A bright light came from behind and hit Ji square between the shoulders. Kat reached out to grab him but missed narrowly, his shirt slipping through her fingers. Carey watched in horror as he fell limply back to earth.

"JI!" Carey cried as she saw him hit the ground.

She went to turn Firefly around but Kat stopped her.

"Carey, no! If we go back now we'll get caught for sure and that's exactly what they want. We'll come back for him, I promise," she bellowed over the howling wind.

Carey turned her head back to Ji. Through the tears she saw him vanish in a wisp of black smoke. "Okay, we'll come back later," she mumbled through the terror that had gripped her, and she turned Firefly towards a small forest in the distance.

Chapter Nine

Jenny's Treasures

Carey steered Firefly to a clearing just east of the castle that was surrounded by dense forest. There they would hide for the night. In silence, she dismounted, walked over to a soft patch of green grass and flopped down cross-legged; she put her head in her hands and shook it dismally. She heard Kat sit down beside her.

"How will we get him back, Kat?" Carey asked, still holding her head in her hands, staring down at the ground, fighting the urge to scream in despair.

"He'll be all right. He can definitely handle himself. Besides, we don't know what Malevolence wants with him. She might be using him as bait to get all of us."

"We *are* going back for him though, aren't we? Even though it might be a trap?"

"A trap never stopped us before. Don't worry, we'll get him back, Carey," Kat assured her, although Carey couldn't help but notice the slight waver in her voice.

"But what if we *do* get caught?" Carey asked, running her fingers through her hair in distress.

Kat gritted her teeth and breathed in slowly. Carey knew she was thinking back to the day their families were taken captive. Carey turned to face Kat and squinted at her through the darkness. "What do you think saved us from Malevolence that day, Kat?"

Kat was silent for a moment. "I've been thinking about that, ever since you killed that Dæmon. You have a unique power, Carey, something Ji and I don't, and it's powerful. Look what you were able to do, even when that thing was blocking our powers. You weren't hindered in the slightest. Perhaps, back then, it was you that saved us. You must have been thinking about us – Ji and myself – when you knocked us out of the way of that curse. Your power covered us, but not our families; they were left the victims."

Carey listened dumbstruck. Could she really posses such powers? But then a horrible thought occurred to her. "I could have saved them then, couldn't have I? I had the power and I didn't."

"It's not your fault," Kat said reassuringly. "You couldn't have known about it back then. We were just children. Even if you did, who's to know what would have happened? Even now you don't know the scope of your power. Who's to say you could have saved them? Look, that's in the past now, you can't change what has happened. We need to look forward. Let's just… let's just think about getting Ji back, all right?"

Carey stared absent-mindedly into the dark then up at the star-spangled sky. "I wish I could remember them. You know, my mother and father."

Kat stopped, her face contorted as though trying to remember something. Then she lifted her satchel over her head and stuck her hand inside. Carey looked on as Kat pulled out a small wooden box and opened it with a tiny gold key.

"I knew I still had it," she said as she handed it to Carey.

Inside was a small silver locket and a tiny gold 'S' shaped pin, placed side by side on the velvet lining.

"These were your mother's," Kat said as she lifted the locket out of the box. "I saved them from your house. After Malevolence sent them to the Mystic Realm she had her soldiers ransack your home. I saved them because I thought that perhaps one day I'd be able to give them back to Jenny. But at the time I never really understood them. I just knew that they were somehow important to her."

"Why did they search the house? What were they looking for?"

"For anything really. Instruments, potions, books, anything that looked remotely important. It was the first place Ji and I went when we escaped because it was the only place we really knew. The village was the one place we always went back to."

Carey examined the two pieces closely. The locket was silver and oval shaped with an intricate floral pattern imprinted around the edges. She opened it slowly and let out a gasp. In the right side of the locket was a black and white photograph of her mother, her face alight with happiness. And there, on the left side, was Carey's father, also smiling, but he had a mischievous twinkle in his eye that made Carey smile a little. Looking closer, she made out the trademark necklace hanging proudly from their necks.

"How long ago were these taken?" Carey asked.

"They were taken just after Malevolence came into power, when they had first formed the Order," Kat explained.

"Oh," said Carey. She looked at the photographs a bit more before closing the locket and placing it back in the box next to the gold 'S' pin. She ran her forefinger over the pin curiously. "What's this?"

"That was given to your mother by a powerful sorcerer, Benjamin Merilius. He was a genius. He was the only one Malevolence didn't have power over. That was true, until Malevolence found his weakness. He was an amazing sorcerer but the People's anger was no match for Malevolence when she took the throne. If Malevolence had the power to destroy such a great sorcerer, what hope did normal witches and wizards have against her?"

She continued reflectively. "This pin gives the wearer the power to shapeshift into any form, animal or human. I saw Jenny use it once, when she posed as one of Malevolence's followers. It can be very useful but extremely dangerous at the same time."

Carey unclipped the pin and held it closer to gain a better look. She was still thinking about the sorcerer, Benjamin Merilius and how such a powerful man had met his downfall in Malevolence.

"Kat, you said that Malevolence was able to kill the most powerful sorcerer of our time. How then do you expect us to defeat her? We're nothing special..."

Kat sighed. "I know that it might be difficult for you to truly understand this, Carey, as much as you want to, but this – us fighting the Empire – it's all we've ever known. It's all we are. We were born unto this mantle. We can't run from it or choose not to fight. It's not as if we can just give up one day and turn to a different life. They would still hunt us and we would spend our lives running. Anyone who isn't a captive slave of the Empire is in perpetual hiding until she is defeated. We might very well be the People's last hope. We have to try, even if it means we die trying."

Kat didn't look at Carey during her speech. When she was finished, she leant forward and lit a small fire and began trying to warm her hands by it. Carey simply stared into the tiny dancing flames reflecting on what Kat had just said. As hard as it was to hear, she was right. She'd been right about Carey not truly understanding. She hadn't grown up running for her life, hoping the Empire weren't just around the next corner. Indeed, she had grown up under the watchful eye of Malevolence, but she hadn't known it at the time, and even though it seemed harsh, in comparison to the life she now led, the ordeals she had faced at the orphanage were trivial. As much as Carey wished it were different, she knew they couldn't run. It just wasn't possible for them. She just didn't see how they could possibly defeat Malevolence and bring down the Empire. It seemed an insurmountable feat.

They were quiet for a moment and Carey looked out in to the darkness. The shadows flickered like quiet Dæmons, creeping forward only to be thrown back by the light of the flames. The deep black of the fallen night swallowed the trees and played tricks on her mind. For a moment she thought she saw a person darting between the trees, a small figure. Carey looked harder, but on second inspection there was nothing. If there had been something it was gone now.

"So how are we going to get Ji back?" she asked, placing the pin back in the velvet-lined box.

"Well, I've thought of something. It's a little rough but I think we could make it work…"

Kat explained the plan she had devised. Carey thought it very clever of Kat to have come up with something so quickly and they spent the night fine-tuning the details. When they finally finished, the sun was beginning to peek over the tops of the trees and the morning birds were starting to sing. Carey stood up and took up her mother's box; she opened it and plucked the small gold pin from the velvet, gesturing for Kat to come closer. Carey then pinned the golden 'S' to Kat's shirt and backed away. Part of the plan involved Kat shapeshifting into a dormouse in order to search the castle for Ji undetected; she would then send some sort of signal for Carey to collect them. This exposed the biggest flaw in their plan as their entire rescue mission rested on Ji being held in a room with a window so that Carey could fly up there with Firefly – if not, then Carey would have to just wait and hope that Kat would be able to fight her way out.

Kat had volunteered to shapeshift partly because Carey believed Kat to be much more confident in her magic than her and partly because Kat blamed herself for Ji's capture in the first place. She reasoned that if she hadn't hesitated, they could have escaped much quicker. She seemed so firm in this theory that Carey dared not argue.

Kat took a deep breath and closed her eyes. Carey watched as she disappeared; now, instead of where Kat the person should have been standing, there was Kat the dormouse. Carey scooped her up and walked over to Firefly, holding Kat in her upturned palm as she mounted and turned to the west.

"Okay, Firefly, here we go. Up to the castle," she whispered in Firefly's ear, and with a great sweep of Firefly's wings, they were on their way.

The sun had now fully risen and several white fluffy clouds were now drifting lazily across the sky. The warm air caressed her face gently, her hair lightly dancing in the wind. It was a typical autumn's day and it begged Carey to forget everything and bask in the withering autumn heat but she shook her head free of any wistful fantasies and forced herself to concentrate on the task ahead. They were approaching the castle fast and she flew low to the trees to keep out of sight, holding on tightly to

Firefly with one hand and clutching Kat closely to her chest with the other. The castle was now very close and Carey directed Firefly towards the dark forest behind it, where the least amount of sun shone, bathing them in cool, dark shadows. They landed silently and smoothly. Carey jumped down and held Kat the dormouse to her face. "Right Kat, we'll wait here behind this oak while you go in. Send a burst of white sparks when you find him," Carey whispered as she put Kat down on to the grass.

Kat squeaked loudly then scurried quickly across the grounds of the castle and out of sight.

"Now all I have to do is wait," Carey sighed nervously as she stroked Firefly's mane.

Hiding behind a giant oak, Carey waited. She was shaking with fear, and not even the beautiful sound of the songbirds or the delicious autumn smell could pacify her. Time seemed to creep by, deliberately prolonging her torment. She kept imagining horrible things that might be happening to Ji. The black spectral figure of the Empress kept floating across her mind and it brought a sick feeling in to her stomach which she just couldn't shake. What did they think they were doing? The thought of fighting Malevolence seemed too much, too out of reach now after everything Kat had said.

Carey stared at the castle, her chest heaving painfully with every crawling second. Just as it was starting to get too uncomfortable, Carey saw Kat's head emerge from a window high in one of the towers to the right; she reached out her hand and sent a shower of white sparks out into the air. Carey jumped up immediately, urging Firefly to her feet. "Come, Firefly! Quickly!" Carey cried as she mounted, trying to keep her voice steady while trying to muster as much courage as she could.

Firefly spread her wings and with a mighty sweep, soared upwards towards the tower window. They came to a stop just outside the window and Carey squinted inside; Kat was untying Ji, her hands fumbling with the knots.

"I think someone's coming!" Ji said in a barely contained whisper.

Carey leapt from Firefly's back through the window, stumbling on the smooth stone floor. She ran over to Ji as Kat sprinted to the door and threw herself up against it in an attempt to stop whatever was on the other side. As Carey fumbled with the rope around Ji's wrists, her stomach lurched with fear; she hoped against hope that Kat could hold off whatever was on the other side of that door. It was at that moment that she noticed that Kat wasn't using any magic. As though he knew what she was thinking, Ji leant forward and said frantically, "It's a bound room; you can't use magic inside it! You've got to help her from out there!"

"What!"

"We have to try from outside the window. If we go outside…"

Carey nodded and with one last tug, managed to free Ji's hands. They ran for the window and Ji held out his hand and practically swung Carey onto Firefly's back. As Ji climbed on behind her, she took a deep calming breath and tried with all her might to clear her mind and summon her magic.

Suddenly the door burst open in a flurry of red sparks, sending Kat sprawling across the floor.

"KAT! Kat, get up!" Carey screamed at her as Malevolence appeared just beyond the threshold, her hands raised.

A low, terrifying voice began reverberating around the small stone room. Malevolence's enchantment filled the room and reached out beyond the window to the others. The wind began to pick up and the sky darkened. Clutching Firefly's mane, Carey found Kat; she lay petrified as Malevolence loomed over her. Carey could see fear in Kat's eyes and it gave her a surge of strength. She drew on her powers like Kat said, reaching down into her very soul and bringing forth every ounce of power that she could. She felt the tingling sensation, but it was too weak – the scene playing out in front of her was too terrifying, too horrific. Malevolence was drawing closer and Carey could see magic dancing at her fingertips. With a deep breath, Carey forced her eyes shut and thought only of Kat. She urged whatever power she had to help her friend, to save Kat, but as she opened her eyes, she saw Malevolence reaching down for her with a skeletal hand.

"Kat! NO!" Carey screamed and a sudden force swept from her body and in through the window. Malevolence was buffeted back and Carey heard Ji cry out triumphantly.

"Kat! Get up! Come on!" she cried and Kat stumbled to her feet, running for the window. Malevolence shook off the enchantment and turned on Carey, the long sweeping tatters of her black garments sweeping around her. She began to chant again and Carey felt her power diminishing. Ji noticed immediately.

"Come on Kat!" he shouted as she climbed onto the sill. "Jump!"

Without a second's hesitation, Kat leapt from the window. The instant her feet left the sill, there was a great blast of wind and Kat was flung forward; Ji reached out and only just managed to grab her by the wrist, shouting in pain as she pulled against his shoulder. Carey gripped Firefly's mane tightly as the Pegasus struggled against the wind; Kat screamed as the wind began to pick up speed around them, whipping them about. From somewhere above them came a loud rumbling as debris swirled about them, making it hard to focus. Carey tried to calm Firefly and regain her bearings but it was proving more and more difficult – the storm that Malevolence had conjured around them was gaining speed and she felt a ripple of something deadly crackle around them.

Then, without warning, a lightning bolt reached down from the blackened sky and touched ground to their left with a deafening CRACK, temporarily blinding the Seekers. Carey flung her arms around Firefly's neck, stunned by her sudden inability to hear or see anything. All she could feel was Ji behind her, struggling to hold onto Kat, and the wind threatening to pull them all down to the ground far below. Firefly bucked and swerved violently and panic rose quickly within Carey's chest where her heart was pounding painfully against her ribcage. She had barely regained her sight when another bolt of lightning struck the ground, this time a lot closer, and Carey screamed, knowing that if they didn't get away soon, the next bolt would find its mark. She turned to see what was happening with her two friends and found Ji straining to hold on to Kat as they swayed violently in the wind.

Twisting Firefly's mane around her wrist for extra support, Carey reached down. "Kat! Take my hand!" she shouted, hoping her words weren't lost to the roar that surrounded them. "Swing up!"

Kat reached up, but her fingers barely touched Carey's before falling back again. "You're too far away! I can't!"

"I can't hold on much longer!" Ji shouted through gritted teeth as Carey felt the ripple of electricity again.

"Come on, Kat! You can do this!" Carey screamed desperately, her arm stretched to its absolute limits.

The wind was a deafening roar now and as Kat swung her arm up again, a gust pushed her forward, giving her the extra lift she needed. Carey cried out in relief as Kat's hand closed around her wrist, and together with Ji, they managed to pull her up onto Firefly. The sky opened up once more, and as the final lightning bolt skewered the clouds, the three Seekers burst from the storm, and not a moment too soon.

Flattened to Firefly's neck, Carey closed her eyes, willing the Pegasus on; the creature responded with enormous speed, and soon they had left the castle far behind. She could feel Kat resting on her back, her breath a ragged mess as she tried to regain her composure. It had been close, but they were alive and together again.

With all three of them exhausted but relieved, they continued north, away from Malevolence for now, but inevitably back to her in the end.

Chapter Ten

Reasoning

The sun was sinking into the horizon when the Seekers finally came to rest in a forest not far from the village of Irvinestown. Carey dismounted the moment Firefly's hooves hit solid ground, her stomach lurching from the long flight. Without saying a word to the others, she threw herself on the ground and hid her face in her hands. What had transpired that very morning still wracked her nerves; her hands were still shaking and images of the Empress were ever present, as if they had been burnt into her irises. Someone sat down softly beside her but she didn't look up. There was silence for a moment before Ji's voice came softly, his dulcet tones soothing her wrecked nerves.

"Carey?" he said quietly, with his hand on her shoulder, strong but comforting.

She didn't know how to put into words what they had just escaped from in a way that wouldn't result in her screaming. It had been a nightmare: Kat's futile effort to barricade the door, Ji tied up, her fingers fumbling as panic had taken her over. That panic – would it ever ease or would it be there forever? Would she ever be as courageous or as confident as her two friends? Carey felt as though she had failed Kat and Ji by being so much less than them, by letting the situation get the better of her.

She looked up at Ji through her fingers and shook her head. Kat had lit a small fire in front of them and she sat cross-legged across the way, her hands clasped with her fingertips together, watching Carey carefully.

Ji moved his hand from her shoulder and gently prised her fingers away from her face.

"Carey, it's over. We're safe," he said gently, taking her hand in his and rubbing it soothingly.

There was something strangely comforting about the way Ji was running his thumb over the back of her hand and the lump in her throat eased. She lifted her head to face the others, shifting self-consciously.

"Sorry," she mumbled, tucking a stray piece of hair behind her ear.

"No, it's fine," Ji said, giving her hand a reassuring squeeze.

"How do you do this? How do you face this everyday and not go completely mad?" Carey asked, trying hard to hide the desperation in her voice. She needed validation that what she was feeling wasn't completely irrational.

Kat laughed, which Carey had to admit was not the reaction she desired.

"If you didn't notice, Carey, I was the one screaming back there. You have to remember that we've been running for a long time. When it comes to it, I put much of our *courage* down to dumb luck and adrenaline."

"But I completely stumbled out there. I couldn't call upon my magic properly at all," Carey said despairingly.

"Like Kat said, we've been running a long time. It also means we've been using our magic a whole lot longer too," Ji said, patting her hand. "Don't worry – you'll get there in the end and you'll be great."

Carey looked up at Ji and was surprised to see him looking at her so intensely. She felt her cheeks flush red and all of a sudden she was glad it was dark.

"I just can't believe Jeremy though. I never thought he'd be one to turn," Kat said, running her hand through her hair. "Of all the people we knew, he and his family were among the most loyal. It still seems so unbelievable."

"He told me everything, as though he couldn't help himself. It felt like he was bragging," Ji said quietly, gazing reflectively into the flames of the fire. "He said he joined Malevolence not long after she banished our families. He joined her purely because he saw she had the upper hand, which I never thought he was capable of. He has no loyalty anymore to what is good, only to what will give him more power. However," Ji paused, "about a year ago, his parents discovered his secret. He told Malevolence and she had them assassinated. They had absolutely no chance. Jeremy's been helping her track us down ever since then. He apparently has eyes everywhere and knew we were coming. Malevolence bewitched the castle so that we would be *attracted* to it. We really have to take more care. I doubt they've left anything to chance; they'll have spies everywhere. They can't afford to have us running around for too much longer."

Ji stared at the flames for a few minutes then continued. "She really doesn't care who she kills or what she does anymore. She thinks she's already won."

"Then why does Malevolence still want us?" Carey asked.

"So she can have total power?" Ji suggested.

"What about the prophecy theory? What if it's not a theory? What if it's real?" Kat said.

"It could answer why she's still so eager to get us. To make sure we have nothing to do with it," Ji put forward.

"But Madame Guise said that Malevolence wasn't one to chase a rumour. Do you think she knows something we don't?" Carey asked, remembering their conversation with the Seer.

Kat shrugged. "Who knows what she knows? I think we got lucky tonight, to tell the truth. The whole situation makes me uneasy."

"Uneasy?" Carey repeated, puzzled.

"She was playing with us, Carey. Malevolence is one of the most powerful sorcerers in known history. She could've killed us there and then, but she didn't."

Replaying the events back at the castle in her mind, Carey realised Kat was right. Not once did she attempt a direct attack even though she had a clear shot. Carey frowned in confusion.

"Why would she do that?"

The three Seekers sat in silence as they contemplated why a sorceress hell-bent on their destruction would simply let them go. The only sound came from a light breeze that danced about them, sending leaves tumbling through the trees.

Carey looked down at Ji's hand on hers and noticed a blood stain on his shirt sleeve near his wrist.

"Ji! You're hurt!" she exclaimed, pointing it out.

Kat jumped up at once and knelt down in front of them. "When did that happen?"

Ji released Carey's hand and crossed his arms so they couldn't see the stain. "It's nothing."

Kat scowled. "It's not nothing. Ji, what did they do to you?"

Ji shook his head, clenching his jaw defiantly; Carey wondered what would have caused Ji to be so resistant. Then he looked up at Kat and her eyes widened in understanding.

"They didn't…" she said quietly, reaching out but stopping short of actually touching him.

Ji nodded; he unfolded his arms and slowly he rolled up his sleeve. There, branded into his skin, was a crude goat's head.

"Oh Ji…" Kat said softly, taking his wrist in her hand tenderly and inspecting it.

Carey stared at it in horror, unable to look away. Ji's skin was blackened and burnt and blood was oozing from the edge where it looked as though the skin had caught on something sharp.

"What is that?" she asked in barely a whisper.

"You heard Jeremy speak of the goat's head?" Kat asked and Carey nodded. "This is it. It's an ancient symbol from the Darklands, the region beyond the lands of the Centre City in the other realm. The Darklands are the centre of black magic within the realms and this was a mark around which dark wizards could gather, to find one another. When Malevolence came to power she brought the mark with her, made it her own. Not only does she brand her followers so that they will never forget where their allegiance lies, but she also brands her victims, so that those who find them are deterred from seeking vengeance. It sends a very strong message: remember who holds the power. She likes reminding people that she owns them, even in death."

Kat produced a long piece of cloth from her bag and tore a strip off. "Here. Let me bind that."

Ji held out his wrist gingerly and Kat carefully wrapped his wound. As she did so, her eyes came to rest on the goat's head and Carey saw revulsion flit across her face. She didn't blame her – even without knowing what it meant, the very thought of them branding Ji like he was an animal was abhorrent.

"There. How's that?" Kat asked as she tied the ends.

Ji nodded with a slight groan. "Fine. Thank you."

Kat sat back down and ran her hands through her hair. "If only we could remove it... but the magic she uses... I'm so sorry, Ji. I wish I could help more."

Ji reached out and rested his hand on Kat's shoulder. "Don't worry. We escaped. If she meant this for you to find, then she failed. I'm still alive, aren't I? It's nothing, so don't give it another thought. It's what she would want; us to be terrified by it."

Kat sighed. As Carey watched, she thought she saw a solitary tear appear in the corner of Kat's eye, but when she looked back up, it was gone. Hatred had replaced disgust upon her face and the flames only made her appear more foreboding.

"I would if it really was nothing. I've seen what follows that mark, as have you. I've seen men and women, great people, become nothing but shadows of their former selves with that mark. We can't dismiss this, Ji. What if she meant it for something more than just a reminder?"

Carey swallowed, her throat dry as she listened to Kat. The hatred that emanated from her was palpable and it made her heart thump painfully against her ribs as she imagined what horrors followed that mark.

"I'll keep it hidden, I swear, and from now on we will have to be more cautious. Trust only ourselves and no one else." Ji reached across and drew Kat into his arms protectively then reached over with his other hand to Carey and took her hand in his. "We will fight this, just as we always do – together. There is nothing we can't do as long we have that."

In silence they sat there as one, with only the light from the flames to frighten away the darkness. Ji's words gave Carey hope; they shone light on what had been a truly terrible day, and she held them close with all her might. The devastation and revelations that had been shown to her did nothing to raise her spirits or give her confidence. Darkness pressed in on her from all sides, but right there with her, were her two friends, who were both her source of strength and her lifeline. This path they were on was never going to be easy; the fight was not only for their survival but for those who could not fight themselves. Carey couldn't let herself be brought down by the evil that surrounded her; she needed to rise above it, become the Seeker they needed her to be. She would find the courage to face what was to come, somehow.

After a while, Kat removed herself from Ji's embrace and stood up.

"I'll make some food since as far as I know, none of us have eaten since last night," she said, stooping next to her bag.

They ate in relative silence until Ji made a proposition Carey found hard to refuse.

"We'll be passing by Irvinestown tomorrow. It was our home town, back in the day. Your old house is still there, if you would like to see it?" he said as he took a bite from a piece of bread.

"My old home? That would be wonderful!" she replied excitedly. Carey had always wondered what her childhood home was like.

Kat was happy to go along with this plan as long as they didn't take too long. "They've had no need to go there for years now but we can't assume they won't be watching the house," she said in warning.

Despite the risk, Carey fell asleep with imaginings of a house with a wide lawn, her parents watching from the terrace as their three daughters played happily in the sun...

* * *

Carey was awoken early the next morning by a big wet muzzle rubbing against the side of her face.

"Ah, Firefly! Leave me alone," Carey grunted as she turned over onto her other side, but again she was nudged stubbornly until she finally opened her eyes and sat up. "Oh I give up. What is it?" she asked, pushing Firefly away with her hand.

She stopped. From somewhere to her left, Carey heard something – the rustling of approaching footsteps. The familiar shock of nerves jolted in her stomach and she wriggled herself free of her bedroll. Crawling on hands and knees, she moved to the edge of the clearing and saw something they had not noticed the night before – a narrow track that carved through the trees. Carey could only guess that it was a trail used by those less eager to travel by the main road, which did not bode well for the Seekers. And there, not more than a hundred metres away, was a small band of travellers.

Quickly she crawled back over to Kat who was still fast asleep, her mouth hanging open slightly.

"Kat, Kat!" Carey whispered urgently, gently shaking her. "Kat, someone's coming!"

Kat's eyes snapped open as if she had never been asleep; she moved instantly over to Ji, who was curled up beside the smouldering remnants of the fire and frantically tried to wake him. Carey gathered up their belongings hurriedly and moved Firefly into the trees before turning back to the track; she approached it with caution.

Carefully concealing herself behind the trunk of a particularly large tree, Carey watched as the group slowly approached in the semi-darkness. They were hooded and cloaked, their faces indiscernible in the dull light, and they moved in a way that gave Carey a horrible feeling in the pit of her stomach. They strode along the path with purpose and in perfect synchronisation.

Kat and Ji joined her behind the tree and peered out at the mysterious travellers. Suddenly Kat grabbed Carey's wrist and whispered tersely, "We need to go."

Carey turned. "What is it?"

"Carey, look closer."

Carey glanced back at the group who were barely thirty metres from them now. Upon their sleeves was the same mark that was branded into

Ji's skin.

"It's the same as Ji's…" Carey whispered as butterflies exploded in her stomach. "Does that mean they're Imperials?"

"I'll bet my life on it," Ji whispered back.

Carey looked back and she felt a tingle run down her spine; they needed to get out of there. The group was very close now and Carey made to follow Ji and Kat only to have her foot catch on a hidden root. Before she could stop herself, a cry of pain escaped her mouth. She slapped a hand over her mouth, but not before the Imperials had heard it. Their heads snapped around at the sound and they instantly found the source. Paralysed by fear, Carey stared back at the faceless men, who were carefully considering her; it was only when Kat screamed at her that she snapped out of it.

"Run!" she yelled and Carey was jolted back to reality. Before she knew it, she was running hard towards Firefly, trying to catch up to the others.

There was a yell and something warm grazed Carey's elbow. Kat and Ji were already on Firefly's back and Ji reached out to take Carey's hand. With one swift movement, Carey grabbed his wrist and he pulled her behind him.

As she looked back, the men had crossed the trees into the clearing; some had their hands raised while others had dropped to one knee. As the three of them lifted from the ground, there came a shout and a stream of curses shot their way. Grabbing Firefly's mane, Kat made to steer her away as Ji shouted, "Shield!"

Ji held out his hand and Carey watched as several of the curses fizzled and popped. The others streamed past them, only just missing them. Carey managed to fight one off but had to duck as another came straight at her head. It whizzed past her cheek, the heat of it burning her skin. As they gained height, Kat turned back and shot a few curses of her own down at the Imperials. One found its target and screams of pain echoed through the woods. Carey watched as he dropped to the ground, writhing in agony.

As they flew higher, they lost sight of their assailants amongst the trees and before long, they were well shot of them, racing through the clouds. Carey took a few deeps breaths to still her thudding heart before she raised her voice in question.

"Who were those people?" she shouted over the whistling of the wind, still a little breathless. She rubbed her cheek, finding it hot from her close encounter but otherwise fine.

"Yes," Kat's voice answered. "Those people, however, were not just loyalists. They were Essedarian, Imperial military. Malevolence's Army, in other words. They're much more organised than the odd Imperial loyalist, and much deadlier. I've seen them destroy an entire underground city before – men, women and children. They show no mercy, especially towards people like us."

"Do you usually just see them out in the open like that? I mean, they weren't exactly trying to be inconspicuous," Carey said, referring to their overly dramatic attire.

"Not normally, but then again, that wasn't exactly the main road back there. If any commoner did come up against them though, I highly doubt they would try to be discreet," Ji answered darkly.

"Regardless of their normal conduct, it merely reinforces how careful we need to be. That was way too close," said Kat as she steered Firefly a little to the left.

Carey closed her eyes and agreed silently. If Firefly hadn't awoken her, it could have been much worse.

"Look!" Ji called out, pointing over Kat's shoulder. "There on the horizon. Irvinestown, Carey."

Carey took in an excited breath as she spotted the church steeple in the distance; soon she would be home.

Chapter Eleven

Sister, Sister

They landed just outside the village, touching down beside the road leading into their old home town. Large, tall pine trees lined the road into town, meeting with a string of small shops that clustered along the main street of Irvinestown. Carey, Kat and Ji observed it silently; a few people were beginning to emerge from their houses, talking cheerfully while going about their morning trade.

The sun was rising heatedly in the east and it cast its rays over the threesome as they walked towards the village.

"It might be better if we leave Firefly here. We could always cover her wings but you never know who might be here," said Ji, walking over towards a clump of thick pines at the side of the road.

Kat nodded her head slightly. "Yes, it's best we do that. We'll attract enough attention as it is. A small town like this – we're bound to stand out."

She led Firefly over to the thick cluster of pine trees by the roadside. "Firefly, stay," said Kat, holding her hand up to placate her. Firefly neighed softly. "Good girl. Okay, shall we go?"

Carey nodded, not sure what she felt more – nervous or excited.

They followed Kat into town and down the main street slowly, surveying the waking inhabitants and the surrounds. Irvinestown was a neat, dull town with residents that wore respectable and equally dull clothing compared to the Seekers' unusual outfits. Carey noticed some women pointing and staring at them as they walked past the butchers; as a matter-of-fact, most of the town folk seemed to have become aware of their sudden presence.

"Kat? Ji? Is it just me, or is everyone staring at us?" Carey asked out of the side of her mouth.

"Just keep walking. We don't want to look any stranger than we already do. This town has a *very* medieval attitude towards witchcraft and wizardry. In fact, they have a very medieval attitude towards *anything* outside their conservative lifestyle. We found that out when they discovered what we," she indicated herself and Ji, "really were. They burnt our houses to the ground. Your family was travelling at the time and we managed to save your family's home from the mob," Kat said, keeping her head forward as she spoke. "I despise this town. Hey Ji, remember Isabella Dellarois? She was always snooping around, trying to find out why we weren't in school. She was the one that found out what we were. Urgh, she was such a busybody."

"It was amazing how Isabella happened to be the Mayor's daughter. It would have been so easy to have made her accidentally *disappear*," said Ji, smiling dreamily.

Kat gave a throaty chuckle as they turned off the main road and into a side street.

An increasing number of people leaving their houses were stopping to stare at the three, whispering conspicuously and making Carey feel increasingly anxious. "Are we getting close, because I *really* don't like the way these people are looking at us." She grabbed Ji's arm for security.

"Here we are," he said, tapping her hand.

A long, white paved path led the way up to a beautiful two-storey wooden house. The veranda that had long been taken over by ivy and flower vines held several broken timber chairs and a number of cracked potted plants. In the vast garden that was overgrown with grass and weeds stood a variety of oak trees, pines and rose bushes spreading out from the path. Carey walked slowly up to the house as Ji and Kat followed at a distance. As she drew closer, she noticed that several of the windows, including the attic, had been smashed and the light blue paint that layered the exterior was starting to peel and show the wood's brownish tint underneath. Kat followed Carey's eye line.

"The Empire, I'm afraid. All the windows… after our families were taken it was searched. Maybe they thought they'd find something, but to tell you the truth, we never really spent much time here."

It was sad to see something that may once have been a happy place for her and her family look so derelict. She raked the building with her eyes, taking in every detail, willing the memories connected to it to return to her, but nothing came. Out of the corner of her eye she saw a very old swing suspended from the branches of one of the trees. She walked over to the large tree and placed her hand on the rough, weather-beaten seat.

"I can't even guess how old that swing is. It was the best fun though," Kat looked down at it fondly as Carey sat down on the swing. She gazed up at the treetops.

"This place… I wish I could remember it. I want so badly to remember," Carey said longingly, running her hands down the ropes that suspended her there.

She looked back over at Ji. He was standing back on the path, his cool demeanour replaced by something nervous and twitching.

"Ji, what is it?" Carey asked as she stood up from the swing.

At her words, though, Ji immediately ceased his nervous shifting and gave a wide grin. "Nothing. I was just making sure we hadn't been followed or anything."

Carey frowned; it hadn't looked like nothing to her.

"Did you want to look inside?" Kat's voice interrupted her thoughts, making her start.

"Oh! Of course, yes," she nodded, turning back to the house. "Are you coming too?"

"No, I think I'll stay out here with Ji and keep a lookout. We're still not far from Jeremy's castle and we can't take any chances. You go ahead," Kat said as she sat down on the bottom step leading up to the house.

Taking hold of the handrail, Carey made her way up the stairs, each one of them creaking dangerously under her weight. Looking along the front veranda she saw the trail of destruction that had been left by the Empire; broken glass, smashed pot plants and ruined furniture lay rotting on the floor. Carey reached for the door handle to turn it, but it too had been damaged. Slowly pushing the door open, Carey glanced back at Kat, who gave her an encouraging nod, waving for her to go on. She took a deep breath and walked inside, taking care so as not to tread on the glass that had been knocked out of the front door pane. She had walked into what looked like the living room; two large lounge chairs stood in front of a wide stone fireplace. They looked as though they may have been comfortable once but now had deep gashes and rips in the soft fabric and black mould eating at the edges. Ornaments and photo frames lay smashed and shattered on the floor and in the hearth, and a tattered rug spread before the spoilt chairs, choked with the dust and dirt that had flown in through the windows over the years.

Carey tiptoed over the splinters of glass and looked down at the photographs that had settled, spoilt and ripped on the dirty floorboards; most of them were faded or had been reduced to pulp by the moisture. Moving one of the lounge chairs out of the way, Carey discovered a perfectly preserved black and white photograph of herself and her family – her whole family. They seemed happy; her younger self stood between her two older sisters, smiling ridiculously into the camera. Her parents' hands rested on their eldest daughters' shoulders protectively. Her mother and father were laughing at some forgotten joke, broad grins on their faces while Jody and Laurel stood happily along with the rest of their family; the family they would one day betray.

Carey pocketed the photograph then turned to explore more of the house. Glancing across the room, she saw, built into the wall, a spiral staircase, enclosed within a glass case. Beside the staircase was a bedroom. Clothes and other objects were strewn across the room, just like the living room. Carey sat down on the bed and ran her hand over the bed's quilt, pushing the dust aside. Delicate patterns had been stitched into the fluffy feather down. The dresser still held a number of unspoilt pieces of clothing which she supposed were her parents'. Tired of her orphanage pinafore, she stuffed some of the clothes into a brown saddlebag that hung from the door frame.

Seeing nothing else of interest or importance, she turned her attention to the stairs. They were an unusual design; she had never seen anything quite like them before. She gently opened the glass door and stepped up onto the first step.

A shout echoed from outside and Carey jumped in surprise. "Geez Kat, couldn't you settle your disagreements with Ji a bit more quietly?" she said disapprovingly, closing the glass door behind her and starting up the staircase.

She looked up as she saw the second floor appear, presenting a number of other rooms. A repeat of the mess downstairs could be seen through the open doors and objects from ripped pages to toys were scattered across the polished wooden floor. Carey clutched the glass door's handle and tried pushing it open, but found it was stuck. She lent up against it gently and pushed a little harder, but it wouldn't budge. Running her hand around the edge of the door, she tried looking for the reason it was stuck, but the door had a small gap all the way around and nothing seemed to be or could possibly be blocking it except for –

"Magic, it must be magic," Carey concluded, standing up immediately. Without a moment's hesitation, she turned and ran back down the stairs. Clasping the door handle at the bottom, she found it also sealed shut. Carey rattled the door in frustration and growing anxiety.

"Kat! JI!" she yelled, her voice echoing and bouncing off the glass interior. No one came.

Carey laid her palms on the glass and pressed her face up against it. She couldn't see Kat or Ji, and as the moments crept by, her situation seemed more and more dire. She would need to figure this one out on her own. She took some deep calming breaths.

It could be nothing, she told herself. *Could just be some strange accident... or something else.* But her instincts were telling her otherwise – something was wrong. Kat would have checked on her by now, surely.

Carey closed her eyes and bowed her head to the ground. She tried to summon her magic like Ji and Kat had taught her but her concentration was interrupted when a foreign smell drifted up past her nostrils. Her eyes flew open to find something that made her heart stop and her head spin; someone had fired four flaming arrows into the room beyond the glass and flames were flaring up from their heads. One of the arrows had embedded itself in the chair closest to her and it erupted in a flurry of flames, engulfing it in a great fiery ball. The dust-ridden rug was disappearing quickly, the scattered photographs exploding with loud audible *pops*. Carey fought the panic that was spreading from her chest; smoke was starting to fill the room, and if she didn't do something quickly, she would suffocate. As she tried to calm herself, another two arrows flew in through the window, landing only a few feet from her and instantly covering the floor with glowing red flames.

Relax, relax, I need to concentrate. Carey closed her eyes, forcing the sight of the burning room from her mind. With great difficulty she cleared her thoughts and brought her magic to her fingertips. She concentrated it on opening the door, and as it burst forth, the sparks flying at the glass, she opened her eyes.

The sparks hit the glass and ricocheted, narrowly missing Carey as she ducked out of the way, flinging her arms over her head. She let out a scream as it grazed past her ear and continued to bounce off the glass. The charm eventually hit the ceiling with a *crack,* splitting the plaster. The instant it stopped, Carey jumped back up and pushed frantically against the door but it didn't budge. It was as solid as ever.

The fire had now spread right across the room, obscuring the front door completely. Smoke was rising in great toxic plumes and was beginning to seep in through the gaps in the glass. Carey's heart was pounding painfully in her chest and she was trembling in fright. Panic was spreading through her veins as fast as the fire around her; it took her over at a rate so fast that she lost control. She grabbed the door's handle and rattled it so hard that it nearly broke off. "Come on, come on, come on!" Carey screeched as she pushed and pulled on the door in desperation.

Breathlessly, she leant back against the stairs, her head swimming from the smoke that was filling the staircase. Sweat poured down her face as the heat rose in the narrow space. She looked over at the front window, trying to see if she could make out Kat or Ji, but she couldn't see past the shattered glass panes. The shattered glass… Carey considered this thought for about half a second then aimed carefully at the door and swung her foot fast and furiously at the glass. The glass was thick but the heat from the fire was weakening it, and as her foot hit, a small crack formed at the base. Carey's heart leapt with elation. She pulled her foot back and kicked out hard again. This time the break splintered and a web of cracks spread out from the impact.

"Come on!" Carey screamed as she kicked out one last time. With a loud snapping sound, the glass fractured and fell out onto the floor, showering Carey's outstretched leg with sharp fragments. Blood spilled out onto the ground. With pain shooting up through her limb, Carey kicked out the remaining glass.

She climbed through the broken door, anxious to escape, and in her haste, clipped a piece of glass that was still hanging from the frame. It ripped open her sleeve, tracing a deep cut just above her elbow. Carey yelped as hot blood began to flow from the wound. She clasped her arm to stem the bleeding as she edged along the wall. She was now faced with a new problem – getting through the inferno that had swept through the entire lower part of the house. The fire was raging, leering at her menacingly. She stood in a small patch that had yet to be taken over by the flames, but she guessed that it wouldn't be long before it, too, would be consumed.

Weakened by her wounds and the smoke swirling around her, Carey knew she didn't have the strength to summon her powers again. A flare threw a wave of heat over her and it was then she felt the strange tingling sensation again. The same feeling that had taken her over as she faced the Dæmon. It began as a spark in her chest, then, with surprising rapidity, it spread, reaching all the way to her fingertips. Her head cleared and the pain from her wounds instantly subsided. Emboldened by it, Carey reached out to the flames. They licked her skin but she felt nothing except a soft, flicking sensation. Steadying herself, she clutched her bag and threw herself into the flames. It was if she had been enclosed in a warm, fuzzy cocoon.

The fire raged around her but she was remarkably unharmed. She reached the door and kicked it open, half-running, half-collapsing out on to the veranda.

A huge explosion of heat and flame burst from within the house and sent Carey soaring down the front steps, landing her head first into the pavement.

"Ouch!" Carey exclaimed, holding her forehead in pain as a trickle of blood ran down from her hairline.

The tingling sensation had disappeared along with any protection it had given her. She looked back and saw that her childhood home was now a fiery inferno, tongues of flame protruding from the windows of both the upper and lower floors.

The scene swam before her eyes and she saw blood. Then there was nothing but darkness...

* * *

"Carey? Carey?"

Feeling heavy-headed and terribly dizzy, she tried to open her eyes. "Ah, geez," Carey groaned, her head aching painfully as she looked upwards.

She was lying on her back, facing a blurred sky.

"Carey? Are you all right?"

Carey felt the pavement beneath her as she reached for whomever it was that was leaning over her. Her vision was beginning to clear and she was able to make out Kat's face. Carey rolled her head to the side and saw Ji kneeling beside her. His face was etched with worry. "Carey?"

Seeing their faces calmed her. She was afraid something had happened to them while she had been in the house. The scenery swayed and shifted in front of her eyes and she closed them again. "Carey, Carey, keep your eyes open! Try to stay awake!" she heard Kat whisper and Carey felt the gentle blows of her slapping her face.

She struggled to keep her eyes open as Ji helped her up into a sitting position. Kat produced a flask of water and held it to Carey's lips. Carey let the water trickle down her chin and onto her dress as she tried with all her might to stay awake; the ground was still moving beneath her and the constant dizziness was testing her vomit reflexes.

"Ow!"

Carey's head gave a sharp stabbing pain to her forehead and she clutched it with her hand, trying to stem the pain with some pressure. Kat or Ji had wrapped her arm and leg wounds with clean clothes' scraps but there was still a dull throbbing. She squinted up at the sky, still holding her head, and saw that the sun was slowly setting in the west, casting long shadows over the three.

"How long was I out for?" she groaned, following the shadows with her eyes.

"You hit your head pretty hard, Carey, harder than I first thought," Ji said, placing his arm around her shoulders to hold her upright. "It took quite a while to wake you up."

Taking her eyes off the sun, she became aware that the town below them was quite busy, their voices and sounds carrying up the road to where they sat.

"Didn't they notice the house burning?" asked Carey, faintly.

"I doubt they can even see it. Your sisters probably bewitched it so no one would notice what was happening," said Kat, suggestively.

Carey turned to her, instantly forgetting her headache. "What do you mean, *my sisters*? What have they got to do with it?"

"Well, when you were inside, Jody and Laurel… they arrived, and before we could do anything, they attacked," said Ji, rubbing his arms.

"How?" Carey asked, thoroughly bewildered by this turn of events.

"They attacked me first, bound me with a rope–"

"Then Laurel came after me. She was so quick but I managed to hold her," Kat said, a tiny hint of exhilaration passing over her face. This was what Kat thrived at – combat. "I didn't even see them appear. It was only when Jody hit Ji with those ropes that I saw them."

"I couldn't fight back – the ropes stopped me from using any magic," Ji explained, rubbing his arms where the ropes had obviously restrained him.

"I watched as Jody sent some kind of curse at the house. I yelled out for you but I'm not sure you heard."

"No, I heard. I just assumed you and Kat were having another argument about something." Carey rubbed her eyes, thinking back to that moment and silently chastising herself for not being more vigilant. "And that curse was to trap me in the staircase. She sealed the doors shut. Then it was Jody who set the house on fire with the arrows, wasn't it?"

Kat and Ji both nodded.

"But… what were my sisters doing here and why were they trying to kill me?"

"They could have been anywhere. They may even have been waiting here for us, even though we've done nothing to suggest we would even come this way. Short answer – they're with Malevolence now and they don't care about anyone anymore. They only follow what she says and that's it. They *laughed* at our families before they were given up to the Empire – laughed! Do you really think they'd be any different now?"

Kat said this so obviously and matter-of-factly that Carey was quite taken aback by it.

"Do you really believe they are as bad as that, even now?"

"Tigers don't change their stripes, Carey. Your sisters did the unforgivable that day, and nothing since then has lead me to believe otherwise."

"But don't you have any doubt?" Carey looked into her friend's eyes and saw nothing but cold hatred. Carey might not have the memories they did, but she remembered that day clearly enough, and after so long of having no family to call her own, she could not write them off so easily. It was true, she could not deny what had just happened, but there was something within her that couldn't quite justify the hate Kat was displaying. Something was holding her back from renouncing them and casting them aside, and because of this, Carey couldn't just let Kat speak of them that way.

"Maybe not, but does that mean we just give up on them?" she said, forgetting her headache.

"Are you serious?" Kat spat in disbelief. "They don't deserve a second chance, Carey. Who knows what our families have had to endure because of them, what *we've* had to endure! They gave up their right for forgiveness a long time ago. Besides, they just tried to kill you – how can you even think of forgiveness?"

"Maybe you don't understand, Kat, but say that were your father, or even your mother? Wouldn't you want to know why?" Carey's voice was getting louder and irater. Ji, who had been quiet throughout the whole exchange, was watching them with wide eyes, unwilling to interject. "Would you be so cold with them?"

It was as though she had slapped Kat in the face. "Cold? You think that's what I am?" she said in a quiet voice. "I might be a lot of things, Carey Lee, but I don't think I would classify myself as that. Perhaps it's because you weren't fighting for your life when you were nine-years-old. Perhaps it's because you didn't spend your childhood scavenging for food, afraid that each meal would be your last. Or perhaps it's because you didn't have to fight back the nightmares of your family's torture every night. Whatever it is, Carey, I have every reason to hate your sisters. Maybe you should look at those who actually care about you rather than trying to show compassion towards those who want you dead."

Kat's words stung and Carey's fight died in her chest. Everything that was holding her back, everything that made her feel less of a Seeker, Kat had laid out bare. The fire inside her was extinguished and what replaced it was the singular, penetrating feeling of inadequacy. Carey shrunk back, her eyes falling to the ground. When she failed to say anything in return, Kat turned on her heel and stalked away.

Hugging her arms, Carey felt Ji's hand on her shoulder; she didn't look at him.

"Carey?" he said tentatively. "Are you all right?"

Forcing her face to remain impassive, she gave a non-committal nod. Ji bowed his head so that he could see her face. "She didn't mean it like that, you know that, right?"

Carey straightened up and looked into his eyes. "How do you know that? It sure sounded like she did," she returned, defensively. Ji sighed, ignoring her hostility.

"Carey, you have to see it her way. Try to imagine it."

"I do, Ji, every single day! I try to imagine not being caught, growing up with you two by my side, being able to remember it all, but I can't. There's just no way I can do that, just as there is no way I can dismiss my sisters like she does. What if it had been your brother, Ji? What if Zacharia had been the one to betray us?"

Ji was silent for a moment, then reached down and took her hands in his. "That's just the thing. He wasn't, so I can't imagine, just as you can't."

Kat was already waiting for them on the outskirts of town, scowling as they approached her. "Took you long enough," she said coldly.

Unwilling to apologise, Carey ignored her and walked over to Firefly. She gave the Pegasus an affectionate pat on the nose and received a friendly nip in return. She was stroking her mane, when out of the corner of her eye, Carey noticed a stirring within nearby trees. For a moment it looked as though someone was standing in the shadows just beyond the tree line, but when she looked closer, there was no one there.

"Carey?" Ji asked. "What is it?"

Carey tore her eyes away from the trees. "Nothing. It's nothing. I thought I saw something, but I guess it was just the shadows."

"I think we should camp over there tonight. It's going to be too dark to travel soon," he suggested, pointing to a small clearing past the first line of trees. As long as they were out of there early they wouldn't be noticed.

"Sure," said Carey, looking over at Kat hesitantly. She nodded tersely before looking away.

"Er... right," said Ji, eager to break the tension. "I'll make us something to eat then."

They sat in almost silence for the rest of the night; Ji tried to make some forced conversation but eventually gave up when Kat gave him the look of death. They didn't even say so much as a goodnight to each other as they climbed into their bedrolls. As Carey lay there awake that night, watching the stars high in the velvet black sky, she wondered if Kat truly had meant what she said and if the resentment that had laced her words earlier was something she carried with her. Regardless of how Kat felt, Carey wasn't going to be the one to say sorry first. In her opinion, Kat should try to understand her perspective, especially if she expected her to do the same.

It was a long time before Carey finally fell asleep, and judging from the absence of Kat's usual loud breathing, she wasn't the only one lying there awake.

Chapter Twelve

Another Strike

The next morning they started out early to avoid the stares and suspicion of the day before. Carey avoided talking to Kat, partly because she was afraid that she would confirm Carey's suspicions about her feelings of resentment towards her and partly because Carey herself was still angry with her. It appeared Kat wasn't about to relent any time soon either, refusing to speak to either Carey or Ji unless it was absolutely necessary. Knowing that it wasn't Ji's fault Kat wasn't talking to him, Carey made an effort to keep up conversation with him and quickly found that Ji didn't care whether Kat spoke to him or not.

"I wouldn't worry too much. She never stays like this for too long," he said as he and Carey kept their distance. "And don't worry about what she said yesterday. I know she didn't mean it."

Carey huffed. "Don't try to stand up for her, Ji. I won't be the first one to say sorry. She'll have to give in first."

She was surprised when Ji laughed. "Good luck with that. If you think you're going to out-stubborn Katrina Lawrence you better have a lot of patience."

Carey sighed, watching the back of Kat's head as she walked stiffly along the road in front of them. She didn't want to fight, but she felt such a burning sense of inadequacy every time Kat glared at her, that she didn't know what to say, even if it came to apologising. She couldn't make up for the lifetime she missed.

"I just feel like she's disappointed with me, as though she expected more," Carey finally mumbled, voicing her fears.

Ji grabbed her arm and turned her towards him. "Don't ever think that way, Carey. Yes, we thought that when we found you, that you would know at least something, and it was a big shock when you didn't, but that doesn't mean you're any less of a Seeker. You were taken from us, and as much as we would love to change the past, we can't."

"But what Kat said yesterday–"

"Was her taking out her anger regarding the whole situation with you, which, to be honest, was completely unfair, and is why I keep telling you not to worry about it. Kat can be stubborn and extremely hot-headed. Makes for a great fighter but an infuriating friend at times."

Carey knew Ji was just trying to be helpful, but it just made her feel even more despondent, especially knowing that they had been expecting a Seeker ready to fight; not some confused amnesia patient.

They stopped for lunch shortly before midday. Kat plonked herself down on a patch of grass without even glancing at the other two, intent on eating her food in silence. Ji, tired of her perpetual need to be stubborn, began singing a rather loud sea shanty as he pulled out his own lunch. Carey couldn't help but stifle a laugh as he reached for a particularly high note, drawing furious looks from Kat. He continued in an overly cheerful manner and it was obvious that he was simply trying to bait her. Carey knew it was childish but couldn't help but watch in amusement as Kat became more and more incensed by his exuberance, to the point where she threw an apple at his head. Catching it deftly, Ji thanked her for the fruit before taking a large, exaggerated bite from it.

"You're really enjoying this, aren't you?" Carey asked Ji as Kat turned her back on them.

Ji shrugged. "I can't help it. She's just too easy to bait. Apple?"

They sat in silence while they finished their lunch, occasionally taking a peek at Kat who had made up her mind to fully ignore them altogether. When Ji had finished his last biscuit, he pointed at Carey's brown saddlebag and asked, "What's in there?"

"Oh, just some clothes I collected from my parents' house. I thought I might need them."

"Well, put them on. That pinafore is looking a bit grubby. So is that shirt."

She had to admit that she was looking a little dirty, especially after the fire. "All right, just don't peek!" said Carey, picking up the bag and stepping behind a wide tree.

She slipped her pinafore off over her head and unbuttoned her shirt that was once white but now black and red with dried blood and flung it onto the grass. She ripped off what parts weren't filthy and replaced the bandages on her arm and leg. Kat and Ji had done a relatively good job at healing her after the fire – long raw pink lines ran where the glass had snagged her, a sight better than the gashes that had been there. The thought of Kat's healing brought a sudden wave of guilt, but then Carey thought back to their argument and the feeling dissipated immediately.

"Hey! What you doing over there?" she heard Ji call to her.

"You better not be peeking, Ji Binx, or I'll get you for sure!" Carey shouted back whilst hurriedly pulling out a new set of clothes.

She dragged a clean shirt over her shoulders and smoothed it down. It was like she had shed a dirty layer of skin, and as Carey buttoned her skirt and tied her belt, she glanced down to inspect her new look; she thought she looked pretty good. She was wearing a long, dark-blue patterned skirt that was held up by a thin plaited leather belt and a long sleeved, tan coloured shirt with sleeves that flared out from the elbows. Her new, knee-high stockings were dyed black with flecks of silver through them and they blended nicely with her black buckle-up shoes. Stepping out from behind the tree, she flicked her lapel the way she had seen the dandies do back in Monaghan and Ji wolf-whistled cheekily; she blushed. Kat shot them a disapproving glance.

"Nice outfit," he said, taking her hand and spinning her around. He pulled her in and bowed. "Enchanté," Ji grinned mischievously, bringing her hand to his lips, and then, to Carey's complete surprise, straightened and gave her a quick, swift kiss dangerously close to her lips. He jumped back, grinning playfully.

"Ji!" she exclaimed as he started backing away. "You cheeky, little...!"

Feeling the heat rise in her ears she tried to grab him but he darted just out of reach, still smiling wickedly.

"Hey! We need to get moving," Kat called out to them, scowling as they ran over to join her. "And could you possibly be quieter? I thought we were trying to keep a low profile."

They stuck to the back roads and paths less travelled in an attempt to remain out of the Empire's sight. They needed to be one step ahead and to do so they needed to stay hidden. By nightfall they had reached the town of Ederney. Kat broke her silence long enough to tell them that they were staying at an inn for the night.

"It's safe," was all the explanation she gave as to why they were stopping at what Carey thought seemed a rather conspicuous place. Ji shrugged. "No point arguing with her."

It was completely dark as Carey took Firefly around to the stables. A light breeze fluttered about her, tickling her bare skin and sending chills down her spine.

"In here, Firefly, you have to stay here with the horses tonight. I'll come and get you first thing in the morning," said Carey as she led Firefly into an empty stall.

Firefly nudged Carey's arm then bowed her head to eat the hay provided on the floor. Carey walked out into the courtyard of the inn and started towards the entrance where Kat and Ji were waiting.

She stopped. A harsh cough had sounded from the other side of the stables. Carey squinted nervously through the darkness, a feeling of unease coming over her. Every muscle in her body tensed. *Not now, please not now,* Carey pleaded silently, hoping it had been her imagination. She listened hard for any further sounds of movement but her senses were obscured by the noises coming from the horses in the stables. She waited a few moments longer, and just when she had decided that she must have imagined it, Carey heard it again – a harsh cough, but it was now on her side of the stables.

Thoroughly unnerved, Carey ran. Disorientated by the darkness, she tripped on a stray vine trailing across the ground. "Urgh," Carey groaned as she hit the flag stone ground, grazing her knees and palms as she went. In a panic, she tried clambering to her feet, but as she pulled herself up, a force from behind grabbed her arm and hit her on the back, her knees buckling. She fell back to the ground, but now there was a very heavy person struggling to twist her arm around. Carey tried to push the person off her, turning herself over to try and see who it was but she couldn't see anyone – whoever it was, they were invisible.

Carey kicked and fought to free herself from her attacker who now had her pinned to the ground. Then, as if someone was holding a burning hot coal to Carey's wrist, an excruciating pain ripped through her body, forcing a scream of agony from her mouth. The white hot searing blinded her, black spots swimming in front of her vision. She tried pulling away as they held the object to her arm, but it was unyielding. Her whole body was on fire and her limbs shook uncontrollably. The pain grew steadily, causing Carey's eyes to water, and just when she thought she was going to be sick, the invisible man struck her across the head with something hard.

And as the world dissolved into darkness, Carey heard the harsh echoing laughter of her ruthless attacker.

Chapter Thirteen

Fianna Parnell

Carey's hair whipped out behind her, falling limp then flying back again as Laurel pushed her on the swing. The summer rays were shining through the leaves of the tree, casting a speckled pattern of light on the soft grass beneath Carey's feet. The soft wind tickled her face and Laurel smiled as Carey giggled with pleasure. Laurel's twin sister, Jody, was sitting under the shade of the veranda reading a heavy book and practicing her magic. Carey put her feet down to stop herself and searched the front garden.

"Laurel. Where's Mama and Nanna? I don't see them anywhere."

"They've gone to the Lawrence's, Carey, they'll be back soon. Don't you remember them telling you?" said Jody, impatiently, not looking up from her book.

Carey scowled at her sister. "I didn't ask you, Jo-dee. I was talking to Laurel."

Jody looked up from her book and stuck her tongue out at Carey. Carey jumped to her feet. "Hey! I'll get you—"

"That's enough, you two! Mama will scold us again if you keep fighting," Laurel said, holding back a struggling Carey by the neck of her dress.

"You're so imnachua, Jody!" Carey yelled furiously at Jody, who smiled sarcastically back at her.

"It's immature, Carey. And where did you learn that?"

"Kat told me," Carey answered, shrugging Laurel off.

Jody made a derisive sound from the back of her throat and resumed reading her book, leaving Carey to glare hatefully up at her.

"Come, Carey. Let's go pick some flowers for Nanna," said Laurel, steering Carey down the path towards the rose bushes.

Robert, Carey's father, was tending to one of the bushes, clipping off the old and broken bits carefully.

"Papa, could we have a rose for Nanna? She likes the pink ones," Carey said, pointing to the pale pink roses that were just starting to bloom.

Robert cut one of the young buds off and handed it gently to Carey with a smile. "Careful, honey, those thorns are sharp. Remember what Nanna says—"

"Beautiful, yet dezeeving," Carey grinned. "That's what Nanna says."

"Sure is, sweetie. Now be careful with that."

"I will, Papa. And Papa?" asked Carey, looking up at her father.

"Hmm?"

"Is Nanna really fighting that bad sorceress?"

Robert stopped trimming and furrowed his brow, considering her question. "Yes she is, Carey. She has got many people from lots of different countries right around the world to fight with her, to help her," he said slowly so Carey would understand.

"Is she winning, Papa?"

Robert Lee knelt and gave her a hug. "I think she will, Carey. Don't you worry, all right sweetheart?"

Carey nodded and looked down the path to find a man in a long travelling cloak walking up towards them. She tugged on her father's sleeve. "Papa, look. There's someone here."

Robert stood up and faced the man as he approached him and when the man greeted him with a bow, Carey's father nodded courteously back.

"Excuse me for my intrusion but is Lady Parnell here? I bring an important message from Head General Colles about the Order's position," the man said with a very important air about him.

Robert nodded. "You can leave it with me."

"Of course, Lord Robert. But please, promise me that Lady Parnell will receive this message," the man said urgently.

"Yes, of course. May I ask your name?" Carey's father asked.

Carey looked from the gentleman to her father, confused by the strange way in which they spoke. The man bowed again. "My name is Mikhail Féin, one of the Order's chief messengers from Russia. But please, do I have your word—"

"Yes, yes. I thank you for your troubles. I will get this to Fianna as soon as it is possible."

The man bowed farewell, then with a sweep of his cloak he was gone. Robert turned the envelope over in his hands for a moment as he gazed down the road, frowning. Jody had put her book down and had joined them out of curiosity.

"What does it say, Papa, what does it say? Come on, open it. I want to know what's happening," Jody pleaded while Laurel stood beside her, looking up at him imploringly.

Their father dug his thumb under the seal and flicked it open; he unfolded it and read it silently, then holding it out so that Jody and Laurel could read it too. Carey screwed her face up in frustration and crossed her arms. She didn't like not being able to read yet and she never got to hear what was happening with her grandmother. Laurel groaned with despair and Jody let out a long sigh; by the sounds, it was not a cheerful message. Carey stomped her foot to gain their attention. Jody looked down at her and scowled. "What is it, Carey?"

"I want to hear what it says. What does it say?"

"Carey, this is not for you, this is only for grown-ups—"

"But you're not a growned-up! How come you get to read it?" Carey whined.

Jody let out an exasperated sign. "Fine. I'll read it for you, but you won't understand it."

She smoothed the paper and started reading.

"Lady Fianna Parnell,

We are sorry to bring such bad news at a time like this but I must tell you of the recent occurrences in the battle against Malevolence's Empire. Her forces have taken over and now occupy most of Europe and Asia and we have only just learnt that she now has complete control over the Mystic Realm, taking most of our people prisoners. Major General Kirchov from Russia unfortunately met his downfall when Imperial forces stormed the Russian headquarters. We are arranging a meeting in Beijing at Colonel Ming's palace in two weeks at dusk to discuss your idea of forming groups of 'Seekers'. A number of dignitaries have expressed their interest in this idea and since it would create a new approach to fighting the Empire, you are assured my full support. I also wish to express my interest in the Seekers' group with which you will personally be involved. Oliver Binx and Peter Lawrence have both sent messages to Major McVolern and myself informing us of their withdrawal from our councils so as to join this group. Awaiting your answer,

Head General Colles."

Jody finished the letter with yet another sigh and folded the letter neatly, slipping it back into its envelope. Carey tried to understand all that Jody had said but was distracted when she looked down the white brick path and saw her mother and beloved grandmother approaching.

"Nanna!" Carey cried, running down to meet her, clutching the small rose bud in her tiny hand and holding it protectively to her chest.

Fianna Parnell stopped and waited for her granddaughter to reach her, bending down to give her a big hug. "My darling! What have you been doing, your dress is all ripped around the bottom. Oh, what's this? It's beautiful," she said as Carey gave her the rose.

"It's your favourite, Nanna, remember? And I'm sorry I ripped the dress you sewed me, Nanna. I fell over by accident, really. But I bought you your favourite rose, Nanna, just for you," said Carey, her eyebrows raised convincingly.

Jody had followed her down with the message for Nanna Parnell. Fianna took it from her with a hint of curiosity and thanked her. Carey's mother cleared her throat. "I'm going to get dinner ready. I'll see you in a few minutes, all right? It's going to be cold tonight and I don't want you to get ill again, Carey. Come Jody."

"Yes, Mama," Carey replied.

"Of course, Jenny, we won't be long," said Fianna, standing back up and unfolding the letter. She read it quickly, tut-tutting in disappointment; Carey looked up at her. "What is it, Nanna? What do they say?"

Her Nanna folded the message and placed it back in the envelope just like Jody had. She took Carey's hand in hers. "I'm afraid it's not good news, darling. I have to go away again. The man who wrote me this is arranging a meeting I cannot miss, unfortunately–"

"But you'll miss my birthday, Nanna. And I was going to have a party, too!" said Carey, sadly.

"I'm terribly sorry, dearest, but I promise I will try to return as quickly as possible, just for you all right? Now Carey, show me where these roses are, sweetheart, there love – Aaahhh!"

Fianna was caught mid-step and wrenched from Carey's grip by an almighty force. It threw her back hard onto the dirt. Carey cried out in shock, falling back onto the path. She turned over, her arms outstretched. Trying desperately to ignore the pain of her grazed elbows, she cast her eyes about for her grandmother. "Nanna! Where are you?"

Their cries had attracted Robert and Jenny's attention and they ran to where Carey and Fianna had fallen. Carey bit her lip in an effort to keep herself from crying as she crawled to her feet, her knees and dress all bloodied. She tried to run to her grandmother but stopped dead when six black-clad men appeared out of thin air, surrounding Fianna. Her eyes darted from the men to her grandmother, who was struggling to get to her feet.

Fianna lashed out in defence but two of the men caught her arms, bending them behind her back and forcing her to her feet roughly. Another took the message from her clenched hand and pocketed it. Then, to Carey's horror, one of the men shot a well-aimed curse, point-blank at her Nanna. There was a flash of retina-burning light and a heavy thud hit Carey square in the chest and she screamed in pain. The feeling spread through her entire body, burning in the tips on her fingers and ends of her toes. Her eyes watered. Jenny and Robert had reached Fianna's assailants and were trying desperately to fend them off with great blows of magic. Carey's attention, however, was on her grandmother. Her breath shallow and the sounds of the battle in her ears, Carey watched as her grandmother was heaved over a burly shoulder. Fianna's eyes had rolled back in her head.

"No! Nanna... Nanna, NO!" Carey screamed in a strangled voice as she dragged herself to her feet and ran towards her, not caring about the men that surrounded her.

One of them grabbed her around the middle. His hood fell back and Carey found herself looking into his eyes; they were like ice, burning with madness.

Ruthlessly he dragged her backwards, throwing her onto the white path. Carey screamed in agony as she hit the stone but she wasn't about to give up. With much difficulty she pulled herself to her feet once more, wanting desperately to reach Fianna.

"Carey, Carey! Are you hurt?"

Jody and Laurel had come to her aid and were now struggling to drag her back up to the house.

"No, No! Let me go! Let... me... go!" Carey shrieked hoarsely, tears streaming down her face. "Nanna... Nanna... NANNA!"

There was a crack like thunder and the men were gone but so was her Nanna. "Nanna, come back. Nanna... Nanna... come-come back."

"Carey, Carey. Wake up. You're dreaming. Carey!"

Someone was shaking her gently by the shoulders. She opened her eyes and found herself face to face with –

"Ji!" Carey gasped in surprise, putting her hand to her heart. "Where am I?"

"He was trying to wake you because you were screaming and kicking something horrible. Were you having a nightmare?"

Kat was sitting by her bed, her face white as ash. Carey sat up, feeling a twinge of humiliation. She didn't answer. Kat pursed her lips. "Fine," she said, standing up, flicking her hair and walking away stiffly.

"Care-ry. Why can't you two just get along again? She just wanted to know how you were. She hates herself for not being there when you were attacked. She's already beating herself up about it," said Ji, sounding slightly annoyed.

But Carey wasn't listening; her wrist had just given her a harrowing shock.

"Ah," she winced, seizing her wrist convulsively to try and stop it hurting.

She looked down at it fearfully and she slowly removed her hand. There, black on tender pink skin was the mark that she now shared with Ji; the Empire's goat's head. Closing her eyes to block out the image, she took some deep breaths, letting herself flop backwards so she was looking up at the ceiling instead.

"Great," said Carey, still staring up at the rafters. Not that it was great – she just couldn't think of anything better to say at the time that didn't involve more colourful language.

"She's branding us, Carey. One by one, I'm sure of it."

"But why? Why doesn't she just kill us if she can just find us so easily?"

"Maybe she's got a plan in mind."

"Well that's just fantastic," Carey retorted acidly. "What about this, then? Can I get rid of it? Will I ever be able to get it off?"

"It's tattooed with magic unfortunately."

"So it won't come off," she deduced glumly.

"Sorry," Ji grimaced.

"Don't be, Ji. I shouldn't have stayed there. I should have run when I had the chance. Ugh, I'm so dumb!" Carey said angrily, smacking her forehead. "Wait… wait a second. Ji," she sat up, throwing her legs around so that they dangled over the side of the bed, "did you see the person who attacked me?"

Ji shook his head.

"I only remember that I could feel him, but I don't remember seeing him. Do you think it's possible for someone to be… invisible?"

"It is possible. I know that the Empire's got witches and wizards that are Inimici – ones that can make themselves invisible. There's not many left now – so many were killed in the Dark War. Witches and wizards can only master Shrouding through the dark arts. They pride themselves on this – having the ability to become invisible – and the few that are still alive hold distinguished positions on the Empire's High Council," Ji explained, handing a cup of water to Carey, who accepted it gratefully.

Carey sat silent for a few minutes, mulling everything over in her mind. The thought of invisible people chilled her to the core, so the idea that there weren't many left provided her some comfort.

"Ji. The dream I just had. I was at home… my family's home… and Laurel and Jody were there… they were very young… twelve… perhaps – and I was playing with Laurel. Then I asked my father for a rose to give to my Nanna. Then… this man came and brought a message from some head general and it explained how – how the Order was going in some war. Ji, how important was my grandmother? What was her position in all this? All you've really told me is that she formed the Order. Who was she really?" Carey asked imploringly.

Ji nodded and gritted his teeth, trying to find the right words to describe it. "You know the Dark War we keep referring to?"

"Uh-huh."

"Well, your grandmother – she was the leader of the side – our side – that was fighting against the Empire. She had groups all around the world fighting. The groups of people that were specially formed from these were called Seekers. The Seekers were a more defined sector of the Order… a more focused way of fighting the Empire; a special society that would whittle away at the Empire until it finally reached its ultimate goal – Malevolence. After our people were forced into this realm, some witches and wizards tried setting up councils in different countries. For a few years they were successful and many kingdoms were founded in secret, heads of councils elected and leaders established, but these were short-lived and most were forced into hiding indefinitely after they were crushed by the Empire. But if the countries could have had a leader after all of this, it would have been Fianna."

"But in my dream, we weren't Seekers yet."

"Groups of Seekers were only properly formed after – after…"

Ji was struggling to say what came next, but Carey already knew.

"After she died," Carey asked, witheringly.

Ji frowned. "How did you know?"

"I – I saw how she died in my dream," Carey said slowly, trying to keep her voice steady.

Ji was silent. Carey could tell that her statement had surprised him.

"Ji,–"

"That doesn't sound like a dream, Carey. Everything you've just said… you would have had to remember it from

somewhere–"

"But I lost my memory–"

"The attack – I've heard that an event like that can force someone to relive past traumas. Like a key to a trunk, unlocking forgotten or lost memories... Perhaps that's why you've suddenly remembered this," Ji suggested shrewdly.

Carey sat pondering Ji's theory when a short, plump woman appeared at the door.

"Excuse me. Supper will be served in a few minutes' time if you would like to join everyone in the dining room," she said politely before moving onto the next room.

"Feeling hungry?" asked Ji, standing up and holding his arm out.

Knowing that it would take her a while to consider all that she had just learnt, she decided to put it all aside for the time being and linked her arm with Ji's.

"Ravenous," she answered.

Chapter Fourteen

Madame Salisbury's Inn

Downstairs, Ji and Carey found themselves in a roomy inn filled with long, wooden tables. Candles lit the room with a dull glow and a haze of pipe smoke hung over their heads. As Carey looked around, she saw that many of the patrons gathered there were most definitely magical folk; in fact, there were several dwarfs at a nearby table, three women across the room swapping small glass bottles that were emitting tiny sparks, and sitting over in the corner was a short, green-faced creature that Ji said was a hag from the high mountains. A few of them noticed their entrance and conversations immediately halted. There was a deafening silence and Carey could feel all the eyes in the room focus on them.

"Come on," Ji muttered, taking her hand and leading her over to the table where Kat was seated.

"Is this such a good idea?" Carey asked as the conversation began to fill the inn again. "These people know who we are. Won't that be dangerous?"

"No it's fine," Ji replied, but before Carey could enquire any further, the woman who had summoned them for dinner, sat down at their table across from Kat; she had a kindly face, brown hair flecked with grey that was tied back in a tight bun and she wore a number of heavy talismans and amulets around her neck.

"Ah, welcome! Please, sit down and have some supper. Persia!" the woman called across the room to a small, dark-haired woman before turning back to Carey and holding out a hand. "Madame Maria Salisbury is my name, but you can just call me Maria. I'm the landlady of The Mystique," she said as she shook Carey's hand.

"So, this is an inn just for people like us?" asked Carey, looking over at the witches who were now showing each other small orb-shaped objects.

"That it is, my dear. All are welcome here."

"What? Even Imperials?" Carey asked in alarm.

"Oh heavens no, my child! This place, to them, is impenetrable. This building has been here for an exceedingly long time and the magic within it acts as protection. Whoever holds this place has the power to admit anyone they like. As it falls to me, I simply make it known that no Imperials and no Commoners shall enter forthwith and it becomes so! You are plenty safe within these walls."

"Then how did that Inimicus attack me if they cannot enter this place?" Carey said, rubbing her arm subconsciously.

"Aah, unfortunately the magic does not extend beyond the walls of this inn. I was surprised he was able to stay so long though. Any who are not permitted here are affected by the magic and are usually driven away. Imperials especially – they can't withstand the affects even for a few moments," said Maria, sighting a group of elves that were sending small, green flames into the air. "Ugh, not again. Excuse me for one second. I have to go settle the rowdy ones."

Carey watched as Maria strode over to the elves and told them to stop their noisy games or she would have them thrown out of the inn.

"But we've paid!" squeaked one of the elves as he stood on his chair to come even with Maria.

"I don't care! I'm the landlady of this inn and if you don't stop conjuring fires and aggravating my other customers I'll have you thrown out on your tiny rear ends! Now stop it!" Maria shouted, throwing her hands up in the air.

The elves gave her a furious glare then sat back down at their table and resumed gabbling quickly in a loud, indistinct language.

"Is she serious?" Carey asked Ji. "Is this place capable of what she just said?"

"It's been like this for years. It's one of the only inns we'll stay at," Ji answered.

"Pardon moi, but Ai haf your supper for you."

Carey looked up, or rather down, at the person who had spoken and sighted the short, dark-haired woman Maria has called to before. Up close, she saw that the woman was really quite pretty with brown, almond-shaped eyes and a small pursed mouth.

"Thank you, err–"

"Persia, miss. It is a pleasure ta see you all again," she said, acknowledging Kat and Ji whilst lifting a large plate of bread and a haunch of meat up onto the table. "Ai will be back with some drinks."

Ji watched Persia walk back to the bar.

"You know her?" Carey asked, following his gaze.

"Oh, for years," Kat said through a mouth full of food. "Though Ji, you seem a little more interested tonight than usual."

Ji wrenched his eyes away from Persia at Kat's sarcastic suggestion. "What? I am not. I just tend to think she's a nice person, that's all."

Kat murmured something under her breath.

"What did you say?" Ji demanded.

"Hmm, nothing," said Kat, staring guiltlessly across the table.

Ji poked his tongue out in a fit of immaturity before falling silent once more. Carey felt an odd sensation in her chest, a nauseating lurch as she watched Ji.

"'Ere is your drink, madam – sir."

Persia had returned with several mugs of brown ale. She looked over at Ji with a smile.

"Yes, thank you very much," Carey said, trying to break Persia's gaze with Ji's.

"Mmm, thank you," Ji said in a forced voice.

Carey snorted contemptuously at him as she took her mug and drank deeply from it. For the rest of the night Carey entertained herself by watching the other patrons. A group of dwarves and the elves started a boisterous game of what looked like marbles flying around above their heads. After a few narrow misses, Maria had had enough and with a thunderous voice, threatened that if they ever tried it again, she'd do more than give them a warning. Shaking their fists, the elves shouted angrily at her then began a game of dodge with the dwarves that included bright blue sparks just to spite her. The three witches had begun conjuring smoke formations from their orbs, adding colour to the grey pipe smoke that filled the air. A number of people began dancing energetically to a leprechaun's music; Maria gave up trying to restore order when the crowd began singing loudly, drowning out her protests.

Carey watched in amusement until she could barely keep her eyes open. Leaving everyone behind, she made her way upstairs, away from the noise and merriment. Standing in front of her mirror as she washed her face and brushed her hair, she wondered if everyone had been as happy and as fun-loving as those she had met downstairs before Malevolence and the Empire had come into power. It was no doubt what those people downstairs hoped for; she could see it in their eyes. They expected Carey and her friends to be warriors, to be their champions.

But if the Empire had never come to power, never prompted the formation of the Order, then Ji, Kat and herself might actually have been normal teenagers with normal families. *Families.* All these *ifs.* But how had it come to this? Why was it like this? Carey couldn't even imagine what had started it all, why they were here, why the Empire had formed in the first place. But most of all, she wanted to know why Malevolence was who she was. She had started all of this. She obviously came from somewhere – no one was like that without reason. Malevolence had a lot to answer for.

Carey grasped at her stomach; a wave of nausea swept over her and she stumbled over to the dresser. Clutching the wooden edge, she looked up into the mirror to a pale reflection gazing back at her. Carey glared back, willing herself to be stronger.

"Come on, Carey. Pull yourself together. You need to, if not for yourself, at least for the people downstairs," she spoke into the mirror, trying to raise her confidence. "They deserve freedom. They deserve to be happy."

"But you deserve freedom too, you know," her reflection whispered distantly, looking back at her meaningfully.

Too tired to even react she merely stared back, unable to reply. She didn't know how.

* * *

Carey woke the next morning to find Ji sprawled out on the floor, half-covered by a thick, patched blanket.

"That's interesting," Carey muttered, rubbing her eyes and climbing awkwardly out of bed. Stretching her arms, she reached up and wrenched open the curtains.

"Carey, it's too early," Ji mumbled thickly, covering his head with his pillow.

"Well it's time – to – get – up!" she said with every nudge she gave Ji with her foot.

"Leave me alone Carey, I'm really tired," he grumbled, his voice muffled.

"And why is that?" Carey asked, turning to him.

"I danced all night."

"With Persia?"

"Yes, *Persia*."

Carey grunted scathingly, pulling the sheets up on her bed.

Rolling up her sleeve, she inspected the tattoo; it had gone a greyish, smoky colour and, surprisingly, no longer caused her any pain. Carey tugged her sleeve back down then bent over and slipped on her stockings and shoes, kicking Ji as she stood up.

"Get up – now! I am going to go and wake up Kat, and if you're not up by the time I come back…" she said, pointing at him threateningly.

"All right, all right," Carey heard him grunt as she walked out into the hallway.

"Boys," she muttered as she knocked on Kat's door.

The door creaked open and she came face to face with a very exhausted looking individual.

"Yes?" Kat asked, bitterly.

Carey sighed resignedly. "Can we stop? This needs to stop. After all that's happened, I don't think it'll help anyone if we keep on like this. I'm... I'm sorry." Without waiting for Kat to respond, Carey kept going, asking the question that had been plaguing her the past few days before she lost her nerve. "There's just one thing I want to know. Did you really mean what you said back there?"

Kat opened her door and stepped out into the hallway, shaking her head, her expression softer now. "Of course not. I said all that because I was bitter, Carey, I was jealous. It was difficult for Ji and I, having to grow up alone. We had hoped you would remember us and the Order and the Seekers. What we didn't count on was you not remembering anything, not even us. I would say that I envy you, but I know how much you hate not being able to do so. I would love to have your optimism when it comes to your sisters, but I've had too much time to consider what they did. But I need put aside my own prejudices." Kat took Carey's hand. "I'm sorry too."

Carey breathed a great sigh of relief and giggled nervously. "You have no idea what that means, Kat. I was so worried..."

"How about we forget about the whole thing?" Kat said as they walked back down the hallway.

Carey nodded in agreement. "Deal. So... did I miss something last night after I went to bed?" she asked, thinking of Ji.

"You have no idea. Ji must have grabbed the wrong mug by accident and he sculled a tankard full of something – some kind of potion I'm guessing. Maria almost had a fit and Ji went absolutely *crazy*. He and Persia did this funny kind of jig thing which looked really strange what with Persia being about a foot-and-a-half shorter and all. Then everyone else decided they would join in too but by that time I could hardly keep my eyes open so I retreated. Not much use though. I couldn't really get to sleep because they were all so very loud. I'm surprised they didn't wake you up. I only heard Ji come up to bed about two hours ago–"

"You're joking! No wonder he wouldn't get up," Carey exclaimed, walking over to her room and pushing the door open.

Ji was still lying on the floor so Carey threw off his blanket and grabbed him ruthlessly by the ear.

"Ow! Carey, come on! There's no need–"

Persia had stuck her head around the side of the door. Ji quickly brushed Carey off and she crossed her arms.

"Er, excuse me but breakfast is ready," she said timidly before running off downstairs again.

Ji coughed in embarrassment and pushed past Carey to the door. Kat raised her eyebrows at her, to which Carey replied with a "What?" Kat turned on her heels and Carey followed her down to the inn's dining room.

The air was tense as they hastily ate breakfast. Carey kept glancing at Ji, who was watching Persia quite openly. She couldn't help but feel a twinge of annoyance, though what Ji did really shouldn't have concerned her so much.

As they left the inn behind with Persia and Maria waving them farewell, Carey voiced a thought to Kat and Ji.

"Don't you think it's dangerous, us staying at that inn last night?"

"Why do you say that?" Kat enquired as she waved back.

Carey frowned. "Well, what if those people are found out by the Empire? Who knows what might happen to them?"

Kat shook her head. "They don't know anything. We didn't say anything about where we're going or what we're doing."

But this did not slake Carey's concern. "They saw us though. I thought that would be enough for the Empire to…" she trailed off, the thought of what may happen terrifying her into silence.

"Carey, if they *were* caught, do you really think that seeing us or not would make a real difference?" Ji interjected.

Ji's voice made Carey's stomach drop and she was suddenly and inexplicably infuriated.

"Well it's not just that. What about the people we leave behind, the ones who we become *friends* with?" she said, struggling to hold back this sudden surge of anger.

Ji came to a halt. "Carey, what is this really about?"

Carey looked at him square in the eyes and her confidence suddenly waned. She shook her head. "Just what I said," she mumbled. "Those people, like Maria, what if something happened to them?"

Ji continued to survey Carey with a slight frown. Kat cleared her throat.

"Don't worry, Carey. We've known Maria for a very long time. She can look after herself," she said, steering them away from another possible argument.

Ji agreed and followed Kat, leaving Carey to the mercy of her confusion, unsure of what had just passed between them.

As they left Ederney, a vast, dark and menacing storm cloud spread across the sky, casting a dark shadow over the countryside. The wind rustled through the long grass, tickling their ankles and sending shivers up Carey's spine.

"Great. This storm looks like it won't give up easily," Kat groaned, gazing up at the heavy sky.

And indeed it didn't; for the next fortnight it rained, drizzled, thundered and poured. The three of them traipsed through the sodden country, unable to fly or stay still. Their only reprieve from the elements was a small abandoned barn in which they spent a day trying to get dry.

"Well, thanks to this absolutely hideous weather, we haven't encountered any Imperials for a while," Carey said as she and Kat peered out an open window, watching the lightning split the sky.

Ji laughed as he flopped back into a dry pile of hay. "Silver lining indeed!"

Chapter Fifteen

To Mark with Evil

T he rain finally receded after what seemed like a never-ending string of storms. Carey was extremely relieved to see it at long last come to an end; it was becoming rather uncomfortable travelling in wet clothes. Kat had insisted that they continue travelling, even through the pouring rain. She didn't hesitate in saying at least fifty times that the winter snows would be much worse to travel in if they failed to reach Donegal before them. They could easily survive a little rain. Carey's definition of 'a little rain' was obviously vastly different to Kat's but she didn't argue – the very thought of having to travel through snow kept her moving despite her discomfort.

To take up time and keep their mind off their sodden garments, Ji found and invented ever more comical and ridiculous ways of keeping dry, and although mostly unsuccessful, it did succeed in diverting Carey's attention. Although she was still perplexed by what had passed between them back at Maria's inn, Ji, it seemed, had forgotten about it completely. He barely let on that he had noticed anything unusual. Whether he did so on purpose or not, Carey was unsure, but in any case, she didn't bring it up again. It was very possible that she was reading a little too much into it so she decided to follow suit and pushed it to the back of her mind.

Carey had also developed a nervous habit of tugging on her sleeve. The mark that hid beneath made her itch involuntarily and it made her sick every time she laid eyes on it. It remained faded but was finely etched into her skin in a way that made it stand out, as if it was begging for attention. Ji's suggestion that it was part of a greater plan made her feel uneasy to the point of nausea, wherein which she would find herself clutching at her wrist as if to restrain it.

They reached Donegal two days later and, after much discussion, reluctantly stopped at a public inn.

"We need to stop, there's no point in arguing. We're starting to resemble the wildlife around us which only serves to attract more attention than we already do. We need a proper clean. The locals might seem a little suspicious of us but at least we can handle them," Kat said finally.

It wasn't ideal, but Carey agreed that they all needed a good scrubbing. She was sure that even Firefly was able to smell them now.

As Ji stowed Firefly away in the stables, Kat managed to get her hands on a local newspaper with some silver she found in the bottom of her saddlebag.

"Look at this," she said as she threw it onto the table in front of Carey and Ji. "Look! Disappearances, suspected murders, and *magical sightings*! We're getting close, I can feel it!"

Carey thought Kat was being a little too enthusiastic about disappearances and possible murders, but a spark of hope flickered inside her chest which was quickly followed by a shiver of terror. Close meant the Empire. Close meant having to fight Malevolence and she still had no idea how they were meant to do that. From what she had seen, Kat and Ji were skilled wizards, but they weren't particularly exceptional.

You're exceptional, a voice noted and Carey's mind was drawn to the magic that had rippled under her skin, first when facing the Dæmon in the clearing and then again at her family's home. She shook her head. *That was nothing. I can't control that. It only happens when I'm in danger.*

The voice echoed back at her. *What do you think facing the Empire will be like? A walk in the park?*

Wow, Carey thought. *I can be really sarcastic.*

Ignoring the snarky voice in her head, she reached for the paper and smoothed out the front page of the *Donegal Journal*; spread across the top of the page was the headline *Strange Happenings Cast Shadow Over Ireland.* This must be the article Kat had been excitedly referring to. Ji pulled it across the table and read it out loud for Carey.

"*Strange happenings and unexplained phenomena have been occurring throughout Ireland this past week, disturbing the quiet lives of Monaghan and Clones. A number of terrified witnesses to these events are currently in hiding, in fear of their safety, believing that Black Magic is the cause.*

"'*There was a woman. She was screaming words and there were these strange flashes of light. I only just escaped. I'm so afraid to go outside because they might be waiting,' said a witness to the Monaghan attack.*

"*Although there is doubt to the level of truth in these accounts, the towns, which had been plagued by these unwarranted and unprovoked attacks, have been almost destroyed. Villagers claim to have seen strange folk at the times of these attacks, dressed in attire reminiscent of medieval folklore pertaining to witches. Others have said to have witnessed secret meetings and even encountered these individuals by chance, often barely escaping with their lives. A number of towns are seriously considering witch hunts after it was banned almost a century ago in order to stop these kinds of assaults. Public punishments are also being considered as a possibility if indeed the perpetrators do engage in or support Black Magic.*

"'*Something has to be done about this menace,' said the mayor of Dublin when he was asked of the possible introduction of public punishment. 'We cannot and will not let such people get away with these monstrosities. They must be dealt with.'*

"*Townsfolk have been cautioned against approaching any people they witness participating in suspicious activities to avoid any violent repercussions. However, until a decision is made by town leaders, there may be more attacks. Some also believe that Travellers may be helping the perpetrators by giving them disguises and safe passage. Given the deceitful nature of Travellers, this statement can almost certainly be assured.*

"*Despite the attention these incidents have received from local law enforcement, the people of Ireland will continue to live in fear of the certain evil that threatens them. No doubt there will be a greater push for hunts and burnings to satisfy the public's yearning for vengeance.*"

Under this rather short article was a picture twice its size of a ruined village, smoke rising in great plumes from the rubble.

"Kat! How can you be so excited by something like this?" Carey cried emphatically.

Kat waved her remark away. "I'm not excited about the attacks. I'm excited because she's never been this conspicuous before."

Carey stared at her.

"Don't you see? She's letting herself be seen by Commoners! Malevolence has always been so careful. She knows as well as anyone that Commoners are prejudiced against our kind. She needed to stay hidden if she wanted her campaign against us to be successful. Witch hunts never were very successful but if they were reinstated, it would delay the Empire for a little while and perhaps give us a chance!" Kat said, trying to keep herself from shouting in excitement. "Listen, we'll stay here for tonight and we'll get an early start tomorrow, all right? I'm going to send a message to Madame Guise and tell her all about it!"

Kat turned and disappeared up the stairs to their room. Somehow Carey didn't think Malevolence was losing control at all; she had a feeling that this was all intentional. Although why Malevolence would want to provoke Commoners into bringing back the medieval practice of witch burnings was beyond Carey's understanding.

She scanned the newspaper article again. "They don't seem to think much of Travellers, do they?"

Ji grunted. "Some Travellers, like some witches and wizards, give bad reputations to the rest of them. Stuff like stealing and rowdiness. The thing is that many witches and wizards that disguise themselves as Travellers, like we do, for safer passage through the land. If we travelled like the Essedarian do, in hooded cloaks and robes, we'd have every village inspector and any other suspicious busybody after us. We can't very well dress as ordinary Commoners either. How many Commoners have you seen travelling the highways by foot? We can't afford such things as carriages or a team of horses so we have dress to suit our means. We take cover as Travellers, even though prejudice sometimes make us targets of angry Commoners.

It's nothing we can't handle though."

Carey nodded, not questioning Ji's logic and why would she? She wasn't the one who had been hiding most of her life.

They both sat quietly for a while and looking around, Carey spotted a tall, red-haired waitress attending to a large, muscled customer. Carey turned to Ji and smiled.

"What?" Ji asked her suspiciously.

She put her finger to her cheek and raised her eyebrows. "I rather like this inn," said Carey, feigning thoughtfulness. "Pity it doesn't have any *Persias*," she said with a smirk.

Ji pointed his finger at her in warning and Carey laughed. As she got up from the table she patted him on shoulder and said, "It's okay, Ji. You can't have something clever to say all the time, you know. I'm going up to Kat. Now don't go talking to any strange people, okay? Especially that red-head waitress over there."

Carey laughed again as Ji sat lost for words, unable to counter her attack. She heard him yell "Hey!" after her as she walked up the stairs shaking her head, but he did not follow. Carey walked to their room and knocked at the door.

"Kat? Kat, can you open the door?"

Carey tried the doorknob and, to her surprise, it opened easily. Kat would never have left the door unlocked. She frowned as she opened it up wide to find Kat lying unconscious on the floor with the red goat's head mark burnt distinctly onto her neck.

* * *

Carey's screams had Ji stumbling up the stairs in a mad rush to find her trying desperately to lift Kat onto her bed. He took over as Carey grabbed the washcloth from the basin, lifting her onto the bed with one swift movement. Carey hesitantly dabbed at the glowing mark on Kat's neck, listening to it hiss slightly at her touch; she winced with each tiny wisp of smoke that curled up into the air. The mark was deep in her skin, deeper than Carey's or Ji's and bruises were beginning to blossom up and down her arms, dark purples and greens. As Kat lay battered and broken, Carey's fear was overtaken by confusion.

"Ji? How is it that the Empire keeps finding us? We've been careful, we've stuck to back roads, and yet Kat's attack is an obvious sign that we haven't been careful enough. How are they doing it?" Carey asked Ji as she sat clutching Kat's limp hand.

Ji was staring at the bed and started at the sound of her voice. He shook his head. "I really don't know how they're doing it. We've always been able to stay hidden. I don't know what's changed."

"But if they're able to find us so easily, how come they haven't just killed us? Why bother branding us?" Carey asked quietly, rubbing her wrist again.

Ji frowned, turning his gaze to her. "You think there's something else going on?"

Carey stopped rubbing her wrist and buried her eyes in the heels of her palms, suddenly extremely tired. "I don't know what I'm thinking."

Carey volunteered to watch over Kat for the night, too scared to close her eyes. Ji agreed reluctantly and left them to find a doctor who would give him some salve for Kat's wound. It had begun to weep and he was convinced it would become infected if they didn't act quickly.

Kat was unconsciousness for almost three days before she finally woke. The mark remained a bright red and had slowly begun to glow an eerie yellow, making Carey and Ji increasingly uneasy. Ji had found the envelope to the letter Kat was in the process of sending to Madame Guise when she was attacked. The letter was nowhere to be found.

"Do you think they took it?" Carey asked in a whisper one day as they sat watching Kat sleep. She turned the envelope over in her hands. "Do you think they took the letter?"

Ji grimaced. "There's a very real possibility that they did. I've been thinking that we should alert Madame Guise. They could find her based on that letter." He sighed. "Even worse, they could know what we're doing or where we're going."

Ji looked back down at Kat, who was starting to stir. Carey grabbed her shoulder and shook her gently, persuading her to wake. "Kat, Kat. Wake up, Kat. Come on."

Kat's eyes flew open; her pupils were dilated so much that barely any of the white was visible. Her body convulsed violently and she was flung up into a sitting position, clutching her cheek. Carey tipped backwards in fright, clutching the back of her chair in an attempt to stop herself from falling over. Kat's eyes began to roll about in her head, wide with unimaginable terror. She was screaming, panting for breath, her body shaking uncontrollably.

Ji was standing over Kat, trying frantically to think of something that might calm her.

"Carey, help me! I'll hold her down and – and try to calm her. Do something that might stop her!"

"What? How? What can I do?" Carey cried, her heart bashing against her ribs, her mind flying about wildly.

"I don't know!" he yelled over Kat's screams as he struggled to hold down her arms. "*Try something! Anything!*

Carey's ears were ringing with Kat's screeches but she tried to block them out. Kat was bucking against Ji's restraint, tossing her head from side to side. Carey grasped it with both hands, straining to hold Kat still and closed her eyes. She wasn't entirely sure what she was doing but she fought the urge to panic, swallowing back the force rising in her throat. She concentrated on where her hands made contact with Kat's temples.

Kat was bucking hard against Ji and with an almighty grunt, kicked him hard in the stomach.

"Urgh!" Ji uttered, doubling over, releasing Kat.

Kat was still screaming at the top of her lungs and she lashed out dangerously at Carey.

"Ji!" Carey pleaded.

Ji clutched the bed, trying to regain his breath. With great effort he managed to regain his grip on her flailing arms. After some tussling, Ji was able to force her to lay still. Carey held her hands steady and focused once more. She reached deep for the magic to calm her friend and it came to

143

her, prickling from her fingers to her toes. It danced down her fingertips and she felt Kat begin to settle; she stopped struggling and her breathing slowed. Suddenly, a small surge pulsed at her fingertips and Carey released Kat in surprise.

"Carey?" Ji asked with concern as he released Kat's wrists slowly.

She shook her head. "No, it's fine. It was nothing."

That was different. Carey had not yet got the hang of this power – it was still so strange and unexpected. She wasn't sure what its capabilities were but so far she had been able to fight off a Dæmon and calm Kat in the throes of a violence-induced fit. Frankly it was frightening.

Ji and Carey backed away from Kat, watching her closely. She sighed deeply, her chest rising and falling peacefully, a completely different being to the one that had inhabited the room only moments before. Slowly, her eyes flickered open and she turned her head towards Carey and Ji. Her eyes welled with unexpected tears.

"You're still here," she said in a rasping whisper.

"Of course we are, Kat," Ji answered softly, moving to her side and helping her up slowly. "You can't get rid of us that easily."

"I saw… such horrible things… what they did to you…" Kat mumbled disjointedly as Ji helped her over to the basin.

She moved over to the mirror, tilting her head to the side in an effort to see the goat's head mark branded into her neck more clearly. Silently she examined the mark, running her finger gently over the raised tattoo now permanently etched into her skin. The tears in her eyes trickled down her face. She turned to Carey and Ji, her face taut with unspeakable pain. She opened her mouth to speak but then suddenly threw her hands up, gripping her head in anguish. Kat cried out, ripping hair from her scalp as an invisible tormentor tortured her from within. Carey ran to her friend but Kat struck out at her violently.

"Stop it, *stop it*!" she screeched, hitting out at someone only she could see. Her face was an image of absolute terror, stretched and contorted.

"Ji, what's happening?" Carey cried desperately, ducking out of the way of Kat's flailing arms.

She tried again to grab hold of Kat, but again she was forced backwards by Kat lashing out as she stumbled around the room in a blind panic. She crashed into the side table, knocking it to the floor with a board-shaking THUD. Her screams were reaching ear-piercing heights, forcing Carey and Ji to clap their hands over their ears. They needed to calm her down as soon as possible or the townsfolk downstairs would become suspicious; at that moment, Carey could not think of anything more terrifying.

"Ji! We have to stop her! They're going to hear her downstairs!" she shouted over Kat.

"I really didn't want to do this!" Ji hollered over the racket as he raised his hands.

A spell erupted from his fingertips just as Kat stopped, the clouds lifting from her eyes. She threw her arm up in useless defence but was hit full in the face.

"Kat!"

She fell to the floor with a dull thud. Ji cursed his stupidity before rushing to her side and lifting her carefully on to her bed. Kat groaned.

"Kat? Can you hear me?" Ji whispered tentatively.

Kat opened her eyes. "You used… magic on me… Ji Binx?"

Ji sighed with relief as Kat propped herself up. She was gasping for breath, as though she'd just run a marathon.

Carey padded across to the door and opened it a crack, peering nervously into the corridor. There were no Commoners outside ready to lynch them, but it was unusually quiet downstairs.

It's nothing, she told herself as she shut the door again. *Maybe it's just quiet down there.*

It was little comfort, but Carey swallowed her fears and turned back to her friends.

"Kat, what was that?" Ji asked, sitting down beside her on the bed. "What just happened?"

She shook her head, trying hard to catch her breath before answering. Her face was bright red and tendrils of hair stuck to her hot cheeks. Every breath she took caused her pain; her chest heaved awkwardly with every short, sharp breath. She opened her mouth and began to speak. Her sentences were broken and difficult to understand, hampered by her stunted breathing. It was as though she was trying to run and talk at the same time.

"I don't know. Someone caught me by surprise... I didn't have time to react... I felt it... a searing pain on my neck... it hurt, so much... then... I... I blacked out. Next thing I heard was... I could hear... Malevolence. She was... was talking... to... to me... I think. No. No, that's not right. She was talking *about* me... about *us*. This mark allows her to... enter my mind..."

Ji and Carey glanced at each other in alarm.

"She'll know what we're planning," Ji said, running his hands nervously through his hair.

"But that's not the only thing," Kat wheezed.

"What else does she want?" Carey squeaked, still trying to wrap her head around the first terrifying thought.

Kat's eyes were wide with panic and terror. "She's... she laughed. She said... she said that this would make it... so much easy – easier for her to..."

Ji took her hand in a desperate attempt to comfort her. "Do what, Kat?"

Somehow Carey already knew before Kat even opened her mouth.

"*Destroy me.* Take my powers. I'm sure she intends to kill me using this..." Her hand wandered to where the mark glowed on her skin.

Carey's sight darkened. The world around her seemed to grow very tight and suffocating. She thought she had imagined every possible evil Malevolence was capable of but this took her to a whole new level. The Dark Magic she wielded seemed even more impossible to Carey, especially if they were to defeat her...

"Telepathy," she heard Ji pronounce.

"What?" she asked, pulling herself back to the moment.

"*Very* strong telepathy. That must be her connection. But I didn't know Malevolence was a telepath..." Ji said, more to himself than anyone else.

He passed a cloth to Kat. She accepted it gratefully and pressed it firmly to her forehead in relief, leaning her elbows on her knees.

"If all that magic *didn't* give her telepathic powers I'd be amazed," Kat said weakly as she wiped her face.

"Telepathy…" said Carey absently, still contemplating the full extent of Malevolence's powers. "How strong does it have to be to…?"

"It's beyond strong," Ji interjected. "It's complete."

"Joining my mind to hers," Kat surmised miserably.

"There has to be a way to break it though, shouldn't there be? If it can be made, it can be broken, right?" Carey asked desperately.

Surely there had to be a way to reverse the effects of the telepathic connection. With what she understood of the power, it was often a two-way street. What kind of power would be needed for such an attempt though? They would need help.

"Madame Guise."

"Hmm? What about her?" Kat asked.

"She might know something, I mean, about the connection and how it might be blocked."

"You're right. I am far from being an expert on the workings of telepathy and we could use all the help we can get," Ji nodded.

Reaching into her bag for some paper, Carey's stomach rumbled in protest. They needed food, which meant going downstairs… She quickly went over their options and came to the conclusion that it would be better if Ji remained with Kat and she would venture downstairs. Carey figured that she wouldn't be able to handle Kat in the throes of magical psychosis but she could probably handle a room full of non-magical Commoners, should they try anything. She mentioned this to Ji who reluctantly agreed, telling her how to send a message to Madame Guise.

"Be careful," Ji said as she left, his worry clear on his face.

Carey entered the main room of the tavern to find the number of townsfolk had swelled as the regulars came in after a day of work. Several heads turned as Carey walked to the bar and ordered some food and they followed her as she took a seat at a table in the back corner. Ignoring them as she tried to act calm and indifferent, Carey pulled the piece of paper from her pocket and began detailing their situation to Madame Guise, asking if there was anything that could be done to help Kat. Folding it tightly, Carey held the letter flat between her palms and directed her thoughts to Madame

Guise. She watched in wonderment as the letter seemed to melt between her hands and then it was gone. She felt as though magic would forever hold her in a constant state of awe.

Carey waited impatiently for the food to arrive, avoiding with much difficulty the ever more apparent stares from many of the other patrons. Their eyes were trained on her, not bothering to hide the blatant suspicion that lined their faces. She could feel their gaze as if they were hot red beams on her skin. Carey was silently pleading for the cook to hurry up when there came a strangle tingling in her hand. Almost immediately, a small pale envelope appeared in her hand.

"Oh!" Carey exclaimed and a number of heads turned. She quickly hid it under the table, hoping no one in the tavern had seen it.

She opened it and found a short letter written on a torn piece of paper.
"Dear Carey,

I will make this quick as I have very little time. There have been several Imperials poking around these parts and I have no doubt I am the target of their investigation. They must therefore know that I have aided you, which you already know is a dangerous thing to do in these times. Therefore, I am going into hiding with some other refugees near Dublin to avoid capture and my escort will be arriving soon.

Regarding the connection that has been forged between Kat and Malevolence – the only way I know that could possibly break the connection would be to get some Silver Water for her to drink. The attack caught her off-guard and so I believe Malevolence was able to form this connection while Kat's powers were still in shock. This way Malevolence was able to suppress them. Silver Water would freeze the mark and give her powers time to heal and overcome the connection. The Silver Water can only be found in a small pond behind the Artesian Falls. This location is a well guarded secret of the Order's. Until then, if Kat's powers continue to weaken, create a Tear Globe. Ask Ji if you aren't able to. This will protect her. Good luck on your journey and please take care when contacting me in the future.

Yours, Madame Guise."

"So we have to get some Silver Water, do we?"

148

Carey jumped with fright at Ji's sudden presence.

"Ji! What are you doing down here? Why aren't you upstairs watching Kat?"

"I was just coming down to check on you. I was worried," he said earnestly as he took the seat next to her.

Something in the way he spoke sent a ripple of nerves fluttering and Carey shivered, caught out by this sudden wave of emotion.

"Carey?" Ji was looking at her, his bright blue eyes seemed unnervingly perceptive and Carey hoped he didn't notice her discomfort.

Avoiding his gaze, Carey put the letter away. "How is she?"

"She's fine for now."

Carey sighed, exhausted. "How have you handled this for so long, Ji?"

Ji looked down at his hands. "To tell you the truth, I don't know. We just have. It's…well, it's all we've ever known, I suppose." Carey's despair must have shown on her face because he quickly added, "But look, Carey. Everything is going to be fine as long as we're together. That's all that matters."

Carey smiled half-heartedly at his reassurance. Ji must have sensed her despondency for he moved to her side and pulled her into his arms. The emotions from a few moments ago flared again and she found herself feeling comforted by Ji's embrace in a way that she had not felt before. It was not merely soothing but filled her soul with a warm comfort that gave her hope and something she had never experienced. Before Carey could explore this feeling further, they were interrupted by a familiar cry; Kat.

Howling in pain, Kat came stumbling down the stairs, her head in her hands.

"Oh no," Carey murmured.

The talking and noise in the tavern ceased immediately and everyone watched in fear and apprehension. As Kat staggered into the middle of the room, a tall red-haired man with a round, protruding stomach stood up from his table.

"She – she's possessed!" he shouted as he pointed at Kat with an accusing finger, sloshing the ale he held in his other hand down his front.

A wave of nervous murmuring spread through the room and Carey looked at Ji. His face was fixed on the man, his hands flexing at his side ready to defend Kat. The townsfolk were beginning to rise from their chairs, their eyes locked on Kat as she continued to writhe in pain. One of them lifted a knife into the air and in a booming voice, cried out to the others in the bar, "She's a witch! They all are! That girl and the other two in the corner there! They're the ones after our families! They must be stopped before their evil spreads! Quick, get them now before they bewitch us all!"

Many of the bar's clientele were clearly hesitant at the thought of attacking the witches but a handful of the men growled angrily and started to advance on Carey, Ji and Kat. An animalistic fury was etched on their faces as they gathered up various weapons that included a broken mop handle and a brass candlestick. The red-haired barmaid screamed and ran into a back room. The sight of the advancing mob gave rise to the strange tingling magic within Carey and her confidence was instantly bolstered. She knew what she had to do.

"Ji. Grab Kat and get out of here now. *Now!*" Carey hissed from the corner of her mouth.

Kat was slowing now with heavy breaths and Carey could see she was weakening; her legs were straining under her weight. Ji saw it too and dived to catch her, sweeping her out of the way of the livid townsfolk. Angry shouts sounded around the room as Carey fought around chairs and tables to get to the door. Kat considered the commotion surrounding her in a daze as Ji carried her, making his way along the back table away from the advancing horde. The men were crying like wild animals as they closed in around them. Carey saw Kat and Ji make it through the door ahead of her. She leapt over a chair and was just about to join them when she was knocked aside by a force from behind. Before Carey knew what was happening, she was being pulled back into the bar. The door was slammed shut to prevent her escape. Then they pounced. The mob crashed on top of her, smothering her; Carey attempted a scream but the air was being pushed from her lungs like a set of bagpipes.

They were all trying to get at her, their fists and boots connecting with various parts of her body. From somewhere she felt the cold stab of metal in her thigh and she yelped in pain as a distinct burning sensation engulfed her, emanating from the point of contact. She kicked out, groping for something that she could pull herself out with. The mass of bodies confused her and she cried out in surprise when someone dragged her out from beneath the pile of men and threw her up against a wall. A hand struck her hard across her head, bringing her to her knees. As Carey gasped for breath, the man took advantage and picked her up by her collar, throwing her roughly to the side, sending her crashing into a set of tables and chairs. Carey's head smacked up against wood and a splitting headache instantly set in. Weakly, Carey tried desperately to pull herself up off the ground when yet another strong hand wrenched her to her feet and pushed her back up against the wall. A surly-looking man with a wiry beard held her there with one of his massive hands while he lined up his other fist with Carey's face. The moment between this and when her attacker swung his fist in towards her face, gave Carey's magic the chance to surge forth, clearing her mind and wiping away any pain that had crippled her instantaneously. She shifted her feet ever so slightly and locked eyes with the bearded man. With a howl, his fist flew at her and in a movement so swift onlookers would debate later whether they had actually seen her move, Carey held her hand out in front of it and cried, "STOP!"

Quite unnecessary though it was to be so vocal, she succeeded; the man froze completely, stuck in the moment. The other men stopped, confused by this sudden development. As Carey tried to pull herself free however, the other men began to shout again but this time with a little trepidation. Those who had hung back to begin with were now edging back away from the fight, afraid that they may be the next to suffer at Carey's hand. Bleeding profusely from her leg and head, the adrenalin produced by the magic was beginning to ebb and Carey was suddenly able to feel every ache and pain. She finally tore herself from the man and ducked quickly as another tried to grab her. She picked up a walking stick that was leaning against a table, and using several quick moves Ji had showed her, she soon had two of the men on the ground, moaning in pain and anger and the rest backing away.

When Carey had finally reached the door, she turned to the remaining men game enough to still be pursuing her and held out her hand, sending a stream of angry red sparks into the air.

"Stand back! If anyone makes one wrong move, I'll send you all to the Darklands!" she spat, holding her injured leg.

The sparks had forced the pack back and Carey took the chance to escape while they were still deciding what to do, slipping out the front door. Ji was waiting outside on an anxious Firefly with Kat sitting weakly in front of him. Grabbing Ji's hand, she swung herself up behind him as he gave Firefly a nudge.

Looking back at the tavern, Carey sighted the rabble emerging from inside, shaking their fists and cursing fluently. Carey looked back at Ji. "That is the last time I *ever* go into a public inn. Urgh…"

The wound to her leg gave her a sharp pain and she rolled up the hem of her skirt. The wound was deep and blood was flowing freely from it.

"What happened?" Ji said, looking down at her bloodied thigh.

"I think someone stabbed me. It feels really deep," Carey said through gritted teeth.

Ji reached around her and placed his hand over the wound. A cool green light flowed from his hand and spread over her thigh like a cool breeze. It soothed deep into the wound and Carey breathed a deep sigh of relief. She looked up into Ji's eyes; there was warmth there and a certain something else. The corner of his mouth curled ever so slightly into a smile and heat rose in her face. She had the simultaneous urge to move closer and push him away, and as he opened his mouth to say something, she looked down, breaking the strange tension that had so quickly built up between them.

"Wow! I didn't know you were such a good healer, Ji," Carey said, her voice breaking slightly as she looked down to find the wound completely healed.

Ji shrugged, the words he wanted to say gone with the moment. "I really only know the basics," he said dismissively, turning back to the front. "What's going to be hard is making sure little Miss Psycho here doesn't fall off. I think her mind is weakening. She looked at me before and said:

'Thulaño a Venthera'."

"Meaning?"

"*To Defeat is to Rule.*"

"Where's that from?"

"They're the words of the Empire. It's in the ancient language of Gadælic. Gadælians were the first to form the Central council of the Mystic Realm."

"So Kat will be speaking Gadælic from now on," Carey guessed, as Ji steered Firefly a little further north.

"Who knows, with Malevolence's connection getting stronger..."

"Then we must get her powers into a Tear Globe as soon as we can or she'll become too weak – or have no powers at all. I've been meaning to ask you. How does a Tear Globe work?"

"I'll show you later. Right now we have to find somewhere safe to camp. Near the Artesian Falls even would be good, then we would be able to retrieve the water easily without much delay."

And so they flew west towards the Artesian Falls, soaring high over the dark and forbidding earth, the shadows chasing them as so much else did.

Chapter Sixteen

Wanted Secrets

I t was almost dawn by the time they found somewhere to rest. Fog hung thickly in the air and dew had begun to form, a thousand tiny droplets shimmering in the moonlight. They had landed in a dark forest, the trees so close together that it seemed even darker in there than night itself. Carey dismounted and immediately she noticed something very different about this forest. The trees were completely still; no animal sounds big or small could be heard. The customary rustling of a hundred different creatures was missing and Firefly stamped her hooves nervously, mirroring Carey's own emotions. The only sound she could hear was an intermittent hum that sounded vaguely like a ship's foghorn.

"Ji," Carey said, staring into the pitch-black of the strange forest. "Are you sure this place is safe? I mean, can you hear those sounds?"

"Trust me. We've been here before. There's nothing bad here, it's just a little strange. Go see for yourself. I'll stay here and set up," he said with his back to her, helping Kat dismount from Firefly.

Kat had begun muttering to herself in a language Carey could not understand, her lips moving constantly with streams of nonsense. Her eyes were wide like a mad-man's, rolling about, unfocused and unseeing. Carey didn't really want to leave her but she knew Ji would look after her, just like he had done for most of their lives.

"All right then. I'll be back in a bit," she called to Ji as she walked away from their camp.

The fog was slowly lowering itself like a great blanket over the forest and was growing thicker with every step Carey took. She touched a nearby trunk and found it damp with dark green moss and dew. She doubted very much whether this part of the forest saw any light at all. The deep rumbling sounds grew louder with every moment that passed and Carey's imagination ran wild with what could possibly be making them. The fog obscured her view and she stumbled a few times on hidden roots and rocks, hardly able to stop herself falling flat on her face as she grappled with the slippery trees. She continued, though, determined to find out what was making those mysterious foghorn-like sounds. Carey was struck by a sudden thought – what if some creature was making these sounds? She was a very easy target and would have little luck in a quick escape, especially the way she was going. Perhaps if she were less conspicuous she'd be safer...

Carey reached into her satchel and felt around for the small wooden box that contained her mother's precious shapeshifting pin and locket. She opened the box carefully with the tiny gold key and unclipped the small pin from its soft velvet bedding, looking at it in the thin moonlight. Tucking her bag out of sight under a giant root, she then attached the pin to her shirt, taking extreme care not to drop it. Then, once making sure it was secure, she set her mind on a shape that would make her as inconspicuous as possible. Almost instantly she transformed into a small brown field-mouse. The transformation took away her breath for a moment and it was with a thrill of excitement that she squeaked, amazed by her new-found perspective. The world towered over her, a giant's landscape. The treetops were almost impossible to see from where she now found herself, hidden beneath fallen foliage. Her long whiskers made her nose twitch as they scraped against leaves and the forest floor, sending shivers through her tiny form as the tiny tendrils helped her feel her way through the undergrowth. In this shape, Carey was glad to find that she was now far beneath the thicket of fog and had a clear view of the way ahead. Her only misgivings were that she would meet other more unpleasant forest floor dwellers.

As the tiny rodent, she began to weave her way along the forest floor.

Carey marvelled at her speed and dexterity, squeezing under roots and threading her way through the maze of foliage that now surrounded her. The booming sounds were louder now and they filled the air, causing the ground to quiver beneath her paws. It wasn't long before she found the source of the vibrations – she had reached what she assumed must be the Artesian Falls. A great wall of rock rose up before her and reached far to the left and to the right, disappearing into the dense trees. A pool of deep, dark-blue water stretched out from the base of the Falls, water so clear that Carey could see right to the very bottom. An elegant cascade of water fell from the heavens with a gentle hiss, the very top obscured by mist and fog. Carey's eyes followed a wide ridge that ran along the rock wall, a rough ledge that disappeared behind the wall of gently falling water. The serenity was compounded by the broken reflections of stars upon the water's surface, creating a heavenly scene. It would have been perfect had it not been for the beasts that stood watch over it.

They were the strangest creatures Carey had ever seen. They had the scruffy-maned head of a bedraggled lion, the hair knotted and limp, the shaggy-coated body of a giant mountain goat and the long snaking scaly tail of what Carey could only imagine would be what a dragon's tail looked like. The one to the right was standing on its four thin legs, watching over the Falls with bright green eyes as it let out another low resounding bellow. A great orange ball of flame lit up the forest around them, the monster's nostrils smouldering as it closed its great jaws. Even though she was very much camouflaged as a field mouse, Carey scurried backwards and hid beneath a large fallen leaf. Those fireballs were much bigger than her current form and she planned to keep herself un-singed. She turned her attention to the other monster; it was lying down, its hairy head resting on its bent knees and its slanted eyes as watchful as its companion's, though strangely unfocused. As they moved their gaze over her hiding spot, she saw an almost human intelligence gleam within those deep pools of green that sent a shiver down her tiny spine.

Carey observed them for a short while from beneath her leaf, watching the flames as they illuminated the forest around her and the beasts as they continued to sound their warnings into the silence.

The fog thinned around the Falls for a moment and the rock wall behind them suddenly became visible to Carey. Rough carvings were etched into the stone, ancient symbols that looked almost haphazard in their arrangement. It was on either side of this wall that the creatures were stationed which could only mean that this wall was the entrance to where the Silver Water was. To be able to bypass those creatures though, Carey would need Ji's help.

By the time Carey left she had a complete mental image of the Falls. She wasn't sure how Ji would approach this given that the entire time she sat there watching, the beasts did not cease in their flame-throwing over the Falls. Having seen enough, Carey started back to where she had stored her bag beneath the tree roots. With a cautious glance over her shoulder, Carey changed back into her human self. She removed the pin and carefully placed it back in its case before stuffing it down the bottom of her bag for safekeeping.

Back at the camp, Carey found Ji watching Kat over steeped fingers. Kat was moving three small stones around in front of her, placing them then replacing them purposefully in smooth, fluid movements. The effect was strangely mesmerising as she muttered the same strange language as before, her eyes misty and glazed. Carey noticed that even though her movements were swift and her speech strong and full of intent, Kat appeared weak.

"Ji," she said as she sat down beside him. "What is she doing?"

Ji frowned over his fingertips. "I'm not sure. It's not any ritual I'm aware of. Whatever it is though, it's making her weak."

"Have you created a Tear Globe yet?" Carey asked, looking about as if to find one.

"No, not yet. I was waiting for you to return," he answered, rubbing his hands together. "Best we do it now. She won't last much longer like this. Just... keep as quiet as possible..."

Ji closed his eyes and made a movement with his hands, slowly drawing them up from his sides and bringing them into a peak above Kat's head. In barely a whisper, Ji began to utter an enchantment. A string of unintelligible

157

words flowed from his lips and Carey was entranced by the intonation, the rise and fall of the sounds as they tumbled through the air, alighting on something instantaneously wondrous and daunting. A shimmer caught her eye and she gasped in amazement. Tiny particles began to appear, drawing in around Kat, swirling about in the air like a tiny flurry of stars. Slowly, in harmony with Ji's enchantment, they drew themselves inwards until they joined together to form a small tear-shaped globe of glistening light.

Ji did not touch it. Instead he made a motion with his hands, coaxing it into position just above Kat's head. Carey opened her mouth to say something but Ji held up his hand to silence her. He closed his eyes again in concentration and Kat looked up from her stones briefly, a blank stare of indifference her only expression, before diverting her eyes once more.

Then Ji reached out and closed his fist in the air, just in front of Kat's chest. He tugged. Kat gasped, dropping her stones in a clatter. Ji pulled back slowly and gently, his other hand enticing, stroking whatever it was that he was drawing from within Kat. Carey watched in awe, sensing that whatever it was that Ji was doing, it deserved reverent silence. A light blue mist followed his hands, emerging from Kat's person, encompassing her in a cocoon of gently cascading light. With a delicate flick of the wrist, the mist filtered up into the beautiful glittering casket and there it stayed, casting a faint spirit-like light over its host. Ji let out a long sigh and got to his feet. He rubbed his eyes as if he had just woken from a deep sleep.

Carey looked back at Kat, who had resumed shifting the three pebbles around, the globe hanging eerily over her head. "That's it? What did you do?"

"I drew her magic from her and encased it in a Tear Globe. Without her magic, Malevolence can't inflict as much damage on her. It's all we can do for now, until we get our hands on some Silver Water."

Carey nodded. "But she is going to be all right, isn't she?" she asked, sitting down by the fire with Ji.

"She'll be fine. Just don't touch the Globe. As long as no one touches it..."

"Why is that?"

"Well, its taboo to possess another's magic, to hold or capture it. I've captured her magic within the globe but I have not taken it from her, if you know what I mean. What I've done isn't taboo, but if you took it for your own use... well, that's something completely different. If it's taken away, a wizard can live but they cannot define meanings, movements, actions or sounds. They are indifferent to everything around them. Their actions are merely echoes of memories. For Kat, those actions are just vague repetitions – she's not even thinking about them. She probably won't even remember doing it when she's better. But even with the globe, we still have to get the Silver Water soon. The globe isn't strong enough to stave off Malevolence for too long," Ji said, staring into the flames.

Carey was contemplating Ji's words when the bushes behind Kat shifted and a shadow flitted across the tree trunks. Carey stiffened.

"Ji," she whispered.

"Hmm?" he muttered, not taking his eyes off the fire.

She scanned the trees but there was nothing else. Whatever had caused the disturbance was gone. "Nothing." *Perhaps an animal?*

After a few moments of silence, Ji asked about her trip to the Falls. With much difficulty, Carey tried describing the creatures to Ji.

"They sound like chimeras," he declared, and when he saw Carey's bewildered look continued. "They're guardians – extremely good ones, very intelligent. And one bad encounter can be fatal. Damn, I should have expected something like this. It's going to be hard getting past them, but we have to," Ji said, running his hand through his hair absent-mindedly.

"And how exactly will we do that?" Carey asked with just a hint of reluctance.

"That's the catch. We can't. You cannot defeat a chimera without the sword of Garidor, and the Empire has that."

Carey let out a breath of despair. "That'd be right. The Empire attacks Kat and the only way to save her would be by getting help *from* the Empire. Great," she sighed heavily as she looked over at her unfortunate friend.

They were silent as Ji sank into a deep train of thought, which Carey could only hope was leading him to some fantastic way to bypass the chimeras. She could think only of the razor-sharp teeth of the Falls' guardians.

"You could trick them," he said quietly.

Carey turned her head sharply, the thought of painful death vanishing instantly from her mind. "Trick them? The chimeras? But how?"

"Jeremy once said–"

"*Jeremy?*" Carey spat, the very mention of his name irritating her.

Ji shook his head. "Jeremy *pre*-insanity told me. Chimeras are blind, apparently, so their other senses are extremely heightened."

"Blind," Carey repeated, thinking back to their bright green eyes and how they seemed un-focused but yet still so alert.

"Yes, blind. If we create enough chaos…"

"We could distract them," Carey finished.

"Exactly. We need to disturb their other senses. I think I might be able to do that but it might get noisy," he warned. "So while I do that, you can get the Silver Water."

"You make it sound so easy, Ji!" Carey cried, incredulous at his rather cavalier disposition.

"Well, I could make it sound harder and list everything that could go wrong, if you like," Ji suggested smartly.

"Actually, I think I'll pass," Carey sighed. "If only I knew how to get past that wall…"

"Wall? What wall?" Ji asked with a frown.

"There was a wall of carved stone behind the Falls. I couldn't quite see the symbols on it though I doubt I would be able to read them even if I could. Is there any way to know what it says?"

"Depends on what language it is. If they're an old wizard's language I might understand a tiny bit but I'm definitely no expert and it probably wouldn't help much anyway. The best thing would be not to touch it. Use magic to open it because if it was sealed by a wizard, which it probably was, it may be cursed. I'm going to go and have a look at the Falls, to check it out. You can stay here with Kat," Ji said as he got to his feet.

"All right, but don't be too long. I don't feel as safe with Kat like this. And please, be careful," Carey pleaded, looking up at him.

Ji placed his hand on her shoulder gently and beamed a confident grin.

"Of course," he said reassuringly and he walked into the forest, the rising sun alleviating the darkness at least.

Carey stared after him, his smile still lingering in her mind. She sighed, gave Kat a worried glance, then turned back to stare into the dancing orange flames.

* * *

The pain from his wounds was intoxicating. He grimaced and renewed his silent vow to not give in. Her torture methods were slowly but surely wearing him thin, but he would not give in. The rope binding him to his chair was starting to cut into his wrists. They burned against his raw flesh. He had given up trying to escape long ago, instead pooling his efforts into resisting the effects of his interrogation. Her visits were always short but then again, she didn't need much time.

He was suddenly drawn away from his thoughts by the sound of someone approaching. He was instantly alert. The darkness was thinning and he could see light flickering on the walls of the corridor outside his cell, the sound of soft-soled shoes echoing faintly off the stone. Then she was there. No matter how many times he saw her, the sight of the ghost-like Empress never failed to send a chill down his spine. A guard stood sentry outside the cell, the light of his blue-flamed torch casting an eerie glow through the bars of the door.

Malevolence crossed the room to where her captive was bound. He glimpsed a flash of red where her eyes might have been and he suppressed his terrified emotions. There was a whisper, one only he could hear and it pierced his ears and made his eyes water.

"Come, you know what I want, boy. You can end this. There is only one thing I desire… The prophets and oracles predict a Liberator. This can all end if you tell me who it is. All I need is one name…" The voice resonated deeply in his mind.

He grit his teeth. "You know my answer."

He had never heard of this prophecy before but the instant she had told him he knew exactly who it was referring to. He kept this thought carefully guarded though. Who knew what Malevolence had access to every time she entered his mind?

"Besides, what happened to Jody and Laurel? Why don't you ask those witches?" he spat contemptuously.

"You question me?" The voice bit at his mind. In the blink of an eye, she was behind her quarry. A mysterious wind began to blow, creating a whirlwind within the circular chamber. The prisoner closed his eyes. He wasn't going to let this affect him.

"They are useless to me. Their minds are lost. They were not strong enough to withstand the magic I imposed. Now it has fallen on you to tell me. How much longer do you think you'll be able to endure my pressure, boy?" she hissed, the sound blurring his senses. "As Jeremy cannot yet tell me, you will!"

A flash like lightning split the room and he was blinded. The noise was building inside the tiny room but the snake-like voice of the Empress sounded clearly in his head.

"Never. I will take it to the grave," he muttered through clenched teeth.

Malevolence was standing over him now and she pointed ominously. "That is somewhere your family will be visiting soon if you continue to resist," the voice said as bright orange sparks danced about her outstretched hand.

With nothing to say to this threat, he leant forward and spat at Malevolence's feet. Malevolence merely hissed.

"So be it."

She drew her hand across in front of her young captive's face as punishment, creating a long, deep cut beneath his left eye. He wanted desperately to cry out, but that would only give her satisfaction. As warm blood began to run down his face, she turned to leave.

"Continue this charade and you will be stripped of everything you know. The people you care for will perish and it will only be in the afterlife that you will *ever* see them again. I will make sure of it."

The spectral Empress disappeared through the door and with her, the wind and deafening roar. It was silent once more. The light faded and he hung his head in grief as the room dissolved again into darkness, leaving him with only his pain and fear.

Chapter Seventeen

Falling

Kat's eyes snapped open. The dark outline of someone sitting nearby came slowly into focus, blurred slightly against the flickering orange flames of the campfire. Her limbs were numb and were moving involuntarily. She tried controlling them but then she felt something else; her magic. It wasn't there. How she knew this, Kat couldn't tell, but it was as obvious as though she was missing a limb. Slowly, she put her head back and gazed upwards. There it was – her magic. She felt nauseatingly sick. Her head swam and for a moment she almost faded back to that blank void from which she had emerged. She struggled against the pull. Her eyes focused and she realised the figure sitting by the fire was Carey. She had to tell her what she had seen; it was important that she did. Kat forced herself to focus and tried to speak; it was painful and unnatural but she had to warn Carey.

"C-c-c-care-a-rey-y!"

Carey spun around. Was that *Kat* trying to say something? She scrambled over.

"Kat? Are you trying to say something? What is it?"

The goat's head mark on her neck was strangely grey, as if the evil had been momentarily extinguished from it. Kat's eyes were bulging as she fought to form her words, and a bead of sweat trickled from her hairline. Whatever she had to say, it was costing her a great deal of energy.

"M-m-m-must t-t-t-t-tell," Kat struggled. "J-j-j-ji-ee n-no-ot–"

"What? Ji? What about Ji? Kat! Ji's not *what?*" Carey gripped Kat's shoulders; the glint of consciousness was disappearing from Kat's eyes.

"N-no-ot J-j–"

The mark began to glow again and Kat went silent. Her eyes slowly slipped back out of focus and she looked back down at her rocks again.

"No," Carey breathed. She shook Kat softly. "Kat? Kat! What *about* Ji? Is he in trouble? Kat! KAT! Damn it! Ji! Oh, Ji, I'm so glad you're back! Kat was speaking – well – trying to tell me something – and – I don't know – it had something to do with you, Ji! And the mark – it was grey instead of red! Ji! Ji? What is it?"

Ji's eyes shifted uneasily from Carey to Kat and then back to her, but he collected himself when she spoke.

"What? She spoke? But how could she?" Ji asked, looking at Kat in consternation.

"I don't know but it sounded like it was hurting her to speak. She said something about you – something about you not being something," said Carey. "Ji? Ji, what is it?"

Ji, who had been looking away distractedly and not really listening, suddenly turned and knelt beside her, gripping her forearms.

"We've got to get the Silver Water tonight. The chimeras are pacing, they know something's not right. And Kat's behaviour – I think she's taken a turn for the worst. Do you think you're ready?"

"I – I think so. But what about Kat?" Carey asked uncertainly.

"Here," he clapped his hands together then opened his arms wide. A wave rippled the air.

"Did you just shield her?"

Ji nodded as he helped her up. "That should keep her safe for now at least."

Carey bit her lip – she still wasn't comfortable with leaving Kat all by herself. Ji noticed her discomfort. "Carey, don't fret. The sooner we get the Water, the sooner we can help Kat. Trust me," he consoled, his hands on her shoulders.

His touch seemed to alleviate some of her worry and she managed a half smile. "All right. Let's go."

Carey gave Kat a backwards glance as she followed Ji into the trees; she tried to forget Kat's broken warning and turned her concentration to the task ahead. They trekked for several minutes through dense forest before the trees began to thin, revealing the edge of the pool at the bottom of the Falls. It was true; the creatures were pacing the path now and the sight made Carey's heart start to race.

"Right. Ready Carey?" Ji asked, gripping her hand.

Carey looked at Ji and saw in his pale blue eyes reassurance. With his confident smile, her ears turned red and her stomach gave that strange jolt –

Ji turned his head, interrupting Carey's thoughts.

"I think they know we're here," he whispered.

The monsters had turned their heads towards the two of them; Carey could see their ears flitting back and forth. They had sensed them.

"Carey, I'm going to distract them so get ready."

Ji knelt to the ground. "Wait!" she breathed.

"What is it?"

She took a deep breath to steady her nerves, adjusted her bag and knelt beside Ji. He grabbed her hand. "You'll be great. I'll see you on the other side."

Ji released her and placed his palms flat on the ground. He muttered something beneath his breath and Carey saw the familiar sparks of magic dance around his hands. Then she felt it; a deep rumbling in the ground. The earth began to shake and the trees began to screech and groan. The noise grew until it was almost deafening. Ji glanced up at Carey. "Go!"

She looked up at the creatures. They were stunned and bewildered by the sudden disturbance and were backing up against the rock wall, trying to escape the noise. It was now or never. Dodging falling branches and shifting rocks, Carey sprinted towards the chimeras, hoping that Ji's distraction would keep them from noticing her.

As she slipped past the monsters, she could feel their hot wretched breath against her face and smell the rank stench that wafted from their shaggy hair. Their ears were twisting continuously as Carey dashed past as they tried to regain their bearings. For a moment Carey thought they had sensed her but they made no move. She ran past to the ancient wall. Small rocks were falling into the water and she held her arm above her head in protection. She reached out.

Amidst the noise and chaos, Carey momentarily forgot Ji's warning and pressed against the wall with her left hand. With a huge surge, a flash of white light exploded from the wall and up her arm.

"Aah!" Carey screamed through gritted teeth as her arm went numb from the shock. She glanced at the chimeras – they hadn't heard her. Her scream had been drowned out by the din. Rubbing her arm she turned back to the wall; the many signs and symbols carved into the rock were completely random and made no sense whatsoever to her. She moved her eyes over the carvings until something caught her attention; a triangle- shaped cavity carved into the stone wall. The hole had a slightly darker colour and it was rather small; it looked like a keyhole. Carey searched the ground, her heart beating faster and her palms beginning to perspire as she looked for a stone or stick, but there was nothing to substitute for a key.

With anxiety rushing to her head, the noise adding unnecessarily to it, Carey twirled her finger around her necklace cord until it twisted down to the –

"Triangle!" Carey exclaimed, grabbing the golden charm and scolding herself for not thinking of it quicker.

Careful not to touch the rock, she placed the triangle in the hole and pressed gently. It was a perfect fit. Carey stood back as she watched a swirl of golden light circle the necklace, illuminating the symbols around it. For a second, they glowed brightly then they vanished along with the rest of the wall. The necklace fell to the rocky ground and Carey scooped it up. The wall gave way to a perfectly rounded cave. Clutching her limp left arm and necklace with her right hand, she stepped inside; the noise outside subsided instantly. For a moment, Carey thought something was wrong with her hearing but then realised it must be part of the cave's enchantments. It did little to calm her nerves.

Before her was a small round pool but it wasn't water that filled it. A thin mist of what appeared to be a billion glittering stars hovered just over the top, their light reflecting softly on the walls of the cave. Carey watched in awe as it changed constantly, swirling in tight concentric circles on the surface, merging together into one then breaking up again, a kaleidoscope of brilliance. She knelt down beside it, entranced by its beauty. She leant right over, squinting down through the mist to the bright flowing liquid that lay beneath that was moving in perfect unison with the stars above. She put her necklace down by the pool and ran her hand through it; it felt like the purest of silk and it gave her a tingling feeling as it clung to her fingers, covering them before slowly dissolving. She went to pick up her necklace when she lost her balance, her left arm falling with a silent splash into the water; Carey gasped. At once it began to prickle and, lifting her arm out of the water, she saw that the liquid had covered it completely. Slowly it sank into her pores and with a sudden rush down her arm, she felt all feeling return. She stared at it with astonishment.

A roar from outside brought her back to the present, reminding her why she was there. Carey reached into her bag and retrieved a small bottle; she uncorked it and plunged it into the smooth liquid. After all the bubbles were dispersed from the phial, Carey carefully lifted it out and re-corked it, wiping the bottle clean of the Silver Water before pocketing it and picking up her necklace once more.

A distant cry echoed from outside the cave.

"Oh no – Ji!" Carey muttered, running to the mouth of the cave. She flung herself carelessly out onto the rock path and slipped slightly on the wet moss in her haste. Gripping the rock wall to steady herself, she looked up to find herself face to face with one of the chimeras. Too terrified to scream, Carey tripped backwards as the chimera reared. The rumbling had ceased and the trees were quiet once more. Distantly she heard Ji shouting and Carey, on impulse, turned her head towards his voice. The beast took advantage of this moment and attacked. It brought its heavy hoofed feet down on top of Carey's chest, pushing her over with a painful thud onto the rock floor. The chimera roared with triumph and released a heated ball of flame, barely missing Carey's head as she lay there winded. Carey coughed and gasped for air, momentarily paralysed from the attack. She stared up at the towering monster as she struggled to regain her strength and watched as the chimera moved to strike again. As the chimera bore down on her, she kicked out, rolling out of the creature's path. Her arm grazed its sharp teeth and she shouted in pain. Blood poured from the wound, clinging to her shirt. Carey was struggling to her feet when she felt the tingling of that inexplicable magic gathering again within her but it wasn't quick enough. The chimera charged again. She tried to summon what energy she had left and aimed some curses. The chimera sensed them and dodged every one of them, much to Carey's anguish and dismay. Her ribs felt cracked and bruised and the animal looked intent on killing her as it reared again. Carey cried out in fear for Ji, knowing that he would not make it in time…

She could see the chimera coming down on top of her again. The magic which had saved her before wasn't going to be able to save her this time. There was nothing she could do to stop the creature's attack. It was base human reaction with which Carey flung her right arm up to shield herself and braced for the impact.

As she threw her arm over her head, Carey's necklace swung up and connected with the creature's temple. Carey was knocked back to the ground as a thunderous crack, which was followed by an explosion of blinding light, threw the chimera against the rock wall. It fell to the ground in a gigantic crumpled heap and did not get back up. Petrified, Carey scrambled backwards. With excruciating pain, she managed to pull herself up, her eyes not once leaving the cowering monster. She could hear the roars of the other one and her mind flew to Ji. Carey stumbled down the path, clutching her necklace to her crushed chest, trying to gather up all her strength in order to try and help him. She could hear him shouting feebly at his attacker and a thrill of terror coursed through her body. Carey willed the mysterious bristling magic that prickled her skin to give her strength. The warmth of it centred on her heart and there was an almighty boost. Energy flowed through her body and Carey was completely re-energised;

she sprinted to help Ji.

It had him pinned against a rock, fireballs flitting dangerously close to Ji's face. Carey rallied behind it and picked a large rock up from the ground. Ji spotted her and yelled at her to get back, but Carey couldn't leave him; all the danger in the world couldn't make her abandon him. She aimed carefully and heaved the stone at the creature's head; it struck with a dull thud directly in the middle of its skull. With a roar of anger, it dropped Ji and rounded on Carey, heaving vehemently. Carey stood as steadily as she could, and as it brought its hooves high over her head, she did not hesitate. She swung her necklace hard, and as with the other, it exploded with a flash of light, sending Carey reeling backwards again across the rocky ground.

With the chimeras subdued, the dust began to settle and Ji ran awkwardly over to where she had come to rest, his eyes wide in astonishment. Her clothes were ripped and bloody and she could feel an enormous headache threatening to split her head open. Ji's cheek had been opened up and both that and his forearm were bleeding freely, soaking his clothes with scarlet blood. As he helped her sit up carefully, she grimaced, the pain spreading down her back from the last fall. Carey collapsed into his arms sobbing, her breath short and excruciating. The boost of magical adrenalin was wearing off and she could feel every point of pain acutely. Ji held her as she collected herself.

She wanted to stay that way, unmoving and comforted, but he sat her up to inspect her injuries. "Is anything broken?" he asked softly, his eyes scanning her for any damage.

She pointed to her ribs and he placed his hand on her side. The cool green light flowed again into her body and she closed her eyes in relief, feeling the magic heal her broken bones and sealing her wounds. The pain weakened and she took some deep breaths before she opened her eyes again. She looked up at Ji and somewhere in her stomach she felt a rush of nerves that had nothing to do with what had just happened. With a dry throat she inquired how he was. "Are – you all right?" said Carey.

He smiled. "I'll be fine."

They sat in silence for a brief moment and Carey was suddenly very aware that they were still holding onto each other. Ji was smiling mildly, gazing at her with a sudden intensity that made her feel rather uncomfortable. The silence was stretching as was Carey's discomfort. She cast about wildly for something to say to break it.

"Um... I – I got the Silver Water for Kat – see – ," Carey stuttered hastily, taking the phial from her pocket and holding it with both hands. "And the keyhole – it was the same shape as-as the necklace – *our* necklace – and-and-the creatures, how they-they-" Carey broke off.

With everything that had just happened Ji was suddenly and amazingly calm. It was as though he had forgotten about the chimeras and the fact that they were both covered in blood. His whole reaction struck Carey as rather strange except that what he did next surprised her so much, it made her forget everything as well.

Ji pulled her close and lifted a hand to Carey's face, gently sweeping her hair back from her eyes. His hand traced her jaw bone so that it came to rest on her cheek. Her senses were suddenly acutely sensitive as her skin prickled hotly under his touch and her face burned. She couldn't move; her muscles were tensed with equal measures of exhilaration and sheer terror. Carey felt like the snake being enchanted by a charmer's melody. Her throat constricted, rendering her involuntarily silent.

Ji leant in to her until their foreheads touched and they were so close that the tips of their noses met. His eyes were closed but hers weren't; she couldn't help but stare back at him because in that moment, something changed. It was as if all the thoughts she'd ever had about him were rearranging themselves; changing her perception of every moment. With her heart racing, she lifted her hand to his and he opened his eyes. Ji's face was so close now that Carey could hear his breathing, how it seemed ragged with some unspoken anticipation. With some sudden urge, Carey half expected him to kiss her but he didn't – this gesture was as close as he allowed himself.

Her heart did not stop thumping, even after he pulled away. She was still gripping his hands.

"Ji–" Carey started, but she didn't know what to say. His expression was of calm acceptance and all she could do was smile back awkwardly. This sudden movement was riddled with confusion and Carey's moment of clarity was clouded in insecurity. It was as though Ji had just shown her something then promptly taken it away. She didn't know whether to acknowledge what had occurred or to ignore it. She couldn't be sure what Ji was doing.

He got to his feet, pulling Carey up with him. "Come. Let's go save Kat," he said, and leading her by the hand, Carey followed.

Chapter Eighteen

Calling and Confusion

A grave scene met them when they returned to camp. Firefly was distraught, kicking up clouds of dust in a dreadful flurry and Carey instantly knew something was wrong.

"Oh!" Carey gasped, and she ran over to Kat.

Kat's head was limp and bowed to the ground; her hair covered her face and beside her... beside her were the shattered remains of her Tear Globe. Carey picked up the biggest part of the globe and held it with a shaking hand. She did not dare think of what had happened. Kat wasn't moving. Carey's heart was thudding against her chest with desperate anxiety and heat began to rise in her face as she fumbled with the broken pieces of the Globe. Ji joined her and she could feel his composure evaporate as he brushed Kat's dark hair from her face and touched her ghostly pale cheek.

"Ji?" Carey rasped.

Slowly and carefully, he laid Kat back on the ground. Her arms and head flopped motionless to the grass; her complexion was horrifically pale and the mark glowed a deep red. Carey placed her hand on Kat's forehead and found her deathly cold.

"Oh... no! What happened? How did it break?" Carey asked frantically, looking about for clues.

She looked down and saw something odd – tiny footprints, the size of a child's perhaps. It was at that moment that she saw something move out the corner of her eye. Carey jumped to her feet and faced the trees. Standing there, perfectly still, was a person, but it wasn't a child. She was short and her glare bore into Carey's very soul. Carey remembered instantly that it was the same person she had seen fleetingly back at the village.

"Hey!" Carey shouted. "Who are you? What are you doing here?"

Ji looked up at the sound of her voice. "Carey, who are you shouting at?"

Carey pointed at the trees then stopped; the person had vanished. Carey ran over to the trees. "What? But they were just – you didn't see her?" she asked Ji in desperation. "There was someone just standing there, watching us."

"Carey, please. Kat..."

Carey's breath caught in her throat. What was she doing? Kat needed her and she was chasing a ghost?

"Here! The Silver Water – quick!" she said, pulling the water from her pocket and fumbling with the cork; it popped and rolled away across the ground.

Her hands quivering with nerves, Carey knelt as Ji propped Kat up against his shoulder. She held the bottle up to Kat's mouth and tipped it until the smallest droplet of the healing liquid spilled into Kat's mouth. Carey waited a few seconds then tipped the bottle again. She repeated this several more times until the liquid was half gone; Carey put the bottle aside and Ji lay Kat gently back down. She was still, her limbs unmoving and her face cold and lifeless. Carey rubbed her hands together then held them to Kat's face; she couldn't feel her breathing.

"How long until the Silver Water starts working?" she asked Ji in a whisper.

Ji shook his head. "I'm not sure. I would've thought it would start working immediately."

They sat in silence, Carey with her hands on Kat's cheeks and Ji grasping Kat's hand. Carey prayed silently, pleading for something to happen but as the minutes passed, their hopes were slowly dwindling. Carey held Kat's other hand to her face and she felt the iciness of her skin. There wasn't a single bit of warmth left. A horrible nauseating feeling grew in

Carey's stomach and hot tears pricked her eyes. A wave of light-headedness threatened to overcome her, although it would have been a welcome relief compared to what she now faced.

Kat was gone. Not even the most amazing healing water on earth had made a difference; a loud sob wracked Carey's chest. The Empire had got what they wanted; they had broken them, taken their spirit and crushed it. Ji reached over with shaking hands and pushed Kat's raven hair back from her face, and with this simple gesture, Carey's grief ripped through her. She fell forward onto Kat's still figure and great guttural cries heaved from Carey's chest. The noise echoed through the woods but she didn't care if anyone heard her. Nothing else mattered at that moment, not the Empire, not their pursuit, just their fallen friend. Her tears fell thick and fast, uninhibited. Ji pulled her gently into his arms but she kept hold of Kat's hand. Her heart was ripping in two; her chest heaved with the most unbelievable pain she had ever experienced. She could feel Ji's body shudder against hers and she held back a new wave of tears. They sat in a huddle on the grass beside Kat's body, a mess of tears and blood…

Carey dropped her head and looked mournfully down at Kat's limp form; she gasped in alarm and fell back in astonishment, knocking Ji to the ground. A liquid was emerging from Kat's skin, emerging from her very pores! It was seeping out of her skin, slowly, as if it was squeezing itself from her body. It glowed silver metallic and the droplets swelled together like a small pool of water over Kat's thin figure in a strange motion. As the tiny droplets of the liquid had merged, it spread over Kat's entire body as if it was living matter.

Carey and Ji watched all this happen in amazement. Reluctantly, Carey reached down to touch the odd fluid, fearing that it might be a reaction to the Water. Then she realised what it was – it was the Silver Water itself. Once the water had completely covered Kat, it ceased moving for a moment before it turned completely transparent.

Both Carey and Ji waited expectantly, wanting desperately for something to happen, but nothing happened. Carey's hopes were dropping like autumn leaves. The tears began to well again and she could hear Ji whimper beside her. A new wave of terror consumed her, sending her spiralling again, a rush of anger and uncertainty washing over her. She clung to Ji, wanting him to make it better although she knew it was impossible. But she wanted it so badly...

There was a flicker, the tiniest of movements. Carey pulled away from Ji and stared at Kat. Was she dreaming? No, there it was again – the smallest movement under her eyelids. Carey trembled with hope. "Ji! Kat moved! Her eyelids, look!"

Ji shook his head. "What? That's imposs–"

All of a sudden, Kat's chest heaved as she gasped for air and her eyes bulged; her mouth was open wide, struggling to take a breath. Carey and Ji moved quickly, Carey hooking her arms under Kat's armpits and sitting her up against a nearby tree. Ji took her hands, trying to hold her still. They sat, shaking with surprise and relief, watching their friend with wide eyes. Kat's breathing slowed momentarily and Carey saw that the mark had faded to the same dull grey hers was instead of the ugly reddish-black it had been a moment ago.

There were a few minutes where they were not sure what to expect. Kat was beginning to relax, letting out long, deep breaths. She clasped a hand wearily over her eyes.

"Urgh, what a headache..." She looked up to find the other two staring at her in absolute amazement. "What?"

Carey uttered a cry of joy and threw her arms around Kat's neck as tears of joy streamed down her face instead. Kat was patting Carey's arm, clearly bewildered by this sudden show of glee. Carey pulled away and wiped her eyes and nose noisily on her sleeve. "Kat! You scared us half to death! You're alive, thank goodness you're alive! Are you all right? I mean, you nearly... Your magic! Is it – does it still work?" Carey blubbered, grabbing Ji's hand again by impulse.

Kat held out her hand and without a moment's hesitation, a tiny flame appeared in her palm. Kat raised her eyebrows then asked, "What is this all about?"

"Just then... it was... and you couldn't... breathe or anything. You were...

176

you were almost... but then the Water..." Carey said, feeling a little light-headed.

Kat shook her head. "What? What are you on about? What just happened?"

"Kat... you nearly *died*. Just now, just a few moments ago. We were so worried. I don't what we would have done if you had – died," Carey choked, feelings of distress beginning to surface again.

Kat's eyes widened. "I almost what?" she barely whispered.

Carey and Ji didn't say a word but they didn't need to; the expressions on their faces said everything. Kat laughed nervously but she sobered quickly. "How close... how close was I?"

Ji forced a smile. "Not that close, obviously."

Kat ran her hands through her hair, her eyes vague as she considered something. "Did you say something about water? You don't mean Silver Water?"

"Yes, we had to get some for you. It was the only way to help you, to block the connection," Carey said.

Kat held out her hand. "Let me see," Kat demanded.

Taken aback by Kat's abruptness, Carey handed over the phial. Kat handled it like it was a priceless possession, breakable. She eyed it with extreme interest and incredulity but then she shook her head and shoved it back into Carey's hand. "Get rid of it. You have to get rid of it."

Carey and Ji frowned. Kat looked at them both in disbelief. "You can't keep this with you! You should know better, Ji. If the Empire ever got their hands on it... This is much too powerful."

Carey glanced down at the bottle, closing her hands over the glass. There was only perhaps half left, a few drops. She had seen its power but what could the Empire do with such a small portion?

"I am sorry, Kat. I wasn't thinking. I didn't tell Carey. After what happened, first at the Falls and then, what with you... I guess it slipped my mind," Ji apologised.

"What happened at the Falls?" Kat asked curiously.

Ji began to tell her the drama that had unfolded at the Falls. He told her of their plan and how they managed to deceive the chimeras. Kat coughed in astonishment and held up her hands.

"Wait. You fought the chimeras by hand? Are you insane?" she squeaked, shocked by their actions.

They were instantly affronted. Kat let out an exasperated sigh. "I can't believe that! Ji, don't you remember Madame Guise telling us about the chimeras? What if you were killed?"

"But we weren't!" Carey said, trying to calm her. She told Kat how she had stopped them but all Kat did was scoff knowingly.

"Of course that worked. The Falls are protected by the Order! You didn't think…"

Kat continued to berate Ji for his mistake until Ji apologised profusely. Only then did Kat let him go on with his account. Carey was silent, now thinking about the object still clutched in her hand. *I should keep it, in case something else happens*, she thought, slipping it into her bag without Kat or Ji noticing. She listened as Ji recounted their story. When he reached the part after she had defeated the second chimera, Carey felt red in the face. There was a pause from Ji, whose eyes flickered momentarily to her, but he did not disclose what had happened in that moment. Carey was glad he hadn't. She wasn't sure of what it had meant, was baffled by the feelings that had emerged. The way Ji had held her – she never wanted it to end, wanted it forever, but at the same time she was petrified.

* * *

They slept for almost a day, the exhaustion finally getting the better of them, yet despite the fatigue Carey felt, her body refused to let her relax. Her sleep was plagued with memories of her family and when she woke, her marked arm ached and stung from Malevolence's torture. Kat allowed for them to stay one more day but seemed extremely frustrated by it; she was getting restless, wanting nothing more than to be back on the road. They finally convinced her that one more day would not hurt her considering her recent ordeal. The following night proved to Carey that even when they were trying to rest, it seemed impossible and she should've known. Kat's growing excitement matched only the growing danger Carey soon discovered, and sleeping restlessly by the fire, she felt the first stab of something very strange.

It happened unexpectedly. She wasn't fully asleep but not completely awake when a haze began to enter her mind. It blocked her thoughts and grabbed at her mentally. Carey frowned at it; what was this? Ji shifted slightly beside her as she flinched nervously. She was awake now and she tried opening her eyes but whatever it was had her trapped. She began to panic. It was a peculiar sensation, both foreign and familiar. Mentally she lashed out at it, trying to fight it off; then there was a yell that echoed through her mind. She was hearing something. A moment later a girl's voice called out; Carey sat up, her eyes still closed as she concentrated on the voices inside her head.

"Mama? Mama, where are you going? Mama—"

"Stay where you are Alexander, Seramina. Whatever happens, don't move, all right my darlings?"

"Mama!"

The woman's voice continued but this time she was yelling. "Leave us alone, please! We are hiding nothing! Leave my babies alone! Don't hurt them! They did nothing—"

A cry of pain ended her sentence.

"Mama!"

"There you are – we've been looking for you. Come here!" a man's voice barked at them.

There was the crash of wooden objects and Carey jerked as if she had been hit herself.

"Alexander? Alexander! No! Alexander—"

"Seramina! Help me! No... let go! Let go of me! Sera—"

Another scream.

"No, please! Please, have mercy! Leave my brother! He is – ow!"

"Get out of there, you brats."

"Seramina... Seramina! Help me!"

"I can't, Alexander, I – aaahhh!"

The last scream echoed through Carey's head painfully and she forced her eyes open. The strange sensation evaporated instantly but her ears were ringing. What was that? Had it been a dream? No, she had been awake. And the voices – they were of a mother and her children. And a man. They were being attacked or hurt or something and she couldn't help them. The feeling of absolute hopelessness was excruciating. Who were they and how were they in her head? The children's names were the only clues that were revealed to her. She heard nothing from the man or their mother. She gulped the early morning air and realised she was sweaty and shaking. Ji lay next to her; his eyes were wide open.

"Ji?" she whispered, seeing that Kat was still asleep.

He turned his head, his expression grave. "Did you hear that?" he whispered back.

A shock of relief ran through her body. "Yes," she answered breathlessly. "What was it? Do you know?"

Ji was silent, staring up into the tree tops. Residual echoes of the voices fluttered around in her head and Carey put her hand to her temple. He looked at her. "What is it?"

She put her hand down. "I can still hear them. They were so clear, almost as if they were right next to me..."

Ji sat up and moved over beside her. "You heard them clearly?"

"Yes, so clearly. I could even hear what was happening around them. But... didn't you hear it too?"

He nodded. "Yes, but not as clearly as that. I heard bits and pieces, as if the sound was coming to me on the wind. Tell me what you heard."

Carey told him as much as she could remember, her temples throbbing now.

Ji stared at her pensively. "Did it... hurt?"

Carey shook her head slowly, remembering. "Not when it was happening, only when it stopped. You?" she asked, willing him to say yes. He shook his head.

"No. It was strange though," he said, his tone apologetic.

Carey became more distraught. "But why? Why did it hurt me and not you? I... why... I don't..." she stuttered. "What was it? It was terrifying! I heard the – the fear in their voices and... oh Ji, I couldn't help them! The girl screamed and I couldn't stop the man hurting them. I couldn't..."

She stopped, flustered and upset.

"Oh Carey," Ji whispered as he put his arms about her.

The darkness was thinning and streams of orange light were filtering through the leaves, casting cold shadows on them. Kat was stirring and she opened her eyes slowly. Carey pulled away from Ji, not entirely sure why she was doing so.

Kat had noticed that something was wrong and crawled over to her.

"Carey, what is it? You don't look so good."

Wiping her face on her sleeve awkwardly, she told Kat of what she and Ji had just experienced, pushing away the sudden embarrassment she had felt.

As she told Kat, she realised how much energy the strange calling had cost her; her eyelids were struggling to stay open and her limbs were heavy and sluggish.

"Now that you say that, I did have a dream," Kat said vaguely. "At least, I thought it was a dream. It didn't wake me up though, like it did with you..." Kat faded off into thought. Carey watched her blankly, waiting.

"The girl, the one we heard, must have been a telepathist of some sort," Kat said finally. "The sensation you felt was the same I experienced when Malevolence had me. And when you said it hurt, that's when she must have pulled away. She must have pulled away very quickly to hurt you."

Ji was nodding slightly in agreement. "It makes sense. There are different types of telepathy. She must be very strong to do what she did."

"Why was I the only one to hear it so clearly though? What was that feeling?" Carey asked, struggling to keep her words coherent.

"You must have been the closest one she reached out to, I guess. We might have only heard it because she wasn't truly concentrating on a target and her aim was scattered."

"You make it sound like she was aiming to shoot," Carey commented.

"Well, wasn't she?" Ji said. "A telepathist aims to connect with someone else's mind, just like a hunter aims at his game. If they haven't got a particular person in mind, or target, they're just sending out messages into the dark, hoping that they'll connect with someone. She wasn't close, so you felt that haze. If she was closer, you wouldn't feel it."

Carey found it difficult to take in all this new information. She suddenly wished she knew it already.

"Can we help them?"

She blinked expectantly at Kat, hoping for a positive answer but she found herself sorely disappointed; Kat shook her head sadly.

"It'd be impossible to find them. Maybe if we were telepaths too we might have been able to help, but we aren't. There's no way."

"But, can't we even try looking for them? At least *try*?"

Kat shook her head again. "We wouldn't even know where to start. They might be a hundred miles away in any direction for all we know. I'm sorry."

Carey gritted her teeth in frustration. What good was being a Seeker if she couldn't even help those who needed it? Feeling disgruntled, she leant back against a tree and closed her eyes, desperately wanting to go back to sleep. The events of the last few days were starting to take their toll on Carey's body and she felt horribly wretched and uncoordinated, dreading the fact that she would have to move sooner or later. She sank into a bitter state and a million thoughts, each as resentful as the next, began running through her mind. She dwelt on each of them, making no attempt to push them away. Carey questioned herself, she questioned their mission. She wished for it all to stop but knew what a hollow wish that was. Her skin crawled with frustration and she felt something that she had not felt the whole time she had been with Kat and Ji – hatred. She hated it. She hated the fighting, she hated the running, she hated that she wasn't the kind of person they wanted her to be. She wasn't strong or fearless, yet this is what she was meant to be, what she wanted to be.

Carey cursed herself for being weak and she felt heavy and burdened by these thoughts but she couldn't let them go…

Carey only realised Ji was trying to speak to her when he shook her by the shoulders, almost yelling her name. He had noticed how pale she was and asked how she was feeling. He and Kat had recovered easily from the effects of the telepathy but Carey had not. She loathed her inability to overcome these tribulations as quickly as her companions. Ji and Kat decided to stay just a little longer after seeing how exhausted she suddenly was. A cold wind had begun to blow and although there were no clouds about, the sun offered little warmth. Carey abandoned the tiring dealings of her lot and instead reflected on what had occurred at the Falls. What had happened there still confused her. She wanted to talk to Kat about it but embarrassment stilled her tongue. Didn't she want to feel that way again? She couldn't decide and worse, it felt wrong, as though she wasn't meant to know of it. Why was that?

Carey opened her eyes and blinked hard against the sunlight, not realising that she had fallen asleep. Kat and Ji were beside her, talking once more in low voices.

"You talking about me again?" she said, trying to muster some humour. They jumped.

"Oh good, you're awake! We were afraid the telepathy might have really affected you," Ji said, relieved.

Carey sat up and despite feeling only slightly lighter decided to lie. "No, I'm fine now, perfect actually."

Ji smiled at her but she turned to Kat. "How are *you* feeling?"

Kat waved away her question. "No need to fuss. Despite the fact that I almost died, the Silver Water really gave me a boost. This mark certainly isn't causing any trouble," she said, touching her neck. "Oh, by the way, did you get rid of that Water you had left over?"

Carey tightened her grip on her bag, but only slightly. "Of course," she lied again. She would have to stop doing that.

"Good, because the last thing we need is for the Empire to get hold of it. Just a few drops would be enough to make Malevolence practically invincible and that's all we need right now."

Chapter Nineteen

Sacrifice

Carey felt burdened with an unwanted array of emotions. She felt guilty about keeping the Silver Water but convinced herself that it was for their safety. Could they really risk a close call like that again? In her mind, keeping the liquid was easily justifiable. But her other feelings weren't so easily satiated. She was still aggravated by the never-ending attacks and attention she and her friends attracted and she couldn't seem to let the feeling go. When Carey had escaped from the orphanage, she wasn't sure of what she would find. She had never thought about it before, about the reality Kat and Ji had brought to her. It had only just become clear to her how immense their goal was and she felt completely inadequate in comparison. Carey sighed heavily. They were dodging attacks as if they were bullets, barely escaping with a couple of grazes. They had been way too lucky in that respect and it made her worry about how much longer they'd be able to keep it up.

Then there was Ji. Carey didn't quite know how to act in front of him now. Every time he spoke to her she would become nervous, coming across as too eager or too serious. She didn't know how to arrange her feelings, how to put them in order. She was in such disarray; she wanted to talk to Kat about it but didn't know how to approach it. Luckily, Ji provided a distraction that would perhaps take her mind off her own problems for a while.

"Kat, I want to know something," he said, breaking Carey's line of thought. "What did it feel like when you were, you know... under the power of that mark?"

Kat said nothing at first, her forehead creased in thought.

"It was like... there was a wall blocking me, blocking my thoughts," she said slowly. "Every time I pushed, it would knock me back. It was as if another 'thing' was inside me, trying to control me, so if I did anything weird, trust me, I had no idea."

Carey frowned, her mind flying back to when Kat had tried to talk to her. She had spoken of Ji in those few brief seconds of struggle, but when she queried Kat about it, she shrugged.

"It could have been Malevolence," she suggested but Carey couldn't help feeling that it wasn't the case. Her eyes had been so focused, sharp, alert... Carey suddenly got cold shivers.

"I'll tell you what was really strange though. The wall... you know–" Kat tapped her head " – at one point completely disappeared and I didn't even do anything–"

"Oh!" Carey exclaimed. "The Tear Globe!"

"Tear Globe?" Kat said indignantly. "You put a *Tear Globe* on me? And you were going to tell me this when exactly?"

Carey spluttered, lost for words. She hadn't realised it was such a big thing.

"We had to," Ji jumped in before Kat got fired up. "Your powers would have disappeared before we got the Silver Water otherwise."

"But when we got back from the Falls, it was broken. We don't know what happened – we certainly didn't break it," Carey added, slightly terrified by the thunderous expression on Kat's face.

Kat eyed Ji who shrugged apologetically. "Well at least it makes sense," she muttered.

"What does?" Carey asked.

"Well... I guess when it broke, it broke the wall inside my mind. I sensed it straight away. I didn't know, *of course*, about the Tear Globe, but as soon as it was gone, I rose up to it. I... rose up, I guess, from my sub-consciousness too quickly, trying to wake up, and I could feel myself failing... I froze. I couldn't move. Although, if I had known about the Globe, I wouldn't have been so stupid," Kat glared at Ji. "Then, I felt a larger block form. It trapped me and I knew it was different to the other because of how it felt. It was... strange. It felt... strong but... unstable enough to shatter," said Kat, biting her tongue and frowning at her inability to explain her situation.

"What was it?"

"I don't know, because then I blacked out. I lost consciousness completely... in my *sub-consciousness*."

Kat stopped. She grimaced, confusion clouding her face. Ji grabbed her arm.

"You lost consciousness in your sub-conscious? Wouldn't that mean you were–"

"Dead," Carey whispered.

Dead. Kat *had* died. She *had* been lost to them. But for how long? Had they returned just in time? What if they had taken longer? Their quest could have been destroyed, thrown to the wind in a matter of moments... Would Carey and Ji have been strong enough to carry on? She had a deep wounding suspicion that they might not be and that their goal, their dreams, would be shattered in a moment as spontaneous and exact as the one which had saved Kat.

Carey closed her eyes and sighed. The world hung in an all too dangerous balance of choice and fate and Carey cringed to think she now had such an intricate part in it. *Is this all the fates have in store for me?* Carey mused.

Ji touched her hand gently. "Is something the matter?"

"I can't wait for the day when someone doesn't have to ask me that question," said Carey, thinking her wish quite far-fetched.

Ji gave her an uneasy smile but said nothing. They continued in silence, leaving each to their own thoughts. It was only later that night when they had set up camp that Carey finally got up the nerve to talk to Kat about what she had been feeling.

Kat had posted herself a little way away from their campsite while Ji made himself comfortable by the fire. Carey sat down beside her. There was a moment where she battled with her courage until she finally forced herself to speak.

"Kat," she started.

Without turning her head, Kat answered. "Hmm?"

Carey took a deep breath. "How... how do you know when you're falling in love?"

To Carey's surprise, Kat didn't move. "There's no such thing."

This wasn't the reaction Carey was expecting. "What?"

"*Falling in love*. There's no such thing," she repeated, finally turning to face Carey.

Feeling just a little puzzled, Carey said, "But our parents, they're in love, aren't they?"

"Of course they are!" Kat exclaimed. "But falling in love and loving someone is completely different."

Still none the wiser, Carey waited for Kat to explain. She smiled.

"Oh Carey, I'm sorry! I keep forgetting how much you still don't know!"

Slightly affronted by this statement, Carey opened her mouth to respond but stopped when she realised it was the truth. "Why? Is it one of those I've-been-around-Commoners-too-long situations again?"

Kat patted her hand in support. "Let me explain. We're different from Commoners, right? Witches, wizard–"

"We can do magic," Carey offered.

Kat nodded. "Yes, but we're not just Commoners who can do magic. We're as different from Commoners as, say, cats are from dogs. We might have some things similar but we're almost completely different."

"All right," Carey said, understanding her explanation though not exactly sure what it had to do with her initial question.

"Well, to say someone 'falls in love' suggests they can fall out of it. Commoners are constantly searching for the 'perfect person'. I sort of feel sorry for them. You see, when we're born," she said, pointing to Carey and herself, "a bond is formed between us and one other being. Just one. It's a natural formation, a phenomenon that is hard to explain. We don't know who this person is or when we'll finally meet them. We can only hope that destiny will lead us to them."

"But how do you know it's that person?" Carey asked, both excited and bewildered by the notion that the universe had this one person designed for her.

"That's the thing, though, isn't it? You might know straight away or it might take a long time to fully realise it," Kat said. "I mean, we're all connected. How else would telepaths be able to do what they do? They just feel the connection more than the rest. But this connection we have with that one person is stronger, more unique."

"How do you know all this? You haven't met that person, have you?" Carey asked, curious of how Kat knew all this.

Kat laughed. "Of course not! Carey, once you find this person, you don't leave them! I simply know all this because we all do. We learn it when we're very young because it's one of the most amazing things, something that truly defines us from anyone else. You would have known about this once..."

Carey felt the familiar itch of frustration. She felt so ridiculous having to re-learn everything, especially something like this, something so important. However, for now she forced it from her mind. Kat was still speaking.

"You never leave them once you've found them because you're connected. As soon as innocence gives way to truth, you feel inexplicably drawn to them. You never want to be away from them." Kat face was taken over by a dream-like haze. She frowned suddenly. "Why did you ask me about this?"

Carey was silent, her brain unable to produce a quick lie. She hated herself for being so slow after being able to whip out a lie so quickly before. She could feel Kat looking at her intently. With a gasp of sudden realisation, Kat clapped her hand over her mouth.

"You! You asked because – ! But... Ji! Is it Ji?" she whispered, barely coherent in her surprise and excitement.

Carey shrugged, not confident enough to say yes. "I don't know. It's just... I don't know what I'm feeling anymore. I look at Ji and I can't help feeling happy but at the same time I'm completely terrified. I don't know what it is. I've never felt this before so I thought... I don't know, Kat. I'm not making much sense, am I?"

Kat's hand was still clasped over her mouth, her eyes wide in shock. Slowly she lowered it.

"You're serious," was all she said.

Carey was hoping for something a bit more supportive.

"Yes I am, at least, I think I am. Oh Kat! You have to help me! I don't know what to do," she cried softly, grabbing her friend's hands. This action broke Kat's surprised stupor. She laughed nervously.

"So everything I just said, your question, it was because of this? Do you think he knows? Does Ji know?" she asked, squirming with anticipation.

Carey's insides were writhing. She may have lacked confidence in herself but not in Ji; she was fairly sure he knew. She nodded. Kat squealed in delight.

"Kat! Sshh! Ji might hear you!" Carey said, startled by her reaction.

She had rarely seen or heard Kat express any true emotion. It was as if the long hard years in the service of the Order had forced her to suppress her emotions. She'd only seen Kat express her true emotions once before which seemed so very long ago. Now, however, she was as giddy as a schoolgirl.

"I'm sorry! This is just so amazing and unexpected! Do you realise how lucky you are? When did you know?"

Carey thought she had better tell Kat everything if she was going to help, and so with a deep breath, she told Kat what had happened near the Falls. Kat hung on her every word, a mingled look of disbelief and faint longing playing on her features. Carey began to feel a twinge of excitement herself when Kat exclaimed again the immensity of her luck.

"But the thing is, Ji was this close–" she held her thumb and index finger a few millimetres apart, " – to kissing me, but he didn't," Carey finished.

Kat's reaction changed instantly. "I hope not. He's not that foolish," she remarked seriously.

Not sure whether this statement was meant to wound her or if it was merely a slip of the tongue, Carey asked her why.

"Oh no! I didn't mean it like that! It's just that a kiss is not just a kiss like it is with Commoners. For us it is so much more. We have this connection already, right? A kiss is like the seal. It's what joins our spirits, making it like one," Kat said, but seeing Carey's confusion, she continued. "Everyone is just one half of a spirit. It doesn't seem like it, but we are. You only really feel it once you've found your other half. Ji's your other half and a kiss – a kiss would bring the two halves together and make it a whole. The first kiss brings a bond so infinite that anything is possible. I've heard that some people even become telepathic."

"But if Ji is really my *other half,* then why can't he…" Carey asked, trailing off.

Kat was serious now. "Look inside yourself, Carey. How do you feel about this?"

She knew the answer to this already; she had been thinking about it ever since the moment by the Falls. There was a myriad of feelings but one came to mind above all – uncertainty. Carey didn't know how she felt or why she felt both ecstatic and frightened at the same time. She wanted to separate her emotions and analyse them but she couldn't. They were a swirl of dizzying confusion.

Kat didn't even wait for an answer; she could see it in Carey's face. "That's why. The universe is all about balance. If you don't yet feel one-hundred per cent comfortable with this, then things could go very wrong. You have to wait until you're both on the same plane."

"When will I know that though?" Carey demanded. "When? I don't even know… This is all so… How do I even approach Ji?" Carey was beginning to see the enormity of her situation and begged Kat for the answers that would relieve her predicament.

Kat shrugged. "I'm sorry, I don't know. But I've heard that it'll work out, all by itself."

After some time in silence, Carey left Kat to her sentry duties and returned to the fire. Ji was already asleep and she didn't wake him. All Kat had told her changed everything – this wasn't just about liking someone anymore. She lay down a few feet from Ji, lying on her side so she could see him. Watching his chest rise and fall became oddly calming and she soon began to feel her worries slip away, sleep lapping at the edges of her mind like an incoming tide. She swayed in and out of consciousness, her head contesting between the constant swirl of thoughts and the enticing bliss of sleep. In the end, the allure was too strong and Carey's beleaguered body finally gave in.

Carey blinked; she was standing and it was suddenly very dark, the light from the fire extinguished. She felt behind her and found herself backed up against a cold stone wall, hidden in the deep darkness of its shadow. She assumed she was in some sort of room and it reeked of mould and sweat. Carey wrinkled her nose and pulled her hair away from her eyes. She searched the room and sensed another presence hidden in the darkness. It took a few moments for her eyes to adjust properly to the poor light before she could make out the other person. It was a young man. He was sitting barely a few feet away, his wrists and ankles bound to the chair's arms and legs. His head was bowed to the ground so he hadn't noticed her yet. His bare chest and arms were infested with wounds and his breathing was ragged and sharp. The lower parts of his slacks were ripped and bloodied. He had dirty brown hair that was matted with dry blood and the bindings that held him were cutting into his skin, leaving it raw and shiny.

Carey looked around and saw nothing but a small narrow door with a tiny dark hole at the top that served as a window. She moved slightly to the side in the hope that she might see the boy better when she accidentally kicked some loose pebbles, sending them stuttering across the chamber floor. Their movement echoed loudly around the room and Carey stopped. The boy stirred.

"Taken to sneaking in on me now? Think you'll catch me by surprise?" the boy croaked, looking up.

Carey froze, agape. That voice – she knew it instantly.

"Ji?" she whispered, her voice wavering slightly.

He lifted his head sharply and looked through the darkness at her with narrowed eyes. He was almost unrecognisable. He had deep slashes down the sides of his face, his lips were cut and red and there were bruises around his eyes that made them appear swollen. A metal clasp encircled his neck.

"Carey?" he said slowly, keeping his eyes on her.

His voice was tainted with distrust and he continued to stare at her suspiciously. This didn't deter her though. It was mind-numbing and Carey couldn't accept what she was seeing. His horrifying wounds made her heart ache and she moved towards him with slow, hesitant steps. She fell to her knees and trembling, she lifted her hand to his face. He continued to stare at her defiantly as she gently brushed his hair from his eyes, wary of his injuries.

"What are you doing here?" she asked.

This was a dream, surely, because this could not be real. He continued to stare. "What are you doing here?"

Carey stuttered. "I – I don't know. I just – just closed my eyes. This is just a dream, Ji. This isn't real, this isn't. I'm dreaming because you're not really here and neither–"

Ji shook his head. "No. No, Carey, this is real. I am really here... and you can't be. If you really are you, you can't be here," Ji said forcefully.

"What? Why? I don't understand. What happened to you?" Carey asked, confused by his answer.

His gaze softened but distrust was still written in his features. "What did I do when you first saw us in the Monaghan market?" he asked suddenly.

"What – ?" Carey began but Ji cut across.

"Just answer me. Please," he said in a hopeful tone.

Carey thought back to that day and remembered the moment she'd first laid eyes on her two friends.

"You winked at me," she said.

Ji seemed satisfied with her answer. "I had to make sure. Her mind games... I couldn't be certain."

"I still don't understand," Carey said.

Ji looked around again, searching for something. When he turned his attention back to her, his voice was urgent and fearful. "I was brought here, after I was taken at Jeremy's castle. They've been trying to force me, trying to get me to say who the One is. But–"

"What? What are you saying, Ji? We rescued you. We got you back. At this very moment you're asleep next to me in some clearing. You can't be here, you just can't–"

"But I am here. In Torarn. The Centre City."

Carey bit her lip. What was this?

192

"And this isn't a dream," he added, speaking as if he had read her thoughts. "What I want to know is how did you get here? There must be at least two hundred Guardsmen in the under tunnels."

"I – I don't know, I really don't know. I swear it's a dream, Ji. I just found myself here."

She was getting scared now. This situation was beginning to feel much too real and she looked over at the door in fear. "I have to get you out of here," she said, taking hold of the ropes that bound him there.

Ji shook his head in discouragement. "No. You can't. We'll never get past all the guards."

"But I can't leave you, not now that I'm here! I must be here for a reason if not this," Carey gasped, her heart pounding with grief at the very thought of leaving Ji in the dark cell. "I have to."

"You don't understand. They don't want me, Carey. They want... you. And if they find you here," Ji shook his head, "we lose."

"What do you mean, they want me?" Carey asked imperatively. "And that we lose?"

Ji looked at her with saddened eyes before dropping his gaze to his knees. "The people here believe a force of good will rise against evil with the power of great strength. They have called this person the Liberator or bringer of peace–"

"Wait. And they think it's me? But why me? I don't have any special powers. There must be thousands of others with powers greater than mine."

"It's not a guess. Malevolence has Foreseers that have uncovered signs pointing directly at us – you, Kat and I. I don't know what these signs are, but they've got them. I've listened to what Malevolence has said and I think she means you though she doesn't know it yet. You have a power that neither Kat nor I have. That's why I can't leave. I have to keep Malevolence guessing to give you enough time to get through to this world."

"Guessing?" Carey hissed.

"She's... been questioning me. I've held out, I've given her nothing, so right now, she's just guessing. She thinks it's Kat, but she also suspects you. I don't know her reason and she would never tell me. Despite this suspicion, she thinks you are weaker than Kat, who she merely assumes has the special powers. Carey, you have that power–"

"Which I can only use as a defence..." but Carey stopped. Even as she said this she knew it wasn't the truth. The chimera's attack floated to the top of her mind and she remembered that extra boost of strength the power had given her. Was Ji right in his assumption?

This situation was outrageous though. How could Carey be this Liberator Ji spoke of? Malevolence was right in assuming it was Kat – she was nowhere near as strong.

"You know that's not true, Carey. The thing is she won't stop until she finds out and she's no longer using magic. She started resorting to medieval methods, rods and fire..." he shuddered "but even so, it won't be long until she finds out from her seers. I have to prolong this long enough for you–"

"But you could die before then! The torture will kill you!" Carey spluttered, trying to comprehend what Ji was telling her.

He looked her in the eyes. "This is what I have to do. I'm a Seeker, Carey, as are you. Our freedom, our people's freedom, depends on us. It's not heroics, it's the truth. Now tell me you wouldn't do the same if you were in my place."

Deep in her heart Carey knew he was right. She would never betray them if it was her sitting in that chair and she knew that it was their curse to endure such atrocities.

Before she could say anything, Ji turned his head to the door and hissed, "Someone's coming. You must go!"

Carey jumped. "But I can't leave you here!" she choked.

"You must! For your sake and everyone else's you must! Go back the way you came and leave this place. Please, Carey!" Ji pleaded anxiously.

"No!" Carey cried, tears starting to stream down her cheeks. "I can't–"

"Please, Carey, just go!"

Sobbing silently, Carey touched his cheek in despair, not wanting to leave him. He flinched convulsively as she withdrew, and she sunk back into the darkness of the shadows. Drying her tears quickly, she listened intently and a few moments later, the tall, dark figure of Malevolence entered the room. She was followed in by a stooping character with a bald head. He placed a flaming torch in a bracket by the door, his other hand occupied by a large leather roll. He remained by the *doorway, his gaze upon the floor. Carey stood as if frozen, her muscles tense as she tried to control her breathing.*

Malevolence paced about Ji's chair in silence for a minute or so before facing him. Her voice caught Carey's breath, making the hairs on the back of her neck stand on end in a cold shiver.

"I tire of this charade, boy. I have little patience for uncooperative rebels, so tell me what I require and I will end this," she hissed, a glint of her red eyes flashing.

Ji grunted. "You know my answer."

Malevolence lifted a hand and beckoned the man by the door. He moved forwards and conjured a small table, placing his leather roll upon it. With a flick it unrolled to present numerous implements of torture. His fingers were long and thin and he handled the instruments with delicacy, his movements possessing an almost feminine quality. He selected a small, iron rod and held the point up to the torch until it turned a deep, burning red.

Carrying it upright, he walked to Ji's holding position and stood, waiting for Malevolence's command.

This time, Malevolence's voice echoed but not aloud; her words presented themselves telepathically. "You wish not to betray them but by doing so, you will instead get to witness their deaths. They are not so far away now. They will be here soon and when they do arrive, I will find out. But if that is what you want—"

Ji coughed. "You don't care what I want. And why do you want to know who it is when you're going to kill them anyway? Kill me now if you have no reason."

Malevolence signalled and the man held the rod under Ji's chin. "I have my reasons. I need not explain them to you," she said and the rod was pressed against his skin. Ji moaned in pain and Carey smelt the acrid rancidity of burning skin.

Ji's voice was strained when he spoke next, the pain noticeable in his words. "I think you want me to tell you because you don't want them reaching the Centre City. I think you're afraid – ahh!"

The rod was resting on his forearm this time, thin tapers of smoke rising into the air. Malevolence hissed, almost in amusement. "Afraid? Hardly..."

Yet despite this, Ji continued; Carey admired his nerve. "I think there's something coming, something that will disturb your empire. I bet your seers have seen it. Well, you know what?" he said through gritted teeth, "I'm not going to help you succeed."

The hunched torturer put down his rod and picked up a more sinister-looking device. It was long and thin, the tip divided into five pin-sharp points. He stepped up to Ji and held it in front of his face. His eyes were so dark they appeared black.

Malevolence moved to the side, allowing him space. She bent her knees as if to sit and as she did so, a grand silver chair grew up from the floor like an elegant twist of vines. She leant back, the red again flickering where her eyes should have been. Carey felt sick as she watched her dear friend being tortured while Malevolence sat back like a spectator at the theatre. The whole scene was repulsive. The torturer leaned in closely to Ji and spoke for the first time.

"You are very strong. I was surprised to be summoned, considering who you are. Pity you are not more like your brother," he said in a silky voice that taunted Ji.

"What of Zacharia?" Ji asked with faint disquiet, his bravado wavering at the mention of his brother.

The man smiled wickedly, revealing rows of tiny pointed teeth. "He hasn't been doing so well in the Corigliphs. After a mere week of my attendance he's gibbering incessantly."

"But he doesn't know anything! What did you do to him?"

The torturer paused. "Do you truly believe we want anything from him?"

Ji eyed the sharp tool that was waved dangerously in front of him. "I see what you're doing," he said in a hushed voice. "And I'll say just this – Zacharia is a Seeker, just like me. He would not want me to give up, even if you kill him–"

The barbed instrument was suddenly thrust into his thigh and Ji could not hold back the scream that escaped his lips.

Carey winced, feeling a horrible wrenching ache in her stomach. It was bad enough seeing Ji tortured, but to not be able to help him... It was taking every last bit of effort to stop herself running to him.

"He's strong. Stronger than most," the torturer said, speaking to Malevolence. "He will prove hard to break."

"I will... not break," Ji said painfully.

"Yes you will," Malevolence's voice echoed once more. "What you guard will be mine. It is merely a matter of time. It will be wonderful, watching you die..."

Ji was breathing heavily now, and with much effort he said, "I will never tell you which of my friends is the one that will lead to your destruction, even if it means I die because of it. I would rather die a thousand deaths than betray them. My answer stays the same, Malevolence, I will not tell."

The Empress was at his side in an instant; the chair had dissolved. She leaned in to him, her face inches from his.

"Then you die in vain."

"Never," Ji growled.

Malevolence gripped his neck and twisted. He yelled and Carey felt his anguish stab painfully at her heart and it pulled her out of the shadows. "No, **STOP!**"

Malevolence let go of Ji and rounded slowly on Carey. The man looked up at her in surprise, almost dropping his spiked tool.

"I see you've finally decided to join us," Malevolence said in her harsh whispering voice.

There was a moment of silence in which Carey realised what she had just said. There was a sharp twitch in her temple and suddenly she heard Malevolence slithering around in her mind. "I hadn't expected you to hold back for so long. Did you truly think you could simply hide in the shadows and think I wouldn't notice you?"

Carey whimpered in discomfort.

"Don't tell them anything, Carey!" Ji coughed.

At once she felt a deep, piercing sensation inside her, different to Malevolence's. It was soul penetrating. The torturer stepped around Malevolence.

"It's a Fiorilusa, my queen."

His words sent a shiver down Carey's spine though she wasn't exactly sure why.

"Yes indeed, Liseau, a Twilight Traveller. I expected as much."

"She believes this to be a dream..."

Carey shook her head. The strange delving sensation had been the man, Liseau. He had read her mind. Carey gulped. "This is a dream. This is a dream and I won't say anything, not to you, not to anybody because it's my dream and−"

There was a sharp pain and Carey clapped her hands to her head.

"No, not quite," the Empress breathed. "This is, at most, unexpected but could prove invaluable."

"Say nothing, Carey."

"Liseau..." Malevolence commanded, dryly.

He lifted his iron rod and struck Ji hard over the head. A trickle of blood ran down from his hairline; Carey reached out to him. "Please, stop..."

"As I thought..."

Malevolence took hold of one of Ji's fingers and twisted. "You know what I want, Carey Lee. You will tell me or he will suffer for you." Her voice pitched and whistled around the room.

Ji shook his head pleadingly and Carey's heartbeat quickened. "This is a dream. It's a dream. It's a dream. It's a..." she repeated over and over, willing it to stop.

"No, it's not. Now tell me. Tell... me."

Carey tried turning away but she felt Liseau's mind powers tug somewhere near the top of her spine and she was dragged over to Ji, dangerously close to Malevolence. The Empress looked down at her.

"Tell... me..."

Carey shook her head with wide eyes. Malevolence moved suddenly and she heard a sickening, dull **CRACK**.

Ji yelped. Malevolence had broken his finger and she now moved mercilessly onto the next one. Carey gulped back the urge to vomit. "... a dream. It's just a dream. It's a dream..."

There was another tug and she fell to her knees in front of Ji; a deep sorrow filled her chest. She looked fearfully at Malevolence, but she made no move to strike.

"Why do you not harm me? Why do you not torture me as you do Ji?" Carey asked, her voice cracking with emotion.

"Twilight Travellers only feel what they want to feel and I know you don't want me to torture you. It would be a waste of time trying."

"But you are controlling me–"

"Your mind may be a mere echo, but that is all that's needed... Besides, I do not need to hurt you in order to torture you. Liseau," Malevolence commanded. "Her eyes."

Liseau forced Carey to look straight at Ji; she cried out. They were filled with such a deep pain she could almost feel it. They bulged with agony as another of his fingers broke; Carey's stomach twisted in a heartbreaking knot.

"It's only a small price, Carey..." he whispered, his eyes watering.

With Malevolence's voice all around her and unable to pull away, the feeling was horrific. As the Empress continued to inflict pain on Ji, anger replaced Carey's sorrow. It built up like a dam inside her and the longer she sat there staring at him, the stronger it became. Ji's cries of pain echoed and blended with the demands of the witch queen. Carey's eyes streamed with hot tears and her body shook with fury. She could see out of the corner of her eye the mocking, taunting face of Liseau, his mouth spread in a hungry grin and in that moment, something snapped.

The rage burst forth and Carey screamed in anger, momentarily distracting Liseau. She broke from his control and ran backwards. She saw Ji's head droop and she stumbled in shock. The tears in her eyes blurred her vision. They streamed down her face and she cried with anguish as Malevolence twisted another of Ji's digits. Ji moaned faintly and again pleaded softly with Carey to say nothing. She sobbed as she backed away. "... it's a dream. Just a dream. Just..."

"You can keep saying that, Carey, but the truth is that Ji will die if you don't tell me," Malevolence breathed.

The Empress raised a hand and a wind began to fill the room. Carey could sense Malevolence's anger around her and felt her own vanish in an instant. She backed away further, trying to escape the nightmare that had built up around her.

Ji was groaning in extreme torment and she trembled; her ankles gave way and she fell to the floor as she heard Ji's third finger break. She covered her ears. "No! This can't be happening. It's all a dream. It's all just a dream," she cried.

"Tell me, Carey, tell me or he dies!" She heard Malevolence's voice, shrill as it swirled about the room, carried on the wind that was building.

Ji yelled out in pain and Carey pushed herself back against the wall as the colours of the room began to swirl together, making her sick.

"It's only a dream. Ji's going to be all right. It's only a dream!" Carey sobbed out loud, collapsing to the ground completely.

The roar of the wind and sounds of the chamber churned together and pressed against her ears in a terrible screeching swell. She cried out in panic, holding her hands over her ears as she heard Ji scream, tears from her eyes dropping to the floor.

"This isn't possible. This... isn't... possible..."

She closed her eyes and a sudden sharp surge pulled her from her senses. Everything went black and her stomach dropped steeply from the force. She blinked.

She was back in the clearing. Ji had his hand at her temple; Kat was kneeling beside him, watching her closely. Carey looked about in fright then to Ji as he sat in front of her; she sat up sharply and threw her arms around Ji's neck. Tears were still streaming down her face as she cried in fear, shock and confusion. *He's all right, he's here... he's all right,* Carey told herself feverishly. His arms wrapped around her and he held her while she cried helplessly into his shoulder. He whispered words of comfort into her ear until she finally managed to pull away and face him.

"Oh, Ji, it was horrible! I had the most horrible nightmare. You... you were a prisoner in the other realm and you were being tortured by Malevolence, and the terrible thing was that I couldn't help you, I couldn't do anything! I couldn't..." Carey threw herself around Ji's neck again and he whispered gently into her ear, "Don't worry, it was only a dream."

Carey nodded into his shoulder, sniffling.

It was only a dream, she thought with some comfort, *only a dream.* But from deep inside, a more sinister voice answered, *Yes, but what is a Twilight Traveller?*

Chapter Twenty

Mistaken

She didn't want to talk about it, so when neither Kat nor Ji asked, she was relieved. It had felt so real and it didn't help that Carey couldn't stop thinking about it. It kept playing over and over in her head, again and again, relentlessly tormenting her with images she would rather forget. She kept telling herself it had only been a dream, but something kept urging her to look closer. It had been neither absurd not broken – the closest thing Carey could relate it to was perhaps a memory. Everything made sense, it all fit together, except for Ji. He was here with her, not in some chamber in the other realm. Was it in fact not a dream but a message? But what could it possibly be trying to say? Was it perhaps telling her something about Ji? Was it one of those – what did Kat call them – Premonitive Dreams? It could have been a forewarning of what was to come. It was a possibility. If they were caught…

Still nagging at her though were those names. Ji had tried to convince her that she was some sort of Liberator, that she was special, but she didn't consider herself special. Kat and Ji were easily more capable of stronger magic, so she gave little credibility to this idea. What carried more interest though was what that man, Liseau, had called her – a Twilight Traveller. She'd never heard this term before. Carey wanted to know if this was a real thing, if there were actually people called Twilight Travellers, or if it had been something her mind had made up.

Kat asked her whether she wanted to rest for the remainder of the day, to which Carey answered quite rudely in the negative. It had only been a dream. She couldn't and definitely wouldn't stall the group because she'd had a dream.

Ji estimated that they were still at least a day away from the next town.

"We'll head for that line of trees. It's not far; you can see it on the horizon."

Kat agreed and Carey made no move to interfere. Night was approaching fast yet she was wide awake. She did not want to go to sleep for fear of the nightmare repeating itself. Carey would have been happy if she never went to sleep again. She was silent as she listened to Kat and Ji talk and refused to join the conversation. She felt strangely isolated and could find nothing that she might be able to contribute. To her relief, they reached the edge of the wood just on sunset.

The moment they stepped into the shade of the trees, Carey was hit with a painful force; voices began ringing incoherently through her head, echoing distantly.

"Seramina... No!... Mercy, have... my brother... Help me! ... can't, Alexan..."

These words echoed again and again through Carey's mind. She recognised them instantly. She heard Ji and Kat cry out in surprise and Carey knew they could hear it too. The sounds became louder, the pain in her head throbbing unbearably and she raised her hands to her temples, falling awkwardly to the forest floor. The voices vibrated inside her head as if they were reverberating against her brain. Then they were gone. The echoes stopped, the voices receded. All that she could hear now was a faint bubbling coursing through the recesses of her mind.

Carey lifted her head. Kat was clutching at a branch, struggling to hold herself up. Ji was leaning back against a nearby tree, his eyes wide and his hair tousled.

"Kat? Ji?"

Ji staggered over and helped her up. She shook her head in an effort to clear away the residual voices.

"It was the girl again," she said, finally regaining her balance. "It was the girl, Seramina."

"Yes," Kat concurred, "and I think I know why."

She was staring into the woods and Carey followed her eye line.

"Ji, look."

Deep in the shadows, lying on an old and overgrown track was a wagon, burnt out and smouldering in a charred mess. Smoke rose from the dying fire in curling wisps that twisted towards the treetops. The roof and a single wheel stuck visibly out of the mound, blackened, brittle and glowing red with embers that still burnt within the ashes. The grass surrounding was black and crisp, hissing under their feet with every apprehensive step they took. Ji kicked a block of burnt wood out of the way, sending a flurry of hot sparks into the air. Carey walked around the ruins with a deep sinking feeling. She saw a colourfully dyed silk cloth caught on a nearby branch and, carefully untangling it from its captor, Carey pulled it down. She drew it across her hand; they had been so close.

The three of them were silent as they looked about the wreckage. Carey drifted away from the others and sat down by a large boulder. She shivered violently as the wind blew harshly, stirring a fluster of leaves from their resting place. Blowing to one side, Carey sighted a small brown notebook half hidden amongst them. She frowned. Curiously she dusted it off and with it a name became visible: Seramina Jessup. Picking it up carefully, she saw that it had escaped the fire; she flipped through the pages. The first few pages had been written on but the rest was totally blank. Carey turned to the first page and saw that it was a journal. Perhaps it could tell her something. The girl's writing, Seramina's writing, was small and neat but contained a childlike aspect. Carey began to read.

I am so excited! Tomorrow I'll see the sun for the first time! I wonder if it looks like what father said. I cannot wait! I can't sleep I'm so excited. Alexander is already asleep because he wore himself out playing Roogle. He says he'll probably never get to play it once we go out. They were so rough today, I almost got hit twice. Angus swore it was only an accident but then he tried it again and got in trouble from Father. It's really late now. The torch is almost out. I can hear Mother and Father talking with the Desmonds. Tiana gave this journal to me today. She said she wants to read all about our journey so I have to write everything down. I'll miss Tiana. She's never seen the sun either. I will send her a message when we get to San Veria. Mother says it has very large and beautiful cave flower gardens there. I hope I see it soon. Seramina Jessup.

It was very sad today when we left. Tiana and Eli came to say goodbye and I cried! Angus said that I was a cry-baby so I punched him really hard to show him I wasn't. Tiana gave me this really pretty fairy gold necklace from the other realm. Another present! It was her grandmother's and because she didn't wear it she gave it to me. It has her grandmother's name on the front and on the back it has The Order of the Rose. I was so happy. Father used to be part of that group and Tiana said that the necklace is supposed to protect me from evil. That was a bit scary though. Eli gave me a cave flower. It is a beautiful purple one and he pinned it to my shirt for good luck. After we said goodbye to Nanna and Poppa, some guards took us down to the front tunnel. They did some strange magic in front of the doors and they opened. Then there was this really bright light. It was like a thousand fire torches. It took a long time for our eyes to get used to it. It was the sun! We got in our travelling wagon, which is very bright and colourful with pretty dyed silk streamers flying from the corners. Alexander and I were too excited to stay in the wagon so we ran alongside it all day. We played some tricks on the guards with our powers too. It was so funny! Father said today that when we get to San Veria he will teach me to control things with my mind. He said that Alexander was too young but then Alexander complained and he said maybe. Alexander always has to do what I do! I saw some really strange flowers today as well. They are nothing like cave flowers. They are so much bigger and prettier! I picked a whole bunch. The sun gets very hot after a while, like standing too close to a fire torch. We had supper just before and Alexander and I are sleeping in bunks in the wagon. This is really fun! I love the outer world! Seramina Jessup.

Carey flicked over to the last few entries by Seramina and read with interest the way she wrote innocently about the dangers and the strange dreams that were plaguing her.

Today was very strange. The guards told us not to leave the wagon and Father is walking outside with them. He looks very angry. We went through this village this morning. I got out to stretch my legs and Father commanded me to get back inside so sharply it gave me a headache. A man and some women were looking at us and mother said that people will look at us strangely because we are disguised as Travellers. I was scared when Father hurt me like that. He doesn't even tell us stories anymore of when he was part of the Order of the Rose and how he escaped the Empire. He always used to tell us stories about Lady Fianna and her Seekers. He used to say that they will one day fight the evil Empress again. I'd like to have adventures like he did. I don't know what is going on though. Mother spent all day looking through the curtain of the window. She looked like she was afraid of something outside. I hope everything is all right. Seramina Jessup.

I had this very strange dream last night. I was in a dungeon with a man I saw in the village. He had bright blue eyes that looked like they were made of ice. I've seen a mad man's eyes before and that's what they looked like, but he wasn't mad. In my dream he was a wizard and wore clothes like Father used to. He was nice to start with then he asked me where the other Seekers were. I told him I didn't know. I don't know about the Seekers. But he kept asking me and I kept telling him I didn't know. Then he got angry and I got really scared. I started to cry but he didn't stop. Then I heard a lady's voice. I couldn't see her but she was talking about hurting me if I didn't tell her. I screamed so loudly. Luckily Father woke me. I told Mama about it and she told me not to worry. She knows I'm not a Seer or a Twilight Traveller so it must've just been a nightmare. Thank goodness! It was very scary. I hope Angus doesn't hear about this. Seramina Jessup.

Carey blinked. There was that expression again – Twilight Traveller. Carey's innards squirmed uncomfortably. So her mind hadn't made it up. Carey would have given up speculating right there and then about her dream and turned believer if not for one major detail – Ji. It was confusing but she wouldn't let herself believe something was real when he was mere feet from where she sat. She remained convinced that it had been simply a dream, albeit a very realistic one. Reluctantly she read on.

Something's wrong today. I don't know what's happening but Mother is scared. She keeps looking like she's going to cry. I don't like this. Tiana said this would be fun but it's not. Now I can hear horses outside. They're not ours

Seramina's writing stopped abruptly, mid-sentence. Carey flipped the page but found it blank. She frowned. She wanted to know what had happened to Seramina and her family. Carey called over to Kat.

"Kat, have a look at this," she said, holding out Seramina's diary.

Kat took it and slowly read the pages Carey indicated; she sighed remorsefully. Ji looked over her shoulder as she read.

"What do you think went wrong?" Carey asked.

"Possibly Essedarian, only, this seems a little messy. They're usually a lot less obvious," Kat said, shutting the diary and handing it back to Carey. "When this Seramina girl got out of the wagon at that village they must have seen the necklace. Those people she mentioned – Commoners don't tend to stare. They like to avoid eye contact with Travellers. They must have been Essedarian. Probably thinking she was one of us, they followed and attacked."

"But don't they know there's only the three of us? She clearly wasn't old enough to be mistaken for one of us."

Kat shook her head. "No. But to wear one of necklaces is like putting a target on your forehead. Essedarian wouldn't be privy to such information about us but word spreads. Whether they thought she was one of us or not, they saw the gold and attacked."

Carey ran her fingers through her hair, holding back the impulse to rip it out in frustration. "If only we knew what had happened to them."

Kat stopped in thought. "There is a way."

She searched inside her bag for a moment before revealing a small diamond-cut crystal. She drew back her arm and tossed it into the air. It froze and hovered just above the remains of the wagon. Arcs of light sprang from the crystal, creating a dome-like cascade. The light faded and a number of shadowy forms remained. It was hard to define at first but the shapes soon became more recognisable. It was the wagon, exactly how Seramina had described it. It was merely a ghost, grey and smoke-like. There were people too. Carey realised quickly that she was seeing a replay of events, the last moment of the travellers.

On top of the wagon were the two guards Seramina had described and below was a tall, stern man with a small black beard. He was yelling at something but Carey heard no sound. He was aiming at people not yet in range of the crystal. The guards were climbing down from the wagon when five men on horses entered the picture. They dismounted in one swift action whilst dodging the curses of the tall man. Then something strange occurred. The advancing men stopped as though they had come up against a wall. An invisible force was keeping them back.

Carey noticed how the tall man's face was strained, his body shuddering under some tremendous weight. The attacking men seemed lost for only a moment but recovered quickly. In unison they clapped their hands together, then with a terrible force, struck out at the invisible barrier with their open palms. The man fell backwards, crashing to the ground; his defence was broken. He was quickly dragged aside as the other four shot the guards down. Carey almost cried out in alarm. Their expressions bore into Carey's soul, unearthing something horribly familiar. Were they the same assassins who had killed her Grandmother all those years ago?

The Essedarian reduced the guards to ash with a single gesture, their remnants carried away with the wind. Three of them made for the wagon whilst the other two guarded the man lying on the ground.

As the three men approached the wagon, a woman with long, wavy red hair stumbled down the stairs; she yelled something at the men and held her arms out, barring the doorway. Distress pulled at her face as she stood her ground. One particularly solid man, who seemed to stand out from the rest, laughed as he took hold of one of the woman's wrists and twisted it. Her knees buckled and she cried out as she fell to her knees; the rest of the group stared as the man said something to her, his expression full of contempt. She grasped his hand and tried to loosen his grip, pulling at it with all her might but the man only laughed again, and with one strong movement, he threw her aside into the dirt. Without so much as a sideways glance, he then proceeded into the cabin; the other two men dragged her to her feet and pushed her over to their other captive where they bound her with silver ropes. She struggled against them, but stopped when one of the wizards struck her hard across the head with the back of his hand. A moment later the surly man reappeared from inside the caravan, hauling behind him a girl with red hair and a small dark-haired boy.

"Seramina," Carey breathed.

Seramina looked only about twelve-years-old and her brother about nine or ten. She was holding her journal in one hand, and as the man threw them down the stairs, it flew from her hand over to where Carey had found it. The wizard stepped over them, clipping Seramina with his foot as he went. He turned to her as she pulled herself up off the ground and seized a handful of red wavy hair, wrenching her head backwards. Seramina clenched her teeth and glared at the man with tears in her eyes. He took hold of the triangle necklace dangling from around her neck and tugged it hard, ripping it from her before throwing her down onto the ground. Carey winced. She glanced at Kat and Ji who were watching intently, following every action. Turning back, Carey saw Alexander struggle to his feet and launch himself at his sister's attacker, only to be brushed aside effortlessly by the thug. The whole group was now gathering around Alexander and Seramina and in a blink of an eye, had them bound and gagged and on their feet. Two of them took hold of who Carey knew now to be Seramina's mother and father, and with a single nod from the leader they disappeared. Only one stayed behind to seal the attack, letting the horses loose and sending a flaming ball of fire in through the window of the wagon; within a minute the whole carriage was engulfed in flames. Then, with a sweep of his cloak, the last of the Essedarian disappeared.

Carey was stupefied by what she had just witnessed; her knuckles were painfully white from clutching Seramina's journal. It had all happened so quickly. Kat summoned the crystal from above the ruins and pocketed it, turning away from the remains; Ji walked over to it and kicked a piece of blackened wood aside, this time in agitation. Carey walked over and placed her hand on his shoulder; his head drooped to the ground.

"She thought it would save her, the necklace," he muttered.

Carey looked at him then at the diary in her other hand; it just didn't seem fair. They were supposed to protect and help people, not get them in trouble.

They stood in silence for only a moment. All Carey had been troubled by, all her feelings she had been struggling to sort out, suddenly didn't seem to matter anymore. There were much bigger things to worry about.

She let her hand slip from Ji's shoulder and walked over to Kat; she was biting her fingernail in frustration.

"Why would Essedarian take a whole family hostage?" said Carey.

Kat grunted but said nothing.

"Seramina's father used to be in the Order. Maybe it has something to do with him," Carey suggested, placing Seramina's journal in her bag.

Kat stood silent; Carey prodded her. "Hmm? Yeah, maybe," she said, obviously not listening to what Carey had said. "We need to move on. It'll start getting dangerous – well, *more* dangerous, if we stay here any longer. Come on. We'll set up camp somewhere else."

Carey retired to bed earlier than usual that night, despite her earlier resolution of never sleeping again. Once more she dreamt of Ji in his small cell but this time she was watching herself as well. It made no more sense the second time than it did the first but this time it had the sting of a memory. She rubbed the tattoo in vain. It was confusing but Carey pushed it away. They were reaching the coastal town from which they were to leave by sea to Aran Island and she couldn't allow herself to be distracted.

The air was cold and bit viciously at their bare skin. They had agreed to fly in order to reach the town of Burtonport before the winter snows truly started and they all knew time was running short.

Despite the bitter cold, Carey felt a soaring elation riding Firefly that morning. The rush lifted her spirits and lightened her heart. She would have loved to have kept going, flying forever, but knew it was impossible. Some other day perhaps.

Just a mile from Burtonport they dismounted. Kat wrapped a scarf around her neck to hide the ghastly mark it bore. A sight like that would cause trouble and Kat could not stand to have it seen on her.

Carefully they blended themselves in with a long band of people travelling to the city. The people were a mix of both common and Traveller background and the air was tense with excitement.

An old man leading a donkey and trading cart was travelling beside Carey. She noticed the lack of trade in his carriage.

"Excuse me for asking, but why are you and all these other people travelling to Burtonport? I noticed that you had nothing to trade," Carey said pointedly.

The man looked her up and down with slight distaste then grunted.

"Aye. I am not 'ere to trade. They're makin' an important anuncemen' to th' people. Somethin' to do with th' future of Ireland I've heard."

Carey was intrigued by this. "Do you know anything else?"

But the man ignored her. It seemed he did not favour her appearance. Many of the other common travellers gave them the cold shoulder, visibly displaying their dislike. Firefly made it even more difficult to travel inconspicuously and they were all glad to arrive in Burtonport unscathed.

"I swear, those people looked ready to kill," Ji said.

Kat nodded in agreement. "It's getting almost as dangerous to travel as Travellers as it is ourselves. Now, if I remember rightly, they stay by the shore in a caravan settlement. It's about as safe as we can hope for so we'll be staying there for now. We might even find someone to camp with – Travellers are generally friendly towards us. Similar thought plane, you see..."

The settlement, as Kat described, was made up like a small village all of its own; there were many a rig set up, row after row, wide alleyways weaving themselves throughout. When they reached the settlement, Carey gaped; she never knew there were so many Travellers in Ireland. Coloured wagons of brilliant radiance were scattered in a strange orderly fashion throughout the large green field. Brilliantly dyed silk flags not unlike those of Seramina's rig fluttered in the wind; small private fires here and there were being lit for later heat.

The three of them and Firefly walked quietly through the sprawling maze, watching Traveller children play alongside them and elderly folk smoke long pipes and talk wildly. As they turned a corner, a tall, dark-haired girl ran headlong into Carey, sending them both head over heels.

"Ow!" Carey muttered, holding her head.

The girl stood up and quickly dusted herself off. She held out her hand to help Carey up. "Oh my! I am so sorry! Are you all right? My gosh, I didn't even see you! It was all my fault! I am so – oh!"

The girl had caught sight of Carey's gold necklace which had slipped out over the neck of the blouse, and in excitement, let go of her hand, dropping Carey to the ground again. The girl held her hand to her mouth. "You're – you're a – a–"

"Ji, could you help me up?" Carey said in irritation, her head still ringing.

The girl shook her head. "Oh my. No, no. Here. I am really, *really* sorry about this. I never thought I'd meet a real Seeker," she said, helping Carey up carefully. "Do you have anywhere to stay tonight? Or are you just passing through? You really should stay. You could meet my mother! Come! She will be so happy to meet you! My name's Diira Farro, by the way. I'm a noma-witch. We're here for trading but also to hear about this big announcement. Come! This way!"

"Noma-witch?" Carey muttered to Ji.

"Like us but are nomadic, much like Travellers," he muttered back.

"Oh…"

Breathlessly, Diira led them through a complicated series of passageways, telling them how there were twice as many Travellers and magical people here than usual for this time of year.

"No one knows what this announcement is about, but it has to be important. We only heard about it maybe a day or so ago but it spread like wildfire! I mean, look how many people have turned up!"

Diira continued to ramble as they walked. Kat nudged Carey in the ribs. "Guess we have somewhere to stay tonight then. This should be interesting."

Carey could only nod in agreement.

Chapter Twenty-One

Rumours

"Here we are."

They stopped. They were standing beside a large, beautifully painted and cleverly carved wagon. It was made of a deep dark pine and had a distinct antique air. Diira called out and the door swung open. A woman with the same waist-length black hair peered out into the open air and squinted at her visitors.

"Who is it, Diira? It's not those Clurneys again, is it?"

"No, Ma!" Diira hissed. "This is Carey Lee, Katrina Lawrence and Ji Binx. They're going to stay *here* tonight."

Diira's words were heavy with emphasis, willing her mother to make the connection.

The woman frowned. "Lee... Lawrence... Binx... now, where have I – oh!" she gasped. "The three First Families! But what – how..." She picked up her skirts and petticoats and practically flew down the stairs. "Please, sit. Please!"

Carey and the others smiled and accepted the woman's invitation, each sitting themselves on an upturned stump. The woman looked ecstatic. "This is such a wonderful surprise. What brings you here to this part of Burtonport? My daughter didn't do anything–"

"No no, of course not. We kind of just... bumped into her... She's been quite helpful in showing us around," said Kat reassuringly.

The woman frowned at Diira. *"Bumped?"*

Diira sighed exaggeratedly. "Oh really, Ma, it was nothing. I was just off to tell Crissto something and I was in a bit of a hurry – oh *geez*, I'm late! I completely forgot. Excuse me for a bit. Mother, do you need any herbs? I am passing the Herbalist near Crissto's rig if you want me to collect some. She's got some lavender and witch hazel at the moment. I heard she got them from the Ring of Kerry," Diira suggested.

Her mother shook her head. "No, I'm fine with the herbs, Diira. Just go."

Dirra grinned and hurried off. The woman asked them if they wanted something to eat before setting herself down by a burnt out bonfire. She introduced herself as Anoueshka Farro, a noma-witch from the south.

"It was with much pain that our family migrated to this world. The war left us no choice though. We lived in San Veria for a short while but that wasn't the life for us. We would rather risk everything then be stuck in that city. Being underground wasn't the life I wanted, although becoming a noma-witch wasn't what I wanted either but the rise of the Empire made it our only option. Your families were an inspiration for all of us. What they did to them was terrible."

Carey perked up. *"What they did?"*

Anoueshka frowned at her, unsure of whether she was being sincere.

"You don't know?" she asked almost fearfully.

All three of them shook their heads.

"We know nothing beyond their disappearance," Kat said, her eyes wide. "No one was ever able to tell us what happened to them."

Anoueshka sighed heavily, running a hand fretfully through her long hair. "You don't know… well, I suppose if you don't know… your families," she started. "When we heard of your defeat, the Empire sent out a message, an announcement of sorts."

Ji leant forward. "What was the announcement?"

Anoueshka appeared deeply distressed. "They said that the Order had been defeated and that the Empire now had full control. They detailed the capture of your families and said that they were to be made examples of in the other realm. They acknowledged your escape but they left no hope for us. They said that if anyone tried to help you, they would face the worst kind of treatment from the Empire. Not just for them but their families and everyone they know."

The Seekers were silent. Kat was deep in thought while Ji was staring at his hands, his eyes unfocused and his features pained. Carey couldn't stop imagining how her family was being *made an example of.*

"That's why no one wanted to help us. They didn't *want* to betray us, they were just afraid," Kat said.

"Is this warning still in effect? Because then us being here–" Carey started in alarm, but Anoueshka soothed her.

"My dear, the Empire may be formidable, but if you hadn't noticed, we have quite a legion here. Even the true Travellers wouldn't give you up. To tell you the truth, it's because there's no gold involved. You will be safe here."

Silence again descended on the group. Ji had not said anything as yet, still transfixed in his absent-minded state.

"Ji?"

He jumped. "Carey! What in – ? Sorry. Sorry," he said, directing his apology at Anoueshka. "I guess I'm just a tad weary. I forgot where I was for a moment."

Anoueshka smiled at him sympathetically. "You all look like you've come far. If you're not leaving too soon, we're having a small gathering tonight, maybe some song and dance. You're more than welcome. And don't worry yourself, Miss Lee," she directed at Carey, "We will no sooner give you up than join the Empire."

Kat accepted her invitation graciously before falling silent again. Ji was happy enough to change the subject and carried on talking with Anoueshka. Carey was not as easily satiated. She had an idea. Just as Seramina had done, she too would keep a journal. Perhaps through it she could discern some connections between everything that had occurred, some logic. There must be more to the attacks than simple Imperial hatred. It also would provide her an outlet; to get everything off her chest and onto the page may grant her some relief. Maybe then she could figure out how she felt about Ji…

She excused herself, much to Anoueshka's apparent disappointment, and moved to the far side of the carriage. She suddenly realised she had no quill.

"Well that's clever," she muttered to herself, rummaging through the bottom of her bag. She spotted a woman working at her doorstep gazing inquisitively at her. "Do you have a quill I can borrow?"

The woman nodded and withdrew a quill from within her wagon. She gave it to Carey in silence.

"Thank you."

She simply nodded her acknowledgment before disappearing back into her wagon. Carey watched her move out of sight with curiosity. That was odd...

She shifted her attention back to the journal and opened it to a blank page.

"Now let's see," Carey reminisced, holding the quill to her lips.

First, the villages – but those attacks weren't for them... *Jeremy's castle*, she thought with a shudder... the travelling group, which she must admit was partially their fault... the attack at her house...

Then there was the ambush at the inn. She looked down at her wrist where the horrible mark burned. All up, that had been two assaults aimed directly at her, but neither had succeeded in killing her and neither was as bad as the recent attack on Kat. It was rather strange; the attack was such that their consequences would cause Kat to deliberately fade slowly, whereas the others aimed at Ji and herself had been attempts to eliminate them immediately. Carey sunk into deep thought. If they had wanted Kat to die slowly then either the Empire was waiting for something or they were forcing her and Ji to act upon it. They *had* acted upon it. They had collected the Silver Water for Kat... Heat rose in her face as she thought of the small vial in her bag, its potency and the fact that she'd lied to Kat about getting rid of it. Of course the Empire wanted the Silver Water, but why the charade? If they knew where they were, couldn't they just catch them and interrogate them for the whereabouts of the waterfall?

There were also the witch hunts, triggered by the Dark Witch herself –

there was a plan behind them, Carey was sure of it. She just had to figure out what.

Carey carefully considered the string of events in an effort to find some logical connection, to try to see the reason, if there was any. It was as if they were all parts in a bigger picture that she couldn't quite see yet. What would forcefully branding the three of them with the mark do exactly? Carey's constantly revived memories of her family, memories that sent her back to when she was only young, when the Seekers had only just been formed...

Carey twirled her quill pensively then slowly lowered it to the page.

I wonder. Maybe this has something to do with my family, whether Malevolence is trying to tell me something about my past. A message or hint perhaps. But what would memories of my past and trying to kill Kat have in common? Does she want us to do something?

Carey looked over at the others. Anoueshka was talking animatedly with Ji and Kat. She was giving life to the conversation with hand actions and very loud body language. Carey smiled and put her quill back to her paper.

I wonder if this announcement has something to do with it all? But the Irish don't have anything to do with us, or the Empire. Our worlds are completely different. Our war is not their war. The only thing that is linking us right now is those witch hunts. They don't know what real witches are though so what threat is there?

Carey sat for a long time contemplating the same complicated and seemingly unanswerable questions until it was almost dusk. She tried to remember every conversation they'd had about the Empire, which was proving almost impossible. How many had they had? She wrote down everything and anything of importance, however remote, and went through each and every point. First she considered their encounters, going over again and again what she knew, hoping that something would occur to her. When she found herself stuck she turned her attention to this mysterious upcoming announcement. She made notes and jotted down thoughts but no connections between the magical and the common Ireland became apparent. She became deeply frustrated as she tried to coax some kind of reason from it all and several times threw her quill down in disappointment, convinced that it was useless. Malevolence was mad, so therefore, what reason did she have to do what she did?

Biting her quill, she pushed aside her irritation and kept writing. She was so deep in thought that she didn't even notice Ji standing over her. She gave a start.

"Carey?" he asked with a tone of slight concern.

Carey turned back to her journal. "I've been going over everything that's happened since I've joined you. I can't help but feel like everything's linked, that there is some bigger picture."

Ji sat down beside her. "Maybe. Or maybe it's not linked at all."

Carey frowned, looking down at her journal in consternation.

"Look, Carey, you've been sitting over here for hours. How about you relax, just for a little while? We've been going so hard these last few days I know I need a bit of distraction from the chase."

Ji gave her a small smile.

"Mm…" Carey groaned indecisively.

"Come on Carey, *please*. Just forget about the Empire for one night and try to enjoy yourself," Ji pleaded with her.

Carey sighed. She was a little hungry, but she wanted so badly to find the connection. She tapped the journal with her finger, torn. She glanced over at the fire and was surprised by how many people had joined them. She hadn't even noticed. A large beast and spit had been placed in the fire, a tantalizing smell wafting into the night air. A number of people were dancing and singing energetically by the light of the flames as a handful of Travellers played lively music on a whistle and drums. The festive air pulled at Carey. She sought out Kat and was amazed to see her dancing happily with a rather handsome fellow. Her hair flicked out gracefully behind her every time she spun around and she was laughing. She was no longer wearing the scarf and the mark had faded significantly to a faint pink.

Ji held his hand out. Carey stared at him for a second before taking it.

"All right, you win."

Ji smiled. "I always do," he said and dragged her over to the fire.

A young man approached her as they joined the group. He took her hand. "Would you like to dance? I could show you," he asked, pulling her from Ji rather audaciously.

"Ah, Ji?" Carey said uncertainly.

"Go on, Carey. I won't get jealous," he said with a wink.

Carey poked her tongue out at him and let the boy lead her over to the other dancers.

Her partner would have only been perhaps eighteen or nineteen. His skin was dark and tanned and his long black hair was pulled back into a ponytail that trailed down his back. He led her to the centre of the dance floor before turning back to her.

"I'm not a very good dancer, er... "

"Thanasi," the boy said with a grin. "No problem. It doesn't matter really. Just go with the music." Thanasi put his arm tightly around Carey's waist and pulled her into a waltz position. "Let it guide you."

Carey nodded. "Okay," she said nervously and they began to dance.

He spun her out then back in, taking her for a quick two-step. The wind and music swirled around her as they danced about the fire. The background blended together into a colourful eddy of red flame and bright clothes, making her feel giddy. Thanasi twirled her under his arm and Carey laughed, beginning to enjoy herself as the dance progressed. A few minutes later another man cut in, taking Carey from Thanasi for a fast jig. The people on the outside clapped along with the music, laughing and singing. Flushed and feeling slightly light-headed, Carey spun and skipped around the fire, the music catching her and urging her on. The Travellers really knew how to dance and have fun. The music filled her very soul with something intoxicating that made her want to keep going forever. As one song finished and the next started, a striking youth asked her for a dance. He had dazzling green eyes that sparkled in the firelight and beautifully sun-tanned skin. His features were soft and he flashed her a smile not unlike Ji's. Carey cocked her head to the side.

"Ah, hi. You are...?"

"Crissto. Crissto Sharrett," he said, taking her hand and spinning her around delicately.

"Crissto? Diira mentioned you," said Carey, allowing Crissto to lead.

Cristo nodded and smiled again. "Only good things, I hope. Diira's my one."

Carey almost tripped over. "Really? But how do you know?"

He smiled again as if he knew what she was thinking. "We were lucky. Diira's mother, Anoueshka, spotted it."

Carey spun out. "Spotted what?"

Crissto pulled her back in. "Our joined auras. She's an aura Seer, amongst other things. She can See the life forces that join us to our bond mate. I met Diira at a Spring Festival not long ago and Anoueshka saw it straight away."

Carey raised an eyebrow. An aura Seer. She had never heard of that before. "What does an aura look like?"

Crissto shrugged. "I don't really know myself but Anoueshka's tried to explain it to me. I still don't get it though," he laughed as he dipped Carey.

She laughed as he swung her back up.

"I don't know. They look kind of like an invisible mist that surrounds each person and everyone's is different. Well, that's how I interpreted it."

Carey smiled, intrigued by the idea of knowing one's other half through their aura. *I must ask Anoueshka about them later.* "So," Carey asked, "you're a wizard? Or are you like Diira, a noma-witch? I mean, if it's not too bold a thing to ask."

Crissto shook his head. "Not at all. I'm like Diira. My mother and father thought it would be safer for me to stay with Travellers. Of course it wasn't ideal, but then again, if they hadn't taken me in, I would never have met Diira. I wish they could have met her."

Crissto's smile faltered as he spoke of his parents.

"Wish?"

Crissto hesitated, obviously debating with himself about whether to carry on. He spoke in a low voice.

"My father was in the Order as a kind of double spy. He worked closely with Lady Parnell. He found out some really terrible things, mostly plots against the rebels. The Empire didn't like it when they found out about it...

It was a long time ago..."

Carey's heart lurched at what his words implied. "I'm so sorry..." was all she could manage.

Crissto shook his head. "Don't be sorry. They died fighting for what they believed in and I have no doubt that they died without any regrets. I was only young but I remember wanting to fight for them after they died. The Order fell long before I could reach of age though and I've never had the chance to fight for them. I had my grandmother to care for and everyone knew that if any one of us tried to take up the fight with the Empire, they wouldn't just destroy us but everyone we knew. So many of us would have joined the fight if it weren't for that."

Carey was silent. They had stopped dancing and they were just standing there, Crissto still holding her hands. What could she say? She had nothing to say to Crissto that could possibly bring him any solace after what he and his family had suffered.

"Don't worry though, Miss Carey. Your being here may be dangerous but we are no longer scared. The Empire may own our freedom, but your return has given us hope, and that is more than any of us have had for a very long time."

The song came to an end and Crissto lead Carey back to her seat. He bowed to her again and she thanked him for the dance. She watched him walk away with a feeling of great pity. The war had truly taken its toll. She wanted to make things right but there were scars that she knew she'd never be able to fix. Somehow she felt a part of this was her, as a Seeker's fault – her family's fault. The decisions they had made had determined so much of the war and people had suffered. They had tried to do the right thing and still they couldn't win. Carey was learning that no matter how hard they tried, they couldn't protect everyone. This was what war brought, and no matter how bad it was, they had to continue to fight for the freedom of their people, endeavour to bring them the peace they deserved. Yet what kind of peace would people like Crissto ever have?

Still watching Crissto, someone flopped down beside her; it was Kat and she was grinning like a lunatic. She flicked back her hair and let out a long sigh. "This is unbelievable! I've never had so much fun in my life! Except for maybe the Spring Festivals we used to have. Listen to that music! My mother used to play the penny whistle. *I loved Spring Festivals*. They used to have these special performances and light shows and dancing and the most delicious apple cider and sugar cakes. And the *costumes*! We used to wear the most beautiful costumes, with yellow feathers and dyed scarves and – oh, how I miss it! You know, you'd absolutely love it," Kat babbled on like an excited child.

Carey had never seen her so happy. Her eyes were alight with a crazy kind of ecstasy and even before she had caught her breath, she was up dancing again with a new burst of energy. Carey shook her head – she didn't know where Kat got her energy from. All she knew was that right now she felt exhausted to her very core. She continued to watch Kat dance about for a few minutes, how her skirt ruffled out as she spun around and the way she skipped lightly around the dance floor. She was practically radiating.

"Carey!"

Shaken from her thoughts, Carey looked over to see Ji excusing himself from the group he had been chatting with. Carey squinted at him as he approached. "Yes?"

He cleared his throat. "I saw you dancing with Crissto. You two seemed… close," he teased.

"We were just planning to run away with each other," she smirked.

"Sure you were," he said, rolling his eyes. "Ah… you're going to hate me for this but–" he held out his hand, " – would you care to dance?"

Carey pursed her lips pensively and nodded slowly. "I suppose I could be persuaded."

She took his hand and he led her over to the dance circle. Ji took her left hand and placed it on his shoulder. He placed his arm around her waist then held out his leading hand. Carey took it gently as the musicians struck up a slow tune. Diira and Crissto walked past them and joined them on the dance floor. Crissto caught her eye and inclined his head graciously. She nodded in return and watched him lead Diira to the other side of the fire.

Ji moved his hand. "Shall we?"

Carey looked up at him. "Of course."

They began to dance, rotating slowly on the spot at first before Ji swept Carey away in a graceful waltz, weaving their way through the other dancers. Ji spun Carey gently under his arm and she stared up into his eyes, his smile hypnotizing her. He pushed back the hair from her face and Carey blushed.

"You know, your dancing's not half bad," Ji quipped.

Carey tightened her lips. "Oh really? Not half?" she laughed. "Can I tell you a secret? I've never actually danced before."

"Oh I don't know. You were always dancing circles around me when we were younger."

"Really?"

Ji winked. "Really. So how about you take me for a spin?" he said as the music sped up.

They danced and danced until they found themselves staggering from the dance space in exhaustion. For Carey it had a euphoric effect; it was such a rush. The excitement and joy of those around them was infectious and for a moment she was uplifted and her worries receded.

Walking back to their seats, Carey stumbled in pain. "Ah…!"

Ji caught her. "Whoa, hang on there. Need a little help?"

Carey shook her head. "Ow… I guess I'm just not used to dancing this much. It's my ankle. Ah… I think I'll go – ow – find Anoueshka. She might have something. Sit, sit. I'll be back in a second."

"Don't be silly, Carey. Here – sit over here for a second and I'll go find Anoueshka."

Ji helped her over the far end of the wagon and sat Carey down on a spare log before hurrying off to find Anoueshka. Leaning back against the smooth wooden body of the wagon, Carey closed her eyes. She listened to the laughter and music as it swirled around her, enjoying the atmosphere it provided when she noticed something amiss. Somewhere behind her, away from the party, came the sound of people whispering urgently. Carey opened her eyes and turned slowly; whoever it was, was hidden by the shadows of the rig. The conversation seemed serious and Carey, not wanting to eavesdrop, made to move but stopped at the mention of auras.

"...I Saw their auras and it was the strangest thing. I've never Seen anything like it before."

"Why? Are their auras like Crissto's and mine? What was so strange about them?"

Carey recognised the voices at once despite the noise from the fire; it was Diira and Anoueshka. Who were they talking about so urgently? Forgetting her decision to retreat, Carey moved a little closer to the end of the wagon.

"I don't think they are what they seem. Tifala said something to me just before – I think she noticed it too. I've never seen an undercurrent like theirs before. It was the shape – it was so unusual. Parts of their auras were connected like yours and Crissto's, but there were other parts that weren't. They joined, but not completely. His aura was calm where they were connected but it was fighting where it wasn't. No... not fighting... overpowering. It was trying to overpower hers, trying to... take control of her aura almost. It's almost as if he's hiding something."

"Hiding? Hiding what though? How about hers? Was hers normal?"

"Well that was even stranger. Hers was completely... calm, almost oblivious to the other. Her aura wasn't struggling or fighting. She's either been kept from the truth or been bewitched, which I hardly think is possible considering who they are. There must be something violent or powerful about him though to streak his aura like that. Or he has an ulterior motive she doesn't know about. An aura always shows the person's inner self in a way, inner emotions and intentions. If their auras depict what is inside, then it shows, on one hand, his feelings for her but on the other... some other intention. There must be something strange that Master Ji isn't – shh... did you hear something?"

Carey froze. Anoueshka and Diira fell silent, obviously listening for intruders. Despite a burning desire to let them continue, she couldn't keep eavesdropping. She had to make herself known and just hope she didn't reveal to them that she'd overheard their conversation. She pulled herself up and stepped out from behind the rig. "Anoueshka? Um – I've been looking for you. I – er, hurt my ankle dancing, and I was wondering whether you had anything that might help it – oh, I'm sorry! Was I interrupting something?" Carey said, feigning sincerity.

Anoueshka gave Diira a quick glance then looked kindly on Carey. "Of course I have something for that ankle of yours. Come, I have all my herbs inside. Diira, could you please go and tell the rest of them to settle down? We don't want any sheriffs coming around here with their idea that all Travellers are bad or something... Commoners don't have a clue."

Anoueshka walked Carey around to the front of the wagon, babbling in a way that made Carey feel as though she was trying desperately to act normal as they climbed up the stairs.

"They're already paranoid as it is what with witch hunts being issued. And don't think I don't know where they're going with those either. Burnings. Urgh, horrible things they are. Nearly a whole generation of my family were burnt during the seventeen

hundreds–"

"Burnings?"

Anoueshka nodded. "As medieval as they are, it's the only way I see these *witch hunts* going."

Carey's mind began to race. She suddenly forgot about everything she'd just overheard as she stood in Anoueshka's doorway, overcome with the thought of flames and screams.

"I didn't know the witch hunt idea had actually been acted upon," Carey said in a small voice, thinking back to the article she had read in the tavern.

"Oh aye," Anoueshka said as she rummaged through a cupboard above her head. "They've not really managed to catch any real witches or wizards just yet but it's only a matter of time. They've come close, although how, I'm not sure. Only a witch or wizard would know how to get around the protections we have set up."

Unbeknownst to her, Anoueshka's last statement hit Carey with the force of a runaway train.

"Commoner's have got through?" Carey asked, trying to keep her voice from shaking. "How is that possible?"

Anoueshka looked at her for a moment before gasping with realisation as to what she was suggesting.

"You don't think–"

But Carey was already out the door and racing to find Kat and Ji, ignoring the pain in her ankle.

"Ji! Kat! Kat, come here!" she shouted over the noise, trying to find them within the thicket of dancers.

Looking slightly irritated at having been dragged from her dance partner, Kat walked over to her. They were joined a moment later by Ji.

"Carey, what is it?"

"I think I might know what tomorrow's announcement will be about. Anoueshka said something and I think that might be it. But there's something else. Something worse."

Frowning slightly, Kat crossed her arms. "What did she say?"

Carey took a deep breath and relayed her conversation with Anoueshka. Kat and Ji's eyes widened as she spoke.

"I really hope you're not thinking what I think you're thinking," Ji said without a hint of humour.

"You think the Empire is helping the Commoners," Kat said, laying out bare the terrible thought that had planted itself in Carey's mind. She nodded.

Kat shook her head. "But why? Why would the Empire do that?"

Carey leaned up against a nearby tree and stared down at her hands. "Here's what I think. I think Malevolence provoked the Commoners by attacking villages which has lead to these witch hunts. That's why those men attacked us at the inn; they didn't think Kat was mad – they guessed what we were. Perhaps there is some kind of reward for people who catch a witch. But what if they want to go further than just catching us? What if they want to reinstate burnings? The thing is, Commoners aren't very good at spotting the real deal so rather than actually catching anyone of any real magical background, they're simply executing some poor Traveller or common folk. That's where the Empire come in. There are so many witches and wizards living in this realm that it would be impossible for the Empire to go around looking for every single one. However, give the Commoners the tools to find a real witch or wizard–"

"And they'd be able to do the Empire's dirty work for them," Ji finished quietly.

Kat was pacing now, her head down in concentration. "And once they'd been caught, the Commoners would be able to have them executed by way of burning. And you think that this announcement tomorrow is about that, that they want to bring them back?"

Carey nodded silently. Kat looked back over at the campfire with wide eyes. "If that's true, then everyone here is in danger."

"It's a trap," Ji said as he ran his hands through his hair with a tone of despair.

"That's exactly what I thought," Carey replied as she watched Crissto dancing with Diira. "Look how many have come. Make a big enough deal and everyone will come. As soon as they make the announcement..." She couldn't begin to imagine what might happen. She knew there were some Commoners out there who didn't think this kind of violence was warranted, but they represented the small majority. How many would be out looking for blood? How many would go to any length to avenge their countrymen of the wrongs that had occurred?

"Look, let's not get too ahead of ourselves just yet," Kat said rationally. "This is all merely speculation. That said," she said, holding up her hand as Carey went to interject, "we should get word out. Make sure we tell as many people as we can to be on their guard. Whatever this announcement is, we need to be ready."

And with those words she strode off towards the camp. Carey flopped onto the ground and buried her head in her hands. Ji sat down next to her but she didn't look up.

"Ji, do you sometimes wish everything was different? Don't you wish we could be normal?" she asked as she stared down at the grass.

Ji was quiet for a moment before answering. "I remember something my father once said to Zacharia. He said, 'We cannot afford to waste our time on dreams and 'what-ifs'. If we are to dream, we should only dream of the possibilities.' He was trying to say that anything is possible, even a normal life. But was can't dwell on what we don't have. I try to remember that, every day. I've sunk myself more than once into a pit of despair because I couldn't stop thinking of everything we'll probably never have or that is just out of our reach. But every now and then, I like to think of what it would be like to be normal and you know what I end up realising?"

Carey looked up. "What?"

Ji grinned. "That it would be completely and utterly boring."

She placed her head back in her hands. "Helpful, you are."

Carey had to agree though. She couldn't let her wishes of an improbable life cloud her. She had already tasted the bitterness of that particular dream. Carey had to try and accept what she had been given. Perhaps life had something better in store for her, perhaps not just yet. Now that was at least a dream she could hold on to.

Chapter Twenty-Two

True Powers

"I remember learning about witch burnings in the orphanage. It always seemed to be a popular topic with Ms Rorx, funnily enough. I remember her saying that they were always held in the village square or at least somewhere nice and public for everyone to see. Noon was always a common time for things like burnings and hangings but there'd be an instance every now and then when it would be held at dawn. It depends though. Well, whenever it might be, we have at least two hours to figure something out. What do you think?"

"All right Ji, what type of magic do you recommend for this situation? That is, presuming we're facing a crowd of hostile townsfolk out to watch a burning."

"I was thinking memory replacement. Make them think they're seeing something else other than what is actually going on. I could imagine it all but the power to work it will need the three of us."

"I think we can handle that."

"So how exactly will we do this?"

It was very early morning and the three Seekers were sitting around the blackened coals of the bonfire. The three of them had managed to get the word out to as many as they could about what the announcement might hold and for everyone to be ready to flee should the time come. Carey could feel the tiredness hanging from her eyes, and she was a little lethargic in her movements. Kat and Ji, however, seemed perfectly alert as if they had had a full night's sleep. Secretly she envied them as she struggled to concentrate.

"I'll need you and Kat to concentrate on clearing their minds. I'll plant the memory. I'll make it so they think they're watching the burning when in actual fact they won't be. While they're under the spell, we'll freeze the fire just long enough to rescue the poor person they're trying to incinerate and take them somewhere safe. The townsfolk won't know the difference and what they don't know can't hurt them, or better, us."

"So it's like an illusion," said Carey, impressed by the idea.

"Exactly. We could dance around stark naked and they wouldn't see us," said Kat wryly.

Carey giggled in disgust. "Ah, no thanks. I think I'll pass."

"So after we've extracted whoever it is we're saving, where do we go then? We can't come back to the camp, we can't risk it. We'd put everyone here in danger."

"Oh right," said Kat. "I forgot to tell you. Ji, you really need to pick up the slack when I forget to tell Carey things like this! We know a Councillor from the Centre City who lives nearby. He's been hiding in this city since the war, luckily for us. I don't know what we would have done if this had happened anywhere else. I'm hoping he's Seen us coming." Seeing Carey's look of confusion, Kat clarified by adding, "He's a Seer."

She looked up at the lightening sky. "I think we should leave soon, go and see if we can find anything out beforehand."

Carey nodded in agreement; as she stood she could feel the onset of nerves flickering at the edges of her stomach.

"All right then. Before we leave though, I've got to go and see Crissto," Ji said.

"Yes, and I'm just off to see something," Kat said cryptically and was gone before either of them could question her.

Carey suddenly found herself all alone.

"Well I guess I'll just stay here," she said to herself, looking around.

The campsite was already starting to wake, even at this early hour; energy ran through the air like electricity. Children ran about playfully, laughing and screaming as they tackled each other in a game of tag, blissfully unaware of the dangers this day could bring should Carey's guess turn out to be correct. Adults walked about, the colours of their clothes swirling through the air in a vibrant collage. The brightness did extend to their faces though which were taut with concern. Carey suddenly felt responsible for these people, these strangers she barely knew. She had to protect them from whatever came of today, and everything that followed. Their concerns and fears should be hers, not theirs to be burdened with.

She watched for a few more minutes before taking out the journal.

I can't help thinking I've forgotten something. It was definitely something important but I just can't seem to remember what. All this talk about burnings has made me forget everything else. Such a barbaric thing. What do Commoners think they'll achieve by burning us? And why burning? It's so horrific and I'm so incredibly nervous. What if our plan fails? I know that with all three of us working together we stand a good chance but what if something does happen? What if it all goes wrong? I really hope we've been completely wrong about it all and it's just a simple announcement about taxes or something as equally mundane.

Carey paused and took a deep breath. She placed her quill down on her page and squinted up into the sky. The sun had risen and the greyish tinge and fleeting clouds were the only signs to show that winter was on its way. The temperature had certainly dropped, forcing Carey to don a light cloak in order to warm herself a little.

She looked over at a group of children huddled by a small fire and noticed one of them staring at her. She looked familiar but Carey couldn't quite figure out where she had seen her before. Her small round face held little of childlike innocence; it was dark and intense, different to those around her. She was staring at Carey with a ferocity that made Carey abandon her journal and take notice. Her play-friends hadn't noticed the withdrawal of their companion; in fact, it was as if they weren't aware of her at all. Her clothes and appearance were a stark contrast to the others, all dark and dirty. Carey looked back at her, waiting for her to look away in discomfort but the child kept staring as if she was waiting for something to happen. Her gaze was unwavering and nothing seemed to distract her, not even the shower of coloured sparks that the children beside her had managed to conjure from the fire. She was still and calm and there was something almost sinister behind her eyes and Carey began to feel unnerved by her. It was as though the girl was trying to pull her in, trying to coax something from her. All other things became obsolete as the two of them stared at each other. A strange muteness descended over them and a darkness blocked everything else from her consciousness. Carey stood up, wanting to approach the girl.

"So, are you ready?"

Carey jumped. The darkness lifted and the sounds of the camp came flooding back. Ji was standing next to her.

"Oh! Ji! Umm…" she turned back to where the children were playing but the mysterious girl had disappeared. She spun around, searching for her; Carey wanted to know who she was.

"Ah, Carey? What are you looking for?"

She continued to search. "There was this girl. It was… so strange. She just kept staring at me but now… I can't see her. It's as if she just disappeared. Ji, you should have seen her. It was really–"

"Carey," Ji said, gripping her by the shoulders. "Why are you worried about it? It was probably nothing."

She shook her head. "No, you don't understand. It was as if she knew something."

"But she's gone now, right? We've got bigger things to worry about right now, don't you think?" he asked, releasing her.

Carey stopped. What was she thinking? "Yes, sorry, of course we do. It was just… Where's Kat?"

"Right here," came Kat's voice as she rounded the corner of a neighbouring wagon.

"Where have you been?" Ji asked with a hint of suspicion.

"Just confirming our suspicions," she said as she joined them.

"What?" Carey asked in surprise, all thoughts of the strange girl vanishing in an instant. "You confirmed? But how?"

"Oh, you know, a little bit of coercion, a touch of persuasion and just a hint of luck."

"You found a really thick guard, didn't you?" Ji asked with a smirk.

Kat coughed in indignation but didn't answer.

"Like I said, it's what you suspected, Carey, right on target in fact. They're going to announce witch burnings and apparently there is going to be *a lot* of people out there to hear all about it. We need to move now if we want to get in close though. The announcement is due to happen within the hour so it doesn't give us much time."

"Within the hour?" Carey repeated in alarm, not truly expecting it to happen so quickly.

"Yes, so I think it's about time we said goodbye to Anoueshka and got going."

"Did you know she was an Aura Seer?" Ji said casually as they went to find her.

At the very mention of the word *aura*, Carey had a rush of memories. The whispered conversation between Diira and Anoueshka came flooding back and Carey now remembered what it was she had forgotten. Ji's strange aura had caught Anoueshka's attention and Carey hadn't liked what she had heard. She wanted to know more, find out what it meant but she didn't know how to ask. After all, she had been eavesdropping at the time and besides, did she really want to find out what Anoueshka knew about Ji? Would it be something that she would rather not know? Carey thought she knew him and Kat would surely have told her if something was amiss. Anoueshka had only just met him. In fact, Anoueshka barely even knew Ji. Even if she was some Aura Seer, she didn't know anything about him or what he had been through over the years. All of that could be the reason she had seen something strange in his aura, surely. How could it not affect him?

She was torn. If Anoueshka knew something, she wanted to know, but if it was nothing, if it were untrue, then asking would first of all expose her deception and second, it would harm Ji's trust. She trusted him, more than perhaps she trusted herself at times. She didn't want to insult him by insinuating that he was hiding something from her.

They soon found Anoueshka talking amongst a group of women.

"There you are! I had begun to wonder if you had left without saying farewell," she said, clasping Kat's hand in her own.

"Of course not! It was wonderful meeting you. Thank you so much for helping us."

"Oh no, it was no problem." Anoueshka said as her smile wavered. "And do be careful. If you're right, there could be a lot of trouble."

Kat nodded and thanked her again before stepping aside for Carey.

Carey received a hug, and as Anoueshka pulled away she appeared worried.

"Is everything all right, Carey?"

Carey looked her in the eye and her heart stilled for only a moment. "Yes, everything's fine. Thank you for everything."

She had a feeling that she would regret not asking Anoueshka about what she had overheard but there were more pressing issues to be dealt with at that moment.

After bidding their final farewells, they set off for the main part of town, towards the town square. They made their way through the colourful alleyways and Carey felt a great sadness as they found themselves in the miserable grey streets of Burtonport. The smoke-stained walls of the houses towered on either side of the street and Carey peered cautiously up into the windows. Curtains snapped shut as they passed and she could feel the hostility and danger growing by the minute. She hastened her steps.

"So how are we going to do this?" she asked, trying to ignore the half-hidden glares.

"Well, when it comes to it, I'm going to need to be in between you two," Ji said, positioning himself between them in demonstration. "If you each take one of my hands, the magic will be stronger. Concentrate on clearing their minds and then focus everything you have through me."

"Sounds easy enough," Kat commented confidently.

Carey couldn't bring herself to say anything. She was worried about whether she'd be able to conjure the magic needed when the time came. Ji must have noticed her nervous silence and he took her hand and squeezed it reassuringly.

"Don't worry. You'll be fine," he whispered.

He held her hand a little longer than usual before releasing it. Carey didn't respond but felt comfort replace the usual embarrassment that would have followed such intimacy. She noticed a measure of assurance begin to sneak in. She smiled gratefully at Ji but he wasn't looking. She quickly realised why.

They had come up behind a very large crowd. Carey's stomach dropped a few notches and Kat tightened her scarf cautiously around her neck. There were people of all ages and types gathered, from young school children to elderly men and women, Traveller and commoner. It was loud and buzzing with expectation though Carey noticed the Traveller-folk had placed themselves on the fringe of the gathering mass.

Leaving Firefly behind in a deserted alleyway, the three of them edged their way around the crowd, trying to catch a glimpse of the small wooden stage that had been erected in the centre of the square. It was bare for the moment yet soldiers stood post guarding it, creating a wide berth around the structure.

People in the crowd shouted impatiently at the guards while others waited silently. Carey could feel the tension between the two groups of people and she stayed close to Kat and Ji, afraid that they would become separated amongst the multitudes. The sea of people was growing and it soon became difficult for them to move freely. They managed to get within a couple of metres of the stage before they could move no further.

Then, from across the square came a loud series of shouts and the crowd parted to form a narrow pathway revealing a small band of people, led by a formidable-looking priest. The three Seekers stood and watched as the group approached the platform. The priest ascended the stairs followed by a group of five soldiers. They were surrounding a sixth person whom Carey had difficulty seeing clearly. She stood on tiptoes, trying to catch a glimpse of the victim, but they remained hidden as they climbed onto the platform. The priest signalled for silence; the crowd fell quiet almost instantly, watching intensely. Carey watched the priest as he looked down upon the throng: he was a well-built man with robes of dark grey draped from his shoulders. Atop his head he wore a peaked cap and a rope of heavy beads hung from his neck. These were not, however, what had caught her attention. It was his eyes. They were like ice, so light a grey that they were almost silver and they gleamed with madness, although he seemed quite sane. They reminded her of something but her mind simply refused to remember.

Kat elbowed her in the side, bringing her back to her senses. *"Look!"*

The soldiers had stepped back to reveal their prisoner – a young girl with bright flaming red hair. Carey knew who it was at once – Seramina. She couldn't believe it. From the side of the stage came another two soldiers – one was hauling a roughly hewn post up the stairs whilst the other followed with a bundle of sticks. They set the lot down in the centre of the stage and the town watched in absolute silence as the other guards dragged Seramina to the stake. They began piling bundles of twigs at her feet, ignoring her cries of distress. Tears streamed down her filthy cheeks and her beautiful curly red hair had since been hacked off at her shoulders. Her pleas echoed through the square as the crowd became restless with a mixture of fear, anger and excitement. Some of the crowd were talking anxiously amongst themselves whilst others began yelling and calling out to the people on the stage. Ji gripped her hand and she knew what he was thinking. This could get out of hand very quickly. The soldiers finished piling the wood at Seramina's feet and filed off the platform, leaving only the priest and Seramina in view. The priest cleared his voice.

"Respectable people of Ireland!" he cried, turning around to address all four corners of the square. The crowd became quiet once more. "You have come here, travelled far and wide for this. Today I have an announcement to make on behalf of the King and his church. Over the past year our towns and villages have been plagued by a dreadful force. You have watched your homes burn and your families perish. Why? Because there lives a people amongst us who wish nothing but ill-will and death! We thought we had purged this world of their evil once before but we were wrong and we have paid. But now, *they* must be dealt with.

They must be held accountable for their heathen ways."

He strode over to where Seramina was bound and pointed to her accusingly.

"People of Ireland, we have been taken over by witches once more! Not in more than one hundred years have we seen the likes but here stands proof! Will you stand for it?" the priest roared to the crowd.

A vast majority cried out in agreement but Carey could see the terror in some of her neighbours' eyes. What Travellers she could see were trying in vain to move or make themselves less conspicuous. Carey could only imagine how many of the real Traveller folk would suffer from this instatement. She looked back up at Seramina who was almost beside herself.

The priest held up a silencing hand.

"This witch you see before you has committed the foulest of felonies: the Black Arts! She used her childlike appearance to deceive her victims and bewitched them to obey her every command. This daughter of Darkness has spread her wickedness for too long but today, I will end her evil ways. By the power invested in me by the Crown and the Church, we will begin our purge of this evil. Witch burnings will once again be seen in our lands. Today, she will burn!"

Again the townsfolk cheered. The priest continued. "Witch, what have you to say?" he bellowed.

Seramina coughed through her tears and cried out in a broken voice: "I am innocent! I have done nothing wrong–"

"See how she uses her disguise! With God as my witness, she will burn for her murderous sins!" He paused to accept a flaming torch from one of the soldiers. "Now I return you, *witch*, back to the hell in which you were conceived. Let us see the world into a new era. Let them all burn!"

The priest lowered the torch. Seramina kicked at her bindings and struggled desperately against the ropes. Ji squeezed her hand. "Ready?" he whispered.

The priest sneered as the fire caught and the townsfolk erupted with a tumultuous bellow.

"Now!" Ji roared over the noise.

Carey closed her eyes and reached down deep. She thought only of clearing their minds, wiping their existence from the townsfolk's memories. The magic tingled down her arm and into her hand. She hoped it was enough.

There was silence; Carey's eyes snapped open. The crowd had frozen. Then, with a BANG as loud as a cannon and a blinding flash of white, the crowd resumed its shouting and jeering. Without a second's hesitation, Ji took off, pushing his way through the crowd, Carey in tow. Kat was beside her, fighting towards the stage, her eyes locked on Seramina. They pushed past the guarding soldiers and Carey leapt on to the stage to find herself face to face with the priest. She almost fell back off the platform in surprise but he did not react; the spell was working.

"It's working!" she shouted.

"We know! Now come and help us!" Kat yelled back, making her way over to the burning pyre.

There was something about the priest that caused a stirring inside Carey. It was as if she had seen him somewhere before.

Carey joined Kat and Ji but was repelled by the heat. She tried spotting Seramina amongst the plumes of swirling grey smoke but it had grown too thick. Then there came a shout from behind, a cry that made Carey turn around.

Out of the corner of her eye she saw the priest, bearing down on her, the burnt-out fire torch above his head. He shouted again, but this time he struck out. *"For the Empire!"*

Before she could think to move, Carey was struck hard over the head with the lump of wood. She fell to her knees, the pain blinding her. The crowd swirled in confusing torrents before her eyes, making her head feel thick and heavy. The priest, recovering from the first blow, swung the torch up over his head and screamed murderously. He lunged at her, ready to attack again. Just past him came dozens of Imperials in long capes, pushing their way through the spellbound crowd. Dazed, Carey simply stared. They had escaped the spell. How had they escaped it...?

Shaking the dizziness from her head, Carey ducked just in time, the priest's torch so close that her hair ruffled as it flew past. She screamed for Kat as she scrambled out of his path, stumbling awkwardly to her feet. She raised her hand, trying desperately to steady herself. No priest was going to take her with a piece of wood. From within, the strange magic stirred again but this time, instead of being captivated by it, she used it. Taking hold of it, Carey forced it up and out through her fingertips.

The advancing priest was knocked backwards by the force of the magic, taking out six Imperials that had been making their way up onto the platform with him.

Then there was an odd kind of flickering in the air and suddenly everything froze again. Everyone, including the Imperials, stopped. An eerie silence fell over the entire city that was only broken by the crackle of the fire. Carey whipped around to see Kat standing with her arms outstretched; she had frozen the crowd. Carey could hear Ji coughing within the thicket of greyish smoke.

"Ji…" she said absent-mindedly, but before she had moved a step, there was a loud hiss and the smoke rose away from them in great plumes.

There was a snapping of twigs and murmuring of words before Carey heard Ji holler, "Quick, let's go!" and saw him jump from the stage, Seramina limp in his arms.

Trying to run through the mass of frozen townsfolk proved difficult – the bystanders were as hard as carved stone – yet despite this, the three of them managed it just in time. Freeing themselves from the crowd, they stumbled into the dark alleyway where Firefly lay hidden, and not a moment too soon. As they threw themselves into the shadows, the crowd erupted. Glancing back, Carey was delighted to see the Imperials falling over themselves, confused and evidently annoyed. The priest was enraged and cussing worse than a drunken sailor.

"Well I can tell you this – you'll never see another priest like that in this lifetime!" Ji said, puffing with adrenalin. "Carey, how's your head?"

Carey rubbed it warily and felt a sticky something in her matted hair. She looked at her fingers then wiped them on her skirt, hastily rubbing the blood from them. "It's nothing that'll kill me. I'll survive for now."

"Are you sure?"

"Pretty sure."

"All right, come on then. We have to get to the Councillor's house before the Imperials find us," he said, readjusting Seramina in his arms. "After you."

Firefly was waiting patiently, unperturbed by what was happening around her. Leading her away, Carey kept to the shadows, following Kat as they made their way quickly through the backstreets of Burtonport. The events of the platform kept flashing through her head and only one thing seemed glaringly obvious.

"There was someone who knew our plan back there, wasn't there?"

Kat nodded in agreement. "I was thinking the same thing. How else would they have been able to escape our spell? We really should have been a little more careful back there in the camp."

Ji grunted. "Spies, of course. Our magic was good, but if they had known, it would have been easy to deflect. Although, the way you froze that crowd, Kat. That was incredibly risky."

Carey snorted. "Truly Ji, did you really think that any of that wasn't risky in the first..."

She trailed off. Carey had turned to Ji, who was lagging a few steps behind with Seramina, to find a terrifying vision.

A tall, hooded figure had stepped out of the shadows of a side alleyway. Noticing Carey's expression, Ji tried to turn but he was too slow; the figure raised what looked like a wooden staff and deep red sparks flew from its tip.

Carey screamed as Ji stiffened and fell hard to the ground. Seramina rolled limply from his arms and onto the cobblestones. The man began to laugh and it chilled Carey to the bone. Not discouraged by this intruder's sudden appearance, Kat stepped up, hands raised and ready to attack.

Without even stopping, the man lifted his staff again. "*Freeze!*" he commanded.

Kat halted in obedience. She did not move; it was as if she was set in time. Even the sparks from the curse she was about to perform were still hovering about her hand.

Her heart pounding in her chest, Carey turned slowly back to their assailant, raising her hands in surrender as she did. The man kept his staff pointed at her but did not attack. She could feel him watching her, considering her. He was waiting. Summoning what courage she had, Carey called out to him.

"Who... who are you? What do you want?"

The man took a slight step towards her but remained in the shadows so his face was hidden from view.

"I am a... humble servant of her Majesty, the Empress of the Realms and what I want... is you," he said quietly in a slow, deep voice that floated through the air and made Carey's hair stand on end. "There are many after your head, girl, many whose dying wish would be to see to your death. Some think you powerful, but by what I have just accomplished, demonstrates that you are little more than a name that was perhaps powerful a long time ago. Oh, how my Queen will reward me for ridding her of the last, pestering reminders of your wretched Order. I will finally be welcomed into the Centre Ring!"

Carey gaped. He wasn't even a wizard of the council; he was just an Imperial ally, a follower. Somehow the fact that he wasn't a guard made Carey feel a little better. Only a little though. *I just have to keep him talking,* she thought, keeping her attention focused on her faceless opponent.

"And you just want to... kill us? But there are no witnesses," she said, sickened by what she was saying. "How will anyone know it was you? Wouldn't it be better if–"

"No! Killing you would be the *highest honour.* I would be given prestige to rival the greatest of Imperials. I would be sired amongst wizards as the one who destroyed the rebel order completely!

"And you! *You* I will take first. *You* are the granddaughter of that wench Parnell herself and so the greatest danger. But then again, you could be just like your comrades, simply a name and nothing else," he glared. He raised his staff. "Take guard, *Carey Lee!*"

Carey took a sharp breath in. Almost by instinct she shielded herself, charging her power. The wizard aimed his staff and a bright flash of red flew at her. She stumbled backwards as the curse deflected; the force of his magic was strong.

Then she felt it; that other power. It began to flow through her body as if encouraged or provoked by the attack. It tingled beneath her skin, the power warm as it ran through her every vein. The magic built up inside her and made her feel stronger. It was greater than that which had surfaced back on the stage, as if it knew the enormity of the situation and was compensating for it. The confidence that had boosted her once before spread across her chest. She was ready to face this Dæmon.

The wizard laughed mockingly. "Trying to hold me at bay, are we?" he asked, his voice resonating with deep bass tones. "Why waste your energy? We both know how this is going to end…"

Carey ducked to one side, avoiding another hit. Careful not to draw the fight too close to the others, Carey backed away, giving the wizard a clear range away from Kat, Ji and Seramina. Firefly had vanished.

The wizard continued to laugh. "Running away? Backing out? I don't blame you. You are wise for retreating. Much smarter than your Grandmother. Yes, she was too stubborn and stupid to see that her Order was weak and powerless against the Dark rule."

Excuse me?

Carey had not been prepared for this kind of attack; he was taunting her. What was he getting at? The wizard threw off his hood to reveal a scarred visage, distorted and sinister. He smirked. An eerie darkness grew around them, blotting out the light. Shadows developed in the darkest corners of the alleyway and Carey's new-found confidence faltered. She felt the first wave of panic and fear.

No. I have to keep calm… keep calm, Carey told herself sternly. *I will not give into him.*

"If only you had seen her in the early days, offering her people up for the slaughter. I saw it, with my own eyes. No matter how many people died for her sake, she was never satisfied. She was a sadistic leader. It was almost as if she wanted her people to die by the Empire's hand. She was a murderess."

He had struck a nerve and Carey's anger flared at once. *How dare he...* Deflecting a hit, Carey stood firm, rooted to the spot. She could barely remember her Grandmother but she knew one thing for sure – she was not a murderer. Fianna Parnell had fought for the freedom of the oppressed and whoever may have died had done so for the sake of others. The accusation that she was somehow indifferent to their sacrifices burned at Carey's insides. She could feel the anger coursing through her, but she held it back. She couldn't let her judgment be jeopardized by anger. She couldn't... she wouldn't...

The wizard continued, clearly realising the effects of his tormenting. "Fianna Parnell was so blinded by her own stubbornness that she let thousands of people die needlessly. She even led her own family into her trap."

Carey ground her teeth. *It's not true... He's just trying to disarm you...*

"She must have despised her family terribly if she wanted them so badly in her ill-fated Order."

And with those words, Carey's restraint broke. Anger was now coursing through her and she could no longer control it. The tingling beneath her skin became hot and it was as though her blood had been replaced by fire. The magic kept building but there was now something else; something bigger. Carey was almost overwhelmed by its power as it gripped at her heart, begging to be free.

"Yet as stupid and as stubborn as she was, she was nothing, *nothing* compared to your mother and father, who so willingly joined her."

That was the final straw and Carey screamed in fury. She raised her hands and beset the power tugging at her chest onto the unsuspecting wizard. The force drove itself out of her body. A blinding light streamed from her, engulfing her tormentor. Stunned and horrified, he screeched in absolute terror. Unperturbed, Carey stood her ground. The force was creating a strong, dark wind that surrounded her like a hurricane. It whipped her hair back and ruffled her skirt. The light darkened the shadows of her face as she continued to glare at the wizard...

His body jerked forward and Carey watched as his eyes bulged in alarm, his screams caught in his throat. The searing light was pulling back from him, coaxing what looked like a shimmering vapour from his body. It was dragging his soul from the very centre of his being and, in the blink of an eye, swallowed it ruthlessly.

And then there was nothing.

Chapter Twenty-Three

Missing Pieces of the Puzzle

The wizard slumped to the ground and Carey was immediately sick. She didn't understand what had just happened. What was that magic? What was that power that had forced itself from her? It was unlike anything she had ever felt before. Its potential scared her – it scared her more than anything in her life. She lifted her hands to her face; they were shaking uncontrollably. Her heart was racing and she felt light, like she was going to faint…

Kat and Ji jolted back to life.

"Stop!" Kat cried, and the belated curse went flying past Ji's ear as he stood up.

He started. "What in blazes…?"

Kat spun around. "Carey, what happened? The man–"

"Dear Merlin…" Ji breathed as he knelt beside the fallen wizard's body. "What happened to him?"

Carey shook her head; she was completely lost for words. She knew that if she opened her mouth she'd be sick.

"Carey?"

She gulped back the urge to vomit. "I – I don't know," she said in barely a whisper.

She couldn't explain or even begin to explain what had just happened. She couldn't justify the dark, foreboding power that resided within her.

How could she be capable of such... destruction? It was not only this but the way she had felt at the time – gripped by such certainty and strength. She hadn't felt fear or indecision, just the simple notion that she was doing the right thing, the only thing, to protect herself and her friends. And now she had blood on her hands. This notion was as equally terrifying as the deed itself and Carey didn't want to frighten her friends. No, that wasn't it – she didn't want them to be afraid of her. She had done a terrible thing and what was worse was that she couldn't control it either. The only way she could describe the feeling of it was that of a beast tearing itself free of its cage and she definitely wasn't going to tell them that. How could they understand it when she could hardly fathom it herself? So she lied. Again.

"How don't you know? You were the only one that wasn't cursed, weren't you?" Ji asked as he examined the wizard

"I – I really don't know. It was an accident."

"An accident? This looks like Dark magic," said Kat, joining him.

Dark magic. Carey shrugged and tried to act clueless as her stomach lurched unpleasantly.

"The last curse I used – his must've hit mine and... ricocheted back onto him. He was aiming to kill. His powers were ten times greater than mine... easily," Carey lied.

Kat nodded and Carey's shoulders relaxed slightly. Kat believed her...

After a moment's silence, Ji muttered something and the body shrunk, transforming into a rock no bigger than his palm. He knocked it aside. "There. We don't need anything that could lead those Imperials to us."

Despite this unceremonious disposal of her attacker's body, Carey was relieved to be rid of it. She could not, however, rid herself of the images that were now burnt into her mind.

Ji was looking at her curiously now and she turned away, unable to meet his eye.

Kat stood up and dusted herself off. "That was a close call. That guard nearly had us."

"He wasn't a guard."

Kat cocked her head to the side. "What? Not a guard? How do you know?"

Carey helped Ji pick Seramina up off the ground before answering. "He said so himself. Something about being welcomed into Malevolence's Centre Ring if he got rid of us for her."

Carey didn't bother telling them what the wizard had said about her family. She herself would rather forget the taunts than bring them up again for discussion.

"Umm… did you see where Firefly went?" she said, hastily changing the subject.

Firefly wasn't anywhere nearby. They quickly searched the side roads to no avail.

"Come on, we can't stay here. Firefly will find us, don't worry," Kat said, beckoning for the other two to follow.

Carey welcomed her suggestion – she wanted to escape this place as soon as possible.

Silently and with extra caution, Kat led them all to the Councillor's. His thin two-storey house was not a terribly big place and it was inconspicuous. He had managed to blend in with the other Commoners which worked in their favour. It was down a tight, darkened street and nothing about it seemed extraordinary. Especially nothing that hinted a wizard might live there.

Kat knocked on the door and waited. A moment later, a small panel in the door slid back, revealing a curious eye.

"Who calls?"

Kat stepped up to the door. "We are Seekers of the Order of the Rose. Katrina Lawrence, Ji Binx and Carey Lee. Please, we seek refuge."

The eye behind the door quivered, passing over the three Seekers. His gaze paused on the limp form that was Seramina and his eye narrowed. "And who is the one from which the light is fading?"

Kat looked around, slightly confused then exclaimed, "Oh, Seramina? She is but a child, a victim of the hunts. No harm will come from her."

After a short pause, the eye looked satisfied and the panel slid back into place. There was a sliding and clicking of many locks being unlatched and slowly the door opened. Carey followed Kat into the narrow house, gazing about curiously. There was nothing strange or out of place there, but Carey guessed it was all in an effort to dispel suspicion about the Councillor's true identity. He blended in very well and if Carey hadn't known he was a wizard, she would have thought him to be simply another Commoner.

The Councillor was a tall and rather round fellow and he held out a pudgy hand to greet each of them. His pale pastel-blue eyes surveyed them more closely from beneath a pair of thick ginger eyebrows that twitched involuntarily as he spoke. His cheeks were pleasantly rounded as though he constantly had a mouthful of food and his lips were almost nonexistent beneath a large walrus-like moustache. He wore a nondescript tweed coat, his vest stretched uncomfortably tight over his broad stomach and the chain of a pocket watch dangled from his breast pocket. The only hint of his ties to the magical realm was the familiar gold necklace peeking out from beneath his collar.

He cleared his throat. "Welcome, my friends. I have been expecting you. Also, you may find a certain winged-friend of yours that has been waiting also."

"Firefly?" said Carey, glad that she had returned.

"If that is your Pegasus then yes, she is in the back courtyard grazing on my daisies."

Carey nodded gratefully. The Councillor beckoned them to join him in a small tea room. It was filled with a long cushioned lounge chair, two smaller pouffes and a round polished oak tea table. A tall handsome grandfather clock occupied the far wall with its pendulum swinging lazily from side to side. The fireplace was filled with dancing red flames and was radiating such heat that Carey was forced to remove her warm cloak from her shoulders. The whole house smelled vaguely of freshly cut grass but was welcoming. The Councillor sat down, motioning for them to join him, but Carey followed suit when Kat and Ji remained standing.

"Miss Lawrence, why is it you plead sanctuary? I was under the impression that you had long ago learnt the dealings and lie of this land."

"In all truth, Councillor...?"

"Hecate. Julius Hecate."

"Well, in all truth, Councillor Hecate," she said, "it is not us who requires sanctuary. It is the victim we rescued. She is ill and is being hunted at this very moment. Because of this, we will not be able to accommodate her on our journey. We know we are asking a great deal but we humbly request she stays here until it is safe for her return to the outer world."

Councillor Hecate frowned, but ever so slightly. "I see. And what if the search comes beyond my front door? Will she be safe then?"

Carey could see Kat was doing some very quick thinking. She nodded. "Miss Lee and myself have formed a spell that will keep her hidden from any prying eyes. I assure you, no Imperial Guard or, indeed, no Imperial will find her while she is bewitched."

Carey was very surprised by Kat's answer. What spell? She turned to Ji with raised eyebrows; he looked just as surprised.

There was a long pause in which Councillor Hecate considered his decision. It was like waiting for judgement. He dipped his head in assent. "I will provide sanctuary for her as a guest of the Order. I am not one to stand in the way of its success. If Imperial Guards seek me out, I have been fortunate so far and I will fight. As a devotee of the Order's mission, I will care for the girl, for she never anticipated for her path and that of the Empire's to cross. Forever to Lady Parnell I remain ever faithful."

Kat inclined her head to his answer gratefully, but Carey found his devotion to the Order slightly aggravating. Why was he hiding instead of fighting alongside them then if he was so faithful? She was rather irritated and turned her head away from him to look at Seramina, whom Ji was still cradling in his arms. Her brilliant red hair lined her pale face, the marks on her face shining lurid red. The only good sign was that her breathing was steady. Several nasty wounds on her arms and legs needed desperate attendance though. Dried blood stained her shabby brown dress in patches and Carey felt great sympathy towards the young witch.

"Councillor, we need to move Seramina somewhere more comfortable. Do you have a spare room?"

He nodded and recommended moving Seramina into a room in the back.

Still unconscious, Seramina was transferred to a small, dark room that was so hot it acted almost as a furnace within itself. She was placed on the bed and Kat settled herself down to explain her plan.

The Councillor went to fetch a cold towel.

"Ji, can you distract the Councillor? I know he's a member of the Order but we can't trust him," Kat whispered hurriedly whilst keeping her eyes on the door.

Ji nodded and exited the room, closing the door with a snap.

"We really can't trust him? Even though he's in the Order?" Carey asked.

"Especially because of that," Kat said as she made sure Seramina was comfortable.

Carey sighed. They had gone from almost carefree the night before to a state of complete distrust. It was hard to keep up.

"Kat, he's wearing a necklace like ours. Does that mean he was a Seeker because I thought Seekers were just our families?"

Kat shook her head. "In the beginning, when Fianna first created the Seekers, there were a number of groups throughout the world. Not many knew this outside the Order, which is how they wanted it. Unfortunately, many of these groups were destroyed during the war. Those who escaped, like our Councillor here and the grandmother of Seramina's friend, fled. They were secret groups so very few people knew about the movements of other Seekers. They couldn't just join another group and carry on. Many rejoined their families or went into hiding, as you have seen. The reason why so many people believe us to be the only group of Seekers is because that is how your Grandmother wanted it. There was a lot of secrecy in those days, even within our own ranks."

Carey nodded, feeling properly ashamed of her prior anger towards the Councillor. She could see now why these lost Seekers would rather stay hidden: to expose themselves again would be deadly. Seramina was living proof of that mistake.

"All right. So, this spell I've figured out is one that will protect Seramina from Imperials, any Imperials. I've been thinking about it ever since we found out about the burnings–"

"You've been planning it since last night? Well that's good because I thought you were just lying to the Councillor so he would let her stay," Carey said, impressed by Kat's forward thinking. She had had barely enough thought capacity to deal with the burnings.

"Yes, sorry about not telling you. At the time it was more of a vague idea and I guess I thought we just needed to concentrate on the more pressing matters at the time. I knew there'd be someone we would need to save and if it actually was a witch or wizard, they'd need our protection from the Empire.

"The thing is that I couldn't think of any spell I've used before. We've never had to protect someone like this. So I thought, *what could we shield her with*? Then I thought of something, but it might be a bit difficult. We need to give her some of your power."

Carey stared at her blankly; Kat went on. "Let me explain it a little better. You can shield yourself with that power you have, right? It's stronger than any other shield I know. If we were able to take some of that power and give it to Seramina, we could shield her easily."

Carey's stomach lurched. Kat was asking her to use the magic with which she had just killed someone. The very thought made her ill.

"Is there any other way we can do this? Without using that power?" she croaked, barely concealing her aversion to Kat's idea.

Kat stopped, put out by Carey's question. She shook her head slowly. "Umm, I... not really," she said as she considered Carey with narrowed eyes. "Perhaps if we had help... or more – more time. But we have neither and nor does Seramina," she said, looking back down at the young girl. There was no mistaking the desperation in Kat's voice. It was a vulnerability Carey rarely heard and in that moment she saw what this really was for Kat. It was a chance for redemption, for every person, every friend they never had the chance to save. Who knows how many Kat had had to say goodbye to only to have them live on forever in her memories, haunting her, and with that, Carey realised how selfish her own self-pity had been.

"No, you're right," she said with a hand on Kat's shoulder. "Of course you're right. Ignore me. It's just been a long day. You were saying?"

Kat blinked, the panic Carey's almost rejection had brought disappearing. "I was saying that if we can use some of that power of yours, I think we can shield Seramina from anyone that may be looking for her."

"Like when I shielded myself against that flying monster that time?"

Kat shook her head. "No. If you concentrate on her to shield her, you would have to concentrate on her *all* the time. You'd have no other way of doing anything else, your mind would be devoted only to her. But this way, I'm thinking, will protect her from any Dark Wizards – constantly. It will be a long-lasting, though probably not a completely permanent defence. And you won't have to try and concentrate on her all the time. It will be easier to keep her concealed this way."

Carey nodded her head slowly though still not understanding Kat completely. "All right."

"So to do this we will extract a little of your power and bestow it upon Seramina. This will therefore protect her like it protects you."

"And what will happen to me when you make this *extraction*?" Carey asked, not as sure of this plan as Kat was.

"Well, I'd imagine that your power is so potent that even if you remove just a small portion of it, it would replenish itself. You won't even notice it's gone."

Carey chewed her lip in thought, going over Kat's rationale. "Are you sure about this?"

Kat merely shrugged as she brushed Seramina's hair away from her forehead. "I don't really think we have time to be one-hundred per cent certain. I guess I'm about eighty per cent certain it'll work. I know it's a big ask, but I need you to trust me on this."

Carey ran her hand through her matted hair. The bleeding had stopped but it had now congealed into a thick, stiff clump. This day had given her more worries than she cared for but she trusted Kat. If she couldn't trust her, then who could she?

"So, I'm guessing you've worked out a way of getting this?" she asked, her nerves telling her that it would be much harder than it sounded.

"To extract it, yes. I've already devised a spell that should work for this instance. But after I extract it, you will need to focus the particles of your power on Seramina, otherwise it will just disperse. I can help draw it out but because it's your magic, you'll need to give it to her. If this works, it will make her not only resistant to Dark magic, but invisible to Dark wizards as well. They could look around here all they like and never find her," said Kat.

"That's very clever, Kat–"

"Thanks."

" – but I thought you'd never done a spell like this before. How come you seem to think this will work?"

"I've seen something similar before. It's a way of sharing magic."

"But you've never actually done it before?"

"Should we get started?" Kat suggested, side-stepping Carey's last question. "I need you to put your hands on Seramina's forehead first. Think of your magic. Don't use it, just bring it to the forefront, just enough so I can find it. Do you think you can do that?"

Carey nodded nervously, placing her hand gently on Seramina's forehead, all the while silently hoping this would work. Kat laid a single hand on Carey's shoulder and closed her eyes. She began a whispered chant, her body still and relaxed, centred in a kind of mediation. Her chant became steadily faster as Carey reached for that magic, the magic that frightened her beyond anything else, as drops of sweat which had nothing to do with the heat rolled down her forehead. Then she felt it.

Carey gasped. It was as though something had reached deep inside her. It coursed through her, this strange wave. It stopped in her chest. It started to pull, and her breath caught in her lungs. Like a giant invisible fist it gripped her by the heart and was pulling it slowly upwards. It rose from her chest and formed a lump in her throat. Burning pinpricks filled her throat, making her eyes water uncontrollably. She managed to keep her hands on Seramina's head, blinking back the tears. The lump forced its way up her throat and out of her mouth. Carey gulped; before her was a small orb of blinding gold. It reminded her of a star. Its surface wasn't smooth but tiny spikes of light reached out then receded back in on itself.

Carey took a deep breath and focused the magic on Seramina as her heart raced. It moved only slightly. She focused again, this time ignoring the anxiety pulsing through her body and concentrating all her mental strength to push at it. Slowly it began to move towards the young telepath. Sweat poured down Carey's face; she began to shake from the effort. Every muscle ached from being tensed; her teeth were gritted so hard they felt like they were going to break. Carey's breath became uneven as she focused every last fibre of her being on the golden sphere. Eventually it reached Seramina and Carey saw in her mind's eye her power surging over the girl, creating the protection she needed. Suddenly, with a jolt of power, the magic hit the young girl's body while at the same time sending Carey flying over backwards.

"Whoa!"

THUD. Carey hit the floor hard, landing flat on her back. "Ow..." she gasped, winded.

Kat looked down at her, smiling ecstatically. "It worked! We actually did it–"

A sleepy groan interrupted her; Seramina was waking. Her eyes were creeping slowly open and were flicking from side to side sleepily. Upon seeing Kat and Carey standing over her, her eyes snapped open and she threw off her sheets. Terrified, Seramina began desperately trying to push herself into the corner, away from them. She scratched at the walls and pushed at the bed sheets, kicking out at them. "No! No please! Leave me alone – don't hurt me. Please, don't hurt me!" she screeched hysterically, scratching frantically at the stone.

Carey stayed where she was, holding her hands up slowly so Seramina could see she meant no harm. "It's all right, Seramina. We're not going to hurt you. We're not with the Empire."

Seramina stared. "How... how do you know my name? How... do you know m-my name?"

Kat spoke to her calmly and cautiously. "We found your wagon. And we saw what happened – with the Essedarian."

"You *saw*? But you weren't there... you weren't, were you?" Seramina whispered, confused and frightened, her lip quivering.

"It was only a crystal's shadow, what we saw."

Seramina looked them over warily. "A crystal? You're witches? But not from the Empire..."

Carey nodded. "Yes. We saved you from the burning–"

Seramina shook her head. "No... NO! Why didn't you leave me? Why didn't you just leave me?" she screamed feverishly.

Carey was shocked by her response. What had happened to her that she would rather have burned than be saved?

Carefully, she approached Seramina. "What happened to you?"

Seramina sank back down into her bed. For about five quiet minutes she sat there, chewing nervously on her knuckles before she decided to speak. "They took us prisoner, me and my family. They took us somewhere and we got separated. I was all by myself. I wanted my family so badly. They locked me in a dungeon... it was dark and there were rats and... there was a man. And he had these eyes – these terrible eyes. Madman's eyes. But he wasn't though. He was–"

"The man from your dreams?" said Carey.

She remembered now where she had come across the man with the gleaming eyes before – Seramina's journal. He was an Imperial, no doubt. He had to be the same man who had posed as the priest in the square.

Seramina looked at her in surprise. "How do you know about my dreams? Are – are you a telepathist too?" she asked hopefully.

Carey reached down and pulled Seramina's diary from the bottom of her bag. "I found this."

Seramina was slightly taken aback by its appearance. She considered it for a moment, a grimace on her face before shaking her head. "Please, put it away. I don't want it. You can have it. I don't want to remember."

Carey granted her request and placed it back in her bag. Seramina seemed relieved. Despite this, Carey still wanted to know about the man. She felt it was something important she needed to know.

Seramina coughed. "Could I have some water or – or something..."

Kat stood up. "Certainly." And she left. Behind the closed door Carey could hear Ji and Kat talking fast. She turned back to Seramina.

"Seramina, what did the man say?" she said slowly.

Her eyes red with emotion, Seramina bit her lip. "He was a man from the Empire. He – he asked me all these questions. He thought I knew about the Seekers. You know – one of those people from the Order..."

Her eyes fell on Carey's necklace. "You. Your necklace. You're a Seeker?"

Seramina's face darkened at the prospect, so instead of answering her with the obvious, Carey asked; "Why? What did he ask?" But Seramina wasn't so easily put off.

"What is your name?"

She was watching Carey with extreme sincerity which put her off slightly. Seramina was no longer the innocent twelve-year-old Carey had encountered through her journal.

"You're right, I am a Seeker. My parents are Robert and Jenny Lee–"

Seramina drew in a sharp breath. "It was you! *You're* Carey Lee. That man – that man... he asked about you – you and another – *that* other girl... Katrina Lawrence? That was her, wasn't it? He – he kept talking about a Liberator or something. He thought I knew! Because of my necklace Tiana gave me. I was scared... I told him I didn't know anything about it and he g-got angry," Seramina said. "Then – then he – he–"

She began to rock back and forth; she pulled her knees into her chest and put her head down upon them. Carey had a feeling she knew what had happened, what the man had done. The blood stains on her dress were no accident. "You don't have to tell me, Seramina."

Seramina lifted her head. "It hurt me," she said more quietly. "He wouldn't stop. He kept... he kept screaming at me to tell him but – but I couldn't tell him what... what he wanted. I didn't know anything. I didn't know anything."

She stopped and closed her eyes, a lone tear trickling down her cheek. She took a deep breath. "There was this voice. It came from nowhere, but it was all around me. At first I thought I was dreaming it but then the man answered. It told him I didn't know about the Seekers, that I was just a peasant... one of the People." Seramina's voice became louder. "It told the man... it told him to get rid of me! Then I knew – I realised who it was... the voice was her. It was her and she had a plan. She said she knew where the Seekers were going. She said they were going to be in Burtonport and she wanted to catch you but the man had a different idea. He suggested pushing the witch hunts to burnings. He said they'd use me, they'd use me as *bait*! That's how they were going to catch you, by *burning me*!"

Tears were now streaming down her face but she kept her distance from Carey, who had to restrain herself from rushing forward to comfort her. Seramina wiped her nose; she had more to say.

"They planned this in front of me... said that if I was going to... to..." Seramina shook her head, unable to finish the sentence. "They said it didn't make any difference. I was so scared... I didn't want to... *die*... and it was for something I didn't even know about. My Father only ever told me about the adventures he used to have – and about Lady Parnell. I never knew anything about you or – oh no – *my family*!"

"What? What about your family?" Carey asked.

The telepathist was staring wildly from a face now filled with torment. "The man... he used magic on me to... he showed me pictures of my family. They were hurting and he said it would all stop if I helped him. But I couldn't!"

Seramina broke down completely, unable to restrain herself any longer. Pushing aside resistance, Carey took her in her arms; Seramina did not stop her.

"And the thing is," she sobbed into Carey's shoulder, "I can't find them anywhere. I can't feel them. I can always find them... with my mind, but I can't..."

The door creaked open and Kat entered carrying a mug of water.

"Ji's gone to find a boat – what's going on?"

Carey shook her head to silence her. She didn't think Seramina could handle the pain of going over it all again. Kat handed the mug to Seramina and as she turned to drink from it, Kat spoke to Carey.

"We've been talking to Councillor Hecate and he says we have to leave as soon as possible."

"Did he say why?" Carey asked, wiping a bead of sweat from her brow. She hadn't quite realised how hot it was in the tiny room.

Kat nodded. "Apparently there is a prophecy. In his exact words, *'There will come a liberator who will free the world from the evil,'*" Kat said in barely a whisper. "That's all he said, he wouldn't say anymore. He just told us that we had some important part in this and that we have to leave now."

"A Liberator? Seramina said she had been asked about a Liberator during her captivity," Carey whispered. She didn't say, but she was also thinking back to her dream about Ji which was now seeming more and more significant. "Was this a vision he had?"

"All he said was that he has contacts among the mermaids. I think we should listen to him. I know I said not to trust him before but if the mermaids are involved then I know he's not lying. He can't be."

Deciding to leave her questions about mermaids for later, Carey glanced over at Seramina, who was beginning to calm.

"So Madame Guise was right, then? About there being a prophecy and its influence?" she said quietly so only Kat could hear.

Kat let out a long sigh. "It would seem that way. Don't worry about her. You know how strong that magic is. She'll be fine," she said, quietly referring to Seramina. Carey had just been thinking of how soon it was to be leaving the young witch, especially in her delicate situation.

Carey sighed heavily. "So when are we leaving?"

"As soon as Ji returns."

Seramina dropped her mug upon hearing Kat's words. "You're leaving? You can't leave! What about me? Where will I go?" she asked worriedly.

"It's all right," said Kat. "You're protected. We used some magic on you–"

"Magic? *Magic!* You used *magic* on me!" Seramina shrieked, her calm vanishing.

"No, no, no!" said Carey, waving her hands. "It's good magic. It'll keep you from getting hurt."

"But what if Empire guards come? What if they find me?"

"They can't. They won't. The spell will hide you. They could come into this very room and not be able to see you. It's safe, *completely* safe," Carey reassured her.

The door creaked open and Ji stepped into the room.

"Yes?"

"It's ready. We have a small sailboat waiting for us down at the dock and if we go now, we'll be able to get away without being seen. The guards haven't reached the harbour just yet. Shall we?" said Ji.

Seramina grabbed Carey's hand. "I will be safe, won't I?"

Carey smiled. "I promise." She got up from the bed and walked over to the door. Ji was looking about the room as if searching for something. Carey put her hand on his shoulder.

"What are you doing?"

"Mmm? Oh, nothing. Just looking."

She frowned and looked back into the hot little room. There really wasn't that much to look at. "Come on."

Councillor Hecate was stoking the fire when they came out. Carey approached him.

"Councillor Hecate. I would like to... request that Firefly – er – my Pegasus remains here while we continue on."

The Councillor merely nodded, saying nothing. Carey bit her lip. "All right. Ah – thanks – I mean, thank you very much."

While Kat and Ji bid farewell (with a tad more eloquence than herself), Carey said goodbye to Firefly. The Pegasus sensed the sincerity in her voice and whinnied nervously.

"Settle girl, settle. I'll be back soon, you'll see. Just stay, all right?" she hushed, stroking Firefly's mane.

Firefly listened and watched with sad eyes as Carey left, doing little to ease the situation.

Carey didn't notice how long it took for them to reach the dock. She was too busy sizing up the enormous black clouds that were rolling in from the ocean. She couldn't help the feeling that something bad was going to happen. A growing tick of apprehension was growing in her chest...

The sailboat didn't look too sturdy either – it exuded an air of severe dereliction. She found it difficult to find a spot on the hull that hadn't been patched up. Casting her eyes along the coastline, Carey spotted a number of shallow coves of treacherous rock. She shivered; the dark clouds had brought with them a blistering cold wind and she pulled her cloak around her tightly.

Kat stepped warily into the little boat first. Ji jumped in next but Carey hesitated. Ji took her hand.

"Are you coming?"

Carey creased her brow. "This isn't right, Ji. Something bad is going to happen, I can feel it."

Ji simply flashed a comforting smile and said, "Everything will be fine. Sure, those clouds aren't exactly inviting but we're all together. I'm sure we can handle a little rain."

Carey highly doubted it would be just a little rain, but she couldn't not go; they were so close. So with a deep breath, she stepped off the pier and down into the very questionable vessel. The cold icy water slopped unpleasantly against the sides and Carey dared not risk a glance into the dark, metal-grey waters. The ominous sensation twanged at her insides, threatening her with panic, but she ignored it as best she could. Besides, with Ji by her side and Kat opposite, she couldn't be safer...

Could she?

Chapter Twenty-Four

The Handing of Destiny

Ji tossed the painter rope onto the wharf as Kat laid some spells on the boat. A sudden gust caught the sail, carrying them from the port and out onto the open sea. Ji took his seat beside Carey; she took his arm and squeezed it tight, unable to relax.

"Just beyond those islands there," Ji said, pointing to a number of greyish blobs on the horizon "is where we want to go. There's a passage between the two that we'll take. Once we're through, it's a straight shot to Aran Island."

Carey could do nothing more than nod as she stared off into the distance, willing the tiny boat to go faster in the hope they would reach land before that cloud reached them.

Kat held onto the mast, directing the boat as it skipped across the waves, its speed enhanced by her touch. Carey watched as they approached the first lot of islands, and as they navigated their way through the channel between the two, she had never found the idea of solid land more inviting. The water beneath them swirled, deep and dark, and the idea of falling overboard was accompanied by the unpleasant thought of being swallowed up by the darkness that now surrounded them on all sides.

Aran Island came into sight as they rounded the heads and sailed out into open waters. Left bare of the protection afforded by the islands from the elements, an unexpected gust of wind whipped dangerously across the water and rocked the boat. The great dark cloud was almost now completely upon them and Carey stole whatever courage she had left and held it close to her heart and tendrils of fear and uncertainty tried to pluck it away. A wave sloshed over the side and splashed over their feet. Kat merely looked down at her boots and wiped them off. She was so calm that she almost looked bored, again demonstrating the kind of control and courage Carey knew she seriously lacked. Secretly Carey envied her. Instead of emanating confidence like her comrade, Carey felt like heaving her breakfast all over the deck. The sun was slowly being blotted out by the oncoming storm and as the clouds churned angrily, far off in the distance thunder rumbled and lightning flashed dangerously. Those unexpected gusts of wind were now blowing constantly, rocking the boat dangerously from side to side, letting in more water. Carey moved closer to Ji and he put his arm around her shoulders. The waves began to grow and Carey held her breath every time their little sailboat climbed a wave and crashed down on the other side. She could just imagine it splitting in two which wasn't a far stretch to imagine as it creaked and groaned under the strain of its journey. She didn't want to know how much longer it would hold out.

Suddenly, a fork of lightning crackled, splitting the sky in two, momentarily blinding her, and Carey screamed as waves broke loose of their restraints and the ocean unleashed its fury.

The waters rose up in great tsunami-like swells and thunder crashed loudly overhead. Rain gushed from the sky in great torrents, whipping at Carey's face painfully. Through the downpour, she could just make out Kat clutching the mast tightly, her face the same passive grimace. The sail began to flap about wildly and the vessel struggled against the gale. Gigantic waves were breaking over the sides now, soaking them to the bone; the boat tipped dangerously and Carey screeched, terrified. There came a deafening rip and the sail came away from the mast. It whipped about in the wind, its riggings barely holding it to the mast…

Ji jumped up. "Kat! Carey! Help me tie this down!" he shouted through the roaring winds, struggling to grab at the sail.

Shaking but determined, Carey grasped the mast and attempted a wild swipe for the sail; she couldn't reach it. She pulled herself to her feet and lunged at it, but again, it flicked out of reach. She tried once more, but the sail whipped back at her defensively, striking her hard across the face and she fell backwards. "*JI!*"

A crack of lightning and thunder broke, drowning out her cry. Kat and Ji were shouting to each other as they tried to capture the wild sail. Unable to get back on her feet, Carey wrapped her arms around the bottom of the mast. The wind pressed in on her ears until Kat and Ji's shouts were drowned out and their voices were replaced by the thundering and pounding of the sea.

Another gale rattled the riggings and with it came a slight cracking sound. Carey looked down fearfully at the base of the mast; running horizontally through the base was a long fracture in the weathered wood. The wind blew more ferociously and the split grew longer, spreading to the deck. Another gale of wind would surely rip the entire mast from the boat.

Carey wiped her face. "Ji! Kat! Don't touch the sail! The mast! It's going to break!" she screamed.

Ji flicked his hair out of his eyes. "What?"

"Don't touch the sail–"

"I've got it! I've got it!" Carey heard Kat bellow, and with a triumphant wave she restored it to its riggings.

"Kat, no!" Carey moaned just as another harsh gust of wind hit them. The sound of the mast breaking away rent the air with a resounding CRACK! Ji and Kat were almost thrown overboard as the mast pitched askew. The boat dipped low on one side and began taking on water as the broken mast and sail floundered. It was only a moment before the sail filled with water and began dragging the vessel under. Carey clung to the exposed side of the boat, desperately digging her fingers into the worn wood. She cast about for Kat and found her clinging to the mast, struggling to pull herself out of the swirling grey mass. Carey reached out.

"Kat! Kat, take my hand! Now! Reach for me!"

Her calm veneer had disappeared. A wild, terrified Kat thrashed about, trying to take Carey's hand. "Closer! I can't reach you! Help…" she cried as she splashed about the water, coughing and spluttering.

The rain was now so heavy that Carey was finding it increasingly difficult to see clearly. The wind washed a heavy wave over them and for a terrifying second Kat disappeared. Carey reached out, trying to find her; the mast bobbed above the waves for a brief moment and she reappeared, gasping for air. Rain battered the boat's exposed side and stung their bare skin. The hull was slippery beneath her hands and Carey was finding it increasingly difficult to hold on. Ji reached out for Kat this time but she kept slipping beneath the surface, just beyond his reach...

A massive wave fell and with a final crack, the boat broke up completely. Carey and Ji were thrown from the broken vessel and into the tumultuous ocean. Kat slid from view. Carey tried swimming back to where she last saw her but was swept away from the wreckage by the powerful swell. Confused and deafened, Carey lashed out and, in a stroke of luck, found Ji.

"Ji!" Carey spluttered over the howling wind, swallowing a mouthful of seawater.

Ji put his arms around her waist for support. "Hold on! It's the only way to stay above water!"

Carey put her hands on his shoulders obediently. "What about Kat? I can't see her!"

Ji looked as hopeless as a young child. Carey gazed blurredly at him and right away knew what he was thinking. She was gone.

Another wave engulfed them and Carey struggled to keep hold of Ji. The rain and water splashed in her eyes and again she swallowed a large mouthful. Ji was using all his strength to hold her up.

"We have to find – land... I can't see anything... come on. Try and kick–"

Hand in hand, they struck out, kicking desperately towards what they hoped was land. Water kept filling her mouth and nose and Carey eye's stung from the salt. She kept kicking.

The current pulled them under again and they found themselves swirling about in a grey mass of confusion. Carey kicked hard and resurfaced, gasping for air. A crash of thunder boomed overhead and the roar of the wind was worse than ever. The two Seekers bobbed up and down in the treacherous water, holding one another tightly. Hot tears on her face mingle with the saltwater and rain. She held Ji more tightly as a series of new waves began to break; she felt overwhelming nausea.

"Carey! We have to keep trying!" Ji shouted to her.

They tried again but soon stopped, exhausted and out of breath. They clung to each other, their faces only inches apart. Carey reached out and swept the hair from his eyes. This was all so terribly unfair. There were only a small number of ways this would end and she favoured none of them. This was her last chance. Carey opened her mouth to speak but her voice caught in her throat. She had glanced past Ji's shoulder only to see a monstrous wave building up behind him. A terror like Carey had never felt before welled inside her. Ji followed her eye line and a sharp dread filled his gaze. He looked back at Carey, breathing fast and panicky. He lifted his hand and placed it softly to her cheek just as the wave pushed them under. It was strong, too strong, and no matter how hard they tried, they were torn from each other's grips. Carey was swept about violently in the current, the swirling waters smothering her. The dark waters showed no compassion. Using what little energy she had left, Carey kicked for the surface, reaching out and she surfaced once more...

Everything spun mercilessly, distorted and confusing. Carey cried for help even though she knew no one would hear her. Only the crashing waves and blackened sky answered her pleas. The waters washed over her, the thunder rolled and lightning flashed, and as the cold rain fell down upon her face, everything gradually seeped into darkness. She could not fight anymore: she had no more fight left. Carey took one last, gulping breath and looked up into the storm, her last thoughts of Kat and Ji and how they had failed. Then she sank beneath the waves...

* * *

There was darkness. Carey blinked. That was strange. She squinted. Bubbles floated up around her. Water? She could feel the liquid rippling against her skin. Where was she? Was she dead? A ghost? It didn't seem so, but how was she breathing? She could feel the air filling her lungs but how, she did not know. Carey looked about. There was nothing... wait. Out of the corner of her eye, something silver... There it was again, though this time she saw a fin. A very large fin. Carey's heart skipped a beat.

Before Carey could even think, a ghostly pale face appeared from out of the shadows. She screamed; only, she would have if she hadn't been under water. Instead, a stream of bubbles issued from her open mouth. The face smiled at her and drew itself level; a large silver bubble emerged from Carey's lips as she gasped. The person before her was very strange; in fact, she wasn't a person at all. Her hair was a long blue-grey sheet with a crown of pearls perched upon it. Openings, which Carey assumed were gills, gaped on either side of her neck and seaweed spread across her chest. Silver fins ran from her elbows to her wrists, shimmering and rippling in the water. The woman circled Carey, looking at her kindly. Carey noticed the skin across her back was stretched so tightly that the shape of her backbone could be seen. More flowing silver fins lined her spine, but what amazed Carey the most was that instead of legs, the woman had a brilliant, glittering silver tail. She was a mermaid. She smiled again then opened her mouth. A beautiful, haunting song filled the water, its high-pitched notes echoing around her. Carey narrowed her eyes. In the shadows she could make out more flashes of slivery movement. As they drew closer, she saw three more silver-tailed mermaids. Carey realised they were responding to the first mermaid's song.

The first whispered something to her companions. They turned to Carey, and with a graceful flick of their tails, they surrounded her. Carey could only stare; she was unsure of whether to be comforted or to panic. The chief mermaid came forward.

"Liberator of Earth, Sea and Sky, we have brought you here to tell you that all is not lost. This is merely the beginning. Your destiny is yet to be fulfilled. As daughters of the waves, we are here to help you."

Carey blinked. This had to be a dream. Mermaids, breathing under water, destinies. It couldn't be real. It was all some illusion... or perhaps she really was dead. She was dead and this was what happened when people died. But mermaids? That was a little bit unexpected to say the very least. She had never heard of mermaids appearing after death. They never factored in any of the death-related myths she'd come across. It was supposed to be all clouds and angels – or fire and brimstone.

Yet perhaps this wasn't a dream or some post-demise vision. Perhaps it was real. Perhaps she was floating in the ocean somewhere with mermaids telling her of destiny and Liberators. She shook her head. What difference did it make though? She was no one special; she couldn't even save her friends from drowning. They were gone, most probably dead. Nothing else mattered but them. Destiny or no destiny, mermaids or no mermaids, she couldn't go it alone.

Carey realised the four mermaids were staring expectantly at her and she bit her lip. She didn't want to confirm their presumptions so she asked a question instead.

"How – how can I be here?" she burbled.

One of the mermaids held out her hands. "We have magic also. Wizards are not the only creatures of power. We saved you."

Carey didn't know what to say so she dipped her head in gratitude. It was all she could do. What could she say to the idea that they had saved her, when there was no evidence that they had saved her friends also. The onset of guilt swam in her stomach at the thought. She didn't even have to ask why they hadn't saved Kat or Ji – they had already answered that question. They thought she was the Liberator, the one from Madame Guise's prophecy. As far as they were concerned, the other two did not even exist. Carey swallowed back her emotions.

"Why do you call me that? Why do you call me the Liberator?" she asked, wanting to know the reasoning behind their assumption.

They seemed neither surprised nor upset that she had asked this question. It was almost as if they were expecting it.

"You possess a power as great as that of the false Empress. You do not understand it yet but you will come to learn its true nature. It is the only match to true evil. You doubt it, but you must embrace it or you will fail. That is why you are the Liberator," the mermaid to her right explained.

Carey thought of the terrible power she held within her and said nothing.

It was a terrifying secret that in an instant these mermaids had laid bare. Their claims were sensational; a power to match that of Malevolence's. It was daunting though not completely surprising. She knew it was strong; it was so strong it scared her witless. Carey was confused by it; she was a Seeker, fighting for the greater good she thought, yet the darkness of her power made her feel that it was leading her away from who she was supposed to be. Could evil only be matched by evil?

The more Carey thought of her power, the more she saw how it had influenced her. Everything up to this moment, every escape, she had put down to luck. Had this power perhaps been the reason she had managed it all for so long? She had felt its effects before, not only when she had faced that Imperial, but at the Falls and against the flying Dæmon. It would seem that the mermaid's assumption might not be completely unfounded. But how was she to complete such a task without Kat or Ji? Even if she did possess the true power they said she did, she needed them. She turned to the mermaid who had spoken to her.

"I can't do this. Not without my friends," she bubbled, hoping they would understand.

The mermaid merely continued to smile benignly. "Do not worry. Their part has not yet ended."

Carey was unsure what to make of her response. They were gone. Dead. What other part could they play in her future?

"But what if I'm not this Liberator? What if you have it wrong?" she asked, desperate for some doubt.

The first mermaid stretched out her arm and traced a circle before Carey, a line of bubbles following her hand. "We foresee in clarity beyond any other creature's ability. We have known of your destiny since the day you were gifted to this world. There is no misjudgement." She took Carey's hand. "You will accept this," she said as she lifted Carey up through the water.

Carey's heart sank but she allowed herself to be lead by the mermaid. The others swam alongside them, their silvery tails flickering in the darkness. Just below the water's surface the chief mermaid reached out to Carey's neck and said; "Stay safe, my sister. May your journeys be successful–"

"Wait," Carey interrupted. "Do you… do you know what will happen to me?"

The mermaid smiled once more. "That is for you to discover, for with it will come your power."

The mermaid blew a thin stream of bubbles to where her hand was resting and Carey gulped. Before she knew what was happening, she had sunk back into the pitch-black darkness…

* * *

Her skin prickled as the cold wind blew on her bare limbs. Her wet hair clung to the sides of her face. She opened her eyes and found herself gazing up at the sky. The angry storm clouds had disappeared and stars were winking down at her as she thought to herself how beautiful it all was. The soft bed she lay on was so comfortable she felt no rush of anxiety. She stretched lazily and the dais of bubbles she'd mistaken for a bed broke. With a sharp jerk she fell awkwardly into the water. Spluttering and soaked, Carey was slightly confused. She kicked out and her foot connected with something hard. Sand – hard, solid, glorious sand! She stood up and then instantly dropped back down when she saw where she was. The great cliffs and sandy mountains of Aran Island rose before her in the semi-darkness. Carey had just ducked out of the view of what looked like patrolling Guardsmen walking along the shore. They were peculiar; definitely not wizards. Their dull grey armour was dented and muddy and they were carrying long, crooked spear-like weapons with sharp ends and jagged edges. They were much larger than an Imperial wizard, their torsos short in comparison to their tall, flaring legs that stood like small tree trunks. Their long, gorilla-like arms grazed the sand as they walked with a slight rocking motion. They were only metres from Carey when one of them turned his head her way; she swallowed a mouthful of seawater in surprise.

Its face was a pasty greenish-brown with scab-like marks covering every inch of it. It was stretched over a pointed face that resembled a wild dog, though Carey would have preferred one to this creature. A deep gash took the place of its mouth which was filled with yellow-stained and pointed teeth that poked out from beneath non-existent lips. Black glutinous saliva dripped from them in sickening strings. Metal rings and tacks glinted in the moonlight, protruding from its disfigured visage while glowing beneath wrinkled eyelids were golden pupils, faint and murderous.

Its gaze paused for moment on the spot where Carey was wading, then continued its patrol. Carey breathed – that was close. She squinted and waited till they had disappeared before paddling over to a nearby inlet. She had to get out of the water as soon as possible – it was freezing.

Keeping low to a shadowy cluster of rock, Carey crept into a sandy cove below the cliff. Reaching up to take a handhold, she froze; a soft high-pitched screeching was filtering over to her on the breeze. Quickly, she ducked beneath a small rock overhang. The crunching of metal on sand grew louder and momentarily, two sets of armoured legs came into view. Her heart was racing; she could see in her mind's eye the fetid face of the sentry and she pushed herself further back into the shadows of the overhang, only to send an unfortunate trickle of loose shell into a nearby rock pool. She froze. The screeching stopped and one of the guards shuffled about, searching. Then, to Carey's horror, he bent down. Concealing herself in the dark as best she could, Carey gulped back a scream. The sinister glow of its eyes burned through the night, seeking her out. Carey dared not use her magic; she wanted to escape unnoticed and a fight with this foul creature would see that plan evaporate as quickly as the morning mist.

It sniffed. Any second now it would discover her and she fought against her imagination as it tried to present possibilities of what might happen if it did. The *thing* leant in further and a string of black saliva dribbled from its mouth and landed on the sand with a disturbing sizzle. It peered about the darkness and grunted from its throat. Another glob of disgusting spittle fell from the corner of its crackled lips. Realising how loud her breathing was, Carey held her breath. Suddenly, the other guard barked a series of screeches, calling to its partner. Reluctantly the guard slowly raised itself from Carey's hideout and turned away. As they walked out of sight, Carey let out a giant sigh of relief. She popped her head around the side of the rock and watched the guard's retrieving backs.

Cautiously, she stood up and took a handhold on the rock. Slowly she progressed up the slight cliff, taking care not to disturb anymore loose debris. In the face of the cliff she discovered a small cave. The entrance was only a small crevice, hidden behind a thicket of rough brush. Carey crawled inside and sat right to the back of the cave. Sitting there in silence and the darkness, Carey's grief began to seep in.

The desperate nature of her situation was becoming starkly apparent. She was alone. She was alone and now trying to comprehend how she could possibly complete what they had begun. It was too big, too incomprehensible, too much to even consider. She wanted to believe that she was this Liberator, this person that would bring her people freedom, but she lacked heart. Could she really do this by herself? Carey thought of how Kat and Ji would have responded to this situation but she found herself disheartened rather than encouraged. This was their moment, their triumph after so many years of fighting and it had been cruelly snatched away. Why had this happened?

Carey choked back a sob. She didn't know what to think in her confusion. Her heart felt heavy and sick. She had seen her two best friends drown before her very eyes and she couldn't do a thing to save them. If she really was this Liberator, why hadn't she been able to save them? She had known something bad was going to happen, she had felt it in her gut. They shouldn't have embarked on the voyage. Again, for the second time in as many months, her heart was tearing itself apart and a nauseating sickness filled her stomach. A prickling burnt her throat and eyes and try as she might, she could not swallow it back. An uncontrollable lump rose in her throat and tears burst forth from her eyes. She couldn't stop it. She could only think of Kat and Ji and how she would never hear their voices again, never get to talk and joke and laugh with them...

Suddenly the weight of it all came crashing down upon her. She was suffocating, weak. Every thought, every memory was tainted and the darkness soon blotted out all the light and goodness. Malevolence's evil had finally reached her and she could not fight it. Her mind, her heart, even her soul was heavy with it.

Hugging her knees, Carey cried into her damp skirt. She wanted to scream, doubtful that this pain would ever stop. It felt as though her heart was being strangled, mauled and crushed; it was bursting inside her and the pain was too much. The thought of being all alone was boring into her and she welcomed the deep, dark depression that now consumed her. What awaited her terrified her so much that she preferred the soul crushing self-pity and agony of her sorrows. Everything swirled around in her head, incomprehensible and broken, every word they had ever said, everything they had done. She didn't try to control it or even understand it. She just let it wash over her, as merciless as the storm that had taken them, sweeping her deeper into the darkness...

Time passed. She didn't know how long she sat there by herself in the shadows of the cave. She didn't feel tired or hungry. Outside the world carried on – the moon disappeared and the sun rose triumphantly – but she no longer felt a part of it. There was something that gnawed at her; something that compounded the grief that weighed down on her. She hadn't come to terms with how Ji had made her feel, how his very presence would both excite and terrify her. She knew what Kat had said, that she would find comfort in the idea of her and Ji in time, but what of it now? Would she be doomed to wander through this life alone, knowing that she would never have that moment of clarity? She could still see his face from their last moments together. She could still feel his hand upon her cheek.

Carey lifted her hand to her face and held it there, imaging he was there with her again. He smiled and asked what she was doing. She held his hand to her cheek.

"I don't know. I can't do anything," she whispered back.

He continued to smile and asked her why.

Carey shook her head. "Because I can't. I'm afraid. And because you're not here to help me..." she said, tears beginning to well in her eyes.

Ji moved closer and whispered in her ear so only she could hear. "But am

I not here now?"

Carey blinked; she was alone in the cave. She must have fallen asleep. The dream lingered, Ji's words still in her ear. However, the longing it had provoked had incited something new. Something inside her was rising above the grief and despair, something stronger than either of them – the urge to fight. Despite everything that was weighing her down, it was that one notion that was bringing her to her feet. She wanted to fight. She wanted to fight until she gained what was rightfully theirs. For the first time since emerging from the ocean there was a light, something she could reach for. A faint sense of hope was blossoming and she took hold of it with a growing determination.

Her dearest friends had struggled and died in this battle yet victory had not yet been claimed; she could still carry on. She was the last Seeker and she had survived for a reason, whether it was to fulfil some preordained destiny or to simply finish what had been started. She couldn't desert Kat and Ji, not while she still had life in her. A warm glow spread through her chest as she thought of Ji's words from her dream – a dream it may have been, but they rang true; they were not yet gone. They had taught Carey everything she knew and through her they would see this battle won. They gave her strength and she would not give up when they needed her most. She would not let this be her downfall...

Despite the enormity of what she was about to attempt, Carey set to work on a plan and the first thing she needed to do was observe those guards. She had a feeling there was more to them than their ghastly appearance.

For hours she watched the guards patrol the beach whilst holding back the emotions that continued to threaten her. They were struggling to overcome her but Carey's new- found strength trounced the weaker. She was almost itching to get out there.

Following the progress of some passing patrollers, a flicker of movement to her right caught Carey's eye. She snapped her head to the side so fast she cricked her neck. She stared at the rocks and waited to see if it happened again. There it was; a flash of dark-blue amongst the grey. Then something happened that made Carey choke with surprise – a head popped up over the rocks and looked straight up at her. A girl of about her age with frizzled, black hair and a dark-blue cape was climbing the rocks, heading straight for her hiding place. Carey knelt to one side, watching the girl closely. She had all the looks of a poor street wanderer except for the thick, silvery cuff that was clasped around her thin neck.

Carey moved back further until she could just see the girl from around the side of the cave entrance. Strange as she was, what was stranger was how she'd pause and talk to herself every few steps. Carey glanced around the cave; there was no way out. She was trapped. Carey cursed herself for being so stupid. If she was found she'd have no choice but to fight and run for it and hope the guards on the beach wouldn't notice. But run where, though? Carey turned back to watch the girl but she'd disappeared. Carey's heart quickened; where did she go? Forgetting her cover, Carey stuck her head out from behind the cave wall – she stifled a scream. The girl was next to her, a queer type of smile on her face. Carey could do nothing but stare, the girl's sudden appearance leaving her lost for words.

"Carey Lee, I presume?"

Chapter Twenty-Five

Crossing Over

Carey was momentarily stunned. She was caught, and what was worse, this girl knew who she was. In what would probably be considered a slow reaction, Carey leapt to her feet with her arm outstretched, her hand pointed at the girl's heart. She didn't move as Carey took an extra step back; she gazed steadily into the girl's eyes.

"What do you want?"

The girl got up slowly and inclined her head. "Nothing. I'm here to take you to Terra Saga. I'm here to–"

"I'm sorry," Carey growled, trying to frighten the girl, "but I'm not going to be *taken* anywhere."

The girl smiled placidly at her, unperturbed by Carey's answer. If she was trying to unnerve her, Carey would make sure she wouldn't succeed. She kept her hand steady. *Trust no one.*

"Grandpa Alois told me you'd be like this. He's always right. He told me I'd find you here. I know you're the Liberator. They've all been talking about, you know."

Carey was not expecting this. As far as she knew, even the Empire didn't know she was the Liberator, and it was only a few hours ago that she herself made aware of her so-called destiny. Yet here was this girl, who had appeared out of nowhere, speaking as though it was common knowledge.

Carey shook her head. Surely this was some kind of ploy? Did this girl think she could fool Carey by pretending to be innocent? She could easily be an Imperial, despite her appearance, and Carey wasn't about to let her guard down. She had to test her.

"So, the Empire knows about me then. It's about time. I was beginning to think that they actually were as stupid as they looked," Carey quipped, waiting to see how the girl would react to such a statement.

The girl's reaction was a mix of incredulity and surprise.

"Me? An Imperial? No, no! You've got this all wrong! *I'm* not an Imperial, not by a long shot. I'm here to *help* you."

"Oh, and I'm supposed to believe that? You come out of nowhere to say that I'm the Liberator then expect me to follow you?" Carey said sardonically.

"But we're waiting for you! We all know you're coming and I'm supposed to–"

"We? Who else knows I'm coming?" she hissed, feeling her hopes of an unnoticed entry vanish along with her stomach.

"Oh no, no one. I meant–"

"Then who's *we*? No, I'm sorry, but I can't have people knowing that I'm coming. You knowing is bad enough! I shouldn't even be talking to you–" Carey said, taking a step towards her as she felt her chances of success slipping away with every word they spoke.

"Carey, please!" the girl cried desperately and Carey stopped. "I can explain. My Grandpa is a Seer, a very good one. He was the one who told me you were here. Me and my family are the only ones who know you are here. We're the only ones who know *you* are the Liberator. There have been rumours for months about a Liberator coming but no one else knows it's you. We haven't told anyone either, I promise, so don't worry. You have to believe me," she said, breathless with desperation.

Carey considered her shrewdly but was still hesitant to trust her; she had, after all, appeared out of nowhere and somehow managed to avoid those creatures that were patrolling the beach. She couldn't help feeling that this might be some kind of trap and Carey wasn't about to bestow her trust in someone who generated so much suspicion in her. Carey kept her hand at the ready.

"If you're not an Imperial, then who are you? I know you said you're here to help me but how do I know this is not some Imperial trap?"

The girl reached in to her pocket and Carey tensed. She drew out something that glinted in the darkness; she threw it to Carey. Carey looked down as it landed at her feet; she frowned at it. Making sure her hand was still trained on the girl, she bent down awkwardly and picked the object off the cave floor. When she saw what it was, her jaw dropped.

It was a Seeker's necklace, but that wasn't what had caught her off-guard; it was the name inscribed upon it.

Fianna.

This was her grandmother's necklace. She might have thought it a fake if Kat had not told her once that their necklaces were special, their magic so unique to the point that they could never be copied or reproduced.

"Where did you get this?" Carey asked in barely a whisper, running her thumb over the engraving.

"From my grandfather. He was a friend of your grandmother's. He helped her with something, a long time ago."

Carey closed her hand around the necklace. "But how did he get this? Why does he have it?" she demanded.

The girl was now completely serious, the smile she had been toting before, gone. "My grandfather knew something terrible was going to happen to her. Despite knowing what the consequences might have been if he told her, he warned her of the dangers anyway. Just before she died, Fianna gave my grandfather her necklace."

Carey considered this for a moment. "How do I know this wasn't taken by the Empire?"

The girl shook her frizzy head. "You don't understand. The Empire never keeps these kinds of things. They're considered filth. Back in the day, Rebels who were caught were forced to wear their necklaces as they were stripped of their magic and burnt at the stake. The Empress wanted them to burn with that which had put them there. The Empire sees no use in these necklaces, no matter whose it is or was."

"If it was such a risk, why did you keep it? I've seen the consequences of keeping such a trinket," Carey said, Seramina's family springing to mind.

The girl sighed. "So we could give it to you. My grandfather knew this day would come. Why else would your grandmother have given it to him?"

Carey was slightly mystified by her response. She frowned as she tried to comprehend what this girl was suggesting. Had her grandmother really known this day would come? Had she truly given her necklace to a Seer, knowing that one day it would need to be used to convince her granddaughter of the truth so many years after her own death?

Carey could not deny that it was an amazing story, but she still struggled with the suspicion that it was all just a ruse. Perhaps she could use this situation to her advantage. If this girl was an Imperial, then once she had led Carey to the other realm Carey could escape her and she could continue with her plan. If the girl was indeed who she said she was then there could be more Carey could discover from her. She would have to trust her just enough.

Carey lowered her hand.

"What's your name?"

The girl appeared relieved that Carey was no longer considering her a threat. "My name is Torena. Torena Patroni."

"You're a witch?" Carey asked.

Torena shook her head. "No, not a witch. I'm... something else. I'm a slave of the Empire now though, which has pretty much erased anything I might have been once. My family and I live, or rather are kept, in the Centre City."

Carey frowned. "You're a slave in the Centre City? But how could you have possibly escaped to get here? There must be guards or something at least?"

Torena grinned with pride. "Grandpa Alois. He Saw how I would get here, told me where to go and what to expect.

"Which reminds me..." Torena looked out at the sky. "We've got to go. We've got to go or we won't make it back in time. Come. You can ask questions later."

Torena suddenly reached across and grabbed her by the hand before leading her out of the cave and down the rocks. Taking a deep breath, Carey obliged and carefully climbed down the rocky cliff. Jumping down beside Torena, Carey looked around; she listened for anyone approaching, but all was silent. She made to move but was caught by Torena, who pulled her down; she put a finger to her lips. Slightly exasperated, Carey opened her mouth to argue but then thought better of it. Keeping low, she waited. A moment later, a pair of guards appeared, creeping along in silent stealth. They were screeching in their gibberish, but only just; Torena had closed her eyes and was muttering silently to herself. As soon as the guards had passed, Torena opened her eyes and stood up.

"They know I've escaped. Come, and quietly."

Carey followed her along the beach, keeping to the line of trees and rock below the cliffs. A new wave of questions came over Carey, but she pushed them aside for now. Carefully they made their way up into another cluster of rocks, Torena stopping every so often to enter her strange trance-like state. They climbed the cliff to find a small narrow track; they edged along it, making their way around into the heart of the cliff. Upon entering, Carey stopped, astonished by the spectacle that met them. Two towering stone statues stood either side of a great crevice. The carvings were of a man and a woman, each wearing great flowing robes; their hair hung wild, reaching right down to their ankles. The woman held to her breast a great bow, beautiful jewels and Celtic patterns upon it. The man held above his head a mighty sword where more sparkling jewels glinted at its hilt. The expertly carved stone looked hundreds of years old, spider cracks running through the weathered rock and vines lining them. Elaborate rune inscriptions were etched into a stone arch that stretched between them. Carey's eyes were drawn to the fissure between them – it presented an amazing sight.

Dazzling white smoke swirled within, glittering with the light of thousands upon thousands of tiny stars. It was as though an entire universe was contained within the gap. Colours came and went, shifted and changed. As Carey watched it turned a reddy-orange, as magnificent as the setting sun. It continued to swirl, fading slowly from one spectacular colour to the next...

Torena pulled her down behind the shelter of some rocks as the sounds of footsteps reached their ears; two of the ghastly patrolmen appeared from behind the statues. They came to a halt in front, their jagged spears close to their sides.

"What is it they're guarding?" Carey breathed.

Torena was quiet; she had been observing the two guards, and Carey had a feeling she had interrupted one of her trances.

"That's the gate to the other Realm, to Terra Saga, kept by the Guardians of the Realms," she whispered. "The woman is Taethys, guardian of the seas; the man is Aetherus, guardian of the sky; and the nymph above the gate is Pria, the guardian of the lands."

Carey looked back up at the statues; upon closer inspection she could just make out a smaller figure perched above the smoke. Its features were plain and simple, nothing like its companions, and in its hands it held a small sphere. Just as Carey was watching, it lit up. The sphere glowed a pale yellow and the contents within the fracture began to swirl faster, almost like there was a storm brewing. A green jewel in Taethys' bow flashed brightly as the smoke-storm grew. Following suit, a large blue gem from Aetherus' sword burnt luminously; beams of light from all three flickered over the cave walls like light reflecting on water. The rays were blinding, stretching across to where Carey and Torena hid, threatening to expose their hiding place.

There came a sound like a soft wind and then all at once, the light from all three figures connected, forming a web in the centre of the storm. The runes on the arch glowed blue, burning so bright they soon became indistinguishable. The guards stood steady, seemingly untroubled by these events. On the contrary, Carey seemed the only one in awe of what was happening, and upon realising her mouth was hanging open, shut it hastily. There was a flash of light and four dark shadows appeared from within the smoke. The light sparked again and the jewels faded, the haze returning to a slow swirl. Four more guards had emerged from it, straightening their helmets on their oblong heads. One screeched what sounded like a command and they joined the two guards beneath the statues. Carey groaned; now they had six to get past. She leant over to Torena.

"I might have an idea of how to get past those guards. I have this shapeshifting pin that could get us past and into the next realm if we–"

"No!" Torena exclaimed quietly. "We can't use magic!"

"We can't use magic? Why not?"

"Because of the Örd."

"Örd? What's that?" Carey asked.

"Those things," Torena said heavily, pointing to the guards. "They're Örd, shadow Dæmons. They are loyal to the Empire and they receive certain… benefits for their services," she shuddered. Carey didn't bother asking what these *benefits* entailed.

"They have always existed. They were once only the stuff of legend, scary stories to tell around the fireplace on rainy nights. Very rarely would someone ever see one. They originally lived in dark places, places of great danger or evil, like the Darklands, but now… they are the scourge of our world, the darkest, foulest imaginings. The reason why we can't use magic is because they're attracted to it. If we use it, they'll know we're here and they'll kill us for sure."

Torena turned back to watching the guards and Carey fell silent. She watched the Örd with a sinking feeling. Unable to use magic… She hadn't even thought of it as a possibility. What good were her powers if she couldn't use them? Who was she without them?

She didn't have to wait long to find out what Torena was waiting for. From her left two Örd ran in from the beach and began screeching something to the others; Torena gripped Carey's wrist. One of the Örd signalled for its colleagues to follow and they all trooped out. Carey couldn't believe their luck. As soon as they had passed, Torena yanked Carey out from their hiding place and pulled her towards the arch of smoke.

"Tor – Torena! What are you doing? Wait!" Carey hissed nervously.

Torena answered Carey by pulling her closer to it. Carey resisted a little. "What if there are Örd waiting–"

"*Just trust me!*" she shouted and she threw them both into the miasma.

280

It was like stepping out into a strong wind; Carey's hair flew back from her face and she struggled to stay upright. The white smoke continued to swirl about her, impervious to the force that was trying to knock Carey off her feet, and the flecks of silver she had thought were stars were slowly drawing in on her. She turned her head to the side with much difficulty to see Torena still holding her by the wrist. Her hair had been drawn back from her face also and her cape was flailing about. A high-pitched wailing was pressing in on Carey's ears and she tried desperately to bring her hands up to block them; she was having difficulty keeping her wits about her. The silver specks were now surging around her; Carey yelled in surprise, but there came no sound. There was an explosion of bright light and Carey was thrown forward, almost losing her balance. A roaring screech pounded on her eardrums and she shut her eyes tight. There was another flash of light and Carey found herself able to move; she took a step...

"Oh my..." Carey choked as she fell gasping to her knees.

The air was stifling but not because of the heat. The atmosphere itself was suffocating and held a smoky tinge. A stale breeze blew past her nose. It reminded Carey of a barn that had been shut up too long – it smelt dusty, mouldy and of rot. She gagged, her eyes watering. She hadn't even realised that Torena's hand had slipped from her wrist within the swirling chaos...

Before Carey had recovered, Torena had hauled her to her feet again and dragged her away from the gate. Quickly glancing back, Carey saw a smooth rock face with carvings identical to those in the other realm. Carey's head spun with wonder and confusion. She allowed Torena to lead her to a large dirt mound. Carey watched, faintly impressed as Torena pulled open a trapdoor that had seemingly appeared out of nowhere. Torena led her down into it, peered cautiously back out of the hole, and then shut it, plunging them both into absolute darkness. Torena released her wrist and she stared into the darkness, feeling a little faint.

To her right came a spark; a small fire flared. Torena was holding a large peat-fire torch. She sat down on a large rock indicating that Carey should do so too. When her head had finally stopped swimming and her eyes had adjusted to their new surrounds, Carey turned to Torena.

She was pulling at something in the cavern's roof; with a shower of dust, she yanked a small round metal dial from the rock. A sliver of light shone through the hole, laying a thin line across the dark floor. After dusting it off, Torena held the small metal disk up to the rays.

"Torena, where are we?"

Carey waited for Torena to answer; she shook her head and looked away.

"Torena? *Where are we?*" Carey persisted.

There was a brief moment of silence in which Carey waited impatiently. When Torena finally spoke she did not look up but continued to adjust the small metal disk.

"We are in the hidden city of Dinaght. It was abandoned many years ago when Imperial developments threatened the People's security. However, it was never found by the Empire so we are completely safe. Right now I'm waiting for something. See that tiny sliver of light? By lining it up with the dial it tells the time, like a clock. When it reaches a certain point on the dial, Grandpa Alois said it would be safe to leave the cave, but it has to be exactly on the point or we will miss our chance."

There was a slight note of impatience in her voice.

"And where will we be going?" Carey asked gently, feeling her last question had been a little too demanding.

"We'll be going to my family's house in the slaves' village."

"The village? What, in the *city*? Are you crazy? What if we get caught? People are bound to notice me – it's not as if I'm from around here," said Carey incredulously.

Ignoring Carey's sceptical tone, Torena reached into a pocket and produced a metal ring, identical to the one she wore around her neck. Carey raised an eyebrow.

"I don't think they'll fall for that. I don't even look like you," Carey said pointedly, thinking Torena was going to disguise Carey as herself.

Torena shook her head. "No, that's not what I was thinking. Every slave has one of these. It's what stops us from using our powers. We can't remove it – it is bound to us by magic and since we can't use magic... well, you get the point. My Pa is a blacksmith, and he made this in secret. It will fool the guards, but unlike mine, it won't block your powers and it can be taken off. You might want to dirty-up your clothes a bit more and hide your bag too. Imperials are naturally suspicious but that will really attract them."

Carey unclipped her precious Seeker's necklace and snapped on its replacement. It felt strange against her throat, tight and cold. She lifted her saddlebag over her head and took out what valuables she had – the locket and shapeshifting pin, her grandmother's necklace – and stuffed them deep in her pockets along with her own necklace, before stowing her bag out of sight. She then set about making herself look as derelict as possible. This proved quite easy as her clothes were already starting to fray in spots and her recent dip in the ocean certainly added to the effect. Her hair was an absolute mess and a lump was rising on her scalp from where she had sustained that blow during Seramina's rescue.

They sat in silence for what seemed like ages while Torena vigilantly watched the thin sliver of seemingly unchanging light on the dial. Just as Carey was counting her five hundred and twenty-seventh stalactite, Torena whispered a hurried, "Let's go," took her by the arm and led her swiftly down a dark tunnel. Carey only just managed to glimpse the many rooms and passageways branching off from their own, sighting tall bookcases and impressively carved furniture. It was sad though to see large leather bound books lying ruined on the damp, dark floors. The city had been abandoned in a hurry, leaving behind only vague imprints of its former residents.

The tunnel seemed to go on for ages; if they hadn't been in such a hurry, Carey would have liked to explore them more. Their mystery intrigued her.

Then, without warning, Torena came to a halt and Carey bumped into her awkwardly.

"Oh, sorry!" Carey apologized, stumbling backwards.

"That's all right. We're at the tunnel's end. When we open this trapdoor, we will find ourselves on a hill that overlooks the Mud Pits. It's fairly sheltered so we won't be completely exposed. From there we'll be able to get to the village. Just follow me and we'll be fine. And don't use any magic. There are Örd everywhere, the Mud Pits especially."

She took a deep breath and retrieved the time dial from her pocket. She reached up to the ceiling and pulled another piece of metal from it, allowing a few rays of dim sunlight to pour into the cavern. For only a moment, Torena held the dial up to the light, checking their timing. She nodded then placed the dial back in her pocket and the stopper back in the hole. She moved her hand over the rough stone roof and pulled a trapdoor down.

"Here, I'll give you a boost," Torena said, linking her hands together.

Carefully, Carey put her foot in Torena's hands and reached up. Gripping the dirt edge, she pulled herself out of the hole. She held out her arm and Torena clambered out to join her. Without a single moment's hesitation, she stood up and dusted herself off. Carey, however, did not move.

They were no longer surrounded by the green rolling hills of Ireland, its majestic emerald landscape was now far behind. Instead they were surrounded by a clump of black, gnarled trees; their branches and limbs were twisted and they reached out to Carey. She could feel an evil emanating from them, an ancient evil that sickened her to the heart. Something had happened to those trees to make them that way, something inexplicable. The earth around them was a barren red soil; clouds of brownish-red were whipped about by the wind, creating a haze in the air. It tasted toxic and heavy. It wasn't this, though, that caused Carey to stop; it was what lay beyond the trees...

In disbelief, she staggered to her feet and approached the edge of the brush apprehensively. Stretching out from the valley below was a vast city that covered the horizon, reaching as far as the eye could see. Its outskirts were surrounded by clusters of slab huts which lined more civilised buildings which circled around a towering castle that rose from the heart of the city. The massive structure cast a menacing shadow that spread as far as the sprawling shanty town below.

Casting her eyes down from the metropolis, Carey's gaze fell upon a most terrifying sight. Ravines and mines riddled the earth, covering every square inch of the immediate area up to the hill upon which she and Torena stood. Crude steel constructions emerged from the deep cuts in the ground, their dark, rusted bodies tainting everything which surrounded them. A wood stretched far to her left along the edges of the ravines, its immense blackened trees sentinels for the horrors that lay within. The sky was hidden beneath great clouds of grey, blue, scarlet, and purple that swirled in cyclonic forms. Forks of lightning split the sky and distant thunder rent the air. The high-pitched screeching of shadowy forms joined the rumbling of the thunder, their lizard-like figures snaking across the sky. The air was neither hot nor cold; she could not tell whether it was winter, summer, autumn, or spring, or whether there was a season at all. The atmosphere was electric, filled with the unpleasant tingle of Dark magic. Carey shivered; Torena appeared beside her.

"Welcome... to Torarn, Terra Saga," she said.

Carey continued to stare. She understood now why the People had fled to the other world; this place was a true living nightmare. She looked upon it and all its horror and suddenly felt small. Immense, terrifying evil had created this wasteland. This was Malevolence's world. In the other realm they had almost been equal, but here... this was her domain. Everything she was, all the wickedness and hatred and control that she embodied had been projected outwardly onto this world. Not until now had Carey realised the Empress' full powers and reach and for the tiniest second she felt uneasy about her own abilities. She reached into her pocket and felt the cool of her necklace against her fingertips. She held it in her fist, searching for the courage to go on.

In the last day everything had changed. She had lost her friends, gained an immense responsibility and now she stood alone in a desolate realm, looking down upon a world that she was expected to save. A weight settled on her heart and she could have easily retreated then and there. Yet as she stood there clutching her necklace and Torena at her side, she remembered something, something that had almost been forgotten: her family. She had almost lost sight of the true reason she was there. Hadn't she left the orphanage with the hope of finding them? Hadn't it been the main incentive which had persuaded her to believe Kat and Ji at their very first meeting? For some reason it had been lost amongst the revelations and attacks. Their focus had shifted without Carey even noticing. For months their target had been Malevolence, the prospect of revenge and freedom for their people too tantalizing to ignore. Slowly it had transformed from a fight for their families to a fight for everything. They had taken on the entire Empire without it ever being decided. Now, however, Carey could finally see through the haze and the enormity of what had built up. She may be this Liberator but at that very moment she only had one goal, one thought. She was going to save her family. She didn't have to believe in anything bigger because that one simple goal seemed possible. She could handle that. Anything bigger and she might crumble.

The land before her no longer seemed as terrifying as it had a moment before. There was just one more obstacle. She let go of the necklace and adjusted her cape.

"Let's go."

Torena nodded.

"Now I work over in those mud pits," she said, pointing to their left. "The only way you will be able to get anywhere near the city is if you join one of the work groups. We leave for the pits at sunrise and return home at sundown. They're the only movement between here and the city, which makes it difficult to escape. Without Grandpa's instructions I would have been caught for sure.

"Once we've joined my group though, you'll have to take extra care. That will be as far as my grandfather predicted so just listen to the guards and don't react to anything. Everyone keeps to themselves generally. I know for a fact that you will be safe – no one will expose you. Imperial guards don't reward such acts. They're likely to kill both you *and* the person who gives you up. Just do what everyone else does and you will be fine."

Carey nodded, shaking off her hesitation.

Carefully, Torena led her through the thicket of woods, passing a band of patrolling Örd returning to the portal as they went. The further they went, the more Örd and slaves there were. There were also a dangerous number of Imperial guards striding about menacingly. Carey and Torena arrived at the first of the Mud Pits after an excruciating hour of dodging and hiding, finally ducking behind a large, red boulder. A pair of crooked brown metal poles sticking out of the red soil formed a gate; a fence sprouted from either side, lining the pits and Carey guessed these were more for preventing escapes than to keep people from falling into the deep crevice. Two more Örd flanked the entrance. Within the gates were hundreds of workers, cutting away at the rock surrounding the ravine. Guards were prowling amongst the slaves, their red cloaks billowing out behind them ominously. Torena pointed at the gate.

"We go through there. In about a minute another work group will be entering. We'll need to join them if we want to get past the guards and the Örd. Just follow me and do what I do."

They didn't have long to wait; a small, ragged group of slaves, all with identical neck cuffs, were making their way towards them. Only a single Örd was herding them. As they passed by, Torena and Carey slipped quietly behind the group unnoticed. The other slaves showed no sign of acknowledgement. Carey followed Torena closely, anxiety pressing on her chest. She resisted the urge to touch the cuff around her neck as it rubbed uncomfortably on her skin.

Imperial guards paced about the pits with their silver weapons glinting dangerously at their sides. Carey put her head back and stared up at the enormous metal structures towering over them; ropes and loose metal scaffold dangled hazardously over the workers. They were almost haphazard in their construction. Torena entered through the gate first and without problem. Carey hesitated but only for a moment. She could feel the glare of the Örd upon her; the thought of those deadly golden eyes following her brought beads of sweat to her forehead. Clear of the gate, she breathed a sigh of relief only to realise she'd done so a moment too soon. Carey heard an exclamation from behind. Before she knew what was happening, she was hit with a buzzing jolt of power square between the shoulders. She was instantly paralysed, unable to move. The jolt of power surged through her like hot needles. Her veins burned and her eyes watered as she gasped for air. She gave a choked cry as someone gripped her around the back of the neck and forced her to her knees. Torena turned to investigate, but upon seeing Carey's predicament, kept on turning. The sheer terror in her eyes gave Carey no comfort either. She struggled to maintain her wits as nervous sweat now poured down her face. The strong grip did not release her; instead, it was tightening, slowly, cutting off her air supply. She fought for breath, gulping for air fruitlessly. She had to mentally restrain herself from using her magic. She was a slave... a slave...

Torena bent over and picked up a sharp mining tool from the ground. For a split second Carey thought she was coming to her rescue only to realise she was simply returning to work. Carey's only comfort was knowing Torena was still close by.

The Imperial moved his grip to the base of her skull, and gripping her hair, ripped back her head; Carey winced. A number of hairs parted painfully from her scalp. She could now see her assailant. The man was tall and strongly built. His long dark hair lined his strong square chin; he sneered cruelly with a thin-lipped grin. A long, terrifying white scar ran from his hairline all the way down the side of his face to his chin, crossing through the most unusual eyes Carey had ever seen. His pupils were a burning white that glowed like the sun on a hot day. They shimmered in pools of metallic black, making the guard seem positively demonic. They looked her up and down before staring her straight in the eye. He spoke.

"Identify yourself," he growled in a low resonating voice.

Carey stuttered through the pain; he pulled harder on her hair. "Speak, slave! Identify yourself!"

"Urgh – Seramina," coughed Carey, saying the first name that came into her head.

The Imperial glared. "We shall see. You don't work here. Where are you from?"

Carey choked again; she hadn't prepared for this. She just had to hope the guard couldn't detect lies.

"I – I was – captured, in the other realm and – and sent here," she said hopefully.

The guard squinted in disbelief. "Where did you get your cuff from?"

He eyed the ring of silver clasped around her neck.

"I – I – got it when I came here–"

288

"From who?"

"From who?"

"Yes, filth, from who?" the guard barked.

"My... my captors," Carey said, trying to sound sincere.

The guard snarled and threw her down hard in frustration. "Get to work. I'll be watching you."

He gave her a swift kick in the side before marching away. Carey lay winded on the ground, a dull throbbing pounding inside her head. She pulled her cloak around her protectively, thankful that her pockets remained full, their contents undiscovered and her identity safe. The red dirt mingled with her sweat as she calmed herself, taking a few long, deep breaths. Slowly she got to her feet and staggered over to Torena who handed her a digging tool. Carey was sure her ribs were bruised and her head felt like half the hair had been ripped from it. Her cheek stung raw from where it had hit the ground. But it wasn't these that upset her. What had her rattled was that the guard had frightened her. She had never been truly scared by an Imperial before, but there was something about this one that terrified her...

She felt her rib tenderly. "So much for not attracting any attention," she whispered, now massaging the back of her neck.

Torena looked over her shoulder at the guard. "Please, don't speak to me. The guards are already suspicious," she hissed.

"But–"

"Please," she begged.

Carey bit her lip and yielded. She had to try and trust Torena. Not being able to use her powers left her feeling weak and vulnerable though she knew that if she used even the tiniest bit there'd be more Imperials and Örd on her quicker than she could say 'Seeker'. She couldn't even begin to know what it would be like to feel this way all the time. At least she had a choice – Torena and the others there were trapped. The Empire was doing all it could to trample the spirits of these people. Chipping away at the rock in front of her, Carey wondered if they even remembered what magic felt like or if it was simply a memory, as dead as the look in their eyes.

The other slaves had barely taken notice of their arrival; Carey had the feeling they were actually trying to ignore them more than anything else. She didn't understand until a cold shadow flickered over her and she shivered. The guard with the metallic eyes appeared beside her. Carey almost cried out in surprise when he turned and faced Torena. Torena dropped her tools in fright.

"Where were you, slave?" the guard asked her in a deep, ominous voice.

Torena gulped. "I – I was at th-the other mine," she stammered.

The guard snarled and moved towards her; Torena shrank back.

"I asked you, slave, where you were?" he rumbled and he pushed her hard backwards.

Carey had to fight to stop herself from cursing the guard. Torena fell awkwardly to the ground; tears glistened at the corners of her eyes but she held them back.

"I was at the other mine," she repeated half-heartedly.

"LIAR!" the guard roared and he drew from his hip a long, jagged sword and lay the tip at her throat.

Carey made a move to help Torena but was stopped by another slave. He shook his head.

"Don't. You'll only make it worse."

He laid his hand gently on her wrist and Carey stayed. There was a pleading in his eyes that she couldn't ignore. She turned her gaze back to Torena as she busied her hands with work.

The guard had his blade pressed so hard against her throat that a thin trickle of blood ran down her neck. Carey thought it was a bit barbaric for a wizard to be brandishing a sword so, considering the kind of damage that could be done by magic alone. Carey quickly discovered that it was a useful fear tactic and an effective one at that.

The other slaves, determined to ignore Torena's plight, had begun hacking away at the rock with resolute indifference. Carey was disgusted: not by their reactions but by the Empire. They had beaten and deadened the People so badly that they wouldn't even help one of their own for fear of something worse. The injustice made her blood boil and it was all she could do to stop herself from lashing out.

The guard lifted his sword and moved the tip to Torena's shoulder. Teeth gritted, she fought back a sob. Slowly, and with a manic grin of sadistic satisfaction, he ran the sword down towards her chest. A diagonal line of crimson blood blossomed and Torena could no longer contain her anguish; she let out a scream, the long howl of a wounded animal. The Imperial lifted his sword with a triumphant laugh of derision then struck her hard across the head for good measure. Torena fell to the ground and did not move as the guard knelt beside her and whispered so that only Torena and Carey could hear.

"If you are indeed the rebel I believe you to be, this will seem fickle compared to what I will subject you to."

Carey averted her gaze as he stood up, avoiding his accusatory glare. Once he was gone, Carey turned to Torena and helped her off the ground. Blood soaked her shirt but her face showed no sign of pain; she was adamant in denying the guards the satisfaction.

Back on her feet, Torena picked up her tools once more and resumed her work. Carey's mind was racing; the guard suspected her. She couldn't understand how Torena could simply act as though nothing had happened, as though the guard had never attacked her.

"Torena, are you all right?" she whispered, glancing furtively over her shoulder.

Torena turned away. "I said not to speak to me. It's for your own protection," she said in a forced voice.

"But that guard... He knows," Carey said persistently.

Other slaves around them were beginning to eye them and edge away, obviously scared that they would be preyed upon also if they remained too close. Torena noticed, answering in a rushed whisper.

"He knows nothing. That's the thing about these guards. They are full of empty threats. React and they will know."

There was a tone of finality in her voice and Carey supposed that this knowledge would have to suffice, despite her doubts.

Carey had long abandoned the idea that Torena might be an Imperial; it seemed almost ludicrous after what had just happened. The guard's attack had been unfounded and cruel. Without magic, Torena's wound could kill her. Perhaps that is what the Imperial wanted. Either way, Carey had to tread carefully – empty threat or not, she couldn't take the guard's assumed ignorance for granted. His lack of regard for life was dangerous.

A short while later a bang sounded, signalling the end of the day. The sound brought a great surging crowd of workers slowly towards the gate. Carey helped Torena along; she was now deathly pale but was determinedly resilient. Hundreds of slaves were marching towards the gates at a snail-like pace, pushing past the sentries. Carey looked up at the guards and noticed one that had not been there before. He was talking to the great hulking guard who had attacked her; he then turned and looked straight at her. Carey stared defiantly back at him, not because she challenged him, but because her brain wasn't functioning properly; did he know?

The moments that followed seemed to happen in a strange slow motion: the new guard raised his arm and pointed directly at her. The other grimaced and by the dawning realisation on his face, it seemed he had finally figured out that Carey was definitely not Seramina. He began to make his way through the crowd towards them, his steps strong and purposeful. Torena saw him too.

"Carey, run!" was all she said.

Carey didn't need telling twice; she left Torena and began urgently pushing her way back towards the pits. The Imperial shouted over the crowd and Carey's heart jumped; fear hit her square in the face and sweat began to pour down her forehead again. She bumped into people who walked zombie-like in her path. Other slaves stared at her, dazed as she fought her way through the sea of bodies, yet none tried to stop her. She glanced backwards to see the crowd scatter as the guard pursued her, sending a jolt of panic through her body; she kept pushing, trying to keep some distance between them. "Please, please move... please..."

Once she was free of the crowd, she made a mad dash through the Mud Pits. She ducked quickly under a metal scaffold and then another, swerving around a swinging beam. Running through the dust and dirt, she leapt over a pile of rusted tools; she heard the pounding of the guard's feet behind her and she ran harder. She dodged a hanging canister and rolled under another beam, knocking her elbow hard as she went. Carey had to stop herself cursing out loud as the pain shot up her arm. She thought it strange that the guard wasn't aiming any curses at her. Maybe he was waiting for something. Whatever the reason, she definitely wasn't lamenting the absence of fatal sparks flying through the air.

A stitch was beginning to develop in her side and her ribs were aching painfully. Every breath proved difficult, not quite reaching her lungs, but she couldn't have stopped even if she had wanted to. She swung around a thick pylon and skidded hastily to a stop; she found herself at the edge of a very deep, very dark ravine. Steel structures towered above, trickling down into the ravine itself, but none presented a way to cross it. Carey cast about but found nothing that could help. She heard the heavy footfalls of the guard and decided it was now or never. She bent her knees, swung her arms and took a giant leap out into the nothingness. She reached out desperately for a short beam that hung before her, and feeling the cold hard metal on her hands, she gripped hard. As her legs swung down, Carey heard something unimaginably terrifying; the creak of bending metal. All of a sudden, the end she was hanging from screeched loudly and broke away from the main structure. Carey screamed and slid down to the loose end with a jerk. She strained to hold on, her fingers slipping on the sleek shaft. The black depths of the ravine were creeping up on her as she tried pulling herself back up on to the beam. She reached for a nearby limb but it was just beyond her fingertips; Carey slipped further. Her palms were sweaty and she could feel herself steadily losing her grip. There came a short harsh laugh from above and Carey saw the guard standing at the edge of the chasm. He was watching her with his gleaming demonic eyes. He gripped his cloak and leapt from the edge, landing nimbly and lightly on a beam a few feet above her. It was graceful compared to her awkward leap of desperation. He crouched there above her like an animal of prey as he watched her struggle. Carey looked up at him fearfully, but knew she would not let him win. She was too close now…

Carey grappled for another hold, desperately trying to find a way out. The guard stretched out his hand, and for a moment there, Carey thought that he was going to help her up, though she later realised how stupid she had been to even consider such a thing.

"Did you really think you could escape?" he hissed and a silver mist filtered through the air.

Carey didn't answer at first, watching the mist as it surrounded her. She grit her teeth. "What made you think I couldn't?" she said, trying to sound brave.

The Imperial glared and he clenched his fist. Carey wondered for a second what on earth he was doing before a strong force closed around her throat and she coughed in alarm. She grabbed at it but collected only fistfuls of air, or rather, mist. The Imperial raised his hand, lifting Carey with it. She was dragged upwards until she was just above his eye line; she was slowly choking with every inch he lifted her. She gripped her throat, coughing, debating quickly whether to use her magic or not. If he didn't stop soon, she'd have no choice. His grasp tightened. She was now looking him right in those terrifying eyes and she saw no mercy there. His features were barely human as he snarled, the scar on his cheek illuminated in the dim light. He was going to kill her and the powers within her sensed this. It prickled beneath her skin and she knew that there was no question now about whether she would use it. She closed her eyes and reached for it, feeling the unpleasant sensation of prickling beneath her skin and in her veins. The same deep, dark feeling engulfed her and it fought to get free with the ferocity of a caged tiger.

The guard, not noticing any change in his quarry, answered her question.

"Because you are a stupid witch, one of those suicidal rebels that so unknowingly step where they don't belong. Rebels don't do well on Imperial land."

He tightened his fist further, cutting off Carey's airway almost completely. The animal inside her chest roared to be free but she stayed it. She looked down; there were many beams beneath her and she just hoped she'd be lucky enough to land on one of them. She could feel the blood rushing from her head and Carey spoke to the guard with what breath she had left.

"Do – do you know who I am?" she choked hoarsely.

The guard grinned. "No, but please, tell me the name of the great rebel I am about to eliminate."

Carey looked him in the eyes and she relented. "One you shouldn't have crossed."

The power rushed from her body and with the roaring wind and flash of blinding light, the guard released her. With a gut-wrenching lurch, Carey fell; she reached out frantically and she hit cold metal. Pain split her wrist but she ignored it. Wind rushed about her ears, rock and steel flying past her at an alarming rate; she cried out in horror to think she might end up at the bottom of the ravine when she landed hard on a low beam, flat on her stomach. Fighting for breath, Carey hiccoughed, tasting blood. She hugged the beam and closed her eyes. It took a good few moments before she could see through the agony of her bashed and bruised body. She was aching all over; her ribs were almost certainly broken and she felt her wrist. There was sticky scarlet blood seeping from a deep gash and it was beginning to swell. She groaned; she'd have a hard time fighting now. But despite her many aches and pains she couldn't stay there; there'd be Örd everywhere before long. Carey looked up then down; she gripped the beam hard to stop herself falling from shock. Below her beam was nothing but darkness, the endless black of the deep ravine gaping before her. She gulped; that had been far too close. Never had she been so close to death without even knowing it.

Shaking, she forced herself carefully to her feet, trying hard not to look down. To fall to her death now that she was safe would be disastrous. Carey reached up and took hold of a beam a few feet above her and awkwardly pulled herself up on to it. She rolled onto it, panting hard and gripping her wrist. There were still at least thirty metres above her and Carey moaned in distress. This was going to be hard. Slowly but surely, she pulled herself up, being careful to test each beam before she heaved herself onto it. She kept an ear out for the rush of feet, but thankfully there was nothing. Only the distant call of some lone creature and the grinding and groaning of moving steel-works echoed down to her. The fear of falling never left her, causing her to shake uncontrollably every time she brought herself to her feet. Finally, at the top of the ravine, she crouched on her beam and scoured the land with her eyes cautiously. To her disgust, Carey found the guard's body lying only metres from her on the very edge of the cliff. Looking closer she was surprised to see he was still breathing; his broad chest rose and fell with short, jagged breaths. They were slow and the gap between each one was long. Carey was amazed he had survived. She had felt a slight hesitance at the back of her mind that had betrayed her fear of this deadly force – she hadn't wanted to kill him. Perhaps he had survived because of this. The same anger and fury that had forced her hand before had been absent this time. Did this mean she could control this power? Could she control its destruction?

Carey turned from the guard. Those questions would have to wait. Right now she had to get out of there and the only way to get across was to jump... again. She calmed herself and aimed for a wide piece of metal to her right. She gripped a higher beam and half-swung, half-jumped over to it, landing lightly and with a lot more grace than last time. Crouching low, she proceeded to the next with a wide leap, again landing lightly. Each limb creaked, and with each jump she prayed for the next beam not to break and give way to the bottomless pit below her. With a sigh of relief, her feet connected with the reddish-brown earth and she knelt, wanting almost to kiss it in gratitude. After a moment's rest, she stood and straightened her silver cuff. Hopefully, she'd get out of there before any Örd discovered the guard. It was only a minute or so though before this hope was rudely quashed.

There came the sound of running feet and she whipped around; without thinking twice, she ran. Carey sprinted as fast and as hard as she could and hurdled over the low metal boundary. She ran into the woods and dashed swiftly between the trees, heading towards the shanty town on the edge of the city. She glanced behind her and the sight was surely what nightmares were made of; at least a dozen Örd had arrived and they had begun scanning the area, their weapons ready. Carey turned and kept running. It was slightly downhill, making it easier, but only just. The branches of the twisted oaks were low and she found herself scratched and bruised in no time. She didn't know where she would go after this, whether she'd be able find Torena or not. She couldn't go straight to the castle though, not in her immediate state. She had so little energy left and right now she was running completely on adrenalin.

It was almost sunset and the sky was beginning to darken, the angry clouds above adding to the air of imminent danger. There came a shout. Carey bit down on her lip and ran harder. The crashing of breaking tree limbs behind her willed her on, the stitch in her side and her injured ribs forgotten. A spell hit the tree beside her and it burst into flame. Carey jumped out of its way and hastily summoned the magic that she so feared, to shield her. This was no time to be picky. The tingling sensation quickly spread and Carey breathed as she was re-energized by it. It was refreshing and she pushed onwards, safely guarded against the attacks of those chasing her. She burst from the woods to find herself on the edge of the village. There were people, slaves, everywhere, walking up and down the muddy streets, hanging dusty mats out of small crooked windows and cooking food in blackened tins over open fires. A few people looked up as she burst into the alleyway, tousled and panting, but most ignored her. She heard the Örd behind her and turned to see their ugly faces and yellow eyes glaring hungrily after her. Their screeching and gibberish followed her, echoing off the close-set huts. Their approaching sounds awoke a fear in the people surrounding her and they quickly retreated back into their homes, leaving Carey alone. She sensed their terror and as she took off through the darkening streets, her heart began to pound with something other than exhaustion.

She passed more and more workers, most of whom simply watched her with mild surprise, a sentiment which quickly changed. A few cried out as she brushed past them, but their exclamations of indignation soon turned to terrified screams that resonated throughout the village. Bright bursts of colour followed loud screeches from the Örd. Carey gritted her teeth and wiped her brow; the stitch in her side was creeping up into her chest, making it harder and harder to breathe. She searched for the turrets of the castle and followed them, using them as a guide. She figured that if she got near enough to the castle, where there would be plenty of magic, perhaps the Örd would discontinue their pursuit. It was a desperate theory but she needed it to work.

Trying to find her way through the labyrinth of shacks, Carey took a sharp turn and found herself facing the worst possible thing – a dead-end. She looked around but found nothing that could help her, only the smoke blackened walls at her sides and the mud beneath her feet. The Örd were coming; the screams continued to resonate through the air, mixing with the thunder overhead. Their curses illuminated the sky above the huts. It was a nightmare; she couldn't find any way out of it. She steadied herself, her back firm against the wall. The only option now was to stand and fight. The pounding of her heart and rush of blood in her ears grew with every terrifying second she waited. Carey faced the opening of the alleyway and stretched out her arms, preparing to fight. Just as she heard the Örd enter the adjacent alley, a hidden door to her left swung open and an arm reached out. Before she had time to register what was happening, she was pulled roughly through and into an unknown darkness...

Chapter Twenty-Six

Loyalists of the Order

C arey landed hard on a dirt floor and, by reflex, threw her arms up over her head. She waited for the blow but nothing came. As the moments passed and no curses were dealt, Carey slowly lowered her arms. It was pitch-black and she felt a presence, several actually, but no one spoke. Carey's head and heart were racing as she sat, waiting for her eyes to adjust. The sounds outside were close now, almost right outside, but still no one moved. It was unnerving.

"Who are you?" Carey whispered, eventually finding her tongue.

She waited but no one answered. It was only then she realised she wasn't being kidnapped – she was being rescued. This calmed her a little, though she did not let her guard down completely. The Örd were now right outside. They sat there in the dark for what seemed an age until the noise and calamity died down and the Örd finally retreated. There was a faint scraping and an oil lamp flared; the faces of her rescuers flickered into sight. A tall, dark man with a long black plait down his back and a short frizzy-haired woman stood before her, staring at her with wide, nervous smiles on their faces. In the woman's arms was a tiny baby, snuggled into his mother's chest fast asleep. An old man lay in a bed covered with tattered grey blankets; he was smiling at her contently, his green eyes kind and gentle. A young boy and girl, with hair like their mother's, sat on the edge of a bunk opposite the old man. Both appeared quite scared at the sight of her. Carey looked back at them quietly. She sensed another person to her left; she turned and was instantly struck by a rush of relief.

"Torena! Oh my – I am so happy to see you! I was so worried that those guards – they knew somehow… but you're safe. You're safe! Oh, I don't think I've ever been happier to see someone in my entire life!"

Carey gripped Torena by the shoulders and grinned, her head still swooning from the relief of this revelation. She had been worried about the fate of her new friend and couldn't bear the thought of anything happening to Torena. Her two best friends had already suffered because of her – she couldn't let another come to the same end.

Torena smiled back. "Don't worry about me. I know all the best hiding spots and back alleyways. It wouldn't have been the first time I've given some guard the slip. I'm just so glad you came our way!"

Carey released her and fell back against the wall, suddenly aware of how exhausted she was.

"I think I may be gladder of that fact. If you hadn't pulled me in…" Carey shuddered at the thought. She clutched her wrist and winced. The pain from the recent battering seemed more pronounced now the adrenalin was subsiding. The frizzy-haired woman rushed to her side.

"Oh my, let me have a look at that."

"Carey, this is my mother and father–"

"Dymphna Patroni," Torena's mother said in introduction as she lay her son in a small, roughly hewn cradle so she could look closer at Carey's wounds. "And this is Earc, my husband. My, my, that is a nasty cut."

As Mrs Patroni set about applying a paste of what smelt of fermented beans, Carey looked around at the room's other occupants and caught the eye of the elderly man who was watching her keenly. His hair was frizzy like that of the younger members of his family, but was bright white and so thin that his scalp was visible beneath it. He appeared to be getting on in years but his eyes were as sharp as any.

"Am I right in assuming that you're Torena's grandfather?" Carey asked.

The old man smiled and dipped his head. "Aye. Alois Patroni. She has told you about me then?" he answered, his voice deep and broken.

"Well, let's just say she needed to tell me something extraordinary for me to believe her, and what she said was fairly extraordinary."

Torena's grandfather chuckled. "Indeed, it must have seemed. I am fairly certain that you are unaware of the Vuleta and our gift for Seeing, am I correct?" Carey nodded silently; he continued. "Yes, I thought as much. I don't imagine you would have come across many of our kind. We have been mostly contained to this realm, though had any of us managed to cross over we would have sought to help you in any way possible. We've known of you for quite some time."

"But how?" Carey asked, as Mrs Patroni bound her arm with a strip of clean cloth. "How are you able to know that it is me you are waiting for? How do you know I'm the – I'm the–"

"Liberator?" Grandpa Patroni finished for her. "So you know that this is who you are? You have accepted it?"

Carey stared down at her newly bandaged wrist, not quite seeing it. The events of the past few days flew through her mind as she became aware that everyone was watching her, awaiting her response. Her throat was dry and she answered in barely a whisper.

"Certain – events have led me to believe so, yes."

Mrs Patroni and Torena helped her up and into a chair by their grandfather's bed while there came excited whispering from the two young children on the opposite bunk. Grandpa Patroni took her hand, holding it with both of his.

"I know because I have Seen. The powers which bind wizards are limited when it comes to Seeing. We are not Wizards," he said, answering her look of confusion. "We are, as I said, Vuleta. The Empire may know of our abilities but I highly doubt they have found any who would assist them. My abilities transcend these cuffs that have been so kindly bestowed upon us and since my particular brand of magic is so different to that of an Imperial, I have remained undetected, which I believe has worked most kindly in your favour."

He smiled again but Carey could not return it. A numbing possibility had just occurred to her.

"You have seen my future, is that right?" she asked the old man, trembling as she did so.

He seemed to know what she was thinking and smiled in understanding. "My dear, I know what is in your heart and I know how much you desire it but I cannot tell you your fate. To do so would literally tear your soul apart. If I was to tell someone how and when they would die, I can assure you that that person would spend the rest of their life trying to alter that moment. There are a few people who could ever truly accept it, but these people are few and far between. Besides, despite my level of ability, I have been known to be wrong from time to time." He grimaced wryly. "There are ways to disguise one's true fate so that I may not see it, but this in itself is not a very common ability. Don't worry, my dear," he assured, patting her hand in comfort. "It is better to live, don't you think?"

Carey didn't quite know what to say. Since learning of this destiny she had wondered, *desired,* to know what it led to, what challenges it would present, but more importantly, whether she would survive it. However, no matter how much she wanted to know, she could see the logic in Grandpa Patroni's reasoning. Did she really want to know?

"Come, dear, don't worry yourself with thoughts of a distant future. That is an old man's burden. You must eat, then rest. Your friends will need your strength."

Carey sat upright, ignoring the stabbing pain from her ribs. "Friends? What do you mean, *friends?*"

The smile on Alois Patroni's face faltered. "Your friends, companions. Miss Katrina Lawrence and Master Ji Binx."

Her insides twisted and knotted and Carey pulled her hand from his grasp. It was as though she had plunged into a frozen lake, having managed to tiptoe so far over it already.

"What… what are you talking about?" she gasped, getting up from her place.

Everyone was now staring at her, silent with concern. Torena's grandfather stuttered, thrown off by her sudden change in character. "Your friends. You are here to help them. To… to save them."

"Save them?" Carey spluttered in disbelief. "How can I save them? They're dead!"

There was a moment of silence which was punctured by muffled murmurs from the cradle.

"Dead?"

Torena's father had stepped forward. "How is that possible?"

Confusion mixing with an unusual amount of anger, Carey threw her hands above her head. *"How is it possible?* They're dead! I saw them die with my very own eyes! There was a storm... our boat... we couldn't – we–" and she broke down. She couldn't hold back the waves of despair that suddenly stole over her. Had she not just accepted that they were gone? Why were they questioning it? Did they not know how much pain this was causing her?

There was a comforting hand on her shoulder and with a choking sob, she looked up. It was Torena.

"They're dead, Torena," she whispered, pleading for Torena to believe her. "They can't be alive, they can't. The mermaids only saved me. Just me..."

"I know. But you have to listen to what we have to say. Please. We didn't mean to upset you."

It was now Torena who was pleading with her and Carey suddenly felt a stab of embarrassment. Wiping her brow, she faced Mr Patroni again.

"I'm sorry. I – I don't know what came over me."

He didn't say anything; instead, he ushered her back to the seat by the bed. Once she had completely calmed, he asked her a question.

"Do you know why the People are suffering?"

Carey, thinking this was a trick question, frowned. "Because of the Empire, isn't it?"

Earc shook his head. " No, no. I meant, why are they suffering *now*, at this very moment?"

Creasing her forehead, she shook her head. "I'm sorry, but I don't know what you mean."

Mr Patroni took a deep breath as if to steel himself for what he was about to say. "The people suffer because of Master Ji."

Carey sat stunned as if Mr Patroni had just slapped her across the face. "Ex-excuse me?"

"We heard whispers, rumours, that the Empire had him imprisoned in the castle. These eventuated many months ago, just before everything became much worse."

"Worse?" Carey asked with a tone of incredulity.

Mr Patroni waved his hand in the direction of his eldest daughter. "Torena's misfortune today, yours as well, is a new development. Not long ago Imperials wouldn't even consider touching a slave, but not anymore. Brutality is encouraged, and more than one guard has let slip why."

Not fully understanding, Carey sat silently, listening to Mr Patroni as he continued.

"We hear that he is being tortured – for information. The People believe it has something to do with the Liberator, with you. Don't worry!" he exclaimed at the sight of Carey's shock. "They don't know it's you. The Empire was getting desperate, hoping that Master Ji would divulge the truth. The tale of a prophetic Liberator has been a source of great hope for a long time for many of us. We have gladly endured this cruelty, knowing that as long as we suffered, the secret of your identity had not yet been given up."

"He didn't," Carey said faintly.

"What?"

"He... Ji... didn't give me up..."

It wasn't Mr Patroni's speech which suddenly had Carey feeling weak. She had suddenly recalled her dream, the strange vision of Ji trapped in a dungeon.

"And do you know what happened to Ji?" Carey asked fervently, wanting to know more.

There was a pause but Carey didn't need them to answer; the truth was clearer than her dream.

"I'm so sorry, my dear," Mrs Patroni said softly, apologetically. "But all we have heard are rumours. We cannot be sure of his fate..."

Carey turned to Torena's grandfather but he shook his head. "I'm sorry, but that's not how it works. I wish I could see everyone's future, but for me, I only see that which makes a difference. Your future is significant to us all so it stands out. If I had time, perhaps..."

Carey ran her hand through her hair once more, trying to accept the possibility that perhaps her dream had not been a dream at all. If what they said was true though, it suddenly made everything much more complicated. For one, how could Ji be here when he had been with Kat and her all this time?

"He wouldn't give me up, Ji," she said, wanting to explain. "I – I had a dream, not that long ago. Everything you have said – it's as though you took what was in that dream and just laid it before me as the truth. I saw him, trapped and tortured. Malevolence wanted to know about the Liberator but he refused. And now I find out that not only Ji has suffered for his silence, but you have also suffered."

It was a terrible thought, one that she had wanted to avoid, but it had become something completely out of her control. How many more would suffer because of this destiny?

"My dear, don't worry about us. Despite the horrors, we prefer this much more than the alternative. At least, this way, we have hope of a reprieve. If you were given up to the Empire, then we would have nothing."

"It's confusing though, isn't it?" Torena said. "That you said you saw your friend, Ji, drown, yet he should be in the castle. How can that be?"

It seemed to be something they were all thinking yet something none of them had an answer to. The improbability of it all seemed to hang in the air like a murky fog, blurring what Carey had thought she had known so that nothing seemed straightforward and simple anymore. There was a long silence where no one spoke and Carey was only brought back from her stupor when she felt a tug on her sleeve. The small girl with her mother's hair was staring at her with wide eyes.

"Have you theen butterflyth before?" she asked with a soft, lisping voice.

The question seemed to bring everyone back to the moment. The girl asked again.

"Have you?"

"Lyal, come on now," Torena said reproachfully, picking up her younger sister.

"Well Lucas thaid that I can thee butterflyth in the other realm. Can you?" she asked Carey with wide-eyed hopefulness.

"Yes, you can, and they're beautiful," she answered, causing Lyal to be overcome with excitement. "Every colour of the rainbow."

The little girl wriggled her way out of her sister's arms and jumped on the bed where her brother sat, watching quietly. "Did you hear, did you hear, Lucath? They have butterflyth and *rainbowth!*"

As the small girl ran about the tiny hut, her imagination running wild, Carey watched as her family looked on with a love she couldn't remember ever feeling herself. She saw in the family a closeness and affection that she so longed for, her mind wandering to the photograph in Madame Guise's wagon. Had her own family once known the same bond or had something happened, something so drastic that it drove her sisters to betrayal? She wanted so badly to remember, not for comfort but to perhaps make sense of what had happened. Their actions had changed the course of their lives forever; they were the reason she was here, the reason why the Empire had succeeded, the reason why the Patronis were forced to live their lives as slaves. What had changed in them? When was that moment in time when Jodie and Laurel Lee had made the decision that would ultimately affect the lives of so many? Carey wondered what effect their betrayal and her disappearance had ultimately had on her mother and father. Would they be the same?

Lyal jumped about happily as her mother prepared some food and the others talked amongst themselves. Despite their lot, the Patronis seemed happy and Carey suddenly realised what damage her presence could do to that happiness.

"Torena... Torena. I – I can't stay here. I can't. I appreciate everything you've done, everything your family has done. But this is too risky. Your family–"

"Knew what they were getting themselves into," Grandpa Patroni finished with an odd little smile. "My dear, we know perfectly well the risks of helping one such as yourself. Don't delude yourself into believing we're indifferent to the perils of this situation. Now, you need food and you need rest. Please–" he interrupted Carey's start at an argument, "– you are wounded and exhausted, both of which will play to your disadvantage. Don't worry your head about us – we have already lasted this long. If we are not long for this world, even if I have seen it, there would be little I could do, or you, for that matter, to delay that fact. Death is only a stage – it is never the end."

His last words struck a chord with Carey, their weight reverberating through her body. Their risk and willingness to forego everything for her made her feel uneasy, but at the same time humbled. The Patroni's acceptance of a fate that may yet befall them, one that Carey continued to struggle with herself, bolstered the respect she already felt for the family, realising how little she truly deserved their kindness. She could not argue with them, not when she saw the strength of Grandpa Patroni's conviction mirrored in the faces of his family.

Mrs Patroni presented her with some food and she accepted it graciously. The rest of the family joined her and soon the sound of chatter and the high-pitched laughter of the children filled the hut. Torena sat at her side, eating silently.

"Torena?"

"Hmm?" she mumbled, her mouth full of food.

"How did your family come to be here?" Carey asked.

Torena finished eating before placing her bowl on the ground. "We haven't always been here. We were only sent here perhaps a year ago. I say *perhaps* because you really lose track of time in this place. My mother was pregnant with Hari at the time so that's where I lay my presumption.

"The uprising happened when my mother and father were young. Our village was hidden amongst the mountains so at first it didn't affect them. But it soon spread and they couldn't hide from it anymore. Our people, the Vuleta, are born warriors and so naturally we fought. They fought back the Imperials that threatened us but they were relentless. We would defeat one wave of attacks only to have another come in its place. Our warriors were waning and they couldn't carry on that way forever. So they went into hiding.

"They built a whole underground city that was effectively sealed off from the rest of the world. That's where my mother and father met. They didn't want to have children at first, given the situation, but they, as well as everyone else, soon came to realise that the Empire wasn't going away in any great hurry. The council instated a complete seal, except for a group of explorers, who would go above ground once a month. These exploration groups would collect information about the progress of the Empire and about the world at large. They found that many villages and towns, not unlike our own, had also escaped underground but that the Empire was growing stronger, its reach spreading. The one thing that kept everyone hopeful was the news of the rebellion, of Fiana Parnell and her famous Order. I remember the stories that were told by explorers, of the fights and the wars these gallant people fought. I remember when she came to our village. I remember when your grandmother met my grandfather...

"And then they disappeared... but, I guess you know all about that."

"But, if you were so safe in your underground city, what happened that you ended up here?" Carey asked, slightly afraid of what she might hear.

"Well, after the Order disappeared, after *you* disappeared, there was less and less for the explorers to report. Other than the growing strength and stability of the Empire, which did nothing to lighten our spirits, there was little else. There was this one man, however, who became increasingly interested in the explorations, despite their futility. He volunteered time after time to go above ground. The council, among others, became suspicious of his motives and ordered for the decommission of the above-ground ventures, but not before one final expedition was carried out."

Hesitantly, Carey asked in barely a whisper, "What happened?"

She knew what Torena's answer would be, but knowing didn't make the truth any easier to hear.

"He betrayed us."

There was a short pause in which Torena was playing absent-mindedly with the spoon in her bowl and Carey pondered on how the effects of betrayal had led them both to where they were today. Would either of them have been there if Carey's sisters had never turned the Order over to the Empire? Who would have helped her if Torena's family had never been discovered? She was quickly discovering how deeply complex the business of Seeing might actually be.

Torena sighed a short rattling breath and Carey felt she was battling some inner demons.

"It happened so suddenly; they were so strong. I – I can't really remember… it was so scary…"

Carey had the feeling her friend did remember what had happened that fateful day, but judging from the pain etched across her face, she was trying her best to suppress the memories.

"We were some of the lucky ones. Surviving the raid wasn't our only challenge. Our luck lies in the fact that we managed to stay together."

The high-pitched melody of a whistle began to echo around the cabin; Torena's father was playing for the entertainment of the two younger children as Grandpa Patroni clapped along in time. Mrs Patroni had taken baby Hari from his crib and was rocking him gently, watching her family with a smile of watching her beloved. As Carey sat there observing them, with so many questions and doubts running through her head, she wanted to believe that she could finally bring them the one thing they truly deserved – freedom.

Chapter Twenty-Seven

The Enemy's Hand

Feeling utterly exhausted after the events of the past few days, Carey accepted the Patroni's invitation to stay and retired to a bed of softened bracken and light wool blankets. Despite the many thoughts of dark castles and looming dangers running through her mind, Carey slipped almost instantly into unconsciousness, her body finally overpowering her mind.

Carey woke slowly to find herself no longer in the Patroni's small hut but in a beautiful garden. Lifting herself from the soft, green grass, she couldn't help feeling that she wasn't dreaming – she was having the same sensations as the time she stood in the dungeon with Ji. What had Malevolence called it?

Looking around she had to admit that it was nothing like her last venture into this strange dream-world. Surely such a place as this didn't exist in Terra Saga.

It was just on dusk and the garden was dimly lit by tiny, flickering lights scattered amongst the trees and bushes. The small clearing in the centre was surrounded by small, stunted pines, their needles rustling gently in the soft breeze. The night air was cool and tickled her bare skin. White-gold butterflies floated through the air, spreading with them a sense of calm and peace. Carey looked down at her feet and gasped in wonder at the beautiful flowing gown she was clothed in. Its long sleeves reached down to the hem, each layer of the garment overlapping, fading from a glittering yellow to a crimson red. She breathed in the sweet air as she tilted her head back. She was beginning to wonder why she was there when a voice sounded behind her, making her jump.

"Beautiful, isn't it?" a man asked. "Good evening, Princess."

Carey spun around in astonishment. A man in long, royal-red robes stood just behind her, a hood shadowing his face. He took a step towards her, propelling her away from him. She heard danger in that voice.

"Who are you?" Carey asked with slight trepidation.

It was the most obvious question though one she thought she would not get an answer to. He surprised her.

"Excuse my rudeness," he said politely. "My name is Saar. I am but a humble wizard."

Carey didn't say anything.

"I see I've caught you unawares, Princess. I humbly beg your pardon. I have summoned–"

"Why do you call me that?" Carey interrupted, feeling slightly confused. "Why do you keep calling me Princess?"

She was unsettled as it was far from being a term of endearment.

The man lifted his hands and lowered his hood. His face was lightly tanned and from his chin grew a sharp, short black beard. His black hair was tied back rather messily, loose strands hanging down by his face. But Carey barely acknowledged these. She was instead drawn instantly to his eyes. His pupils were a steely silver, void of any apparent emotion. They were mesmerising, burning with extreme intensity. They were the eyes of a mad man yet he stood there before her, completely calm. Her stomach ached with familiarity but she could not place him. He clasped his hands together calmly.

"Merely a courtesy, Princess."

When Carey did not return his acknowledgment, a look of mild surprise flitted across his features. His smile turned to a sneer of amusement.

"You do not know..."

Carey frowned. "Know what, exactly?"

This man Saar continued to watch her in bemusement. "Well, truly, if you don't know, it is certainly not my place to tell you."

It was a strange thing to say but it seemed this Saar individual wasn't about to indulge her further. He was undoubtedly a dubious character and he failed utterly in gaining her trust with his odd speech. Then again, perhaps he wasn't trying to. His eyes glinted hungrily and Carey felt as though he might lash out at any moment. The garden around her no longer felt calm and peaceful but tense and dangerous. The soft breeze whispered warnings in her ear and the butterflies had retreated. Carey's heartbeat restlessly, fluttering like a caged bird being threatened by a large stalking tabby. There was something about this man that irked her and Carey had to find out.

"What is this place?"

He spread his arms wide in presentation. "Do you like it? I created it just for you, Princess. This is your reality."

Carey squinted at him warily. "Reality? This is a dream, is it not?"

The man looked as though he could not believe his ears; he burst out laughing. "A dream! Oh surely you cannot be so naïve? I heard of your encounter in the dungeons and thought... I cannot believe this! How on earth did you manage to survive this long?"

Indignant and thoroughly unimpressed by this man, Carey threw caution to the wind. "Who exactly do you think you are? You find pride in mocking me and then you proceed to question my abilities? If this is not a dream then I demand you tell me exactly what is happening here at once!"

Saar's expression returned to a silent leer. "Demand? Why then, Princess, I suppose I have no choice, though I am not quite accustomed to having to explain myself. You have heard the term Twilight Traveller, *no?" He continued when Carey nodded warily. "To put it plainly, you are able to transport your subconscious, while you sleep, to a real place. However, it is not you that has brought you here this night – I summoned you. It was incredibly easy, I must say. You really must be more cautious, Princess. It was so easy to bring you here. Just imagine how easy it would be to keep you here too."*

Carey blanched. Looking at this man who was surely as dangerous as she feared, she did not doubt for a second that he meant what he said. His explanation of this strange situation made an even stranger sense. He knew of the dungeon; it would explain how it had happened whilst she had slept, and despite the fact that she did not trust him any further than she could throw him, she felt that she had to believe. Carey took a steadying breath.

"What do you want?" she asked, trying to exude confidence. "You must have brought me here for a reason, and it was surely not to enjoy a moonlit walk."

"Hostility, Princess, never helped anyone," Saar commented, his silver-pupil eyes glinting dangerously. "You want to know what I want? It is something that you may want too, actually. I have a proposal."

There was a pause, during which Carey frowned. "A proposal," she repeated, but when Saar made no indication of continuing, she asked, "What is it you're proposing, exactly?"

He smiled unpleasantly. "You are part of a dying race, Princess, the last of the true rebels. Once you are gone, the Empire will feel no qualms in taking the remainder. With your families under their control, you alone hold the last true threat. However," he paused for effect, "I can help you. I can help you avoid the pain of death and keep you protected from all your potential enemies."

Carey snorted; she seriously doubted that. If Malevolence wanted her dead, she couldn't see this man being able to stop her. Yet despite her misgivings about what he'd just said, she was curious to know the full deal.

"But of course you want something in return. I don't believe this kind of offer comes without some sort of price."

There was a snap like a whip and Saar was suddenly right behind her. She stiffened, not daring to move as she felt his breath on the back of her neck. His whisper sent shivers down her spine and made her hair stand on end.

"I am asking you to join me," he said simply.

Carey looked back over her shoulder; his face was barely an inch from her own. "Join you? Join you in what?"

"The future holds many uncertainties, Princess," he said, going to clasp her shoulders yet not touching her. His hands followed her shoulders, moving down her arms. "In times of confusion, the People will need leaders, ones with power and force who can make finite decisions and think without the need of a, in my opinion, futile council."

Carey whispered furiously, the disdain for his presumptions shining through harshly. "What future are you talking about? How can you begin to talk of such things as the future and possible leaders when the present is already enough to consider? Tell me, Saar, who are you exactly?"

Saar leaned in closer so that his lips were almost touching her ear. "I am but a humble loyalist, second only to the Empress herself."

"S-second to Malevolence?"

Carey's heart skipped a beat. Stepping away from him she gulped back a wave of panic. An ordinary Imperial she could have handled but this was infinitely worse – a high-level Imperial with a plan to usurp Malevolence herself. Not only that, but he could trap her there, keep her for his own purposes.

She looked back at her captor and saw triumph in his face.

"And what would happen if I refused?" she asked a little shakily.

His grin faded to be replaced by a bone-chilling expression. "Let us just say that unpleasant occurrences may come about," he threatened.

The low rumbling of his voice resounded through Carey's memory and an image flashed across her mind's eye. It was the smallest detail but now she knew where she had seen him before.

"The priest," Carey whispered, her lips trembling uncontrollably as the memory came flooding back.

Saar stared. "Excuse me?"

"The priest from Seramina's trial. You're the priest from Burtonport."

"She was a pretty little witch," Saar sneered. "I have to say, you are very clever, Princess, a lot cleverer than most. You have been able to see through our smokescreens – you discovered our true motive for the burnings, even before your friends. And you have a certain mystique about you. What with your lineage and certain... talents... who knows what you are capable of," he said cryptically.

Carey's face burned as he mentioned her friends, but she controlled her anger, not wanting to give him the satisfaction. She began to slowly back away.

"I've seen what you do, what the Empire does. I've seen what they've done to Terra Saga and the devastation they've left in the Common world. You destroy villages, you befoul anything beautiful or good and you've enslaved my people. My people. You keep my family from me and your cause killed my friends. You commit the most heinous and diabolical of acts in this realm and the next, the likes of which I could never have imagined in my entire life. I don't care for your flattery or insinuations. I swore I'd put a stop to the Empire and their crusade, even if it kills me. I am a Seeker of the Order of the Rose and I will not bow to the will of Dark magic. Be sure of it, Saar, I will not join you!"

At her words, Saar's face darkened and whatever courage Carey had evaporated. Her fear turned her breathing haggard and uneven and she couldn't believe her daring. Was she going insane? One moment she felt unbelievably brave, the next she was scared out of her wits.

There was a low rumbling and a sharp, harsh wind blew up around them. Saar's cloak flapped wildly against the wind and his eyes burned dark with hatred.

"If you won't come by invitation..."

Saar held out his hand and produced a crystal globe; it flickered with moving pictures of faces she didn't recognise. Carey watched as they slowed to reveal a single face – Torena.

"You choose your company very recklessly, Princess. An entire family of rebel loyalists have placed their lives in your hands, they trust you..."

The globe dissipated into a thousand particles and Carey swallowed, rooted to the spot in absolute fear.

"Let us see how powerful and brave you are, Princess. Let us see how much they trust you after this."

Carey took a breath. "What are you doing, Saar?"

His eyes flashed. "The Imperial guards are ruthless, Princess, and I have them at my very fingertips."

"No..."

"Traitors to the Empire are not tolerated, no matter who they are."

He clicked his fingers and he laughed.

"No!" Carey screamed. "What have you done?"

"Then join me. Join me and I'll call them to halt."

Carey shook her madly. "No! Never! I will never join you!"

"Then they will die."

There was a crash that resounded all around them and Carey stumbled backwards. "What was that?" she screamed at Saar through the thundering wind. Shouts echoed through the clearing and Carey threw her hands over her ears.

"That would be the guards. They're very, very close."

A crash exploded, reverberating through Carey's body. An ear-splitting scream *followed and Carey closed her eyes, trying to block out this nightmare. She had to get back, she had to save them; she wouldn't let them die at the hands of Imperials. Carey tried forcing herself back, forcing herself to wake, but something was blocking her.*

Voices vibrated in her head.

'Papa! Papa, help!'

'Seize them! Traitors of the Empire, surrender!'

'Torena, no!'

A crash and another scream filtered through the garden air and Carey gripped at her hair in distress. "What have you done? Why are you doing this?" *she yelled hoarsely, practically spinning on the spot as she listened to the distraught yells and cries echoing around her.*

"Because," *Saar bellowed, his eyes flashing wildly,* "I want you to see the consequences of your actions!"

He let out a mad, booming laugh that cut through Carey like a knife.

"C-consequences? These aren't consequences," *Carey choked.* "This... this is blackmail! Stop it! Stop it now!"

Saar's face was set with a merciless grin. "You see, Princess, what I mean by how smart you are? Once again I will ask. Join me," *he hissed darkly.*

Carey shook her head, trembling. "No."

The wind and noise flared. Carey could hear Earc Patroni's desperate calls to his family.

'Carey, Carey wake up! Please help us!' *she heard Torena plead with her. There came a strangled cry, another loud crash and a loud, threatening growl.*

Carey was overwrought. The Imperial wizard before her looked to the sky before turning to Carey.

"Valē, Princess," *he said with a wave of his hand, and like before, the voices, wind and picturesque garden swirled together into one great mass, her head spinning as she returned to the real world. The clamour pressed in on her as she was pulled back unmercifully by the great force, wrenched from where she stood. For a moment she couldn't feel or see anything – it was all just a wall of high-pitched wailing, hurling her through a vast nothingness...*

Carey forced open her eyes just as the sharp pointed end of a spear was bearing down at her head. With a shout of surprise, she rolled sideways off the bed as it hit the wall behind her. She jumped to her feet and out of reach of the Imperial guard as he swung his free arm at her chest. There was screaming, crying and shouting all around the room. Another guard behind her grabbed her around the waist and she stumbled forward in surprise. As she struggled, Carey caught a glimpse of the Patronis. They had been forced into the foremost corner of the shanty and were surrounded by a number of guards. Lyal and Lucas had streams of tears running down their faces as they huddled together –blood was gushing from a deep gash in Lucas' brow. Dymphna was holding Hari protectively to her chest as she tried desperately to shield her children. Earc was yelling at the guards and Torena was clinging to her beloved grandfather, her face pale with wild terror. Carey tried summoning her magic but she couldn't; something was suppressing her powers. She could feel it sparking inside her, trying to ignite but it was as though a damp blanket had been thrown over it. She let out a scream of rage and frustration.

As Carey's guard bound her arms, she watched as Dymphna was struck to the ground by an over-zealous Imperial. She fell to the floor where she lay still.

Unable to bear it, Carey tore herself from the guard only to be stopped by another. "No! Let me go – Torena! No, don't do this! Get off me!" she screamed, pulling against the Imperial's grip.

One particular guard, wearing a dark-blue cloak, stepped in front of Carey, facing the Patronis.

"Slaves! You have been found guilty of aiding and abetting a rebel and of conspiring against the Empire and the Empress. You are hereby condemned to death as punishment for your crimes, as ordered by Lord Saar, and sanctioned by her Majesty, the Empress *Di Mur*."

The guard pointed a hand to the door and his troupe began to retreat, leaving the Patronis in their corner. Torena jumped up and began to push her way to Carey but was knocked back. Still struggling madly, Carey was dragged from them. She dug her feet hard into the ground but the sheer strength of the guard almost broke her ankles. Once outside, the door was shut and bolted, but even then she could still hear Torena's pleas for help and Lyal's petrified cries. They barred the doors before stepping away, hauling Carey back roughly with them. Still straining against her captor's grip, Carey watched in horror as one produced a ball of orange flame and hurled it onto the roof. It hit the house with a flare, quickly engulfing the tiny shack.

Carey was fraught with desperation. She fought with all her might, tooth and nail against the two guards now restraining her. "Stop... no, let me off... please... urgh!" she screamed, but the guards did not falter, nor did they loosen their grip. Again she tried calling her powers but to no avail; she could only guess that the guards holding her were the ones restraining her magic.

A command was called and they moved away from the burning shack at the end of the alleyway. Carey kicked and screamed, grief pounding in her chest and tears running down her cheeks in torrents. She wasn't going to go quietly, not while she still had strength enough to fight. Too many people had died for her already because of what she was. The Patronis didn't deserve this. No one deserved this.

The guards led her through the dark alleys of the slave village, paying no attention to her rage. None of the People looked out in curiosity or ran to the aid of the Patronis and because of this Carey fought even harder. Through her anger she spied a loose beam, held up by a flimsy pole just ahead of them. As the guards drew near, Carey kicked out hard at the centre of the support. The Imperial to her right yelled as the support crumbled, releasing the beam. It swung down and Carey ducked at the last second; the guards released her in astonishment as the metal beam dealt them both a heavy blow across their shoulders. Carey tumbled forwards, dodging the falling wreck.

She thought of her bindings and they instantly fell from her hands. She sprung to her feet. "*Stop!*" she screeched and several of the Imperials froze. From somewhere to her right she saw the glint of a weapon just as it swung at her, scraping her shoulder and knocking her back to the ground. The guard swung the spear again and Carey kicked out. Her foot connected with the man's knee and he shrieked in pain, falling beside her as she scrambled out of the way.

Carey glanced momentarily at the other guards before speeding off down the narrow street. She could hear the remaining Imperials racing after her, their heavy footfalls pounding the dirt. Carey ducked quickly around a corner and found herself leaving the shanty village. Well-kept cobblestone roads and high, terraced houses leered before her, presenting a greater danger. This was Imperial soil.

Feeling another stitch starting to develop in her side, Carey vaulted off a wooden barrel by the roadside and gripped a balcony railing. Hearing the danger closing in, Carey lifted herself up and crouched on the edge of the terrace like a watchful tiger. She watched as the men stopped below her; one shouted in suggestion and they hurried off down another side street. Carey peered behind her into the house, but all was still. After making sure no one was coming back, she jumped down from the balcony and set off towards the castle. She could smell the fire wafting from the village, but with all her strength, willed herself to go on.

Devastated by what had happened, Carey now felt more alone than she had ever before. Torena's screams still filled her head, her face as she was knocked to the ground. The horrors of a thousand nightmares couldn't match what she had just witnessed and she doubted whether she would ever be able to forget it.

As the castle loomed, Carey tried to pull herself together. The castle was surrounded by a monstrous stone wall. Several guards paced the perimeter, their sinister weaponry glinting in the pale moonlight. As if she already knew what to do, Carey ripped the metal ring from around her neck and replaced it with her Seeker's necklace. She then took from her pocket her mother's pin. In a little less than a minute, Carey was crawling over the wall, on her way to face an uncertain destiny. And she was going to face it.

Chapter Twenty-Eight

The Labyrinthine Deceit

The castle loomed darkly overhead, its many turrets jutting towards the sky and its gargoyles glaring into the night. A bolt of lightning split the clouds, its flickering light casting eerie shadows on all below. A small green lizard crawled its way over a large boulder that sat at the bottom of a great ugly statue, hewn from black stone. A twisted and contorted figure sprang from the ground, its face hidden beneath a carved hood. Its arms stretched commandingly towards the heavens as though it wished to control them. The lizard glanced up at the stone figure for only a moment before continuing towards the castle. The expansive courtyard was overtaken by long weeds and tortured trees. The trunks of the latter were gnarled and misshapen, curling protectively along the castle walls, their thorns a pulsating green.

The lizard came to a halt by the large wooden door. Above, walking along the ramparts, were two Imperials. A large cauldron-like fire torch stood burning to the left of them. The lizard gazed at the cauldron and a moment later it tipped sideways, the flames extinguishing as coal and ash flew over the edge of the wall. With a cry of surprise, the guards ran over to investigate. As the Imperials spat and cursed over the upturned fire, a slight, blonde girl appeared at the door below. Unnoticed, Carey crept into the shelter of the door's recess, removing the small 'S' pin from her lapel as she went. Unsure of what to do next, she turned to the door and almost let out a gasp of astonishment.

A thick wooden arm was unfurling from the door. Unable to move without exposing herself to those above, Carey watched the arm stretch towards her; it stopped, its palm facing her as if to call a halt. Upon it was a great blinking eye. It rolled around in the palm of the hand, looking Carey over shrewdly. With a sound of a flame being extinguished, the eye was replaced by a pointed nose. Repulsed and terrified at the same time, Carey stood frozen as the nose sniffed the air. Then with another soft hiss a mouth appeared. Carey's heartbeat quickened. There was a moment where she thought nothing would happen, but then it spoke, and with a long, hissing voice it proclaimed, *"Seeker..."* and before Carey could jump out of the way, the hand reached out and grabbed her by the front of her shirt. Before she knew what was happening, the arm pulled her forward; expecting an impact, Carey flinched, eyes closed, but none came. She looked up and found herself no longer facing the door but in pitch-black darkness. Every muscle tensed, she peered about her new surrounds, aware that an attack may come at any moment. There was a flare of blue light and she shielded her eyes protectively. The light bent and curled, a shape forming within it. Then it was gone and all that was left was a huddled figure crouching in the dark. It whimpered painfully. After a moment's hesitation, Carey approached it slowly, casting about for any signs of a trap. Surely the door's reaction meant it to be?

However, as she came closer and closer to the despondent figure, nothing happened. As she approached the figure, she saw that it was a girl, her dark hair limp and shielding her face. She bent down to try and catch a glimpse of her when the girl looked up suddenly. Her bright green eyes pierced the darkness and Carey scrambled backwards, hardly noticing what was issuing from her lips.

"No... no..."

The girl reached out to her. "Carey... please..." and with a crack and a flash of light she was gone and the room began to dissolve; Carey felt her feet leave the ground. With a scream no one would hear, Carey fell suddenly, but she wasn't falling downwards; she was falling upwards. Her stomach dropped and strange flashes of light flickered around her. Faces and people swirled mist-like about her as Carey reached out for something to grab hold of. No sooner had she thought about it did her hand feel the cold of moulded metal. Closing her fingers around it, the rush of pictures stopped and she flopped hard onto a small stone balcony, her hand around the railing. She found herself sitting above a small dark room; her balcony was round, recessed into the wall and she felt as though she was sitting in a viewing box at the theatre. As her eyes adjusted she saw seven people kneeling on the floor below her, bound and silent. Leaning forward, peering through the banister, Carey thought she recognised them; there was one that, even from this height, looked just like –

"Ji," she breathed.

Ji's older brother, Zacharia, lay sideways on the ground, his long brown hair strewn across the face that was almost identical to that of his younger brother. Her heart skipped a beat when she realised the other six people were those she'd been searching for, the ones for which she had come so far.

As she looked upon their families Carey felt a presence behind her. She whipped around, gasping audibly.

"Sshh," Ji hushed, holding his finger to his lips. Carey's heart leapt to her throat, her brain whirring with confusion and giddiness.

"Ji? How... what..." she struggled to comprehend this sudden apparition.

"Don't worry about that right now," Ji said in a hushed voice. "We have to get you out of here."

"But," Carey spluttered, "what about our families? Zacharia is down there!"

Ji shook his head. "We can't save them. How do you suggest we do it? Can you see a way out?"

Carey suddenly noticed the lack of windows and doors in the darkened room. How were they going to get out? She looked back at Ji, her head pounding. There was only a solid wall behind him.

"Ji? How did you get in?"

In one swift moment, Ji gripped her by the shoulders and pinned her down on the ground.

"Ji! Get off me! What are you thinking?" she cried, struggling against him.

There was something in his eyes, something dangerous, and when he spoke again he sounded different, his voice low and harsh.

"Don't you know how easy it was to track you, to follow you? It was as if you wanted to be found! I think Kat has lost her touch. You made her soft – I don't think she wanted to scare you. It made it oh so easy to find you all, so easy to manipulate. It couldn't have been easier even if you came willingly."

Carey had stopped struggling and was listening with a mixture of astonishment and bewilderment.

"What… what are you saying?"

He smirked. "The truth."

Ji released her and the stone beneath her softened; it began to liquefy.

"What… what is this? J-Ji?" she stammered as she began to sink. Carey looked up at Ji in horror. He winked, and in an instant, was gone. She was in shock and found herself sinking fast. She tried to reach out for the railing but the ground was like quicksand; her arms refused to budge. Panic clouded her and she could imagine herself suffocating. As she watched her body disappear she tried closing her eyes and reached for her magic. She felt something flicker and the strange quicksand released her. She fell straight through the floor and into the light.

Gasping for breath, she blinked, shielding her eyes. Everything was a bright white; she couldn't see any walls or windows or anything else for that matter. It was hurting her eyes. It was like looking straight at the sun.

Carey's head was reeling. Where was she? Was this still the castle? Something was happening here, some kind of elaborate ruse or trap, but Carey couldn't keep up. She wasn't even sure what she had seen was true, especially Ji. She couldn't believe that that had been him. The things he'd said…

Carey got to her feet; as soon as she had, there came a gurgling sound. She looked down, and with a cry of surprise, jumped aside as the ground beneath her feet began to open up, swirling around in a whirlpool-like fashion. It became wider and soon there was a shimmering oval of churning matter at her feet. It wasn't water but something else; it reminded Carey of a mirror.

The light around her was just as bright and it showed no signs of dimming. She was wary of the pool at her feet, but there seemed nowhere else she could go.

Out of the corner of her eye something moved. There was a strange haze to her left; she backed away quickly, moving to the opposite side of the pool. It came towards her, a discernible blob of fuzzy colour. Slowly it became clearer and Carey found herself facing who she thought was Ji once more. He smiled.

"Carey," he whispered, his arms outstretched, but she didn't move.

"Who are you?" she demanded.

She wanted so terribly for him to be real but she couldn't help feeling something wasn't right.

He continued to smile as he reached down and touched the glimmering pool with a single fingertip. Carey watched as a fast succession of images flashed over its surface, the same images that had flown past her as she fell. She could not quite see them clearly but every now and then she saw someone or something she recognised. Gradually they slowed and came into sharper focus until a single image remained. Not wanting to take her eyes off Ji, yet curious of what was moving on the pool's surface, she looked away reluctantly.

The picture was moving, a slightly warped vision of what looked like a memory. Carey's eyes widened as she recognised the scene playing out before her: Jeremy's castle, except it wasn't what Carey remembered. She watched as Ji fell from Firefly and was dragged into the castle by Jeremy. Overseen by the dark shrouded figure that was Malevolence, Jeremy yanked Ji's necklace from around his neck, and as he stood back up his features began to change. Carey put her hand to her mouth, stunned by what she was witnessing. In mere moments, Jeremy's face had lengthened, his red hair fading into a dark brown, short and messy, and he was now a foot shorter. Jeremy had become Ji.

He was exactly the same, right down to the last hair and freckle, and as Carey looked back up she saw that it was no longer Ji standing before her but Jeremy Shultz, the last of his features returning to their original form. She couldn't say anything; she was dumbfounded. Their rescue of who they thought was Ji played out in the pool between them as they stood facing each other. Jeremy surveyed her, the corner of his mouth twitching.

"You've been with us all this time," Carey finally croaked, her voice cracking.

He didn't have to say anything; the truth was written all over his smarmy face. Carey's cheeks burned in humiliation, tears pricking her eyes. It was all a lie, everything.

"Why?"

Again, Jeremy touched the surface. "Please, Carey, there's more."

Fighting back tears and trying to ignore the feeling of her heart slowly breaking, she looked back down. Her eyes followed the progress of their journey as she had never seen it before. She watched in dismay as Jeremy-Ji attacked her by the stables. "Your subconscious gave me new eyes. I could see the inn..."

The spectre of Malevolence appeared in front of a mist, Kat's unconscious body drifting across it. Her voice bubbled up from the pool, a mysterious enchantment and Kat writhed in pain. The mark shone on her cheek already...

It changed and the short, dwarf-like creature Carey had seen way back at the start, in the village that had been destroyed, knocked Kat's Tear Globe to the ground. Carey shivered as she remembered seeing something amongst the trees and how Ji had tried stopping her from reviving Kat. He chuckled malevolently. "Our little friend was so helpful. Malicious species, the Korgin. Always willing to lend their special talents to less savoury endeavours," Jeremy commented casually in a low voice.

The vision shifted again and Carey recognised the scene immediately from her dream. A single tear trickled down her cheek; she couldn't stop it. The pain of seeing Ji suffer for her was too much to relive...

The pool changed one last time to show the mysterious dwarf, rifling through Carey's bag as she slept in the camp at Burtonport. Her hand moved subconsciously to her side where her bag had hung until recently as the dwarf pulled out the remaining Silver Water and pocketed it before promptly disappearing. She hadn't even noticed it was missing...

Carey looked back up at Jeremy, puzzled by this last vision as it flickered and disappeared, the pictures dying as soon as they had begun.

"The Silver Water?"

Jeremy laughed a haunting, sadistic laugh and stepped across the pool, gripping Carey by the wrist before she could step away; he pulled her close.

"It's always been about the Silver Water. The attacks – it was all to lead us there. As I said, you were *so* easy to manipulate. Pity you revived Kat. To be rid of the *Liberator* and to obtain the Silver Water all at once would have been perfect."

The last word escaped his lips as a whisper, dripping with contempt. He tightened his grip and Carey winced.

"But no matter. The third world will soon be ours and your luck is soon to run out."

Spinning her hard by the wrist, Jeremy threw Carey from him; as she fell forward, she found herself in what looked like one of the castle dungeons. Jeremy was gone.

The roof of the dungeon was unusually high and dark stone walls surrounded her on all sides. Green mould stained the walls and the only source of light came from a tiny window in the small metal door. The thin strip of light punctuated the darkness profoundly. Carey's heart was beating furiously, making her feel faint. She was staggering from everything that had just been revealed to her and she cursed her stupidity for not realising the traitor in their midst. She felt cheated and embarrassed by Jeremy's deceit. Was it all just a lie? Her aching heart was surely evidence that it was not.

Her head clouded with confusion, she dropped to the floor, a loud, rattling sob escaping her as she leant against the wall of the labyrinth in which she was surely trapped.

"Who's there?" a voice came from the darkness.

Carey jerked around, staring at the far left corner. Slowly, as her eyes adjusted, she was able to discern the dark outlines of a small group of people. The voice spoke again, this time with more command.

"Who's there?"

Gathering herself, Carey answered. "My name is Carey Lee."

There was a sharp intake of breath. "You shouldn't be here, Carey. I didn't tell them anything."

"Ji?"

Carey didn't know what to believe. Cautiously, she crawled over to where he sat.

He looked terrible; his face was covered in deep wounds, old ones taken over by fresh ones; his hair had grown long and ragged, outlining his swollen face; through the rips and tears in his clothes she could see evidence of his torture. He sat with his eyes closed, yet through it all she could see it was him.

"Oh Ji..."

Carey put her arms around his shoulders. "Here, let me help you up."

As he stood Carey saw the others and recognised them immediately from all the pictures she had ever seen of them. Her heart almost burst as her eyes found her parents, unconscious yet alive. She wanted to run to them but thought it better to help Ji first as he could then help her in return. She didn't realise how wrong she was.

Ji allowed her to lead but with reluctant steps. Making their way to the door, he stumbled, falling to his knees.

"Ji!"

He struck out with his hand as if to grab hold of Carey but missed his mark by a foot; he tried again, but failed to catch her.

"Help me, Carey," he moaned pitifully and Carey fell to her knees beside him.

"Ji? What's happened to you—"

Carey stopped. Kat stood in front of them, wild-eyed and disturbed-looking. For a split second they looked at each other, not quite knowing whether to believe what they were seeing. Then Kat, feeling what she saw was true, let out a cry of relief. Suddenly, a bolt of lightning struck the ground between them, renting the air with an all-mighty crackle. Carey threw Ji aside as a blow of electricity flew at them; she heard Kat scream. An explosion of wind blasted Carey's hair back from her face and she whipped around to see her family momentarily illuminated by the deadly intrusion. She gasped as it created a whirlwind around them; it was drawing something from them. Tiny flames floated up from their chests, hovering just above their limp bodies. Whatever was happening, it wasn't good.

A hand closed around Carey's neck, pulling her back hard, and another grasped her at the waist. A harsh, deep voice spoke in her ear.

"Not so fast, Carey."

To the side Carey saw Kat run to Ji and help him out of the way.

"Let go of me, Jeremy, or–"

"Or what?" he hissed in her ear, his chin against her neck. "I wouldn't try anything. She's coming."

The door banged off its hinges as the wind died and the lightning fizzled out. Black smoke billowed in and great clouds of it filled the room. Carey fought to be free, afraid of summoning her powers in case she accidentally hit Kat or Ji or one of the others. Her chest ached from the panic of her heart bashing against her ribs and she tried to level her breathing.

Then from within the smoke emerged a tall, foreboding sight. She towered above them, the trails of her all-covering cloak fluttering in the non-existent breeze. The sheath of sheer material that fell over her face hid her features from view but Carey imagined for a moment that she saw the glint of an eye, crimson and piercing.

Carey expected Malevolence to approach her, but Jeremy, almost lifting her off the ground by her neck, dragged her back against the wall as the Dark Empress moved to where Kat lay protectively over Ji.

"No... please..." Kat murmured, shaking her head as Malevolence cast her hands over her.

With a swift rising motion, Kat was lifted from the ground, unsupported. A gurgling sound was bubbling in her throat and her eyes were popping in fear as she grabbed at her neck.

"Pathetic," Malevolence said, her voice echoing around the chamber. "How is it possible that any could have believed you a champion?"

Kat dropped to the ground, gasping for breath. Carey could see sparks flickering and dying at Kat's fingertips, unable to fight back.

There was the sound of rushing wind and Malevolence was standing by the silent figure of Jiani Lawrence. Kat whimpered in longing.

"I will break you. I know your heart," Malevolence hissed, extending her hand to rest just above the tiny flame that flickered above Jiani's head.

Carey watched in silent terror with Jeremy's breath on her neck. She looked from Malevolence to Kat, who was reaching out to her mother, unable to speak. Her eyes were wide with unspeakable fear. Her hand was making a grasping movement, trying so desperately to fight but failing.

Then, with the swiftest of movements, Malevolence closed her fist, effectively extinguishing the tiny flame. Kat let out a pitiful squeak from her crushed throat, her body overcome by tiny spasms as she broke down into quiet sobbing. Jeremy was quietly laughing; Carey could feel the heaving of his chest against her back. He pushed his cheek against hers.

"How easy it is to die, don't you see? And how easy she was to break... All it took was a single soul. You Seekers – you are so weak. How anyone believed you could truly stand against us..." he snickered, running his hand up her neck and under her hair.

Carey felt sick. Jiani's body flopped sideways, her breath and her life leaving her. Malevolence had extinguished her soul.

Carey could feel it prickling inside her, her magic finding its way to her fingertips. As if it sensed the injustice, it was trying to fight its way out of her body, agreeing with Carey's heart, wanting to vanquish the offenders of its host. Jeremy held her tight, whispering one last farewell.

"Goodbye, Carey. It was good, while it lasted."

There was another great rush of wind and Carey was suddenly free; Jeremy was gone, but so were their families. Kat and Ji were still with her and she rushed to their aid as the room shifted and changed. The walls rounded, the roof lifted and they soon found themselves at the bottom of what seemed like a giant well.

"Kat? Ji? Are you all right?" Carey whispered urgently.

Ji grunted and Kat looked up at her with a tear-stained face.

"Mother... She – she's... Carey!"

Before she had time to react, Carey was pulled back away from her friends and thrown hard against the wall. As stars swam before her eyes, she saw Malevolence advancing on Kat who was trying feebly to fend her off. With great sweeping motions Malevolence summoned two globes of burning black light and she lifted them above her head. The walls of the room began to move, circling around them and picking up speed. Carey crawled towards Kat and Ji, trying to ignore the building commotion. Malevolence was muttering strange words, incantations, as she held the glowing orbs high; the walls began to roar, deafening Carey. She glanced up as Malevolence whipped a hand around her head, bringing one of the orbs straight down at Kat.

"No!" Carey screamed over the din as she flung herself at Kat.

The orb exploded over their heads and Carey heard a high-pitched scream of amusement.

"Carey Lee!" Malevolence's voice sounded, clear even over the roar. "This is no time for acts of valour. Katrina Lawrence will die, whether before you or after you, it is of little difference. However, if you prefer..."

With a single gesture, Carey was lifted off the ground and smashed against the wall once more; it came to an instant halt although the thunderous sound continued. Her head throbbed and something warm began to seep down from her hairline. She felt battered and bruised as she coughed up blood but she could also feel her magic racing all over her body, numbing her pain and injuries; it was giving her a fighting chance. Carey could sense it building in her chest, the lion ready to pounce; it was trickling from her very pores, running onto the stone. She rolled her head to the side and saw in amazement web-like cracks of light spreading across the walls, working their way up to the ceiling.

"What is this...?"

Malevolence had noticed and, abandoning her quarry at her feet, she summoned Carey to her. Carey lifted from the wall and flew into

Malevolence's outstretched hand. Gripped by the front of her shirt, Carey was now face to face with the evil Empress. The magic was still building within her; it was itching to be released and Carey realised it was now a matter of when, not if. An uninhibited confidence had taken her over. She knew, in her heart, that she would not miss, that Kat and Ji would be safe. She was certain beyond question, more certain than she had ever been in her entire life.

It sparked impatiently behind her eyeballs as Malevolence drew her close.

"What is this persistence?" she hissed, entering Carey's mind, reverberating through her head. *"What exactly do you wish to achieve?"*

With a sudden great surge of power through her body, Carey gasped.

"This," she whispered, and with a force so strong that it tore at Carey's every fibre, the magic blasted from her body and hit Malevolence with its full strength.

The grip on her shirt slackened and Carey fell to the floor, unable to move. There was a great flash of light, an earth-rendering crack and Carey thought she saw something fly over her; great white wings. Then there was nothing.

Chapter Twenty-Nine

A New Beginning

"Welcome to the future, Princess."

Saar stood before her, shrouded in all his darkness. He grinned and Carey clenched her fists.

"What future, Saar? For all I know, I'm dead."

Saar laughed in amusement. "Dead, Princess? Oh no, you are far from that."

Carey stopped.

"You really didn't think I'd bother talking to you if you were dead, did you? Only the living are useful," said Saar, his eyes taking her in hungrily.

"If you're going to ask me to join you again, you can forget it. I don't want anything to do with the Empire—"

"The Empire," Saar interrupted, "no longer exists, thanks in a large part to you. No, I am asking your assistance in establishing a new beginning, a new existence. I have seen now what you are capable of, a power even beyond my reach, and a soul such as yours would be... invaluable."

Nails cutting into her palms, Carey stood her ground. "No."

Saar cocked his head to the side. "No?"

"That's what I said: No. I don't care if it's for the Empire or not. I will not ally myself with you. I remain loyal to the Order."

Saar's cold eyes glowed icily as his anger flared. "Stubbornness killed your grandmother and it destroyed her sister because they both failed to accept the inevitable," he snarled.

"What?" Carey asked, confused by this statement. "Sister? What sister?"

But he did not answer. Everything blurred and Carey blinked; there was bright white light. She blinked again.

Carey found herself lying flat on her back. She was surrounded by soft white sheets and it took her a moment to see that she was staring up at a dull grey ceiling. A head of flaming orange hair popped into view and panic shot through her body.

"Argh! Jeremy! Get away from me, get away–" she shrieked, striking out.

A pair of hands gripped her forearms. "Whoa! Wait a second!" a thick-accented voice came. "It's all right Carey, no one's goin' to hurt you 'ere. Settle."

The man's face came into view and Carey saw that it wasn't Jeremy, though she wasn't at all convinced.

"Who are you?" she asked, unable to keep the demanding tone from her voice.

He had a young face with a strong chin and kind eyes. On closer inspection Carey saw that his hair wasn't orange but a multitude of colours, from a dark crimson to a bright yellow. He smiled knowingly.

"Don't worry," he said, releasing her arms and going to pour a glass of water from the pitcher beside her bed. "I know what yer thinkin' and I can safely say that the shapeshifter you're thinkin' of is safely locked away in the castle dungeons. My name is Rupert Tagore. Here," he offered Carey the glass but she refused. "You have nothin' to fear, least of all from me. I'm merely a healer."

He smiled pleasantly but Carey was disinclined to reciprocate.

"Jeremy's in the dungeons? How is that possible? Where am I?" she asked him, unable to make sense of anything.

She looked around and saw a number of other beds lining the walls. It reminded her of a hospital.

"Yer in the Healer's Ward of the castle. You've been out of it for almost a month. I don't know what you did to yerself but it's been a worryin' time," Rupert said. "You were quite unstable for a good while but we got it under control, obviously."

Carey gaped. "A month? I've been unconscious for *a month?*" She closed her eyes and took a deep breath. "You said we were in a castle."

"Yes, in the Centre City. Which other castle were you thinkin' of?"

Carey's eyes snapped open and she sat bolt upright.

"The *Centre City?* Are you mad?"

She couldn't believe it; she had to get out of there. Carey made to get out of bed but Rupert stopped her.

"Please, Carey! You mustn't get up. You've only just woken up–"

"To find myself in the Centre City and in the castle no less! What are you – an Imperial? Is this another trick?" Carey asked firmly, staring defiantly at Rupert.

He seemed lost for words and extremely confused by Carey's outburst. At that moment, the heavy wooden door at the end of the room creaked open and around the side poked a familiar face: Katrina Lawrence.

Kat let out a cry of excitement and positively sprinted to Carey's bedside. Rupert sighed in relief and stepped aside to let her through.

"Oh thank goodness you're awake, Carey. We were starting to get really worried," Kat said, hugging her tightly before taking a seat on the side of the bed. "We didn't know what had happened to you."

Seeing Kat alive and well, soothed Carey greatly. "Kat… you're alive! That's – that's–"

"The desired outcome, I should hope!" she said with a smile and put her hand on Carey's arm affectionately.

"Kat, what is going on? Why are we in the castle still? Does that mean… did we…?"

Rupert cleared his throat noisily. "Ah, I'll just be next door, if – if you need anything…" he announced awkwardly before turning and leaving the room.

Kat waited until he was gone before answering Carey's question.

"We did it, Carey, or rather, *you* did it. The Empire's gone, it's finished!"

Carey was silent, the enormity of what Kat was saying taking an awful long time to register. "It's – it's gone? Really?"

"Really," Kat confirmed. "What you did, that – that magic you used, it certainly did the job."

Carey's heart leapt uncomfortably. "You saw…"

Kat was now serious, her face displaying a look of sombre curiosity. "What was it? Was it that power, the one that shielded you before?"

Carey nodded slowly; Kat's eyes were wide in amazement.

"I didn't know it was so strong. Why didn't you tell us? Surely you must have known."

"I… I guess I didn't want to – to scare you," Carey said in a small voice.

"Scare us? Carey! Why did you ever think that?"

She didn't want to tell Kat about the man in Burtonport, how she had been the one who had killed him. Despite what it had achieved for them she was ashamed of this power, that such a terrible thing lived within her.

"I – I was scared of what it might do," Carey said. She was only bending the truth slightly; she wasn't lying completely. "And, as you saw, I think my feelings were completely justified. I killed Malevolence."

"*Killed Malevolence?*" Kat said, almost laughing, though Carey heard no humour there. "No, Malevolence isn't dead."

Carey jumped as though a giant shock had been sent through her body.

"What? But you just said the Empire was finished!"

"No no, the Empire *is* gone, disbanded. I meant that Malevolence is not dead *yet*," Kat said in a hurry. "You didn't kill her but when you blasted her with that power of yours, you destroyed her body but her magic remained. No one knows how this is possible but no one can destroy it either. It's as if she made her magic indestructible somehow. But that's all she is now – just magic."

Carey's chest was heaving from the shock. "Where is her magic now?"

"We caught it – it's trapped. When you passed out I watched Malevolence sort of… disintegrate. All that was left was a flame, but it wasn't like the ones our parents had. It was black. We couldn't let it escape, so we put it in a Tear Globe. It's here, in the castle under heavy guard."

Carey could see Kat struggling with the thought of comparing Malevolence's soul with that of her parents'. Jiani Lawrence had died that day, her life ended in a split second. Carey's heart ached for Kat, realising how unfair it was that the essence of such an evil person had been allowed to survive whilst Kat's mother had perished. She didn't quite know what to say.

Something sparked in the back of her mind, something she had almost forgotten about.

"Kat? What happened to the Silver Water? I didn't get rid of it like you said and then Jeremy…"

She stopped. She couldn't carry on with what she was going to say because her throat wouldn't let her. Kat, however, seemed not to notice.

"You don't need to worry about that anymore. We found it and destroyed it sufficiently enough so it is now completely irrevocable."

Kat noticed the pained look on Carey's face and smiled gently. "Hey. I said not to worry."

Carey shook her head ashamedly. "I put us all in danger by keeping that stupid stuff and… imagine what Malevolence could have done with it! I practically handed her the greatest weapon she could have asked for! What kind of Seeker am I that I can't even see the dangers, can't even judge the potential of something so potentially devastating?"

Carey threw her head in hands, trying with all her might to push the outward pain and shame she felt back inside. She didn't think she could possibly cope with those emotions right now too.

She felt Kat's hand soft on her shoulder and it calmed her. She took deep breaths, slowing herself. The air flowed back to her lungs, Carey unaware that she had almost stopped breathing in her panic and was hyperventilating. She could see the cool red of the light behind her eyelids and concentrated solely on her breathing. Everything else could be dealt with later.

They sat like this for a while until Carey had herself under control. She was grateful for Kat's patience. How much of a burden she must already be bearing…

After a period of calming silence, Kat spoke again, her voice more jovial this time in a clear attempt to cheer her up.

"Your mother and father will be so happy you're awake," Kat said. "They would have been here but the Council is in session."

"So the Council has reformed then?" Carey asked, curious about what had happened over the last month and anxious to discuss something that didn't rip up raw emotions within her.

"It happened so quickly I couldn't believe it. It was as though the whole city, the whole *country* had an enchantment lifted from it. I wouldn't be surprised if it had, actually. Everyone just came flooding back – you could tell they had been waiting for that day, preparing for it. Ji and I managed to find healers like Rupert who helped our families. The Imperials here didn't put up much fight, except for a few. The ones we caught are in the dungeons – the others fled to the Darklands. Our People in the city here really took up the challenge of rounding up Imperials once they'd regained their powers. They've helped us so much.

"Your parents have been named the new Imperials too. It was absolutely unanimous, given what your family has done in the past. I didn't doubt it for a second."

Carey froze. She stared at Kat, barely aware that her mouth was hanging open in shocked surprise. Kat giggled at her reaction.

"Wow, Carey. I didn't think it would come as that big of a surprise," Kat said, eyeing Carey's expression with a mixture of amusement and confusion.

She closed her mouth and shook her head. It wasn't her parents' appointment that set the warning bells ringing in her head – it was something else, something much more sinister. The memory assaulted her, smothering her with a cloud of nausea. Saar's leering features drifted mockingly in front of her eyes.

"Imperials? So that would make me a… a princess, right?" Carey asked in a strangled voice.

Kat's mouth turned up into a kind of smirk. "And who would have thought?"

Under any other circumstance this would have seemed quite funny but it couldn't be farther from it. His words came echoing back at her, twisting her insides.

"Why do you call me that? Why do you keep calling me Princess*?"*

"Merely a courtesy…"

Despite her response to his latest proposition, Carey doubted it would be last time she would see Saar. He didn't seem the kind of person to give up easily. He was determined and it was clear now that he knew something she didn't. Saar had addressed her with her new title long before it had even been conceived or considered and this unnerved Carey greatly.

Carey was suddenly aware that Kat was staring at her and that she had been silent for a good minute or so. She wasn't ready to say anything about Saar yet – she wasn't even sure who he was – and so she directed the conversation away from herself and for the time being, banished any thought of Saar from her mind.

"But what about you? Surely I'm not the only one to have to be called *Your Highness*?"

Carey asked with the most convincing disdain.

Kat laughed. Small lines appeared at the corners of her eyes and the sheer pleasure that lit up her face comforted Carey, filling her with warmth.

"Oh dear… no… I've not been forgotten, though no one will be calling me *Your Highness*. That apparent pleasure has been reserved for you only," Kat tittered with a wide smile.

"What then?" Carey coaxed.

"I've been given the title of *Keeper of the Realms*."

Carey frowned. "What does that entail?"

Kat shrugged, seemingly unworried by the fact that she had no real idea of what her new position meant. "Not so sure about that yet. Perhaps they just didn't want me to feel unimportant, what with a princess for a best friend," she grinned.

"Urgh! Please, Kat, keep the *princess* business to a minimum."

Kat laughed again at the look of disgust on Carey's face.

"Fine, fine. If it really bothers you that much."

As Kat laughed, Carey thought of something Rupert had mentioned. It made her stomach contract painfully but she had to ask. When Kat had finally released her final chuckle, Carey fidgeted uneasily.

"Kat?"

Kat smoothed her hair and answered with a "Hmm?"

Carey bit her lip and her friend noticed the change in her instantly, turning to her seriously.

"Carey, what is it?"

Carey didn't want Kat to realise the true anguish this caused her, so she pulled her face into a look of careless concern and forced her voice to be as light as she could make it.

"I heard about Jeremy. Is it true you have him down in the dungeons?"

Kat squeezed her hand. "He's in one of the cells. He's refusing to tell us anything but we've already managed to work most things out."

Kat scanned Carey's face and Carey knew what she was thinking. She hadn't fooled her for a moment.

"Carey–"

"Don't... don't worry about me," she said, forcing a smile. "As long as Jeremy is locked away..."

The very thought of Jeremy made her nauseous. His deceit was still fresh in her mind and it made her burn with hatred and shame. The feelings she had felt were real, she knew it, but now she was unsure at whom those feelings were directed. She wanted it so much to be Ji and shuddered at the alternative. Carey could still hear his voice in her ear, feel his cheek pushed up against hers.

Kat was watching her but Carey couldn't look her in the eye; she stared down at her hands, wanting nothing more than for these feelings to disappear. She didn't even know how she was going to face Ji. Ji...

"Where's Ji?" Carey asked, wondering where he was and why she hadn't noticed his absence sooner.

"Oh, I think he's in a meeting with someone," Kat said, looking around the ward. "He's usually here though, visiting Zacharia."

She pointed to the bed at the far end of the room and Carey saw for the first time the still figure of Zacharia Binx.

"What happened to him?" she whispered.

Kat sighed hopelessly. "He's in a bad way. We found him like that, discovered he'd been subjected to the Corigliphs." She shuddered. "Don't ask – you really don't want to know. Rupert's done everything he can for him. He's a miracle worker, that one, but with Zacharia… He doesn't even know when or even *if* he'll wake up."

Carey stared at Zacharia. Yet another casualty.

"How's Ji?" she asked Kat, tearing her eyes from the devastating scene. "How's he coping?"

"He's… he's coping, that's all I can say really."

There was something else in Kat's voice that made Carey suspicious.

"Kat? What is it? Is Ji all right?"

Kat was fidgeting with a loose thread in the bed sheets.

"Kat?"

She looked up at Carey and grimaced. "He's… he's not completely…" she took a deep breath. "You've got to understand. What they put him through was really terrible. He has some injuries that will never heal."

Her heart was pounding with a ferocity Carey barely knew. Kat's speech made her almost not want to know, but she had to ask.

"What happened, Kat?" she asked, her voice shaking uncontrollably.

Kat looked her straight in the eye.

"He can't see anymore, Carey. He's blind."

* * *

Carey remained in the Healer's Ward for another month until Rupert was completely satisfied with her recovery. He was quite the character and had a knack for cheering her up, which proved a welcome distraction. His younger sister, Kyna, came by the ward a number of times a day, proving to be more of a mischief-maker than her older brother. They were enough to divert her attention during the times she had no visitors.

Ji's first visit came on a cold winter's morning not long after she had awoken. He sat by her bed where Carey could now see his horrible afflictions up close. His hands were scarred and the wounds upon his face, although healing, were still quite pronounced. The one thing, however, that almost broke Carey's heart was his eyes. No longer a sparkling blue, they were smoky, like a clear blue sky obscured by an intrusive cloud. It was all she could do to stop herself reaching out to him.

She found it difficult to talk at first; it was hard to find something to say when many of her memories of them together were only hers. Would she ever be able to forget what Jeremy had done? Would she and Ji ever be able to have anything of their own now that her thoughts and feelings for him had been tainted? Jeremy had permeated every last corner of her being. Carey felt repulsed by every leap of her heart, every thought of desire that spiked in her whenever Ji was near. She just could not manage to separate Jeremy from Ji and yet with this confusion, she felt a deep aching sympathy. This wasn't Ji's fault and she feared that he might sense the way she held back from him.

None of this was fair on him. Carey didn't want him to suffer anymore than he already had done.

Ji often spent hours with Zacharia in the hope he would wake; hours in which his silence was most profound. His presence both broke her heart and made it whole. His hope, his compassion, his strength. His devotion… It was so difficult. However, by the time he left, they were almost able to talk freely again despite the muddled feelings Carey had that surfaced at his mention.

The first time she met her parents was an odd occasion. Although she barely remembered them, it was as though they had never parted. They sat for hours talking and laughing, all uncertainty and pain disappearing. Carey couldn't remember a time when she had been happier; she cherished their hours together, awaiting the times they'd return. Her mother, although still thin from her imprisonment, was full of life. She joked as she stroked Carey's hair, taking in everything Carey said, as if making up for the years of not hearing her speak. Robert could not wipe the smile from his face, having eyes only for his daughter.

Even though they did not show it, Carey could feel that they were capable of great things. She now understood why they had been named as the new Imperials. They exuded a confidence free from arrogance and their passion shone through in their obvious affections. They tried their best to appear bright and cheerful but Carey couldn't help noticing an edge of sadness to their voices at times. She hadn't asked them but Carey had a feeling it had something to do with her sisters. No one had heard anything about Jody or Laurel; it was as if they had never existed. The Imperials they had questioned divulged no clues as to where they might have disappeared to and there was no trace of them within the castle. Carey thought it would have been better to know, even if it meant the worst. Surely her parents had suffered enough.

Chapter Thirty

Traitorous Reality

His pounding footsteps and heavy breathing echoed in the confined space of the stairwell. With the piece of paper in hand, he flung himself out onto the seventh floor and sprinted towards the large double doors at the end. It was dark and the only light came from the moonlight that filtered in through the windows. Two guards stood watchful and they called him to halt as he approached.

"What is your business here?" the taller of the guards asked, blocking his way.

"Please... I must see... the Emperor... or Empress," the man panted, holding up the piece of paper in his hand. "It is urgent. It's regarding... the prisoner..."

The two guards looked at each other then nodded. The shorter of the two gave the doors a sharp knock.

"My Lord and Lady. You have an urgent message from the dungeons."

There was a moment where the man tried to compose himself after his desperate sprint. Then came the clicking and clunking of locks and the Empress emerged, her hair slightly tousled and dressed in a long blue night-robe.

"Yes?"

The man glanced sideways at the guards. "Milady, I have some news, but..." he hesitated.

Jenny cleared her throat. "Would you mind giving us a few minutes?" she asked the guards.

"Of course," the taller said with a bow before leading the other away.

The man waited until they were a safe distance away before turning back to the Empress.

"Milady, something terrible has happened down in the dungeons. It's Jeremy Shultz," he said in a quavering voice.

"Jeremy?" Jenny said sharply, any sign of tiredness disappearing in an instant. "What about him, Sheldon?"

Sheldon took a deep breath in an effort to calm himself. "He's dead."

Shock flitted across Jenny's face. "Dead? How is this possible?"

"We don't know, Milady. It's looks as though he may have taken his own life though we can't seem to find any evidence of this. That being the case, we cannot find any trace of poison in any of his food and no one has been to see him. The guards are positive," Sheldon said in a rush to explain. "We don't know how it could have happened."

Jenny was silent, contemplating this news. Sheldon carried on.

"He must have known though, because he left a message."

Jenny frowned at him with a look of deep concern. "Message? What did it say?"

With a shaking hand, Sheldon handed the piece of paper to the Empress. "We weren't sure of its meaning so we wrote it down. We didn't want to get it wrong. We found it written on the wall of his cell."

Jenny took the paper. "On the wall?"

Sheldon nodded. "Yes. In his own blood."

Jenny looked down at the note in her hand, flipping it open with slight trepidation. Upon it were six words – the last thoughts of Jeremy Shultz.

"What does it mean, your Majesty?"

Jenny Lee shook her head, staring at the words. She had a sickening feeling in the pit of her stomach, a feeling that told her something terrible was going to come of this.

"Thank you, Sheldon. You did the right thing by bringing this to me. I will see you in the morning."

Sheldon bowed, taking this as his cue to leave. "Milady."

Jenny closed the door and returned to bed. Her husband was sound asleep and she thought it best to leave it until the morning to tell him. Besides, there was nothing more they could do tonight.

She placed the paper on the bedside table and returned to the warmth of the bedcovers. Her eyes upon the note, she sighed heavily as the moonlight passed over it, illuminating those six words.

The third world will be opened.

* * *

"Ooh, where are my shoes!"

It was the night of the Spring Festival the council had planned – a sort of long-awaited celebration for the city – and Carey was late. A number of important councillors and even some foreign delegates were going to be there and it was an important night for her mother and father. She really didn't want to disappoint them. She had initially planned to be on time, but that schedule had quickly gone out the window. She didn't know how she could have done it but she had dozed off over her diary. Carey was only woken when a harassed-looking Kat came banging on her door, wondering why she was taking so long.

"I can't believe you're not ready! Everyone's already starting to arrive!" had been Kat's wake-up call from the corridor.

Now she was rummaging through her room, trying anxiously to find her shoes, knowing that she was already horribly late for the introductions.

As Carey looked in her closet, she suddenly felt a hand on her shoulder. Not even thinking, Carey spun around and flung a curse at the offender.

Kat deflected the yellow sparks with amazingly quick reflexes. She raised an eyebrow.

"*That* was uncalled for. I did knock."

Carey clapped a surprised hand over her mouth. "Oh, Kat, I am so sorry! I mustn't have heard you…"

Kat glanced around at the mess that was Carey's room. "Obviously. I must remember to knock louder next time. You almost took

my head off – do you realise how long this hairstyle took me to get right?"

Carey looked at Kat and was instantly sick with jealousy. That girl could pull-off the high-society majestic aura that was clearly expected of herself, yet Carey just couldn't manage it as easily as Kat did. Her long hair had been styled beautifully, cleverly tended so that it covered the dreadful mark on her neck. Her long, olive-green gown was a beautiful, classical style and Carey suddenly felt ludicrous standing next to her.

"Wow, Kat. You look beautiful. I don't know why I even bother."

Kat sighed in exasperation. "Because you're the Princess, that's why! And despite your less than willing attitude to match said description, you have to and it's up to me to somehow make you! Now *please* tell me you're ready. Everyone's downstairs ready for the introductions."

Carey bit her lip, trying to ignore Kat's rant about her newly gained status and shook her head meekly. "I can't find my shoes…"

Kat almost exploded. "*What*! You cannot be serious! I had them laid out for you yesterday next to the door. All right. How about you search under the bed and I'll look over here in this mess?"

Kat stalked off to the other side of the room. Carey almost suggested just going barefoot out of sarcasm but quickly decided against it. She didn't need Kat to have a heart attack just now.

Awkwardly she got to her knees, pushed the many layers of her skirt out of the way and ducked into the narrow space under her bed. The floor was covered in dust and Carey had to squint to see through the darkness.

Moving her hands over the dark floor, knocking non-shoe items out of the way, she brushed over an empty space.

"Oh!"

She quickly withdrew her hand, goggling at the patch of floor she had just touched.

"Carey? What is it?" came Kat's voice from over head.

A thin line of blue light was shining through from the floor. As Carey watched, the light carved a small square, outlining what might have been a tiny trapdoor. Hesitantly, she stuck her hand out and waved it through the beams. Nothing happened.

"It's… there's… I think I've found something."

"If it's not your shoes, I don't want to know."

"Oh come on, Kat. I think you should see this."

"Ca-rey," Kat pleaded impatiently.

"Ka-at," Carey whined back at her.

Grumbling irritably, Kat squeezed under the bed next to her, pushing Carey's voluminous skirt out of the way. "I can't believe I'm doing this in *this* dress. Now *what* is so important?"

"Here, look at this. What do you think?" Carey said, pointing at the square in the floor.

Kat squinted and frowned, all thoughts of ruining her dress gone from her face. "I don't know. Looks like a hiding place or something. Or maybe it's a distraction," she added sarcastically.

Ignoring her, Carey examined the square of light a little closer. There seemed nothing evidently malevolent about the beams of light; Carey watched as tiny dust motes danced about them, breaking the rays momentarily. She could feel Kat beside her watching the light as eagerly as she was and Carey knew she was just as intrigued by this mysterious apparition.

Carefully, Carey reached out; her hand passed through the beams and touched the centre of the square. Kat held her breath in trepidation. With a *pop* the small square of floor within the light disappeared at her touch.

Looking at each other, Carey and Kat wriggled in closer to get a better look. Sunk into the floor was a small chamber; in its corner was a blood-red stone. It glinted through the dark.

"Wow…" Carey breathed.

Kat, however, was eyeing it suspiciously. "I don't think you should touch it, Carey. We don't know what it does."

"Oh come on, Kat. It hardly looks dangerous."

"And you should know by now that you can't go on appearances alone," Kat argued.

"Thank you for reminding me," Carey mumbled, and ignoring Kat's cry of protest, reached into the chamber and lifted the stone out from its resting place.

"See? Nothing to worry about."

It was an unusual stone. It was smooth and round, about the size of a quail's egg. It was a dark-red, yet on closer inspection Carey noticed something moving inside it. Tiny flecks of light merged and faded, shimmering on the surface for a moment before disappearing into the dark depths. The body of the stone was encased in a swirling cap of gold that coiled around it like tentacles. Etched into it was minute writing in a round, spiral-like language. From the top hung a long heavy chain; it was a necklace.

She showed it to Kat, who was a little reluctant to touch it.

"Do you know what it says?"

She shook her head. "I can't see it in this light. Maybe if we get out from under here I'll be able to see it properly."

Together they squirmed out from under the bed, rearranged their many layers and dusted themselves off. Kat took the necklace carefully by the chain and held it up to the light.

"It's Gadælic," she proclaimed.

"Can you read it?" Carey asked hopefully.

Kat shook her head. "No, I don't think anyone can," she said much to Carey's disappointment. "All books and scrolls written in Gadælic were banned and burned by the Empire. No one was permitted to speak it even. Maybe that's why this was hidden. The owner didn't want it destroyed."

For a moment they stood staring at the curious find. Then from somewhere in the distance, a fanfare sounded. Kat and Carey started.

"The Festival!" they said at once.

Snatching the necklace from Kat, Carey stuffed it under her pillow, making sure it wasn't showing before making for the door.

"Argh, my shoes! I still don't have–"

"Here," Kat said, pulling Carey's shoes out from under her cupboard and throwing them to her. "Now let's go!"

Shoving her shoes on her feet, Carey sprinted down the hall after Kat. Hiking her dress up over her knees, Carey jumped down the stairs leading to the castle gardens where the festival was being held.

"Come on, Carey!" Kat called, waiting for her at the double oak doors.

Carey pulled up beside her, clutching her side. "Do I look okay?" she puffed, straightening her dress.

"Your circlet's a little lopsided," Kat pointed out, and as she adjusted it, Kat knocked on the doors and they opened.

The sight was magnificent. Garlands of purple pine flower hung from the split stairwell's banisters, lit by thousands of fireflies that fluttered about lazily. A beautiful rose statue stood in the centre of the dance floor: a memorial for those who had perished under the Empire. Elegant figures spun gracefully around it in time to the music of an orchestra of fauns, the haunting sound of their pipes floating over the crowd. Small round tables lined the dance floor, bunches of shining Gold Peliers in the middle of each surrounded by bowls of glorious-looking food and pitchers of Cerulion cider. The air was fresh and cool, the late dusk sky a dark purple and blue.

A Herald stood to their right, dressed in traditional Council robes of embroidered material. He bowed briefly to them, then knocked his staff against the stone floor in proclamation.

"Her Highness, Princess Carey and Lady Katrina Lawrence!" the Herald called and Carey walked side by side with Kat as they descended the stairs.

Kat was instantly distracted from their late arrival by the general splendour. She tittered and gasped excitedly as they walked down the stairs, pointing and commenting on everything she saw. They were met by various members of the Council and, after a round of greetings, Kat left Carey at the invitation of a willing dance partner. Happy to have Kat take the dance floor ahead of her, she found Ji on the far side of the courtyard and sat down next to him in relief.

Smoothing out the glistening silver layers of her skirt, Carey settled down in her chair with a relaxed sigh. The next moment, Ji had turned to her, holding out his hand.

"Yes?" Carey asked cautiously.

"I know you're going to hate me for this, but would you care to dance?"

It was lucky Ji couldn't see her face because she couldn't stop herself from cringing. Those words, those *exact words* brought the night at the camp in Burtonport flooding back. A lump rose in her throat and she swallowed it back down painfully.

Ji shifted impatiently (or was it nervously?), his hand still outstretched. Carey bit her lip, took a deep breath and told herself firmly that this was Ji, not Jeremy and she had to forget the past, forget those memories. She had to learn to put the past behind her...

Carey smiled and took his hand. "I'd be delighted."

Walking to the floor, a familiar jolt of nerves fluttered in her stomach; they tingled in her fingers but she quickly pushed them away.

Ji took her hand and put it on his shoulder. The fauns struck up a gentle waltz and they began to dance slowly on the spot, moving only slightly at first. Ji was looking down at her with his smoky blue eyes, a small smile playing on his lips.

Carey smiled back, though hers was tainted with bitter sadness. They moved gradually across the floor, Carey impressed by how Ji was doing.

"You've been practicing," she commented, as they passed Kat and her partner.

"Hmm, sort of," Ji said. "I've been training, actually. One of the Council scholars is helping me."

"Helping you with what?" Carey asked curiously.

"Well... he's been helping me see again. No, not *actually* see," he corrected with an odd smile. "I can't see details like faces or anything. Though, it would have been nice to be able to tonight."

Carey dropped her gaze, hoping in equal measure that he was talking about her, yet not.

"What... what's it like?" she stammered, trying with all her might to hide the embarrassment in her voice.

"It's... interesting. I can see shapes and outlines, almost like shadows. It's not dark though, everything's surrounded by light. Bright sparks and shimmers. It's not my eye, though – it's what I hear. I hear the vibrations, the sound reverberating when people move. It's like, in my mind, I see what I hear... So right now I can *see* you and I'm able to know where everyone else is too. It's actually quite spectacular," Ji explained, sweeping her around the statue in the centre of the floor. "My teacher says I still have a long way to go though. It's difficult and I'm afraid my concentration is not quite–"

Carey was stunned. "That's incredible, Ji!" she beamed and Ji smiled back.

"It's a start. By the way, I hear you look quite the part tonight."

There was some of his old cheekiness and Carey smiled secretly to herself.

"Oh, you know, it's nothing," she said in a would-be casual way. "I just had this old thing lying around – hey!"

Ji dipped her suddenly and Carey gripped her crown as he swung her back up.

"Don't worry, *Princess*. I won't drop you."

They laughed as they regained their balance. Ji pulled her up so his face was right next hers.

"Even if I can't see you, I bet you look gorgeous," Ji whispered so only Carey could hear.

She didn't know whether to take him seriously or not. Her heart beat hopefully. As he pulled away Carey saw that same mischievous grin he wore when he was playing around and her heart fell. He was just being cheeky.

"Charming?" he answered.

"You wish," she bit back.

The next song started but Ji gave no indication of moving from the dance floor. They had slowed now, no longer sweeping adventurously through the crowd. Carey was quiet, listening to Ji's breathing as they swayed in time, content with merely staying like this. She was almost disappointed when he spoke again, an emotion that quickly turned to horror.

"I heard about Jeremy."

Carey tripped slightly on her ball gown, unable to hold her composure at this sudden unwelcome turn in conversation. She stared at his chest, not wanting to see the expression on his face, not wanting to know what he might be thinking. Carey wasn't ready to have this conversation, least of all with Ji. Would he ever know what effect Jeremy had had on their relationship? Would she ever want Ji to know how that wretched man had potentially destroyed how she viewed him? Carey hoped not, yet with his other senses now so heightened how could Ji possibly be imperceptive to her sudden physical reaction to his words?

Carey could feel the rigidity of her body in his arms and was sure Ji would sense the sudden hostility emanating from her. She hoped he would take it as a sign to abandon his pursuit of this conversation but she also knew Ji wasn't so easily put off. She wasn't disappointed in her judgement.

"Carey... I know you don't like to... talk about him–"

"Then please," Carey croaked, her voice barely steady enough for this short plea. "Please don't."

She had tried so hard recently not to think about Jeremy. The news of his demise had been so widespread though that there was barely a person who wasn't talking about it. As a result, Carey had found it very difficult to be around anyone other than her two best friends, who knew better than to say anything. For such a long time Carey had imagined what her reaction might be if something were to happen to Jeremy. She had expected relief, perhaps a release of this weight that plagued her heart. Instead, Carey found something that made her feel even worse – resentment. She resented the fact that he had escaped so easily, that he wasn't feeling any of what she still felt. Carey had wanted him to experience what she had to bear every single day. She wanted to tear at his heart, hurt him worse than he had her. Now, however...

Carey still didn't look up at Ji. She wondered vaguely if anyone had noticed them still and tense in the middle of the floor. She concluded that even if they had she didn't really care. All that mattered was Ji. Carey hazarded a glance up at his face and immediately wished she hadn't. Ji no longer had his head inclined towards her; his expression was vague and impassive. Carey caught a look of despair and for an instant, anger, momentarily contort his smooth features; a painful stab in the region of her chest gave her momentary breathlessness. Unable to bear the sight of Ji's distress, she quickly diverted her eyes and found herself watching Kat dancing joyously with a new partner. She gracefully flitted about the floor in contented bliss and Carey found herself hopeful. Kat had surely suffered much more than she had. Carey wouldn't soon forget the anguished sobbing that filtered from Kat's room in the middle of the night when she thought everyone else was asleep. Kat had lost a part of her, a most beloved one, yet she was able to be happy too. Carey's heart swelled with optimistic expectation. Perhaps this pain and awkwardness wouldn't last forever.

She closed her eyes and took a deep breath.

"I'm sorry," Carey whispered to Ji.

Ji inclined his head to hers again but said nothing. Carey could feel the tension beginning to lessen; she noticed her muscles unwinding and the stiffness in Ji's shoulders ease under her hand. They started dancing again, revolving slowly on the spot.

After a few minutes of dancing in silence, Ji's brow puckered. "You know things are going to be better from now on?" he asked seriously in a low voice.

Carey searched his face. "You can't know that," she whispered.

He shook his head as if trying to avoid hearing her words. "No, it will be. I promise."

Carey frowned. Could she afford to believe this unfounded promise? She wanted to so badly but her rational mind wouldn't let her do so. Ji brought his face closer to hers and spoke in a low, persuasive voice that made Carey's stomach leap and heart quicken.

"I have a proposition," he breathed.

Carey blinked, unsure of where this was going. There was no trace of humour on his face.

"How about we forget about everything, *everyone* and pretend it's just you and me tonight?"

Carey bit her lip, watching Ji's face. He was waiting for her to answer, his clouded blue eyes searching, intense. Forget about everything? Forget Jeremy, Malevolence and Saar and the unyielding weight that rested on her shoulders?

Carey raised her eyes to his, wishing more than anything that Ji could see her right now.

"Just you and me?"

Ji smiled softly. "Just you and me."

Carey nodded slightly and smiled back.

"That would be nice. I'd like that."

Carey rested her head on Ji's warm chest and sighed; his arm tightened around her waist and the weight of her worries lifted from her heart. She liked Ji's proposition, even if she knew it wouldn't last forever. Even if it was just for tonight.

Carey grinned to herself.

Just for tonight.

About the Author

Alysha King is a Young Adult fiction author who lives in Canberra, Australia with her husband, two young children, a very large dog, and a sneaky white cat. She began writing the Rose Chronicles in high school after being inspired by such writers as Eoin Colfer and Isobelle Carmody. She revels in fantasy and sci-fi and has a soft spot for Enid Blyton, citing her works as some of her all-time favourites and of which she has quite a large collection of in her home library. Alysha also enjoys historical fiction and is currently collecting research for a future planned novel.

When she is not writing or collecting vintage copies of works by famous English writers, Alysha can be found indulging in any number of her other hobbies which include cosplay costuming with her son and daughter, baking overly sweet treats, and collecting Harry Potter paraphernalia.

Alysha can be found on social media and via her website www.alyshaking.com.

www.ingramcontent.com/pod-product-compliance
Lightning Source LLC
Chambersburg PA
CBHW030347120726
47901CB00007B/1940